"Recommended."
—*Library Journal* on *The Island Snatchers*

"This romance has volatile emotional chemistry [and] interesting conflicts . . . sparkles with humor."
—*Romantic Times* on *Home Again*

"[An] explosive, fast-paced thriller."
—*Romantic Times* on *Lifesaver*

Janice Kay Johnson

The Island Snatchers

TOR®

A TOM DOHERTY ASSOCIATES BOOK
NEW YORK

This is a work of fiction. All the characters and events portrayed in this book are either products of the author's imagination or are used fictitiously.

THE ISLAND SNATCHERS

Copyright © 1997 by Janice Kay Johnson

All rights reserved, including the right to reproduce this book, or portions thereof, in any form.

A Tor Book
Published by Tom Doherty Associates, LLC
175 Fifth Avenue
New York, NY 10010

www.tor.com

Tor® is a registered trademark of Tom Doherty Associates, LLC.

ISBN: 0-812-55527-9
Library of Congress Catalog Card Number: 97-1869

First edition: August 1997
First mass market edition: November 2000

Printed in the United States of America

0 9 8 7 6 5 4 3 2 1

For Dad, who took me along on his quests to faraway lands. Here I am, still exploring them! Thank you for opening my eyes, and for your constant love and support.

Prologue

Autumn 1847

Anne Cartwright sat in the room's single wooden chair, her back straight and her hands folded quiescently in her lap as she contemplated the body of her husband. He was laid out on a nine-patch quilt on the bed where he had died, the victim of consumption. Around her fluttered other missionary wives, kind, but sounding to her like the *'i'iwi* birds—though the women with their long dark skirts and high lace-edged necklines would be offended to be compared to creatures so colorful.

Her gaze strayed to the small-paned window. Through the wavery glass she saw the round-leafed *hau* tree and the long-leafed *hala* tree; beyond, the night-blooming cereus crept over the coral-stone wall that separated the mission compound from the street. Despite the neat white picket gate, the view through the window was exotic, not to be mistaken for her native New England.

Anne felt a pat on her hand. "My dear, take comfort in knowing that Mr. Cartwright walks now in the eternal light. We may mourn his loss, but we must rejoice in the knowledge of his triumph above."

Anne wrenched her attention back to the small, spartan bedroom with the simple wooden bedstead and commode, and summoned a smile of sorts for the well-meaning Lydia Griggs. Perhaps it was just as well that she completely misunderstood Anne's emotions.

"Yes, of course," she agreed, as expected. "It's not as though I haven't known the end was coming."

The other woman's brown eyes were unexpectedly shrewd. "But you didn't expect to be crushed by a sense of aloneness. No, you mustn't feel selfish. It's natural, or so I was told. My marriage to Mr. Griggs is my second, you know. My first husband was killed in a wagon accident."

"I had forgotten." Now she did feel selfish.

"It was a long time ago."

"He looks so peaceful," said another of the wives, squeezing Anne's hand.

John Cartwright had been in his late thirties. Always tall and gaunt, he had lost weight during the long voyage around the Horn and across the wide Pacific Ocean to these tiny specks of land where he had intended to continue the noble work of leading the natives from their heathen ways to civilization. They had all lost weight on the voyage, despite the forced inactivity; moldy flour and hardtack scarcely tempted the appetite. But the rest of the missionary company, sent in the year of His Grace 1847, were not seized by great racking coughs. And once on land, their sea legs steadied and the nutritious—if alien—diet having brought color again to pale cheeks, they were given great energy by their joy at arriving and by the zeal of their convictions. But by that time, those coughs splattered his handkerchief with blood, and exhaustion confined John Cartwright to bed. His wife dutifully nursed him, as she had nursed her invalid mother during a much slower death.

He died while she slept in the chair beside the bed. She hadn't heard the last wheezing breath, didn't see whether he was awake and conscious of his departure. For that she was grate-ful. Which would have been worse? To see bitterness and ha-tred in his eyes, or a plea for forgiveness that she would never have given, even on his deathbed?

Perhaps she would have been unaffected by either, as she seemed to be by his death. Anne felt remarkably detached. She could gaze at his pasty, bony face, utterly immobile in death, and feel no more than if he had been a mannequin at a wax museum. She'd helped wash him and dress him in his best shirt and dark frock coat, even tied his cravat, all without feeling anything at all.

Not even relief.

They were talking again, those other women who would be shocked by her thoughts. Their soft voices agreed that it would be best to book a place for her on the first ship sailing for Boston.

". . . nothing for her here now," one said.

The ripple of agreement might have been a rustle of their black silk skirts.

". . . home," said another.

The surface of Anne's calm was disturbed, as though a rock skipped over it.

She stood. "No."

"What?" Uncomprehending faces turned to her.

"But, my dear," began Lydia.

"No. I won't go home."

"Is it only that you can't face the voyage yet? I do under-stand—it was harrowing—but surely you long for your loved ones now."

The voyage. She would let them think she dreaded it. They would understand that. They, who eagerly awaited every packet of letters from home, would never understand that she hated hers. She had married a man she didn't know to escape; paid an enormous price. Go home now? Never.

"I'm certain that I can make myself useful," she suggested, letting her voice falter the tiniest bit. "Until I feel ready."

How willingly they agreed, with such understanding. She would make herself indispensable, until they forgot they had ever intended to send her away.

One

D r. Matthew Cabe stood at the rail as the brig *Minerva* was
towed by native double-hulled canoes through the narrow
entrance into the Honolulu harbor. The rigging creaked above,
and the deck rolled under his feet. He felt as much dismay as
he did satisfaction in his arrival. After 147 days around the
Horn, he was of course glad to be here at last. Glad that he could
get on with his business, the sooner to hope for a hasty departure, perhaps on a whaler returning to Boston loaded with
sperm oil.

Earlier, when the *Minerva* had rounded Diamond Head,
the shoreline at least had been pleasing: coconut palms fringed
a white beach on which the surf gently rolled. But here the thick
crumbling walls of the fort reared over the harbor, though
Matthew could see that no cannon had replaced those spiked
and dismembered by the French in a fit of pique. Some sub-
stantive structures stood out: churches, the hip-roofed palace,
the pretentious new government building on the waterfront.
There were more European-style houses than he had anticipated; clearly a building boom had taken place in the past year
or two. Yet, still sprinkled throughout the town were the pecu-

liar grass huts of the natives. He remembered his father describing Honolulu as bare of vegetation, too, but the foreigners had planted gardens that were beginning to clothe the town in greenery, at least behind the walls that lined the straight streets.

Why in God's name had he come? he wondered, taking in the pleated, barren mountains rising beyond the dry plain behind the town. The Punchbowl loomed over Honolulu, a gaunt dusty guardian. Matthew felt a spasm of longing for home.

Of course, he knew the answer to his own question. He was here to regain what ought to be his; not because he cared for it, but because he owed as much to his father. His conscience would allow him no other course. When homesick, he need only remind himself that his stay would be short.

With the other passengers, Matthew descended to a boat and made the trip to shore. There distaste joined his other emotions. The waterfront looked much like those of San Francisco and San Diego: ramshackle wharves, slaughterhouses, and fish sheds projected over scummy water, and warehouses were crammed between cattle pens and pigsties, adding their reek to that of oakum and dried fish. Grog shops invited the sailors, and nightfall would no doubt bring out women plying their ancient trade.

The industry evident here was impressive, however; loaded drays arrived at and departed from warehouses, boats shuttled to and from the twenty or more ships at anchor in the harbor, and wharves were stacked with barrels. Presumably because a ship had just stood in, hacks and warehouse vans waited, with a dozen or more horses tied to rails and lampposts.

Matthew studied the natives with interest. He had expected a coarser appearance, but those he saw were handsome though dark, with open, amiable countenances, disfigured only by pervasive skin disorders. All wore European clothing. Those who met the incoming boats were as eager to provide transportation and goods as were the residents dependent on trade in any port.

His intention had been to get a hack to the Commercial Hotel, which he understood to be respectable. He had it on the best authority that the establishment offered hot, cold, and shower baths as well as having a particularly fine billiards room.

A fellow passenger, Elijah Freeman, had offered him accommodations, but Freeman was given to making intemperate speeches about the need for revolution in the Sandwich Islands and the clear absurdity of any white man's accepting laws promulgated by a brown-skinned savage with no concept of civilization. Matthew thought it wisest to stay dissociated from the man for the present. Matthew's father had refused to sign the oath of allegiance to the Hawaiian kingdom, but more because his family was still in Massachusetts than out of disrespect for the native rulers. Matthew had no opinions on the Hawaiian political situation and no wish to become entangled in it.

He had no sooner set foot onshore, his trunks at his feet, than Freeman, portly and self-satisfied, bustled up to repeat his offer.

"Sure you won't reconsider? You'd be more comfortable . . ." He glanced over his shoulder. "Ah, Mr. Griggs." His tone had curdled, making his antipathy plain.

The slight, soberly dressed gentleman inclined his head, his glance chilly. "Mr. Freeman." His voice warmed. "Dare I hope this is Dr. Cabe?"

"You're acquainted?" Freeman said in surprise.

"We've corresponded," the missionary explained, though sounding grudging at the necessity. Clearly he wished Freeman would take himself off. Matthew wondered at the antipathy: Were spiritual matters or politics at the root of it? "Dr. Cabe's father and I were good friends. Perhaps you knew Captain Cabe of the whaler *Warwick*."

Matthew shook the narrow, bony hand that gripped his. "It's kind of you to meet me, sir." He was genuinely surprised; he had intended to call on the missionary, but the exchange of several courteous letters hadn't led him to think his visit was warmly anticipated.

"Of course you'll stay with me, at least until you get settled." Griggs apparently considered it a matter of course. "Is this all your luggage?"

Matthew was tempted to argue, preferring the independence and solitude of a hotel room, but saw no way to refuse without being rude. He asked, "I won't be putting you out?"

"I'd be insulted if you refused." The Reverend Mr. Griggs glanced dismissively at Freeman. "I fear I have no room to offer you a ride."

"I'm being met." Freeman held out a hand to Matthew. "Dr. Cabe, I trust we'll encounter each other again. Perhaps dinner some evening? Ah, good. Until then."

Matthew took stock of his host as he accepted assistance with his trunks. A large man himself, Matthew towered over the missionary, who was short of stature and narrow of chest and shoulder. His color was not good, either, Matthew noted from long habit; might he be consumptive? Perhaps it was only that the tropical clime did not agree with him. His face was thin and intelligent, more zealous than kindly, although he had been everything that was civil thus far.

They deposited the luggage in a cart pulled by an unprepossessing animal the Reverend Mr. Griggs remarked was typical of island horseflesh. He waited until Matthew was seated before he snapped the reins. "Some of the chiefs and wealthier foreigners have better, but on the whole the horses here are a pitiful lot. I'd say they're suitable for the slaughterhouse, but few carry enough meat to make them welcome there! The Hawaiians are enamored of horses but care for them poorly. This specimen belongs to one of our native teachers, a fine fellow but for his pleasure in Saturday horse racing."

"Do the natives bet?"

"He doesn't, but of course a good deal of gambling goes on despite our best efforts to discourage it."

As they rode, Matthew observed that there appeared to be no sidewalks, and the adobe walls were disintegrating, their mud oozing down to deepen the layer in the street. Here and there the adobe had been replaced by rough blocks Matthew knew to have been cut from coral, or by wooden picket fences. He was agreeably surprised by some of the houses, two-story frame structures with wide verandas and well-laid-out gardens. Yet the cart also passed pigs wallowing in mud holes, and once a native strode past completely naked but for a hat, an embroidered waistcoat, and a scanty swatch of fabric wrapped about his hips. He grinned amiably, but what caught Matthew's physician's eye was the scabrous condition of his skin.

"Are venereal diseases prevalent here?"

"Disgracefully so!" exclaimed Griggs. "During the whaling season the women sell themselves and then take home the diseases. The race is nearly dying out, with that the primary cause. You can see why I hope to persuade you to stay. There are too few doctors here. Those we have must often travel to the other islands. Several are away right now. I could bring you twenty patients tomorrow!"

He paused as half a dozen untended cattle thundered by, slipping in the mud and shaking their long horns at the horse and wagon. Apparently the occurrence was too commonplace for comment, for when the lowing of the agitated beasts diminished, he continued, "And matters may worsen. I hear that two native washerwomen over on Maunakea Street have been stricken with smallpox."

Smallpox. Matthew felt a chill at the very idea. His father had written of how susceptible the islanders were to white man's diseases, how often they were fatal. During a measles epidemic in 1848, in one day alone three hundred bodies had been carried off Waikiki to be disposed of at sea. Smallpox was a scourge even in Boston, where vaccination was commonly done; it was still one of the largest killers of children. But here, where neither adults nor children had had a chance to develop resistance! The Hawaiians could be decimated.

"What measures have been taken?" he asked.

"Ships arriving are warned, and any ill passengers or sailors are quarantined. The yards and adjoining lots were fenced off so that the grass huts and contaminated clothing could be burned, and I understand that a commission of health has been appointed. What they will decide, I don't know."

Surely the obvious action—a program of vaccinations— could be taken without lengthy, or even brief, deliberation. When Matthew said so, the missionary sighed.

"Such ignorance still prevails among the natives, I greatly fear for them. They persist in going to their native *kahunas*— no better than witch doctors—in preference to our physicians. They may be frightened by the idea of having their arms scratched to inoculate them with one pestilence to banish another. And will they understand the necessity for quarantine, or for burning all the possessions touched by those stricken?"

Burning the homes after the victims died would be too late to stop the spread of the disease in any case. Thinking aloud, Matthew said, "A quarantine hospital should be established immediately. Do you know the makeup of your commission?"

"Two of the three are physicians. Drs. Judd and Rooke."

"Then they must have anticipated this crisis. It was inevitable that smallpox would arrive. Unfortunately, vaccine matters doesn't always travel or keep well. We can only hope that sufficient is available." Privately, Matthew wondered why some effort to vaccinate the natives hadn't been attempted before a crisis made all frighteningly urgent.

"Indeed," the missionary agreed. "Or that it isn't needed. Smallpox first appeared in February, when a passenger became ill on the *Charles Mallory* out of San Francisco. But he was quarantined and made a recovery, and no one else was stricken. Perhaps this outbreak is separate and can be contained as easily."

"Let us hope so," Matthew agreed, too courteous to express his reservations. "And I'd be willing to see some patients while I'm here. But I should warn you that I intend to depart by September at the latest. Your persuasions will be for naught; I must return to my practice."

"Yes, of course," his host agreed blandly. "Though you mustn't expect me to abandon trying! Ah, here we are."

The small frame house could have been transported wholesale from any New England village. Perhaps it had been. Matthew recalled that, because of the shortage of lumber here, a few houses had been built in the United States, carefully dismantled, and then sent to be reassembled by the missionaries.

The interior was as familiar and as lacking in any hint of the tropical setting. Only the unpapered walls had the crudeness of the frontier. But several portraits and landscapes hung thereon, and the furnishings were similar to those of any parlor in Boston. Mrs. Griggs bustled out of the kitchen to greet them. She was a sturdy woman several inches taller than her husband and considerably more substantial. Though they looked odd together, affection seemed to exist between them. She accepted with equanimity the addition of a visitor to the household, and both Griggses showed him to a bedroom that probably belonged to a child.

Observing the bat and ball in one corner, Matthew said, "But where will your son sleep?"

Immediately he felt from the silence that he had spoken

tactlessly. He turned to see the unalterable grief of parents who have lost a dearly beloved child. Griggs tried to disguise it, speaking bravely.

"We lost Owen just this spring. A terrible pain in the stomach, a high fever . . ." The missionary's throat worked. "Dr. Alexander cupped him, but to no avail. We console ourselves that he has been transported to Heaven, beyond the reach of temptation and the ordeals of life. He, in mercy, is spared its dangers."

"I'm sorry," Matthew said gently. "You must miss him nonetheless."

Mrs. Griggs blinked back tears. "We shouldn't have left his room the way it was. Of course I've given his clothes to the needy, but I kept a few of his possessions . . . If they distress you . . ."

"Not at all," he said, feeling inadequate.

Mrs. Griggs gave him a shaky smile and abruptly turned and fled the bedroom. Griggs cleared his throat. "I apologize. He was our only child, and we still feel the loss deeply."

"No, it is I who must apologize for imposing. Are you certain . . . ?"

"Yes," the missionary said firmly. "The company will do us good, give us something to think about. Come, let's have some luncheon and you can tell me what it is you hope to accomplish here and whether I might be of assistance."

The meal was simple, but gratefully received. Fruits and vegetables were scarce on a sea voyage, and the array of fruit Mrs. Griggs set out was as heaven to a dying sinner. Matthew had never eaten watermelon, and oranges and bananas but rarely. These bananas were baked, and tasted somewhat like apples similarly cooked.

Eventually sated, Matthew said, "You're aware of the failure of my father's sugar plantation."

Griggs rested his elbows on the table. "Yes."

"Father was . . . stunned that his fortunes could be reversed so quickly." So stunned that he had killed himself, Matthew thought grimly, though in writing the Reverend Mr. Griggs he had not explained the cause of death. Feeling a share of the responsibility for his father's choice of suicide, Matthew wasn't yet ready to explain the hopelessness that had led to such a desperate act. He said merely, "His distress played a great role in his death. Obviously he was prevented from coming himself to check on matters. I'm here in his stead."

"Many of the planters have suffered similar reversals." Yet the missionary wasn't meeting his eyes. "Sugar brought high prices in California while the rush for gold was on, but that market has largely dried up. Those prices have plummeted."

"But according to Father's partner, they had not suffered as much as some of their fellows. The investment they'd made in machinery for more efficient milling of the cane seemed to have been a wise one. My father felt sure the superior grade of sugar they produced would allow them to survive until a treaty to reduce the U.S. tariff is negotiated. Then to have the government foreclose on their loan!"

"I understand it must have been a shock."

It was information Matthew sought, not sympathy. "My father's partner was Mr. Edward Landre. Is he still in the Sandwich Islands?"

"Regrettably, yes." The missionary's mouth had tightened. "Since your father's departure, Landre has become an assistant minister of finance for the government."

Matthew said incredulously, "They foreclose on his loan and then appoint him, a failure as a planter, to oversee the kingdom's money?"

"That, despite disgraceful conduct of his personal life. He lives with a young Hawaiian woman without benefit of marriage and has fathered a child by her. We do not see *him* in church on Sunday! I told your father at the time that I thought he had made a mistake in his choice of business partner." Griggs leaped to his feet and paced, face flushed with the force of his feelings. "Landre is precisely the kind of white man who undermines our every effort to awaken the Hawaiians to a sense of moral values. On the one hand we preach, and on the other they see the conduct of men such as he, respected in the foreign community and even among the chiefs." Bitterly he added, "If only the plague would cleanse these islands of the bloodsuckers like Landre, we might welcome it with gratitude rather than fear!"

Matthew wondered at the strength of his response. This was no gentle, forgiving man of God, but rather one with the wrath of the Old Testament Jehovah.

Shaking off his surprise, Matthew fastened on one part of this tirade. "If Landre is so respected—even to the point of being offered a post in the government—how is it that his loan was foreclosed on?"

The missionary's chest heaved, and he said acidly, "I do not understand it, but he was able to recover. You should know that Mr. Landre is again in possession of the plantation. This time, as sole owner."

Out-and-out thievery! A controlled man, Matthew was disturbed by his reaction to the news. His hands involuntarily curled into fists. By God, he wanted to knock the bastard down, see blood spurt from his nose. In the most primitive way possible, he wanted to punish his father's trusted partner for his betrayal. Even Matthew's awareness that his anger burned hotter because of his own share of guilt didn't serve to cool his temper.

He shoved back his chair. "I believe he owes me an explanation."

"Yes. I can loan you the horse and give you directions now, unless you'd prefer to wait until tomorrow . . ."

"No," Matthew said with resolve only hardened by the dif-

ficulty and delay of traveling halfway around the world. "The
sooner the better."

Honolulu House, the building in which the government ministers had their offices, was a handsome structure of the ubiqui-
tous coral blocks quarried from the reef in front of the harbor.
Matthew's father had written that the stone was soft when cut
but hardened quickly on exposure to air. The government building stood on Merchant Street near the wharves; Matthew entered the small yard surrounded by a wall through an arched
stone gateway topped by a large gilt crown.

Several white men were leaving just as he arrived. Having
no idea what his father's former partner looked like, Matthew
nodded. "Good day. I wonder if you could direct me to Mr. Edward Landre."

"His office is upstairs," one of them said willingly enough.
"Second door on the left. But I don't believe he's there."

"Are you new to Honolulu?" inquired another, a stocky man
of middle age. Though not physically prepossessing, he had
piercing eyes that commanded attention.

"I arrived only this morning," Matthew conceded, "on the
brig *Minerva*. My name is Cabe. Dr. Matthew Cabe."

This answer was seized upon. "Ah! A medical doctor?"

"Yes," he admitted somewhat warily. "I'm told you have a
shortage."

"A desperate one," the gentleman exclaimed. He held out a
hand. "I'm Dr. Gerrit Judd, Minister of Finance. Perhaps you've
been told that smallpox has made its appearance here?"

"Yes. If I can be of assistance . . ."

"Have you any experience preparing vaccine matter?"

"In a small way, but I'm primarily a surgeon."

"Ah! Better yet," Dr. Judd said with evident satisfaction. "I can refer several patients to you, if you would be willing to see them. Perhaps you'll dine with me tonight? I must hurry right now, but we could talk then."

"I'll look forward to dinner," Matthew said. He couldn't help being interested in the chance to observe for himself the man scathingly called "King" Judd by those infuriated by his autocratic manner. Yet this was the same man who had put the Hawaiian kingdom on a sound financial footing and steered it through the dark days when independence was threatened first by the English and then the French.

Directions in hand to Dr. Judd's home in the Nuuanu Valley behind Honolulu, Matthew asked, "Where might I find Mr. Landre?"

"Try the Customs House," Dr. Judd said as he turned away. "Or even the courts. He's taken on many of my duties to free my attention for the medical crisis."

"Thank you," Matthew said.

The men departed, and, placing no dependence on Judd's vague suggestions, Matthew continued into the government building. Upstairs he found a clerk who thought Landre might have gone home.

Half an hour later, Matthew dismounted in front of a handsome house on the *mauka* side of Beretania Street. Already he had discovered that directions in Honolulu did not consist of turns south or west; rather, *makai* was toward the sea, *mauka* the barren mountains, *Waikiki* toward Diamond Head, and *ewa* for the opposite, which he judged to be roughly northwest. Thus he had taken a number of wrong turns from the difficulty of remembering whether he was to turn *mauka* on Fort Street or *ewa* on Hotel, and what the devil each meant anyway. But he thought this must be Landre's house.

Two storied, it had large windows flung open to receive the day's pleasant breezes. A lanai—another new word—flung its shaded arms around the house. A wall built of coral block and topped by wooden pickets separated lush grounds from the muddy street. There seemed to be smaller structures in back, for what purposes Matthew had no idea.

He tied his horse to a hitching post and strode up the walk past roses in bloom, their scent mingling in the warm air with that of other, more exotic flowers. His knock on the carved front door was answered after a long silence by a young Hawaiian woman.

She was astonishingly pretty, with liquid dark eyes that fastened themselves inquiringly on his face. Aside from the dusky hue of her skin, she wouldn't have stood out in any drawing room back home, except by virtue of her beauty. Glossy black hair was skillfully confined in a heavy chignon on her neck, and a high-necked green silk gown rustled over layers of petticoats when she opened the door wider.

"May I help you?" she asked.

It would have been rude to express his surprise at her facility with English, so he confined himself to inquiring, "Is Mr. Landre at home? I'm Dr. Matthew Cabe. I must speak to him."

"Yes, he is. Come in." When he followed her into the pleasantly shaded interior, she gestured gracefully with one slender hand. "Please, have a seat. I'll tell him you're here."

This must be the native woman of whom Griggs had spoken. No wonder Landre hadn't been able to resist her charms!

It appeared that he could afford the best. Certainly no sign of financial difficulties showed here. Woolen carpets covered the floor of the room that ran the length of the house. A piano reposed at one end; Venetian blinds could be lowered over the tall casement windows. An elegant rose-and-black striped sofa was coupled with two black-and-rose patterned wing chairs before a fireplace.

He didn't want to leap to conclusions. The sugar plantation might not have been Landre's only investment—although if he'd had other resources, why hadn't he met the loan obligation?

When Matthew heard a footstep behind him, he turned.

Edward Landre had the looks and air of a European diplomat. His black frock coat and trousers were well cut, and his boots gleamed with a polish Matthew never achieved. Vivid blue eyes were a startling contrast to his handsome, sundarkened face. One hand extended, he advanced smiling, teeth a flash of white below a full mustache.

"Napua called you Dr. Cabe. Can it be that you're William's son?"

Matthew did not smile or accept the handclasp. "That's right. I am."

Landre's face sobered and his hand dropped. "I'm sorrier than I can say about your father. He was a fine man. I regret the end of our association. In fact, I've been hoping . . ." He hesitated.

Matthew lifted an eyebrow. "Hoping?"

"That he hadn't received my news about the plantation before he died. I thought perhaps he'd been spared that."

"I'm afraid not." Matthew made no attempt to disguise his anger. "In fact, the news was what precipitated his death."

Looking troubled, Landre searched Matthew's face. At last he said with a groan, "Dear God, I feared as much. I knew he hadn't a great deal of other income."

So little that the loss of the plantation meant he would be dependent on his son. Apparently death had been preferable to that. The knowledge that his own bitterness had led to their cool relations would haunt Matthew for the rest of his life. Perhaps it was absurd to think that he could atone in some way by recovering his father's share in the plantation, but working to that end was the only action he could take.

"How did it happen?" Matthew asked quietly.

"You cannot reproach me more than I do myself!" Landre said in agitation, then broke off to draw a deep breath. "Please, sit down, Dr. Cabe. You have every right to hear the story, but it's a long one."

A soft, feminine voice interrupted. "Is everything all right?"

Matthew turned to see the young Hawaiian woman standing in the doorway with her hands clasped before her and her expression faintly anxious.

The reason for her anxiety became clear when Landre frowned and snapped, "Yes, yes. Haven't I made it clear I prefer you not to interrupt when I'm conducting business?"

She flushed and glanced quickly at Matthew, betraying her shame, before her dark eyes returned to her paramour. "I'm sorry," she said with stiff dignity. "I thought . . . Excuse me." Head held high, she exited the room.

Landre said smoothly, "I must apologize. A man needs feminine companionship, but I try not to put my fellow countrymen in the position of having to treat her with the same civility they would my wife, had I one."

"I hope common courtesy isn't too much to ask of your countrymen."

A ghost of some emotion that might have been anger passed through Landre's vivid eyes, but he easily mastered himself. "I treat her very well."

Just as stiffly, Matthew said, "That's between the two of you."

"I shouldn't like you to think . . ." The man stopped. His well-shaped mouth twisted, and he regarded his visitor ruefully. "I fear we've gotten off to a bad start. Please believe I was trying to save you from discomfiture, not cause that very thing."

Matthew saw no alternative but to say with reasonable grace, "I didn't intend to imply criticism."

"Well. Shall we take up where we left off? I believe I had just invited you to have a seat."

Matthew chose the sofa, where he crossed one leg over the

other. "You were going to tell me about the downfall of my father's sugar plantation."

"Indeed." His host sat in one of the wing chairs. "Perhaps we might not have come to such a pass had your father been here. I tried to persuade him to stay, but he was eager to see you and your mother."

Eager? Matthew thought the word too strong to describe his father's occasional duty visits home. Matthew's entire childhood had been spent without a father. William Cabe was a whaler who regularly embarked on two- and three-year voyages around the Horn to the killing waters of the Arctic and the Sea of Japan. Brief fall or spring respites would be spent in Honolulu, where barrels of oil could be transferred to another ship to be carried to New England and the whaler restocked with potatoes, onions, pineapples, cabbage, and beef on the hoof, enough to last another season hunting the behemoths of the ocean for their blubber. Captain Cabe's visits home were fleeting, his letters about the wonders he saw a poor substitute. The boy Matthew had considered that he might as well not have a father for all the use the man was to his wife and son.

He had become a planter instead only the last few years, but even that had been half a world away from his family. The last visit had been too late to see his wife again. The cholera had taken her along with many others that winter, too swiftly for her to summon Matthew to her side. She'd died alone, and Matthew had only rage left for the father who professed grief and a desire to become close to his son.

Landre had continued talking; he'd had business in Honolulu even as he tried to run the plantation, he said, and had been distracted, traveling back and forth over the Pali as often as once a week, but in his absence the foreman had encountered continual difficulties.

"Machinery broke down, we had to wait for parts and meanwhile weren't producing sugar—we had such bad luck I even wondered about sabotage. And labor is a perpetual problem here, you know. The Hawaiians, when you can get them to work at all, are like children, completely undependable. The overseer turns his back and they instantly drop their hoes and pull out their pipes. Weeds cripple the cane while they tell yarns and laugh at the *haole*, as they call the white man! Last year we imported some Chinese contract laborers, who are superior, but there are too few, and even they, though diligent, are not swift. I tell you, it seemed for a year or more as though we were cursed!"

His manner was sincere, but Matthew was not a credulous man. He would require far more than this story to let go of his suspicions.

"And then someone in the ministry of finance decided to call in the loan," Matthew prompted the man.

"My fault as well!" Landre said with a grimace. "I made the mistake of inquiring about borrowing a yet greater amount. I can't blame Dr. Judd for fearing that meant we were on the verge of disaster and the kingdom might never see its money again. His first loyalty must be to the government; he has worked hard to set the treasury to rights and dares not take foolish risks only because he wants to extend a helping hand to friends."

Had Judd nonetheless extended a helping hand to a friend, once the partner, perhaps not as well liked, was no longer involved?

Matthew was careful that his tone be no more than dry. "Yet you have obviously recovered your personal fortunes." He gestured about him, at the elegantly appointed parlor.

Landre's cheeks flushed and he surged to his feet, hands curling into fists. His first words were wrathful, as an innocent man's might be. "Do you dare imply . . . ?"

Matthew didn't move. "What might be presumptuous under other circumstances is surely understandable given my father's association with you. Can you blame me for being . . . curious about your apparent prosperity?"

A muscle jerked in the other man's cheek; his fingers flexed. At last his mouth twisted and he abruptly sat down again. "No." His voice was harsh. "No, I cannot blame you. Were I in your position, I would ask the same questions."

"Then perhaps you might answer," Matthew said coolly.

"I had other investments—I'm a partner in a mercantile firm here in Honolulu, Marshall & Sinclair, down on Queen Street, and had sunk some money into a whaling ship as well, the *Kona*, with Captain Barlow. When the troubles began, I regretted extending myself so dangerously, but what could I do? The *Kona* was beyond reach, the store in the midst of stocking up for the winter business . . ." He stood again, as though jerked to his feet, and began to pace. "I've told you how bitterly I regret failing William. Then, when it was too late, the *Kona* arrived with twelve hundred barrels of sperm oil, and a record number of other ships, equally successful, wintered here in Honolulu. Our shelves and warehouse at Marshall & Sinclair were left bare. Both ventures were profitable beyond my dreams! But I had already writ your father, already lost both his money and that I had invested in the plantation."

Grudgingly, Matthew accepted that it was possible. All might have happened just as Edward Landre described it. William Cabe had been foolish to invest so heavily in a business as uncertain as island agriculture. He'd let the high prices sugar was bringing in California blind him to the temporary nature of a fevered rush for gold. As quickly as the gold played out, so did the prices for goods to supply the miners. Had his ruin been no more than the result of bad judgment and bad luck? Matthew wondered.

And had *he* let emotions as blind drive him to make this ill-considered journey, when the same answers—answers that proved a man's innocence—could have been obtained by patient correspondence?

Or was Landre playing him as skillfully as a master pianist performed a long-rehearsed piece?

Well, there were ways to find out. He would make other inquiries until he was certain in his mind, and then apologize if he must. But if Landre had lied to him today, Matthew would make it his business to destroy him.

He, too, rose to his feet. "I've taken enough of your time today. I hope you won't be offended if I question others."

"Would it matter if I was?"

Matthew held his gaze steady. "No."

Landre gave a short laugh. "Then I'll try to accept the inevitable whispers with as much grace as possible. Let me see you out, Dr. Cabe."

They did not shake hands at the door that closed firmly behind him. Swinging a leg over his horse a moment later, Matthew glanced up at the house. In one of the tall upstairs windows stood the Hawaiian woman, watching his departure with grave, dark eyes. He inclined his head, and she hastily stepped back, out of his line of vision.

He couldn't help feeling sorry for her, a proud woman who must accept constant humiliation from the *haole* who dressed her like a beautiful doll but who would never love her. But perhaps she didn't think she had done so badly; after all, she lived in one of Honolulu's finest mansions, wore silk and ate European delicacies. She was undoubtedly better off with Landre than she would have been selling herself to the sailors on Nuuanu Street.

Dismissing thoughts of the young Hawaiian woman, Matthew turned the horse's head toward the harbor. Despite Landre's explanations, he still felt the stir of anger. The origin of his dissatisfaction was easily identified.

For all his lamentation and apparently ingenuous explanations, Landre had been careful not to mention that he owned the plantation again. Did he think Matthew wouldn't find out?

But what bothered Matthew the most was a question he had to ask himself. His father's former partner had detailed his failures and frustrations as a sugar planter; he had admitted that sugar prices were still depressed. So why had Edward Landre chosen to sink his newfound wealth back into that particular mire?

Two

Napua didn't know why she felt unsettled, why she lifted her head from her quilting at every small creak of the house. Edward often went out in the evening without telling her where he was going or when he would be home. His was a life lived in two parts: his *haole* friends, and business, and her. She had once thought the two halves would be joined like an oyster shell, with their love the pearl inside. But she knew better now. She who had once been prideful, who had no small names among her ancestors, had become little better than a *kauwa*—a slave—there to meet his needs when he wanted her, and invisible the rest of the time.

He had promised to marry her, when she first came to live with him. She wouldn't have come otherwise. Too many had wept tears when she gave up her virtue to this *haole* man. She'd disappointed the missionaries, who had been so good to her. To them, marriage meant respect.

But his promises had come to nothing, and she realized she had been a fool. The last time she asked when he would marry her, Edward had laughed derisively.

"When Boki comes back. Isn't that how the natives say it?"

Boki had been *alii*, a high chief who in 1830 fitted out a ship and went off looking for an island across the sea that was said to grow thick with the much-prized sandalwood. No word of him or his ship was ever heard again. Boki wasn't coming back; everyone knew that. It was a mocking way of saying: *Never.*

But what was she to do now? She had a son with this man who had not kept his promises, and no family to return to. Her mother had died with the squatting sickness, *ka mai oku u*, five years ago; her father had gone off in a whaling ship even longer ago, and like Boki had never come back. Those who once would have made up an extended family had all died. The missionaries had become her family, but she had disappointed them. Would they welcome her back? Would they accept her *hapahaole* son, or despise him?

The stitches she set in the quilt were tiny and patient, not like the anxiety in her heart. This quilt was the first she had made that was hers alone, that spoke of her people and the islands. The missionary women made their own kind of quilts: they cut fabric up into small pieces and sewed them back together to make patterns. But Napua had seen immediately that patterns could be made with big sweeps of fabric, patterns that would look like those her mother and mother's mother had stamped onto sheets of *tapa*.

And so she created this quilt that remembered the leis made of the rich feathers from the *mamo* bird, which her people had always worn on ceremonial occasions. She had cut its intricate pattern from one large piece of red calico, and appliquéd it to a white background. Then she cleaned, bleached, and carded wool and laid it out evenly on the backing. Now she quilted in a frame. Instead of making the stitches into patterns of their own, as on the *haole* quilts, hers followed the edges of the red lei, as the waves echoed the line of the shore, however rugged.

It pleased her, this quilt, which wouldn't shred if it got damp as the bark *tapa* had, but still made her think of the beautifully colored *pa'u* Hawaiian women had once worn as skirts. This quilt might endure past a time when there were any Hawaiians to remember the color-blocking done on *tapa*. So many died, Napua thought these islands would soon belong to the foreigners. Those who had once lived and farmed here would be no more than a memory that crumbled with the walls of the fishponds and the foundations of the abandoned *heiau*, which had been places of worship back in dark and sinful times.

She heard the sound of the door opening and quiet footsteps coming into the room. Napua had gathered several stitches onto her needle, and now she left the needle in the cloth and stood, waiting.

He was smiling as he came into the room, but not at her. No, this was a smile for himself. Something had happened that he was glad about. When he saw her, the smile vanished.

"Ah, Napua. I was hoping you were still up. I wanted to speak to you."

"Has this something to do with that man who was here today, that Dr. Cabe?"

"Dr. Cabe?" His eyebrows rose in surprise. "No, why would you think that?"

She bent her head submissively—she had learned that he liked his woman so. "Only because you seemed disturbed."

Edward didn't want to talk about Dr. Cabe, as he seldom wanted to talk about anything important with her. He spoke brusquely. "No, this is something else altogether. Napua, I'm getting married."

Married? Hope washed over her, like water rushing into a newly prepared taro field. Had he changed his mind? And then she heard him fully. *I'm* getting married.

She lifted her head again and asked carefully, "What do you mean?"

"I've asked Miss Isabelle Gordon to marry me. Tonight she agreed. You must move out."

"You said you would marry *me*." Reminding him would do no good, she knew that, but she felt strange. A mist twined before her eyes, as though she'd become lost on Mount Kaala, where the clouds so often clung. The grayness made Edward look far away.

"Did you actually believe that?"

"Yes," she said.

He had a cruel laugh. "Why should I marry you? I got what I wanted without. You're an embarrassment to me in public, and you bring me no advantages, nothing like a well-bred, wealthy young white woman can."

I got what I wanted without. Foolishly she had given it to him. What was it people said? "Everyone knows that a woman is like an easily opened calabash." She was a gourd that had cracked open at the first tap. Was that her fate, to sell her body over and over so that she and Kuokoa could survive?

In desperation, Napua cried, "We have a son."

Edward's mouth curled in contempt. "A half-breed. What would I want with him?"

Her rage came like the *kona-hili-maia*, the banana-thrashing wind that storms down from the mountains. He thought he could throw her away, a thing of no consequence. But it was not so. She had weapons, ways of fighting back. She could make it so this wealthy young *haole* woman, this *Miss Gordon*, didn't want him anymore. She could make sure that he lost some of what she knew he had snatched from others. Like this Matthew Cabe, the tall blond doctor. She had heard what was said, as she had heard other conversations. She knew the lies that were spoken.

But she would wait and see, letting the rage blow itself out for now. Like the *kona-hili-maia*, it would come again. Perhaps he meant to take care of his son, even if he was ashamed of him.

"When do you expect me to leave?" she asked, her voice as

calm as though *pilikia*, the trouble, had not come. She was proud of that voice.

"Tomorrow. The sooner the better. I don't want Miss Gordon to hear about you."

Panic fluttered in Napua's chest. "But where can we go?"

Edward's eyes, so blue, raked her. They saw only the surface. "You're a good-looking woman, Napua. I'm sure you can find another protector."

"I am not that kind of woman."

His mouth curled. "If you weren't before, now you are."

Was it true? she wondered in shame. Was she the whore the Reverend Mr. Griggs had named her? Once her *makua*, her father in all but blood, he had turned from her in disgust when he found out she had gone to live with Edward. Confused then, she had wanted to cry, "If not this, what am I to be?" She had not even known *who* she was. Good Christian? *Haole*, beneath the dark skin? But if so, why despite all her learning and fine manners did the *haole* not treat her as an equal? Why did even the missionaries talk about her as though she were a child, forever needing guidance and gentle chiding?

Was she Hawaiian still? If so, why did she look with scorn and pity at those who still scooped their poi from a communal calabash as they clustered in a filthy thatched hut, at the mothers who fed their babies the traditional way, *ho'opua*, by chewing the food until it was liquid enough to run into their babies' mouths? Why had she abandoned worship of her *aumakua*?

If she was neither Hawaiian nor *haole*, what was she? Where did she belong? She knew no more now than she had then.

"You have a son," Napua said desperately. "You cannot say he isn't yours."

Edward sneered. "You want money."

She held her head high. "Yes."

"I'll give you enough to rent a room." He jerked his head

toward the door and spoke with an awful coldness. "Now go. Pack. Do what you must to be out of here tomorrow morning."

The habit of obedience was strong. She went, climbing the stairs slowly, like an old lady. She ached with hurt and fear and the dread of telling Kuokoa their fate. He was a handsome boy, and she had tried to raise him to make his father proud. His skin was lighter than hers, though still there were *haole* who would call him "nigger." She had heard the word and knew it to be an insult. But the ones who had used the word had been strangers, not the boy's own father! Edward had never been a fond parent, but Kuokoa was young still. She had thought someday he would go to work in his father's mercantile house, or become *luna* on the sugar plantation. She had never thought that she alone would have to provide for the boy.

It wasn't right! A father had a duty to his children, just as a mother did. He should share that fierce need to protect that burned in her breast.

Opening her wardrobe, she stared unseeing at the contents. She would not let Edward abandon their son, Napua resolved. For herself, she might not have used those secrets she had learned. But for Kuokoa, she would do what was necessary.

Sweet Home, Dr. Gerrit Judd's house in the Nuuanu Valley above Honolulu, had an entirely different atmosphere than Matthew had imagined. It would appear that no dinner there could be called intimate; Judd's large family was joined by several guests. The finance minister presided at one end of a long table, his wife at the other end.

Mrs. Judd easily awakened Matthew's respect, which would take little more to warm to liking. She was a commanding figure of a woman, nearly as tall as her husband, with a stateliness of carriage and an engaging manner. Her dress was severe, as befitted a missionary wife, although Matthew couldn't help noting that the young ladies of the family wore more fashionable gowns, with the exception of one introduced as Nellie, who was in mourning.

Only after the ladies, chattering, had left the table did Dr. Judd lead Matthew out into the cool evening air on the veranda. No brandy was offered, just as water only had been served at the dinner table.

Settling into a comfortable chair, Matthew looked across the smooth lawn past flowering shrubs and tall trees toward town in the distance at the foot of the valley, refreshingly green compared to the plains below, where Honolulu was situated. Sweet Home was aptly named, he thought, a sprawling two-story house of surprising elegance and yet clearly home to a loving, close family. Thus far he had seen nothing of the "despotic" Dr. Judd so despised, nor of the temper said to flare at any disagreement.

"I apologize for not realizing that you must be related to Captain Cabe," Judd said. In the quick oncome of night his features were becoming indistinguishable. "I'm afraid I was distracted—have been nothing but distracted! Ten more cases of smallpox were diagnosed today. By the time the first two were discovered, it was too late. We mark the houses of those who fall sick with scraps of yellow cloth, so everyone knows to avoid them. I fear by the end those scraps will hang outside every yard."

"Have you begun a program of vaccination?"

"Yes, but we're desperately short of vaccine matter. I'm ashamed to confess that I even vaccinated a cow in hopes she would become infected and provide pus from her lesions! Ashamed, because I have since read that passing the virus through the cow weakens it, and it would have been useless in any case."

"Did you succeed in infecting the cow?" asked Matthew, interested.

"No, the wretched beast remained determinedly healthy," Judd said wryly. "In the end I fear we will have to inoculate from those who have mild cases of smallpox, rather than wait to increase our supply of the cowpox vaccine, despite its greater safety."

Matthew had never seen an epidemic of the disease, and he didn't envy Dr. Judd, who had been charged by the government with battling its awful advance.

"I shall do my best, but I fear that won't be enough." Judd shook his head. "I have enemies, who will doubtless use any failure to undermine me. What galls me is that their concern is not for the population at large. Or for the pitiful remnants of the Hawaiian race, who might face extinction despite our best efforts. No! My political opponents worry only about their own financial well-being! If smallpox still lingers come fall, the whalers won't put into Honolulu, and the merchants will be ruined. Or so they say."

Seeing his chance, Matthew asked, "Is Mr. Landre among those who fear ruin? Or does he support you?"

He felt Judd's scrutiny, his quickened interest, though he had asked the questions mildly. After a moment the minister of finance said, "I believe him loyal, though it is true that he derives his income from a merchant house."

"And a sugar plantation."

"These days, those are rather a drain than a source of profit." He grunted. "I should know; I'm making an amateur's attempt to grow cane myself, over on the windward side of the island."

"You know that my father and Mr. Landre were partners in the plantation?"

"So I understood, and that your father chose to withdraw—perhaps wisely!—when prices fell."

So easily had his inquiries borne fruit—though bitter fruit. That bitterness sounded in Matthew's voice. "Withdraw? Not willingly! Rather, when the government called in the loan to him and his partner, my father had no hope of recovery. Yet somehow Mr. Landre has not just survived, but prospered!"

Judd leaned forward. "What do you mean, called in the loan? We have extended the terms of our agreements with most planters. Times are hard; it's in our interests to help them survive until either annexation to the United States takes place or we can negotiate lowered tariffs. There may have been exceptions in those instances when the holders of the loans were known to be indolent or wastrels, but your father was hardworking. Are you sure you're not mistaken about the circumstances? Did you succeed in finding Mr. Landre today?"

"Yes." Matthew sat silent for a moment. In these quarters, he was reluctant to voice his suspicions until they were substantiated. "It may be that I asked the wrong questions."

"Indeed." Though darkness had rushed over the valley with startling speed, the other man's voice revealed a frown. "Mr. Landre has held his post in government for over two years, and in that time has never given me reason to doubt either his ability or his ethics."

"Forgive me," Matthew said. "I had no intention of questioning either at this point. I seek only to find out what did happen."

With stiff courtesy, Dr. Judd said, "Then if I may be of assistance . . ."

"I shall certainly call on you," Matthew agreed gratefully. He cast about for a change of topic, recognizing that tact required it. Almost at random, he asked, "Is it true that so few physicians practice here in the Sandwich Islands?"

The subject succeeded admirably in distracting Judd, who rose to pace as he launched into a monologue on the reasons medical men had not settled here. Conditions were primitive; the climate did not agree with all. An ambitious man was unlikely to become wealthy attending the natives or the legion of ill sailors left behind when their ships sailed. Yet the need was great.

"I differ from my colleagues in not utterly condemning the native healers," he declared, rocking on the balls of his feet. "Rather, I believe we ought to endeavor by the best means in our power to correct and modify their practice. It is out of the question for us to think of putting down the native practice unless we are able to attend all the sick ourselves, and to do that we would require twenty—thirty!—physicians for every one now practicing here. No, the *kahunas* may do some good if we can introduce them to the basic principles of Western medicine. Their ignorance is understandable, and some are intelligent men. It is my goal to establish a medical school here for native pupils; they have shown their ability to learn geometry and Greek. Why not anatomy and pharmacology?"

"Why not, indeed," Matthew agreed. "My father had a high opinion of the ability of the natives. One that I gather is not shared by all."

The moon must have risen. Despite the early hour, night was fully upon them, and at a season when days were lengthening in New England. Though the veranda was in darkness, silvery light fell across the lawn and through the gnarled limbs of the tall trees that cast twisted fingers of shadow. Dr. Judd gave a brief, humorless laugh.

"You traveled with Mr. Freeman, I understand. The man is one of the breed who hopes to incite revolution. Annexation is not for them! They fear Hawaii would be admitted as a state, giving citizenship to the natives, whom they despise. They hope to profit by controlling the government, perhaps in the end by selling the islands to the United States. They imagine that they operate in secrecy, but nothing in Honolulu is truly secret."

Matthew fervently hoped that was true, although the secrets that interested him had to do with greed, not revolution.

Dr. Judd suggested they repair to the parlor, where he began to describe several patients he hoped Matthew would consider attending.

"Those who would normally perform surgery are fully occupied with preventing the spread of smallpox. We may need to recruit you to that effort, too, but in the meantime if you could treat patients suffering from other ailments, it would be a burden of worry lifted from the shoulders of those conscientious physicians like Dr. Rooke who dread losing someone from neglect."

Shortly thereafter Matthew took his leave, in his pocket a list of names and directions for patients begging medical advice. In a foreign community as small as that which existed in Honolulu, some of these patients might have known William Cabe, and would surely know Edward Landre. A doctor, needed and welcomed into the home, would receive more candid answers than would a stranger, calling with his questions.

Though it went against his principles, he must ruthlessly use his entrée to gain information and introductions. In return, Matthew vowed, he would do his best to bring relief from suffering.

Anne had to duck her head to enter the low doorway of the thatched hut on Fort Street. Inside was a horrific sight: in the dark, foetid confines of the small hut, half a dozen adults and one child lay on filthy mats in similar poses of wretchedness.

Anne moved swiftly from one to the next. All had fevers and the characteristic pustules that gave smallpox its name. They formed as well on the inside of the mouth and throat, sometimes swelling to prevent breathing. Already air whistled in and out of the child's chest, which heaved with the labor. Anne doubted the boy would live through the day.

Nonetheless, she did what she could to relieve these victims, the first she had seen. Leaving the curtain pulled back to admit sunlight through the door, she brought in a basin of cool water and sponged faces in an effort to lower the fever. She spooned cornmeal gruel into those mouths that would open to receive it.

She had sent a message requesting a wagon to carry the sick to one of the hastily established quarantine hospitals. She had no idea how quickly they would respond. She'd heard of only a scattered few diagnosed with smallpox thus far. Had the Commission of Health taken any real steps to combat the epidemic? Were transport and hospitals a reality, or as yet only a conception?

Two cases in May; now, on June 3, a dozen or more were dead of the disease, the number ill unknown. Despite precautions, including inspections of arriving ships and the beginning of general vaccination, even these small numbers hinted at horror ahead. If each of the sick had infected even one or two others, and those infected one or two, the epidemic would grow with shocking speed. In fact, given the Hawaiian's communal living, each victim might infect a dozen or more! How many families like this one, every member felled, had not yet been discovered?

She had been summoned by a frightened neighbor who found these people but was afraid to nurse them herself. With reason, for the young woman had not been vaccinated either. Anne had hastened there, sent word for the wagon to come, and now was determined to stay until it did.

Her arm grew weary as she sponged feverish foreheads with water that became lukewarm. Yet, whispered gratitude and moans would not let her leave. It was the child in particular who tore at her heart. These days, so few babies were born to the natives, each was doubly precious, and yet so vulnerable.

Living conditions such as these horrified Anne, who had been raised to believe that cleanliness was next to godliness. The woven grass walls and ceiling were alive with insects, every item of clothing and bedcover in here so dirty Anne would have thrown it out rather than attempt to wash it. What daylight penetrated came through gaps where a cow had grazed upon the thatching. One huge calabash had been the only dish employed at mealtime; undoubtedly the first person who had fallen sick had continued to dip his or her hand into the poi along with the hands of the healthy.

The hut and everything in it would be burned. It could be rebuilt if any of these smallpox victims survived. But they were unlikely to. This whole family would probably be wiped out, as many others would be after them by this *haole* pestilence.

It was so unfair! The Hawaiians had been a healthy, contented, even prosperous people until Captain Cook lowered anchor at Waimea, Kauia, in 1778. The natives thought him the god Lono because he came from the sea, as Lono had promised to, and because his ships had tall masts and white sails, like the banners of *tapa* cloth carried in the yearly *makahiki* procession to announce the presence of Lono. They had worshiped the strange white man at first, but what was his legacy? The venereal disease. Since then, the numbers of the natives had declined, with this latest cataclysm perhaps the race's death knell.

There were those among the missionary faction who believed the Hawaiian warrior who struck down Cook was only a tool of Jehovah; that Captain Cook had committed such blasphemy in allowing himself to be venerated as a god, he had offended the one true God.

Yet in the end, the greatest sufferer was not the white man who had discovered these islands and been murdered on the beach at Kealakekua Bay, but the native people he found in these islands. Innocents, like the child in this hut whose breath ceased between one heartbeat and the next.

As with her husband, Anne didn't see the instant life was snuffed from this boy. Her back was turned. But she heard it.

"Oh, no," she whispered, and stumbled to his side, where she dropped to her knees.

His eyes were closed—swollen shut—face grotesque with the pustules, thin chest still. Tears ran down Anne's cheeks as she offered a prayer for the salvation of his soul—for the salvation of his people. Then she gently crossed his hands over his chest and pulled the ragged blanket over his small form.

Feverish though she was, one of the women half sat up and cried out at that moment, a long wail of anguish and loss. And then she, too, died, as though her will allowed her to choose the time.

Another still form to be covered; two more bodies to be carted off to an anonymous burial. There would be no one to grieve at the graveside, no names on stone markers. Any remaining relatives would be too frightened to claim them.

But Anne Cartwright grieved, and was angry. She had come here six years before to, in the words of the original order, "cover these islands with fruitful fields and pleasant dwellings, with schools and churches, and to raise up the whole people to an elevated state of Christian civilization." She hadn't come to see all those hopes buried, along with the natives.

Matthew laid his fingertips on the cool, soft flesh of the woman's breast and stroked in a circular motion. She had unbuttoned her dress to bare her breast, but her face was averted and her cheeks flushed.

He found the lump immediately. It was alarmingly firm and large—larger than he had been led to expect. He pressed harder, defined its outline.

Creases forming between his brows, he sat back. "Mrs. Phillips, would you mind lifting your arm? Yes, like that. Thank you."

He slid his fingers from her breast to the yielding flesh of her underarm, probing gently for the glands. With a breast lesion, the glands often became enlarged, too. In her case, thank God, they felt normal. In another case he had removed the glands as well as the breast, but increasing the size of the wound and the length of time the surgery required also made the danger greater.

With a nod, he said, "I'm done, ma'am. Would you prefer I step out?"

"I . . . Yes, please," she whispered, not meeting his eyes.

She came to him in the parlor, accompanied by her husband, who had waited outside the bedroom while Matthew examined his wife, chaperoned by her native lady's maid.

Hugh Phillips was a wealthy English storekeeper, a solid man with bushy russet side-whiskers, a florid complexion, and a peremptory voice that revealed his more humble origins. He led his wife to a chair and solicitously seated her before he straightened and said, "Well, Dr. Cabe?"

Mrs. Phillips had lifted her head as well and gazed anxiously at him. Matthew would have given a great deal to be able to offer a different verdict. Yet they waited only for him to confirm what they already knew.

"I'm afraid I agree with Dr. Rooke," he said straight out. "The lesion will undoubtedly grow and spread to other organs."

He wished she had been referred to him sooner. He had been in Honolulu three weeks now, and seen dozens of patients, but none who awakened his pity as she did. The lesion had probably not measurably grown in so few weeks, but how greatly she must have suffered from anxiety!

Mrs. Phillips didn't so much as blanch. In contrast, her husband's face twisted and he uttered a ragged sound. As though to disguise the terror he had revealed, he spoke loudly, even aggressively. "And if she chooses not to submit to surgery?"

It was to the narrow-shouldered, pale woman who sat

with such dignity beneath her husband's protective hand that Matthew looked. Gently he said, "My guess is that you would have perhaps a year."

"Have you done such an operation before?" she asked, her voice a mere thread, though steady.

"Yes, several times." He did not add that only one of those patients had survived beyond a few weeks. Yet that was one more than would have lived without the surgery.

"Is it . . . very painful?" Her eyes, a calm, pale gray, searched his.

"There will be a degree of pain afterward," he said honestly. "You will be unconscious of the surgery itself, waking only when I am done."

Her forehead crinkled. "I cannot drink spirits."

"We have new methods," he assured her. "A gas called chloroform, when inhaled, renders the patient unaware for a time. With it, women have borne children without pain."

"You so defy God's will?" her husband asked in incredulity. "Genesis 3:16: 'I will greatly multiply thy sorrow and thy conception; in sorrow thou shalt bring forth children.' He chose to punish Eve for her transgression. And you would circumvent His command?"

For the first time, Mrs. Phillips flinched and seemed to shrink.

Angered, Matthew retorted, "Yet Genesis 2:21 declares: 'And the Lord God caused a deep sleep to fall upon Adam, and he slept; and he took one of his ribs, and closed up the flesh instead thereof.' We might consider that God Himself was the first surgeon to use anesthesia."

His patient gave a timid peek up at her husband. "I remember that passage."

"Queen Victoria herself has used chloroform in her *accouchement*," Matthew told them. "Surely you wouldn't question her devotion."

Apparently, Mr. Phillips wouldn't. Whether he had been persuaded by Queen Victoria's example or his wife's frightened eyes, he gave a brusque nod.

Matthew felt compelled to say, "The greatest danger is not the operation itself, but the infection that so often follows. You must be prepared for that possibility."

"I've heard that Dr. Judd removed the"—her voice seemed to catch on the rarely spoken word—"breast of a chiefess by the name of Kapiolani. That she seemed to recover fully, but weeks later died of erysipelas."

Matthew nodded. Erysipelas was the dread of every surgeon. The patient would appear to be recovering, all would be well, and then deep-red inflammation would appear, spreading as if it had tentacles that strangled the life force from its victim.

"That's not unknown," he admitted. "Yet some patients are free of the infections that claim the lives of others. I won't deceive you: you would indeed be taking a risk. If you decide against surgery, you might have a relatively pain-free year. Yet I believe the end to be certain."

"Then there really is no choice at all, is there?" she asked. She reached over and squeezed her husband's hand. "How soon can you do it, Dr. Gabe?"

Matthew glanced around the bedroom chosen for the surgery. Preparations were nearly completed; the room had been thoroughly scrubbed and the furniture replaced by a reclining Chinese chair, a table for his instruments, a washstand, and a rack to hold the two dozen clean towels his assistant was presently laying out.

He watched her work, assessing how reliable she would be. Normally at least one other physician would have been present. The urgent need for the services of those few in Honolulu meant Matthew would both anesthetize his patient and com-

plete the surgery with only the assistance of Anne Cartwright.
She was a widow who had practical experience in nursing and
a reputation as an accomplished midwife, gained in the six years
since her missionary husband died of a tubercular disease, leaving her to make her own way so far from home. Dr. Judd had
recommended her.

"I believe she would have made a fine doctor," he had said.
"I know she's assisted the mission physicians during amputa-
tions. I assure you, she won't faint at the sight of blood."

It wouldn't be the first time a bystander had crashed to the
floor when Matthew made his initial cut. Relatives sometimes
insisted they could help, and in the days before he'd used ether
or chloroform, he'd needed several able-bodied men to hold
down the patient when limbs convulsed in agony.

Thus far Mrs. Cartwright had been efficient and self-
effacing. He had no sense of her personality. He guessed that
she was perhaps twenty-six or -seven years of age. Physically she
was of medium height, somewhat plump, with unexceptional
features in a pleasantly rounded face. Hair of a chestnut brown
was center-parted and drawn severely back over her ears into a
bun in the common style. Her gown was long-sleeved and high-
necked despite the warmth of the day, and she had added a crisp
white apron to protect it. He was glad to see that she was neither tightly corseted—which made fainting more likely—nor
wearing multiple petticoats, which in these close quarters would
get in the way.

"Mrs. Cartwright."

She turned to him with her brows raised above fine gray
eyes, perhaps her best feature. "Yes, Dr. Cabe?"

"Before we begin, please wash your hands in this basin. It
holds a chlorinated lime solution that offers the most scrupulous cleanliness."

She gave a nod that he thought held approval. "I use something similar when I assist women in childbirth. I've read about the success Dr. Semmelweis has had in Vienna in curtailing puerperal fever thus."

"You're well informed," Matthew said in surprise.

"I have made nursing my life." She spoke primly. "I should like to do it as well as possible."

Would that men—and women—of all professions shared her laudable ambition. He had met entirely too many physicians, well trained but too lazy to stay informed on modern developments or to take the care that extra cleanliness required. What role that cleanliness played in the success of an operation Matthew didn't yet understand, but he was convinced of its efficacy and appalled when he saw surgeons cleanse their lancet by wiping it on a dirty shirtsleeve, or hold tools between their teeth for ready availability rather than laying them on a clean cloth nearby.

Gravely he said, "Then I'm fortunate to have your assistance today."

She contemplated him, neither thanking him for the compliment nor simpering. Rather, he had the sense that she was assessing him much as he had her, and that he could expect her gaze upon him as he worked to be a critical one.

"Are you ready for your patient?" she asked.

He agreed, and she departed to fetch Mrs. Phillips. He had been thinking Mrs. Cartwright was an unusual woman, but when she returned with the patient, he couldn't help admiring Mrs. Phillips's composure as well. She came steadily to the reclining chair and settled herself on it with no more than the shakiness of her smile to betray her fear.

"How different it looks in here!"

"It makes a fine operating room." He took her hand in his. "Mrs. Phillips, you haven't changed your mind? You are determined to have the lesion cut out?"

"Yes," she said, with resolve that only deepened his admiration. He was glad she was his patient and not her husband, who would have been far more difficult.

"Very well, then. I'm going to place this pad over your mouth and nose. What I need you to do is deeply inhale the fumes. Try not to hold your breath or cough; either will contribute to your discomfort and delay the coming of sleep. I promise you, the worst of the pain will be past when you awaken."

She bit her lip and nodded. Mrs. Cartwright stood silently to one side, holding the patient's other hand. Matthew laid the cloth over Mrs. Phillips's face and carefully poured the first few drops of the liquid chloroform, watching as they soaked into the gauze. Her chest rose and fell, rose and fell. Her eyes were wide but unafraid. He let another drop fall, soothed her as she gagged, murmuring reassurance until she breathed regularly again. She was a small woman; he hesitated to use too much chloroform. At best, it would leave her nauseated after awakening; an overdose could kill.

But today the process went smoothly. Her eyelids fluttered shut, she sighed, the hand that had been gripping his assistant's went slack. When Matthew was certain she was unconscious, he looked across her at Mrs. Cartwright. "I shall attempt to work quickly, but you may need to administer more of the chloroform. You must proceed very carefully; a drop at a time, merely. Be careful yourself not to inhale the fumes." Despite an open window, the smell in the room was overpowering; he breathed through his mouth by habit.

"Yes, I watched," she said. She gently laid Mrs. Phillips's hand at her side and unbuttoned the front of her dressing gown, separating its folds to bare her pretty breast. He regretted the mutilation he must perform, but what was it compared to a life? He only hoped that, if she survived, her husband agreed and was not repulsed by her deformity.

He washed her breast with the chlorinated-lime solution, then picked up his scalpel. He made the first cut to one side of her breast, the second on the other side. Both cuts were clear and decisive. Blood spurted and he concentrated on tying off blood vessels with the lengths of catgut handed to him at precisely the right moments by Mrs. Cartwright. Once an artery shot hot blood into his eye and he had to step back, shaking his head. Immediately his face was wiped with a damp towel and he was able to return to work.

He had never been more grateful for the chloroform that allowed him to take his time. Without anesthesia a surgeon's first requirement had been speed. Pain and shock had been so great for the patient that any prolonged operation usually resulted in death. The best surgeons could complete an amputation, including ligature of the bleeding vessels, in thirty-five seconds or less; Matthew had heard of one man who could cut out a bladder stone in under a minute. Yet that cutting, however swift, must also be accurate, despite the shrieks of the patient. Now at last— thank God!—a surgeon could work without inflicting such pain and could take the time to proceed more cautiously, more thoughtfully.

Yet he was done with this patient in twenty minutes. Only once had she stirred slightly. With a nod he had signaled Mrs. Cartwright to administer another drop of chloroform, and deep sleep had been restored. One clean cut removed the patient's breast tissue with its malignant tumor, leaving the muscle beneath and a wound six inches across. With Anne Cartwright's deft assistance, Matthew sewed the incision closed, taking care that his stitches were as fine as any skilled needlewoman's. Bandages covered the whole, and he observed his work with satisfaction before plunging his hands, bloody to the wrists, into the washbasin.

"She may be ill when she awakens," he said. "Have a basin at hand and be prepared to gently lift her."

Mrs. Cartwright was gathering up the bloody cloths that had protected the patient's garments and the reclining chair. She nodded. "And for the pain?"

"I see no harm in using some opiates. But wait until her stomach has emptied itself."

"Very well," she agreed. Briskly she bundled away the blood-stained towels, then removed the splattered apron. Without it, she managed to appear as severe and crisp as she had before they began. Not a hair was out of place, not a bead of perspiration trembled on her high, curving brow.

Matthew was momentarily seized with enthusiasm. What a woman! Nurses were so often slovenly or lazy. Certainly they were seldom as efficient, neat, and well educated as Mrs. Cartwright. Perhaps he should persuade her to return with him to Boston to work in his office. Though if he tried to steal her out from under Dr. Judd's nose, the minister would no doubt see that Matthew was lynched before he could set foot on the ship. She was needed here—and how fortunate the foreign community was to have her.

"I thank you for your help today," he said. "I have rarely had a more skilled assistant."

"It was a pleasure to see you work," she returned with composure. What a melodious voice she had, he thought, still gripped by his postsurgical elation. It was low and somehow musical, pitched to be soothing to the feverish ear.

"Will you be free to assist me again should I need you?" he asked.

"It would be an honor," Mrs. Cartwright said, "although I'm attending two pregnant women near their time."

"Any complications?" he asked, even as he checked Mrs. Phillips's pulse.

"Both confinements are progressing normally, although one of the women is anxious. The child will be her first, and I believe her to have been sheltered."

As Anne Cartwright, whatever her upbringing, clearly had not been. He found he was curious about her. According to Dr. Judd, she had come to the Sandwich Islands in 1847 with the last missionary company. Her husband had died within months of their arrival, but she had neither returned to New England nor remarried in the intervening years, although opportunities must have been ample. She was plain, but nothing in her appearance was offensive. And unmarried white women must be in short supply. Yet she seemed to be making her way very well without a husband. Perhaps she had loved Mr. Cartwright too deeply to forget him so easily.

He left the room to speak to Mr. Phillips, who was pale and humble. He returned to find his patient still asleep. It was some time before, as he took her pulse, he felt her arm twitch. He promptly put his speculation about his assistant out of his mind. Within minutes, his patient was awakening. As he'd predicted, she vomited before consciousness had fully returned. Fortunately she'd obeyed his instructions and had little to eat, although dry heaves continued after the watery contents of her stomach were gone.

At last, pale, she lay back and opened her eyes. "It's done?" she whispered.

"Yes." He held her hand in a reassuring clasp. "It went well. Now you have to concentrate on resting and regaining your strength."

"Please God," she murmured, before her eyelids sank shut as though too heavy for her to master.

Please God, he echoed silently. *Let the pus that will inevitably leak from the wound be white and creamy, not thin and malodorous. Please God, let this deserving woman survive my interfering hand.*

Three

Anne and the tall blond doctor hovered outside Clara Phillips's bedroom door. The hallway was otherwise empty, although Anne could hear Mr. Phillips's voice coming from the parlor, where he was issuing orders to a servant. She would have come to dislike that voice, had his attentions to his wife not been so tender.

Twenty-four hours had gone by since the surgery. Dr. Cabe was making his first postoperative visit. Anne, of course, had stayed; that was her life, moving from household to household, depending on need.

As a result, she knew every doctor in Honolulu and had consulted with all of them just as she was at present with Dr. Cabe. So why did she feel so conscious of their aloneness here in this hall, of the way he had of dominating any space?

She knew the answer perfectly well: he was exactly the kind of man she had watched from afar, wistfully, when she was still young enough to dream impossible dreams and foolish enough to believe other men were not like her father. Dr. Matthew Cabe was the kind of man who had never even glanced her way, and never would. She ought to thank God that he wouldn't. Her experience suggested that, however fine the facade, men were all cruel, whether unthinkingly or maliciously, when it came to dealing with their wives.

Well over six feet tall, with sun-streaked hair and strong bone structure, Matthew Cabe was not, Anne suspected, vain. She had found him thus far to be a proud man, even a little stiff, conscious of his skill and integrity. He would be morally unbending and unlikely to change opinions once formed. He might age into pomposity, if he was too admired, and hadn't someone who occasionally, for his own good, punctured his sense of self-worth. He would not deliberately hurt his wife, she thought, but for all that, he would be master and she must bend to his will, whether it broke her or not.

"The dressing remains dry," Anne said, quietly enough not to be heard through the portal. "No pus, laudable or otherwise. I've been anxious." Absurdly so, considering how well the patient did. Yet Anne had been taught to watch for the creamy, whitish discharge that was most often considered a hopeful sign of healing.

"But she's not feverish?" Dr. Cabe asked.

"No, Mrs. Phillips feels well despite some pain. Her spirits are excellent. I didn't know what to do . . ."

"Nothing is the best course," he said, to her surprise. "I'm inclined not even to remove the dressing to take a look. So often after one does, infection creeps in."

"You believe there's a connection?"

"Have you ever seen a microscope?" he asked.

"No. I've read—that is, if I'm thinking of the right apparatus. You can place an eye to the viewer and see minute particles in amazing detail?"

"Indeed!" His enthusiasm was obvious. "One of the more intriguing sights is the animalcules, the tiny, seemingly living creatures that appear to be everywhere. What role they play is still obscure. Perhaps none at all. But I wonder if we won't find they are beneficial or harmful to the open wound. Either way, the air might let them in, or permit them to escape. I should like to leave well enough alone, so long as all *is* well."

"You may determine that for yourself," she said, opening the door.

She liked the frank way he dealt with Mrs. Phillips, just as she had yesterday been impressed by his skill with a scalpel and his quiet requests to her that replaced the angry demands and impatience that were so often her lot. He had explained instead of assumed, and accepted her competence as though he'd expected it. Men so rarely *did* think women were competent.

Now he pulled up a chair to Mrs. Phillips's bedside and talked to her. No, more to the point, he listened to her. How did she feel? Where did she experience pain? Any shortness of breath? Nausea? Could she move her arm comfortably? He took her pulse and listened to her heartbeat with his stethoscope.

At length, he nodded. "Mrs. Phillips, I'm delighted with your progress. I see no sign of infection as yet, which gives me hope there will be none. You may trust Mrs. Cartwright"—he gave her a warm look—"and call for me should you need me. I'll be back tomorrow."

Mrs. Phillips's cheeks had blushed a soft shade of pink, like the shy appearance of the wild violet. Anne understood the reaction. When Dr. Cabe laid a hand on her arm a moment later as they exited the room, she feared her own cheeks might be warming even as she stiffened, anxious to pull away.

"Yes?" she murmured, as coolly as she could manage. She stole a glance upward to see that the doctor was frowning as he looked down the hall toward the parlor. In the hall, dim light lent shadows to the strong features of his face, giving it a harsh aspect.

Rather abruptly, he said, "Her husband . . . he isn't upsetting Mrs. Phillips?"

"Upsetting?" Anne repeated. "To the contrary, he's been very kind. This morning I heard her crying that he would no longer find her pretty, and he . . ." Oh, how to describe the sweet scene she had accidentally overheard? "He soothed her fears," she concluded rather lamely. Men must often express tender sentiments to women they courted, but to hear a husband, married ten years, tell his wife that she would always be beautiful to him, and in such flowery language, had surprised Anne. No, surprise was too mild a word; she had been stunned, moved. And obscurely frightened, for how could a woman resist such blandishments?

"Ah." Dr. Cabe contemplated her, unreadably, with his blue eyes. "You've put my mind at rest. Well." But he didn't move.

What was he thinking? she wondered, as he stood there gazing down at her. She imagined that he was girding himself— to say something? But what? Anne found these close quarters unnerving; it was peculiarly hard to breathe with him looming over her. In her mind's eye, she had a sudden, unpleasant glimpse of another man looming, and she took an involuntary step back before she recollected herself.

Her indrawn breath had sounded as a small gasp. For a moment they stared at each other, and then a mask seemed to settle over his face.

"I'm sorry, was I frowning fiercely at you? I tend to do that when I'm thinking. I'll go speak to Mr. Phillips now. Continue your good work. Call if you need me."

A few long strides and he'd disappeared into the parlor. Anne felt like a fool. What on earth had come over her? He was nothing—nothing!—like her husband, and the circumstances couldn't be more dissimilar. Dr. Cabe had no more personal interest in her than he did in Mrs. Phillips! To him, she and the other woman were nurse and patient, no more. His expression when speaking to either had never been other than detached and sympathetic. Her fear was absurd.

Yet Dr. Cabe awakened something in her—curiosity, she told herself. She had no business eavesdropping, yet she neither removed herself to the bedroom nor retreated down the hall. From here, she could just make out what the men were saying.

Mr. Phillips sounded uncharacteristically diffident. "I'm more grateful to you than I can say. My wife has been so frightened—you have given her hope, at least."

"More than that, I believe," Dr. Cabe's deeper voice responded. "She isn't safe yet—I can't make any certain promises until several weeks have gone by—but right now I'm optimistic."

"If there is anything, anything at all, that I can do," Mr. Phillips said gruffly. "The payment seems so inadequate."

She expected polite protestations, but instead heard the way the doctor's voice hardened. "There is something you can do. I'm told you're prominent in this community, know everyone. I've been making inquiries about someone. If you would tell me what you know . . ."

Mr. Phillips's words became muffled, as though he had turned away to pace or gaze out the window. Even so, she could hear his caution. "Who is it you want to know about?"

"He is an assistant minister of finance. Mr. Edward Landre."

Anne's interest sharpened. Dr. Cabe was interested in the man who had just cruelly turned Napua and his own son out of their home? She had a reason for listening now. The young Hawaiian woman was her closest friend, despite the difference in their stations. If she could find something out to Napua's advantage . . . Anne took a couple of silent steps closer to the parlor doorway.

"I believe him to be an intelligent businessman," Mr. Phillips said, in the tone of one summing up a man's entire character. "I lent him money myself, a year or more ago, and received a handsome return. He had just joined the government and had an opportunity to buy a plantation in which he'd formerly been a part owner. Apparently, Judd had made it a condition of employment that Landre settle his debt, and he couldn't do that. Nor could his partners, however many there were. But once the foreclosure was complete, the only thing stopping him from buying the plantation back at a cut-rate was his lack of funds! He convinced me that his other investments would protect mine and paid me back once the whaling season was over. The end result was that he owned the plantation for less than he had owed on it."

Dr. Cabe asked sharply, "He was already a member of the government when the foreclosure took place? You're certain of that?"

"Yes, quite certain."

"There didn't seem to you to be any . . . impropriety in his taking advantage of his position in that way?"

Anne winced. Unless Mr. Phillips was impervious to the tone of sarcasm, he would surely take offense.

As he did. "Are you criticizing me, sir?"

"It's Mr. Landre's conduct that concerns me."

"And why might that be?" Phillips asked.

The gentleness the doctor displayed to his patients was nowhere in evidence. His voice was as cold as the New England winters she would never forget. "You were willing enough to help me a moment ago."

"I know nothing to Mr. Landre's discredit."

"Yet you tell me he used his office to engineer the dismissal of his legitimate debt to the government—and neatly dispose of his partner. You do not consider that to his discredit?"

"I didn't say that he used his office—merely that he took advantage of an opportunity." The merchant's words lacked conviction.

"I understand that even Dr. Judd's worst enemies don't question his integrity. Do you think he would look on Mr. Landre's seizing of a 'business opportunity' with the same approbation?" Dr. Cabe demanded.

"I assumed he knew . . ."

"Did you?" A pause. Anne would have given a good deal to see the expression on Dr. Cabe's face at that moment. Then she heard him say dismissively, "Thank you for your frankness," and realized she would indeed see his expression in just an instant, when he discovered her lurking in the hall.

She whirled and fled, making it only as far as the bedroom door before Dr. Cabe came out of the parlor. Perhaps he would think she was just coming out. But he didn't even glance her way, merely snatched up his hat from a hall table and departed out the front door. She had only the briefest of glimpses of his countenance, which was gripped with exultation and fury in equal measure. She doubted he would have seen her had she been standing right in front of him.

With a faint chill, she realized that at this moment he was a dangerous man. Staring after him, Anne wondered what he intended to do with his new knowledge, and why it was so intensely personal to him.

Matthew fully intended to wait until his anger cooled before he confronted Edward Landre. He was unaccustomed to letting any emotion—far less anger—consume him so utterly. Given his profession, he couldn't afford to! Celsus, the first-century Roman, had declared that a surgeon must be "filled with pity, so that he wishes to cure his patient, yet is not moved by his cries to go too fast, or cut less than necessary; but he does everything just as if the cries of pain caused him no emotion." Matthew never let emotions drive him. Already he'd been biding his time. Phillips wasn't the first to undermine Landre's story, only the most conclusive. Today was—he had to think—June 6. In the three weeks since his arrival, he'd interviewed half the foreign colony.

He was disturbed to see that his hands shook as he secured his medical bag behind the saddle of the horse he was leasing from the livery stable. Untying the reins, he swung onto the animal's back and turned its head toward town.

King Street was crowded with horseback riders coming and going from the barren plains that stretched from the town's edge to Diamond Head. Races were held there, and even the women, riding in skirts so long they touched the ground, galloped freely in clouds of dust that extended into Honolulu. With the advent of drier weather, the mud that clogged its streets had turned to dust that seeped through clapboards and got into everything. Matthew had seen nothing thus far to recommend this wretched place. He thought longingly of the spring he'd missed at home.

A crowd of chattering *pa'u* riders—so the women in their unusual skirts were called—raced past him, startling his mount into a sideways prance. He started to rein it in, then thought— Why? He'd swallow enough dust anyway, he might as well make the trip as fast as possible. A hard gallop would suit his mood.

"Hiya!" he called and drove his heels into his horse's flanks. Bending low over the animal's neck, his black bag banging behind him, he tore past laughing Hawaiians and a slow dray delivering fresh drinking water to houses with their windows and doors flung open to receive stray breezes—and accept the cursed dust.

He had other patients to see today. Already this week he had drained a neck abscess, amputated a hand, and stitched up a knife wound. But first he would track down Dr. Judd and demand answers. Tomorrow he'd speak to Landre.

Dismayingly few natives were lined up in front of the courthouse to receive vaccinations despite notices that had been posted all week. Had not enough fallen ill yet to frighten the masses? Some had fled town, he knew, despite the government's attempt to keep Honolulu quarantined. But thus far most natives seemed oblivious to the threat, too intent on their pleasures to heed the yellow scraps of calico hanging outside dozens of yards.

Judd wasn't here in his office, so Matthew turned his horse for the nearest hospital, a large thatched hut. As he dismounted, men carried patients from a wagon through the low doorway. All too soon, Matthew thought grimly, most would be carried out again, to be tipped into mass graves.

He was about to duck to enter when a man came out. They checked at the sight of each other. Matthew's courteous greeting died unspoken. Landre.

William Cabe's betrayer bowed urbanely although his face was unsmiling. "Good day, Dr. Cabe."

Matthew clenched his teeth against the rage that rose within him fiercely. Landre was dressed as impeccably as he'd been that day in his home. He was a man to whom appearances—and money—were important enough to justify lying and fraud. Well, by God, this time he wouldn't get by with it!

"Good day?" Matthew said coldly. "I doubt you'll think so when I tell you that I've had my suspicions confirmed. You cheated my father and abused your position in the government. You're a scoundrel, and I intend to see to it that your day, and more, become considerably less satisfactory!"

"You threaten me?" Landre's glittering blue eyes narrowed. "I'll have a constable after you."

"Not by the time I'm done with you," Matthew snapped. He itched to do violence, though he was determined not to make the first move.

But Landre mocked him. "You can't touch me. You're an outsider, nobody. I'm part of the government. You might as well beat your head against the walls of the fort. And for what? Nothing!"

"Nothing?" he repeated, hands curling into fists. By God,

his father might have had his flaws, but he deserved better than this, and from a partner and supposed friend!

The final straw was when Landre laughed. "William Cabe was a fool. Accept that, and go home."

A red mist spread across Matthew's vision, and he swung. His left hook found its mark, landing with a crunch that might have sickened him another time. Blood spurted from Landre's nose, and he cursed. But instead of backing off, he lowered his head and lunged at Matthew, both fists flying.

Before any further blows could land, other men were pulling them apart. Matthew momentarily fought the arms that pinioned his. "Blast it, let me go!"

Landre wiped blood from his face and shook off the hands that held him. Sneering, he snapped, "He's crazy. Keep him off me."

Matthew wrenched free from his captor. From between clenched teeth, he flung bitter words. "You killed him, and I'll see to it that you pay, even if it's with your own life!"

He strode to his horse and mounted, looking down at Landre, whose blood spilled between his fingers onto his white shirtfront, and at the two strangers who had intervened and now listened avidly. Already he was disgusted with himself. He had as little self-control as a drunken sailor drawn into a brawl. All he had succeeded in doing was damaging his reputation. By nightfall every foreigner in Honolulu would have heard about this ugly scene.

I feel as though my death has entered in me with the babe." The dark-haired woman clutched Anne's hand. "That sounds morbid, doesn't it? But I can't rid myself of a dreadful premonition that I won't live to hold my infant. Oh, if only my mother were here!"

Anne sighed and sat back. Nettie Decker was very near her

time; her cervix had begun to dilate, and her back ached without cease, she'd earlier complained, pressing it fretfully. Always anxious, she had lately sunk into a state of intense gloom. Her spirits might have been lightened were she enclosed in a circle of loving female friends and relatives, but instead she must endure her first pregnancy in new surroundings. Her husband had brought his bride to the Hawaiian Islands only this past winter. The one close acquaintance she'd made was with an older woman who was fond of telling horrific stories of childbed disasters.

"I've made Charles promise to name the baby James if it's a boy," Nettie continued in the same melancholy vein, "after my dear brother, whom I doubt I shall ever see again. I've divided up all my little things so that Charles will know who to give them to if I don't survive. I shan't leave anything undone if I can help it."

"My dear," Anne said gently, "I have every expectation that your confinement will proceed normally. You're healthy and thus far exhibit no worrisome symptoms. Why this premonition of tragedy?"

"I don't know." Nettie shuddered, her pretty face pinched. "I know only that I shall soon step into the Valley of the Shadow of Death, and God alone knows whether His mercy will allow me to walk out the other side." She squeezed Anne's hand with convulsive strength. "Once it starts, you won't leave me? Not once? You promise?"

"You have my word," Anne vowed. "But I wonder, to quiet your anxiety, whether you should call a physician when labor commences."

Nettie's brown eyes rounded. "A man? Oh, no! How could I? I could never let him see me—touch me—in that way." Her voice trembled. "Every feeling of modesty rebels at the very idea!"

Anne fully understood Nettie's fear, yet common sense and

medical necessity sometimes demanded that a woman be brave. If only there were women physicians!

She tried again. "But a physician could do things for you that I can't. There are drugs to hasten labor should it go too slowly, for example. He might be able to examine you by touch alone, if it's the idea of him seeing you that is so daunting."

"You're suggesting I let him reach up under my skirts—?" The young woman broke off in horror. "Never! The only man I could ever let see me or touch me that way is Charles, and even with him—" A flush mantled her cheeks. "Even then, we go to bed in the darkness. I have never seen him—not fully— Oh, I shouldn't be talking about such things!" Tears sprang into her eyes. "It's just that I need someone! I'm so frightened."

Remembering the peaceful way Mrs. Phillips had slipped under the influence of the chloroform gas, Anne seriously considered suggesting that Nettie Decker bear her child under its kindly agency. Anne had never seen anaesthesia used in childbirth but had read of the controversy surrounding its introduction. The opinions of the medical profession were widely at variance; some physicians extolled the "sweet repose" that saved women untold suffering, while others argued that numerous women had died as a result of the use of chloroform or ether.

Anne herself hesitated because she preferred that the patient know what was going on. Childbirth was an active process; nature had not intended that the mother in effect absent herself while her baby was born. Might her insensibility not make it likelier that forceps must be used? And who knew whether the gas crossed the placenta into the baby's bloodstream. It could not be healthy for an infant who ought to be fighting for life to enter the world in a stupor.

Nonetheless, might not this be a patient for whom an exception should be made? Anne considered the young woman huddled on the bed, her body swollen, her fingers twining and untwining in a constant dance of anxiety, her eyes rimmed with red.

Yet there was nothing wrong with her! Though delicate in build, she had exhibited no alarming symptoms to this point. She was not tubercular, which increased a woman's risk, nor had she been affected by rickets, which could deform the birth canal. In short, there was nothing in either her history or health to suggest concern. She had worked herself into an emotional state because she was alone too much and was far from home and the comforting presence of her mother and sisters.

"Let me give you a back rub," Anne suggested. "That will calm you and soothe the ache. Here, roll onto your side."

Nettie let herself be disrobed and lay still as Anne's fingers worked deftly at the knots and tension that bound the muscles in Nettie's narrow back. Anne suspected such muscular weakness was the result of corsets and inactivity. Somewhat disapprovingly, she reflected that, in her experience, women who had to work and did not depend on servants for everything were less likely to suffer the adverse effects of childbirth.

Then it occurred to her how ironic that she, who had never been pregnant or bore a child, should sit in judgment on how other women held up under the stresses of an admittedly frightening, if inevitable, part of their lives. How would they feel to know that she envied them? She would not marry again, had no desire to revisit the marriage bed, but she regretted that her brief term as wife had not resulted in pregnancy. At least then she would have a child to raise and love, would know the joys of motherhood firsthand rather than by observing them in others.

She would not complain about her life, she liked the independence, the knowledge that she was useful. She thought of her mother sometimes, though she had been dead ten years, yet otherwise Anne's experience of family ties was not such as to make her miss them. Only occasionally did she let herself know regret: that she would never be a mother in turn, might never have a home of her own. Sometimes she felt invisible, a presence that wafted insubstantially from household to household, needed briefly but not missed when she left. Would anyone even notice if she vanished altogether?

Right now, Nettie Decker would, but their present relationship would not ripen into real friendship. Too large a gulf of society and beliefs separated them. Nettie was a wealthy man's wife; she existed to look well at the head of his table. Anne's somber, dowdy wardrobe would appall Nettie, once she was able to look outside herself. Her time was spent frivolously: dancing, gossiping, flirting. She undoubtedly thought of the natives as her inferiors: adequate servants, if lazy, but shocking to meet in society. Her husband, Anne knew, was an annexationist; probably his wife shared his disdain for a dark-skinned royal family.

Anne would very likely never even have met either of the Deckers had her services as midwife not been recommended to them. Although the foreign community in Honolulu was small—perhaps five hundred in number—sharp divisions in it existed. The missionaries met socially with their supporters. The merchants and whaling captains comprised another group altogether. A man like Abraham Fornander, the editor of the *Weekly Argus,* who had married a Hawaiian woman, was accepted by neither group despite his educational and intellectual attainments; those who looked down on the natives despised him for his marriage, while the missionary faction disliked him for his opposition to the government. And, of course, he was a former harpooner; class distinctions did exist.

Although circumstances had thrown the two women together, pretty Nettie would pity Anne if she knew she had seized on John Cartwright's offer of marriage because, at age twenty-one, it was the only one she'd ever had.

Well, Nettie could change who she was no more than Anne could. Nettie was well born and pleasing of face and figure, thus doomed to a life in which her only purpose was to be wife and mother. It wasn't her fault if Anne begrudged her the chance to be a mother while secretly crying inside, *I would not whimper and complain and dread the birth of my babe!*

Anne left Nettie sleeping, her face relaxed into a serenity that contrasted with her waking discontentment. Downstairs, Charles Decker waited in the library.

At the sound of Anne's footfall, he rose from behind his enormous, highly polished desk. "Thank you for coming. She is so distressed— How did you find her?"

"Frightened, but well," Anne said frankly. "I think she's feeling the distance from home and the familiar. At such a time, it's natural for a woman to long for her mother or sister or dearest friend. But I believe all is progressing naturally. Whatever you can do to calm her . . ."

"I'll do, of course," he hastened to say. He paced away, a large man whose softening waistline reflected the good life he had earned. He turned back to face her and cleared his throat. "Is she near her time?"

"Very, I should say," Anne replied. "Within days, a week at the most."

"Thank God," he muttered.

Anne thought it would be untactful to agree, although privately she sympathized with him. A frightened Nettie was hardly the sparkling companion his wealth had bought.

Although perhaps she did him—and Nettie—an injustice. He must be twenty years older than his wife, but the slick thickening of his body gave him an air of solidity and prosperity that had its own attraction. Anne thought his usual expression smug, but there were those who admired a man who was self-satisfied, confident in his opinions and worth. Perhaps Nettie lacked that same confidence and therefore needed his.

"I wonder," said Anne tentatively, "whether you might not

want to consider consulting a physician. Mrs. Decker didn't like the idea of a strange man touching her so intimately, but if she would be comforted by his expertise, perhaps a few blushes might be worthwhile."

"She knows Dr. Rooke socially. He wouldn't be a stranger. Perhaps he'd come."

"I'm not sure that wouldn't be worse," Anne pointed out. "To know as he's examining her that she might be facing him across a dinner table two weeks from now, or dancing with him . . . You can certainly ask her, but my guess is that a stranger might be better."

Frowning, Charles Decker asked, "Can you recommend someone?"

"There's a new physician in Honolulu who impressed me with his skill. He's primarily a surgeon, but I assume he does obstetric work."

He looked as incredulously at her as if she had suggested he consult a native *kahuna*. "You're not referring to Dr. Matthew Cabe?"

Flustered by his astonishment, Anne answered with less than her usual composure. "Well, yes, but . . . Am I mistaken in him? Do you know the man?"

"No, only heard the talk." He lifted a brow. "I see that you haven't. He may well be a fine physician, but he's also hot-tempered and foolish in where he speaks."

"Hot-tempered?" Anne echoed, feeling stupid. Dr. Cabe?

"He attacked a man and threatened his life the other day. Do you know Edward Landre, the assistant minister of finance? Apparently Cabe's father and he were in partnership, and the good doctor nurses some sort of grudge from that period. He's come over here to pursue it, although evidently not in the courts."

She hadn't forgotten the white-hot anger she'd seen on his face and her instinctive knowledge that Matthew Cabe could be a dangerous man. Yet he also possessed rigid self-control. He could not otherwise have cut as surely and composedly as he had. Was he a drinking man? she wondered, who had let spirits swamp his usual good sense? But she could not imagine that, either.

"He attacked someone?" she repeated. "Forgive me, I don't doubt your word, but if you didn't see the incident yourself . . ."

"All of Honolulu is talking," Decker said with a certain amount of relish. "Witnesses agree that Dr. Cabe struck the first blow and raged threats to Landre's life." His fleshy cheeks quivered as he shook his head. "An ugly scene, but regrettably not unusual for the participants in that absurd charade they call a government."

Ah! So the secret pleasure in his pale eyes had nothing to do with Dr. Cabe, but a good deal to do with his desire to see the members of the government humiliated. Well, for Napua's sake, Anne wouldn't mind seeing Landre humiliated, but she regretted the blot on Dr. Cabe's reputation and would be sorry indeed if Landre came out of the affair looking like the innocent victim.

"I hadn't heard the story," she said, "but I repeat: I believe Dr. Cabe is a skilled physician."

Her patient's husband looked thoughtful. "He may well have a justifiable grievance against Landre. The doctor was an idiot to make his attack in public—that argues a lack of self-control—but perhaps there were circumstances we don't know about. I'll certainly keep your recommendation in mind should Nettie—Mrs. Decker—decide to consult a doctor. You *will* tell me if matters go awry, or beyond your experience?"

"Of course," she agreed. "But as I told her, I see no reason to think they will. Now, if you'll excuse me . . ."

His face sobered. "It comforts her so when you're here, I wonder if you could come to stay until the baby is born, and perhaps afterward for a little. I understand that you do nursing work, not just midwifery. Only tell me what you charge, and . . ."

"I cannot come now," she interrupted. "Mrs. Phillips had surgery only last week and still needs me. Should Mrs. Decker's pains begin, of course, that would be different, but otherwise I don't feel that I can leave Mrs. Phillips just yet. I'll try to call on your wife every day."

When she departed, however, it wasn't with the intention of returning immediately to the Phillips's residence. Six days after the surgery, Clara was doing extraordinarily well, recovering her strength, already rising from her bed to walk short distances and to sit in the garden. She had thus far been free of infection, although she was not yet safe from that dark possibility. Still, she no longer needed Anne in constant attendance. Anne felt she could take the time to see how Napua was making out.

Four

The young Hawaiian woman and Anne Cartwright had become friends almost six years before, when Anne was newly arrived and widowed and Napua yet a child on the brink of womanhood. Orphaned, she was a boarder at the Royal School and joined the family of the Reverend Mr. Griggs on holidays. She was a star pupil whom the missionaries trotted out to demonstrate the success of their educational methods. The pretty, dark-skinned girl was a model of shy decorum, modestly dressed, equally skilled with her needle and at geometry and geography.

Ironically she'd awakened Anne's interest not by her docility, but by her rare rebellion. They'd been on an outing to Waikiki when Anne saw Napua sneak a glance about and then, thinking herself unobserved, slip away. Curious, Anne followed, staying well back. Napua was at an age where Anne expected an assignation of some sort. Instead, she came upon the girl in a grassy grove of coconut palms, where she stood alone facing the ocean. Her posture was odd but graceful; her hands were lifted to the sky and she swayed like a sapling in the breeze. Her slim brown hands took on a life of their own, as if they were small birds fluttering in the branches of the sapling. It was a moment before Anne realized that Napua was dancing—in fact, doing the hula, which the missionaries so deplored. It was heathen and lascivious, they said, its appeal to grossness and immorality. Anne saw nothing lascivious in the slender girl's moving as though she were one with nature.

Anne watched for some time, gradually hearing the murmured chant that accompanied the dance. She hadn't been able to understand the words, but they had a rhythm not so different from the steady shush of the waves on the shore or the rustle of the palm leaves above. Quietly she edged around so that she could see Napua's face, which had a look as though she were dreaming, or sleepwalking. Her feet never moved throughout the dance; she might have been rooted to the earth. At the end the words rose to some kind of crescendo, and the Hawaiian girl folded until she lay upon the grass unmoving.

Surprising even herself, Anne applauded. Napua's head lifted and she gazed with dark-eyed alarm at the young *haole* teacher.

"You saw? It was nothing," she said quickly, but her cheeks were suffused with shame. "I was remembering. Is that so terrible?"

"Terrible?" Anne lifted her skirt and seated herself on the grass beside Napua. "I thought it was lovely! Was that the hula?"

"You aren't shocked?"

"I don't shock that easily," Anne said gently, smiling to reassure the native girl. She knew guiltily that she ought to pretend to shock, even if she didn't feel it. Yet she would not lie. "I'm not a missionary, you know, although my husband was. To tell you the truth, I've been hoping I'd have a chance to see the hula performed."

"Then there would be, oh, rows of dancers." Napua sat up and waved her hands, her voice becoming more animated. "You would see its beauty."

"I saw its beauty today. You're very good, Napua. Did you learn by yourself, or were you trained?"

Napua relaxed enough to tell her about the school her mother had sent her to when she was a young girl, before she had come under the influence of the missionaries. "My *kumu hula*—my teacher—was a man named Halemanu. He composed many beautiful *mele*. That is the true gift, not the dancing, but the words. They can bring on ruin if the meaning is not always right."

"I wish I spoke your language," Anne said. "I couldn't understand what you were singing."

"It was about Pele's sister, Hi'iaka, and how she learned to dance. It was from her that *we* learned." Napua cast her a shy glance. "I could teach you my language. When we have time."

"Would you really?" Anne wished she had the courage to ask to be taught the hula. She had always been ashamed of her own body, grateful to hide it beneath corsets and skirts. Trying to sound matter-of-fact, she asked the girl what it felt like, to move with such discipline and freedom, to feel one's body in such a way.

Napua tilted her head to one side thoughtfully. "I don't know. When I dance, I am not there." Then she blinked and looked frightened. "Is that why the hula is wrong, because when I dance I'm possessed by Satan?"

Anne contemplated her. "Do you think you are?"

Her high, smooth brow crinkled. "We were taught that when we dance, the *uhane*—the spirits—are speaking through us. That we *are* the winds and the rain, the clouds and sea waves. You see? But the missionaries say that there are no spirits, only the one true God, so perhaps it is Satan."

"But God Himself speaks through the wind and rain and waves, so perhaps you are manifesting a part of Him when you dance." Anne refused to let this girl believe she'd done something evil when her dance was both lovely and fitting.

"As though He were the *kumu*—the rootstock—and we are the *lala*—the branches?" Napua's eyes sparkled again. "Yes! That might be! When I dance, something moves in me; it is not me saying how my hands should go. Perhaps He finds this way of showing Himself pleasing."

"I don't think the Reverend Griggs would agree," Anne felt compelled to point out. Was she doing something dreadful in encouraging this pupil to rebel against her teachers?

"No." The native girl's glow dimmed. "He says hula is a waste of time, that it encourages the cultivation of idle minds." She bent her head to look down at her hands, folded quietly on her lap, so still and . . . and *ordinary* without the studied, graceful movements that had given them life.

"Oh, pooh!" Anne declared dismissively, rebelling herself. "If nothing else, dancing is excellent for the posture and the constitution. Only see how straight you always carry yourself. I'm sure that's because of your training."

"Do you think so?" Napua raised hopeful eyes.

"Indeed I do!" Anne said firmly. "And I'd be delighted if you'd teach me your language."

So had begun their unlikely friendship, which bridged a gulf larger than that which separated Anne from Nettie Decker. Yet despite everything, the young native woman and Anne had forged bonds of sympathy and liking that transcended their differences.

The fabric of those bonds was woven of strong threads: curiosity and the shared desire to think independently, to choose a course after deliberation and not because a man ordered it. Women possessed a good deal of freedom in traditional Hawaiian culture, even political power if the woman was a chiefess. As a child, Napua had been taught the arrogance of the nobility, and now she didn't bow her head readily.

Anne was unconventional from a different cause. Her mother had been intelligent and educated far beyond most women. As an amateur botanist, she corresponded widely with men of similar interests who respected her knowledge and discoveries. Anne had never understood why her mother chose to marry Jacob Schonemann, a farmer and man of rigid religious beliefs. In the end, he had crushed his wife's spirit. Anne thought she had gone gratefully to the grave to escape him. Yet, before her illness, Elizabeth Schonemann had encouraged her young daughter to use her mind and to observe the world skeptically. Anne had learned to disguise her thoughts with an outward show of obedience, but those thoughts continued nonetheless. Her father's rigidity and harshness could not trample the seedlings of independence planted by her mother.

Today she drove her pony cart out along cobbled Nuuanu Street into the country. The air was cooler here, the greenery refreshing. Behind her the ocean was so blue it hurt her eyes; above, veils of rain swept over the mountaintops. She saw a rainbow, which the Hawaiians considered a good omen, a manifestation of the *mana*, or spiritual power, present in every created thing.

A waterfall tumbled over the reddish rocks behind the tiny cottage Napua rented. Anne wondered if Napua bathed in it. She herself would have loved to strip and stand beneath a waterfall. To have the force of the falls tingling through her as the cool water slid over her skin— It must be as glorious as dancing the hula!

She had picnicked once at the beautiful Makiki Falls, surrounded by lush vegetation. Her party had come unbidden on a native woman who had surfaced in the pool like a mermaid and raised herself to stand, arms spread, face tilted up and eyes closed, right under the fall. Her brown skin had glistened, her wet black hair cloaking her like a seal's dark pelt. The sight was astonishingly sensual, and Anne, who ought to have been shocked, was instead envious. On that day she had worn a longsleeved gown, tight around the armpits, and a corset, snugly tied. Why, she had wondered in sudden rebellion, would God, who had created man in His image, demand that men and women cover themselves even in the most absurd circumstances?

She had known better, of course, than to voice her thoughts aloud.

Now Anne sighed. If she ever had the chance to do it, she would! She needn't worry about *her* body inciting men to degrading thoughts. If man had been made in God's image, then He must occasionally be plump. Or had she done that to herself, despite knowing that gluttony was a sin?

Anne tied up her pony to a banana palm, whose peculiar fruits hung in heavy bright green clumps. A beaten path led to the front door. Through lace-hung windows, Anne glimpsed Napua sitting, head bent, at her quilting frame, which appeared to fill the small parlor.

At Anne's knock, Napua lifted her head in inquiry and then delight, rushing to the door. She flung it open and hugged Anne. "You've come! Bless you. Kuokoa is sleeping, we have time to talk."

She'd discarded the fashionable clothes Edward had favored for a Mother Hubbard–style gown that fell, waistless, from the yoke and didn't require a corset or multiple petticoats. Anne envied her the freedom. Dependent on the goodwill—and approval—of the missionary community, she didn't dare live the way she would have liked.

In the parlor, Anne settled herself on the other side of the wooden frame and, without asking, reached for a threaded needle. She thought the sinuous lines of this appliqué very beautiful. How often they had quilted together! Many of the Hawaiian language lessons had taken place over a quilting frame.

It had seemed most natural to Anne, for her happiest memories of her former life involved quilting. The task was useful enough that her father had permitted her to go to neighbors'

houses to attend quilting bees. Women might not be able to
lessen the severity of one another's lives, but at least they listened
and understood. She had always gone home with shoulders less
bowed by misery, her determination to escape bolstered.

Today, just like Anne, Napua took up her needle where she
had left it. As was the way of women, they talked while they
worked.

"Edward, he won't even see me," Napua said, head bent
over her tiny stitches. "I've sent notes, messages . . . He ignores
me. I went to the house, and when Leoiki came to the door, she
told me to go away, that Edward doesn't want me there. And
then she closed the door in my face. As though I were nothing,
nobody!"

"He owes you!"

Bitterly, Napua said, "He believes he paid me well enough
for my body. He bought me nice clothes, took care of me . . .
He told me I could easily find another protector. He said I am
a good-looking woman."

Fury poured into Anne's chest like Pele's steam. "You mustn't
let him convince you that you were no better than . . . than a
prostitute! He promised to marry you, said he loved you! You
would never have gone with him otherwise."

Very softly, Napua said, "I told myself that, but what if I lied?
I am either wicked or a fool."

"You trusted him! Is that so bad?" Anne pressed her lips together. The close-quilted surface of the fabric blurred before her
eyes and her hand hesitated. "I must tell you what I've heard."

After she'd related the tale of how Landre had cheated Dr.
Cabe's father out of his share of the plantation, Napua gave a
small, jerky nod. "I wondered— I heard things—" She stopped,
and despair washed over her face. "How could I love him? A
man who did such things?"

There had been a time when Anne had wondered just that.
Edward Landre might be handsome and charming, but she

thought his insincerity so obvious, she hadn't understood the powerful attraction he held for her young native friend.

But Napua had been particularly vulnerable, having no mother to confide in, no father to set an example. She'd been raised in one culture until she was nine or ten, then abruptly cast into another that must still seem alien. Perhaps she had wanted to love a *haole* man so that she might belong in this new world. Landre had preyed on her confusion.

Preyed on her and then discarded her.

"I think that women must close their eyes to the flaws in the men they love." Anne had never loved, but as a midwife she'd heard the stories of so many marriages, she counted herself an expert.

With renewed bitterness, Napua said, "I might have closed my eyes, but I did not close my ears. I heard many things. He was careless. If I must, I will use what I know."

"Use?" Anne echoed in quick alarm, looking up. "Napua, you don't mean that."

Abandoning her needle in the cloth, Napua rose to her feet with sudden passion. "Then what should I do? Find myself a protector? Swim out to the whaling ships when they anchor?"

"I know you would do neither."

"Then what?" Her eyes seethed with anger and bewilderment. "Become a servant? But who would let me bring Kuokoa? And— Oh, it is wrong, I know, but I don't want to wait on other people! Reverend Griggs would say it is a virtue to work hard, but I don't know how! I was raised to believe that others would wait upon me!" Tears spilled over and she scrubbed at them, the motion curiously childlike. "You must despise me. Here I am talking as though I am something special, better than you—"

"You were raised as *alii*, noble," Anne pointed out. "Not so long ago, the common people would have prostrated themselves for you."

"We were not so high as that!" Napua said ruefully. She sat

down with a sigh, the tears past, but she didn't reach for her needle. "The *makaainana* might have given us respect, but not fear."

"Perhaps not," Anne admitted, "but you weren't raised to wait on others. I was. I don't resent the fact that I must. It's understandable that you do."

"But it's wrong!" Napua cried. "I am no better than you, only lazy. Or perhaps I *am* wicked!"

What dreadful things men did to women! Napua no more deserved to feel this guilt than Anne had deserved to feel shame, as though she were something filthy, disgusting. Both, in their innocence, had let men shape their perception of themselves. With time Anne had nearly convinced herself that she hadn't deserved her husband's vilification, and she must help Napua achieve the same understanding.

"Edward is the wicked one," she said strongly, "not you. I hope Dr. Cabe files a lawsuit and wins. I hope he ruins Edward."

"Yes, but then how could Kuokoa get what should be his?" Napua asked logically enough. "I must hurry, before this doctor takes all that Edward owns. It is Kuokoa's right."

"Yes," Anne admitted somewhat reluctantly. Dr. Cabe was an angry man. Would his anger extend to Edward Landre's young son? Or would he see the justice in Napua's claim on Kuokoa's behalf?

"I will send another note," Napua said. "This time I will say that if he won't see me, I will tell one of his enemies something that I know. If he ignores me again, I'll do it."

"But that's . . . that's blackmail!" Anne ought to be more shocked than she was. More disapproving. "It's dangerous. Are you so sure he wouldn't hurt you?"

"I will be careful. I can hide."

"If you once become a blackmailer, you might have to hide forever," Anne pointed out. "Where would it stop? If he pays you this time, might he fear that you would keep coming back for more? Now he is indifferent to you. He would come to hate and despise you."

"I don't care!" Napua's face convulsed and she bowed her head, her voice muffled by the fall of heavy hair. "Why should I care?"

"Because he's not worth your suffering." Anne spoke what she truly felt. "He's a . . . a worm. No, he's like one of those shark-men I've heard legends about. And just as dangerous."

"I would have seen the shark-mouth on his back," Napua said, with near humor. Then her face hardened. "But, yes, he is like them. If they were discovered, they were stoned to death."

A chill whispered over Anne's skin, like the first hint of the "sick wind" of which the Hawaiians spoke. Troubled, she studied the unfamiliar lines of her friend's face. "Napua . . ."

She gave a harsh laugh. "If I were going to kill him, I would have done it that night, in my first anger. You needn't worry. He deserves such a death, but all I want is a son's due."

Anne took a deep breath. "Napua, I had an idea. It's why I came today. You know that the Griggses lost their son this winter. Their grief runs deep. They loved you once; you were like a daughter to them. I think they would take you back, and welcome Kuokoa, if you went to them."

Doubt and longing transformed Napua's face. "Do you really think so?" she whispered.

Napua's hope and uncertainty wrenched Anne's heart. Pray God she was right, for she couldn't help remembering the scene that took place five years ago, when the Reverend Griggs discovered that Napua had gone to Landre.

By chance, Anne had spent the night at the Griggses' house; her bed at the Taft's had been needed for a missionary couple come to Honolulu from Maui because the wife was ill. When Napua didn't appear at the breakfast table, Mrs. Griggs went up to her room. She came down, pale, with a note in her hand, which she silently handed to her husband, seated at the head of the table. As he read it, fury twisted his face.

Anne wouldn't have expected him to be a forgiving man, but she was surprised to see him loosen the reins on his formidable self-control. Throwing down the note, he hammered the table and ranted about the licentiousness of the foreign merchants, their willingness to corrupt the heathens for their own purposes. But it was not Landre alone he condemned; no, in an ugly voice he consigned Napua to Hell for carelessly tossing away the grace extended to her. In the days to come, he publicly trumpeted his renewed belief in the carnal nature of the natives, the weakness that made them choose sin over righteousness. Eventually he'd been quieted by other members of the Sandwich Island Mission, for he offended Hawaiians who were good Christians.

Time had dimmed Anne's recollection of those days that followed Napua's secret departure. Perhaps she hadn't wanted to remember, for she'd been hurt herself that her young friend hadn't confided in her, that she had crept down the hall that night without pausing at Anne's door.

But last night Anne had lain awake remembering, grateful that Napua hadn't seen the Reverend Griggs's reaction. Then, his temper might have made him do something unforgivable had Napua come to him. But time had cooled the hurt; the Griggses' love for their daughter in all but name had been genuine, Anne believed. Surely now if Napua repented, she would be welcomed back, both in the church and in their home.

And so she had resolved to counsel Napua to humble herself to them.

Now she said to Napua, "You are still the child they loved. How could they not forgive? But it's you who must make the first move. Will you go to them and beg their pardon? It won't be easy, but their sternness is only on the outside. If you can bear their reproaches without anger . . ."

"How could I feel anger?" Napua asked simply. "They warned me, and I turned my back on them. But they were right, everything they said was true. If only I had listened!"

"But then you wouldn't have Kuokoa."

"No." Napua fell silent, twisted her fingers together. Thoughts and fears paraded across her face. At last she gave a decisive nod. "I'll go to them, if you will come with me."

"Of course I will!" Anne said in relief. She stood and went to the Hawaiian woman, taking her hands. "I don't believe you need forgiveness, but theirs will be sweet nonetheless."

"If they give it," Napua said. Her chin came up. "If they don't, I must take care of myself and my son the only way I can."

Nothing would do but that Anne and Napua go directly to the Griggses' small frame house, where once Napua had spent so many happy hours. If only she had understood then the value of what she had! But no— Anne was right, Napua thought. For then she wouldn't have Kuokoa, and she would suffer anything for her handsome son.

He was nestled in her arms right now, the liveliness of a strong, healthy four-year-old contained only by his apprehension. For all Napua's effort to hide her own, he had read it as plainly as though she were his primer. She smiled down at him, but he clung all the harder, his eyes dark and grave. He hadn't understood why they had to leave their home, and now everything frightened him.

The two women spoke little; they must be careful what they said in front of the boy, and neither wanted only to chatter. They passed lush green taro fields and, on the *mauka* side of Nuuanu, the cemetery with its gravestones and wrought-iron fences surrounding family plots. Napua never liked to look at the places where seamen were buried in unmarked graves. They had no one who cared enough to put up a stone, or to erect a column and break off the top to indicate grief. It made her feel their loneliness and her own, just looking at the anonymous graves.

Town was, as always at this season, dusty and smelly. With Anne driving, the pony cart rattled past grog shops and victualing houses, bowling alleys, and small stores. Though the streets were crowded with traffic, it was nothing like whaling season, when thousands of seamen would swell the population, wanting spirits and women.

There was Samsing Co., run by *pake*, Chinamen, and then the Seamen's Bethel, solid and white. Beyond bustled a native market, the shabby stalls heaped with fresh produce and fish in crimson and blue and rose and green, shimmering on their beds of *ti* leaves. Tied pigs squealed and chickens squawked in cages. Naked brown children played in the dirt as *haole* and Hawaiian alike bartered over the goods, and horsemen pressed through the crowd.

Though Kuokoa stared, the sight was too familiar to draw more than a glance from Napua. Each landmark brought nearer their destination. Napua's chest tightened and she tasted her nervousness. She shouldn't have brought Kuokoa. She wouldn't like him to see his mother humiliated. But she'd thought he might soften the missionary's heart, so handsome was he with big bright eyes, the fine features of his father, and her wavy black hair.

Now her son was gazing solemnly at Haleakala, High Chief Abner Paki's residence, set inside beautiful gardens. Napua kept her eyes fixed on the steeple of the stone church, rising above the rest of the city. The Griggses' son must be buried there, in the Kawaiahao Cemetery, as Dr. Judd's son had been. Ah, what if she someday had to bury her child? No! She would not think about such a thing.

And finally, there was the house ahead, tall and straight, guarded by the picket fence. Napua's heartbeat quickened as memories rushed in like the tide filling a fishpond. The indoor kitchen, so hot much of the year, but where she had learned to cook *haole* food under Mrs. Griggs's patient tutelage. The spare bedroom upstairs where she had slept, feeling like a daughter. The porch swing on the lanai out back where she had sat dreaming and despairing, knowing herself *huikau*—confused, lost. To think she'd believed she had found the way when she met Edward, when he stole up the porch steps in the darkness to sit beside her in the swing and embrace her. What a fool she had been!

Anne stopped her pony cart in the yard, beneath the shade of a *kou* tree, with its frilled orange flowers. Both women gazed at the blank face of the house.

"He might not be home," Anne said. Napua could tell she was trying to sound as though it didn't matter, as though this was just a visit like any other, but she failed.

Napua held her son even tighter. "It approaches supper time. Mrs. Griggs liked him home then."

They sat there for another moment, until Kuokoa wriggled like a fish and asked, "Where is this, Mama? Why did we stop?"

"I must speak to the missionary who lives here," Napua said. "He and his wife were old friends of mine, before I knew your papa."

"Why . . . ?" he began, but she murmured, "Hush," in sudden panic, for the front door was opening.

Mrs. Griggs appeared first, as large and stately as ever. She had always regretted her size, tried to disguise it. Napua could never understand why. The Hawaiians admired big women. Why, Ka'ahumanu was said to have had thighs as large as tree trunks!

"Anne!" called the missionary's wife. "I didn't expect you. Is something wrong?" She started down the steps from the porch, reached the bottom one before she saw Napua. She stopped abruptly and pressed a hand to her massive bosom. "Napua?" she whispered. "Is that you?"

In that moment, her husband stepped onto the porch.

"Lydia, what is it?" he asked, but unlike his wife, he looked straight at Napua. His face hardened in anger.

She sat frozen on the wooden seat of the cart. Beside her, Anne climbed down. "See who I've brought with me," she said, as though unveiling a pleasant surprise. "Napua has been living alone but for her son in a small cottage. She feels her mistakes of the past so deeply, she didn't like to come to you, but I persuaded her that she would find no greater example of Christian forgiveness than here, where once she was treated like a daughter."

"This . . . this is your son?" Mrs. Griggs asked timidly.

Before Napua could answer, the missionary hurried down from the porch. "Lydia, do not let a soft heart betray you into consorting with a fallen woman." His tone was harsh.

Anne had known Napua better than she knew herself; she had never imagined that she would feel anger. Yet such was the hot burning in Napua's belly. She had imagined the missionary's reproaches would be sorrowful, revealing his hurt, not caustic and uncaring. But didn't she deserve his condemnation?

So she ignored her anger, reminding herself that pride was a deadly sin. She had no right anymore to pride, for her son's sake couldn't afford it.

She gently urged Kuokoa to the ground and followed him. Then she held out a beseeching hand to her father in all but blood. "Reverend Griggs, I've come to ask your forgiveness. I was young and rash, yielding to temptation despite all you taught me. I deserve the bitter lessons I've learned, but I so long for the healing embrace of Jesus Christ—"

No, that was a lie; it was *his* forgiveness and comforting embrace she sought, not his god's. Her faith had stumbled and weakened since the missionaries had all turned their backs on her; she found herself thinking more often of her *aumakua*, the family god she had worshiped as a child, than she did of the *haole* Jehovah, who had never seemed quite real to her. Pele's temper was visible in the burning lava that spilled from the craters, in the smoke and flame she flung into the sky when she was enraged. How could Napua believe that the *haole* god had created the world in six days and rested on the seventh when the Hawaiians could see that the world was still being created, rising from the sea, pouring from the fiery mouths of the mountains, barren until seeds miraculously probed tiny roots into the crumbling lava?

But perhaps it was only that she had turned her back on them as they had on her. Perhaps their forgiveness would restore her faith, and the old ways she found herself increasingly remembering would melt away again, like a mist touched by the sun.

Now was when she had thought to see her *makua* soften, perhaps look reluctantly at her *hapahaole* son and see that not everything she'd done had been bad, that good could come even from great foolishness.

Indeed, Mrs. Griggs had tears in her eyes and her hands reached out as though she couldn't help herself. Napua saw that she *had* changed, that new lines of sorrow were carved beside her eyes and mouth, that her arms needed a child as the beach needs the waves. Holding Kuokoa's hand, Napua took a step forward.

But before she could respond to the hunger on Lydia Griggs's face, the missionary snatched his wife back. His voice was as cold as the rare snow that lay on top of Haleakala.

"Go into the house, Lydia. Now!"

A quiver struck her, a sob aborted, but she obeyed unquestioningly, and Napua saw with numbing shock that it was not mere condemnation this man felt, but hatred. His eyes blazed at her, his mouth twisted into an ugly shape.

"I suppose you've been abandoned now and think to come back, not out of true repentance, but because you are destitute. Apply elsewhere, whore! You had every advantage, every opportunity, all of our teaching and affection, and you chose to reject it in favor of the luxuries a wealthy white man could buy you. Well, you made your choice and cannot unmake it! Begone!"

Napua felt as though one of the gods had turned her to stone, stealing from her the power to turn and flee, as she so desperately wanted to do. She felt sick, dizzy, unable to look away from those blazing eyes. Only dimly was she aware of Anne, making a sound of disbelief, and of her son's hand trembling in hers.

At last that terrible gaze was turned from her. "Mrs. Cartwright," the Reverend Griggs said awfully, "I thought more highly of you than this."

Anger stiffened the face of Napua's kind friend. "I thought more highly of you, too. Apparently I was mistaken."

"How dare you criticize me!" His voice was the rumble of a rockslide. "I give to those whose hearts are eager to turn away from the degradation of their former paths, to those who are mired in wickedness out of ignorance, not choice. You have been fooled by this young woman, as I am ashamed to say I once was, which I suppose serves as an excuse for your action today. Now, I ask that you remove her and her bastard from these premises."

"You have forgiven the king his excesses, over and over." Anne sounded like the teacher she had been when Napua first knew her, one who could make the roughest of boys shrink merely by her tone. "Were your forgiveness and friendship not sincere, but rather politically expedient?"

"His Royal Highness cannot be compared to a pleasure-loving young woman who prostituted herself because the path of the righteous was too straight and narrow."

"Does not His Highness find it so?"

"Anne," Napua said in a low voice. "Please. Don't argue. What is the use? Will you take me home?"

Anne's glittering eyes swept her unseeingly; then returned

to take a more searching look. Her voice changed. "You're quite right," she said. "It is useless. Let's go." She turned her back on the missionary, who neither moved nor spoke, only glowered at her as his god so often did in pictures.

Anne boosted Kuokoa into the wagon and hurried around to climb up as Napua did the same. Anne took up the reins, cracked the whip, and startled the pony into a gallop that took them careening out the gate.

Napua burned with shame and rage. She should never have abandoned her own gods and the ways she had grown up in for the *haole* ones. She saw now that the arrogant *haoles* sought only to put Hawaii under their feet. They wanted the land and humble laborers to farm it. There was no hand extended in friendship; she had been deceived. How right she had been to see that she would never be treated equally! The *haole* and Hawaiians would not become one. Her only mistake had been to turn from one smooth-tongued white man to another. The one had pretended to be righteous, the other that he did what he did *no ke aloha*—for love. They were liars both.

Anne had been a friend, but who knew how sincere even she was? She had talked Napua into humbling herself for the missionary, hadn't she? Perhaps she hadn't done that out of affection, because she thought it best for Napua, but rather because she didn't like the idea of Napua making a fool out of Edward, a *haole* like herself. Perhaps she, too, thought of Napua as a child who must be led, who could not be allowed to make decisions for herself.

Well, this Hawaiian woman would make her own from now on. Tonight she would write a note demanding justice from Edward, and then she would make an offering to her *aumakua* and beg forgiveness.

Five

"There." Puukua waved his hand in a sweeping arc. "That Captain's plantation."

Matthew rested his hands on the saddle horn and surveyed the prospect before him. It was fine land, these acres that had gripped his father so profoundly. Below the steep, fluted cliffs of the Koolau Mountain range, green fertile ground sloped gently toward Kaneohe Bay. The winds blew, rustling the green fields of sugarcane, higher than a man already, and making shiver the leaves of the coffee trees that Captain Cabe had first thought would be his fortune. Breakers shattered on the reef that protected the bay, where the water shone brilliant blue tipped with white caps. Even from this distance, Matthew could see the stone-walled fishponds along the shore. Many of those on Oahu were ancient, he was told.

"See island?" Puukua asked, mock shivering. "That Moku o' Loe. Always *kapus* on it. Moku o' Loe place of evil spirits. No one goes there."

Matthew saw nothing ominous about the small, irregularly shaped tropical island in the bay. At the moment, only one kind of evil interested him.

He'd been fortunate enough to locate a native who knew the windward side of Oahu and who spoke simple but adequate English and was willing to accompany him on a tour of the plantation. Matthew wanted to be able to interview the workers as well as the manager. He assumed the manager would be a white man; if he proved loyal to Landre, he was unlikely to be frank. Matthew intended to find out whether Landre's stories of labor problems and broken-down machinery were fictional, too, or whether the plantation had in fact been profitable all along.

Puukua was married and had a daughter, and his wife's sister and husband and their child lived with him as well. None was sick, he'd said cheerfully. Matthew wouldn't hire him until he'd showed the scratch on his arm where he had been vaccinated. When Matthew explained that he was a doctor—a kahuna for his people—and asked whether Puukua had had his family vaccinated, too, the native guide had widened his eyes earnestly and said, "Yes, they, too." He gestured vaguely at his arm. "Even little girl."

"Good," Matthew had agreed. "You understand what a quarantine is? I couldn't have taken you with me unless you'd been vaccinated."

Oh, yes, Puukua understood.

How could he not, when the disease was spreading despite all efforts to control it? So desperate were the authorities, they had called for a day of humiliation, fasting, and prayer on June 15. In the intervening week, it was clear the destroying angel had not listened to prayers. It was obvious that Matthew would be needed soon to help prepare vaccine matter and oversee a quarantine hospital. Thus his decision to visit the plantation now, when he wouldn't be missed.

Since his confrontation with Landre, Matthew had also found a lawyer—not an easy matter in Honolulu, where at one point they had been so scarce, Judd had commandeered the first to step off a ship and made him attorney general. Matthew was in the process of filing a lawsuit, and it would not hurt to muster every shred of evidence he could uncover proving that Landre had swindled not just his partner, but the government as well.

If Matthew were honest with himself, he must admit that curiosity had played a part in motivating him to make this journey across the Pali. He wanted to *see* this place that had been worth fraud and betrayal and that had killed his father.

Despite the wind, which he was told blew constantly on this side of the island, once he and Puukua turned their horses down a dirt lane between fields of cane, a stillness seemed to descend. The land was lower here, protected by a windbreak of *kukui* trees, and with the sun beating down the air was hot and stagnant.

Ahead a wagon nearly blocked the lane. Hitched to it, a bony horse with ears almost as large and thick as a mule's hung its head sleepily and twitched its tail. They had reached it when from somewhere in the field Matthew heard a voice raised in anger, the language unintelligible. He glanced at Puukua.

The native's broad, dark face was expressionless. "He say, 'Get lazy ass back to work. Ten strokes of lash if you not finish row quick as Huki finishes his.'"

Matthew grimaced in distaste. "Finish?"

"Here cane grows too thickly to need *hoe hana*—no weeds. Maybe they are stripping leaves from cane. *Hole hole*, that is called."

Matthew grunted and swung his leg over his horse's back, tying the reins loosely through a metal ring on the long wagon.

"I want to see the work. And I might as well meet the overseer."

"Cane will cut you . . ."

Matthew raised his brows. Puukua sighed and dismounted as well. "Hallo!" he called.

"Yes?" the voice bellowed. "Oh, hell, I'm coming." The unseen speaker added a string of what must have been orders in

Hawaiian before the shaking and crashing of cane indicated that someone approached down one of the rows.

He emerged with startling suddenness, shaking like a dog ridding himself of water. Shreds of dried leaves and dust flew from him.

"Who the devil are you?" he asked scowling.

Matthew took stock of the man, short and bullish in build, with shaggy dark hair and a face made villainous by several days' growth of beard, his disagreeable expression, and the tobacco he chewed.

"How do you do?" Matthew said civilly, despite the temptation to be otherwise. "My name is Matthew Cabe. I'm Captain William Cabe's son."

The expression didn't change. "I knew Cabe," he said flatly. "He don't got nothing to do with this place no more."

"I've filed a lawsuit to reclaim his share of the plantation. It might be wise," Matthew suggested, "for you to look on me as a future employer."

"Yeah?" The overseer spat a dark stream of tobacco juice onto the ground, just missing Matthew's boots. "Maybe I'll quit then." He grunted with amusement. "Way the courts in this nigger kingdom work, you might be waitin' fer the next ten years or so fer some judge to hear you. Right now, I work fer Landre."

"Are you the manager?"

"Bauer's that." He jerked his head *makai*. "Might find 'im at the mill."

"Right now, I'd like to see the crew at work."

Another stream of dark liquid struck the ground. "Second I turn my back, them lazy niggers are all sittin' on their haunches gabbin'. You want to see me get them sons-a-bitches moving, why not." With that he turned and strode between two rows of canes, vanishing.

"Do you want to wait here?" Matthew quietly asked Puukua. The native's expression had closed until it was as blank as the long walls of Honolulu's fort, and as friendly. "I wait," he said stolidly.

Matthew hesitated. He wanted to say, *We foreigners are not all alike*, but judged it unnecessary. He had gained the impression that Puukua was a shrewd man, well able to understand that all races had the same mix of humanity that ran the gamut from noble to contemptible.

"I'll be right back," he said at last and plunged into the cane after the overseer.

He had to hold up his arms to protect his face from the sharp-edged leaves of the cane, which also seemed to be covered with a fuzz that felt disagreeable when his skin brushed it. Under the thick growth it was green and hot.

Finding the overseer was no problem; already he was bellowing at his workers. When he sensed Matthew behind him, he glanced over his shoulder. "Lazy bastards. Hardly moved. You can't take your eyes off of 'em."

The nearest worker was a Chinaman, garbed in traditional costume of tunic and full pantaloons; his black hair was braided in a queue down his back. In the next row labored a Hawaiian, a mountainous fellow with curly hair and fleshy features. The greenery rippled as others worked beyond, stripping dried leaves from the cane. All wore long-sleeved garments and cloths wrapped around their hands, but still Matthew could see the fine cuts in the skin that bled in red droplets. Their faces were covered with dust and sweat, the gazes they turned to Matthew dull and incurious.

The overseer had produced a short riding crop from his belt, with which he lashed out at a worker who straightened as though unkinking his back. "Lazy, no-good . . ." he muttered.

Matthew would have liked to dash the crop from his hand but knew the act to be worse than useless; in a temper, the overseer would be even freer with the lashes.

Without a word, Matthew turned and pushed his way back

through the dense growth of cane. It whipped at his face, and he was breathing hard by the time he emerged into the lane.

Puukua started at his appearance. "You okay?" he asked uncertainly.

Matthew growled an answer. "Let's find the mill."

The cane fields alternated with groves of guava and coffee trees, evidence of attempts to diversify. There were even rows of grapes, carefully tied to frames. The fields were all weed-free and thriving, but Matthew, thinking of the workers in the cane, couldn't help wondering at what cost.

The house was white frame, unlandscaped, and curiously bare-looking.

A few hundred yards away, the mill sprawled along the banks of a fine stream, which combined the force of half a dozen of the waterfalls that tumbled down the steep Pali before emptying into the bay. The trade winds battered themselves against this back side of the Koolau Mountain range, and most of the moisture fell here, further eroding the Pali and keeping the windward landscape rich and green. Although sugarcane could be grown in the fertile valleys carved into the leeward side of the island, more irrigation was required. Here the rainfall was great enough to nourish the cane.

The huge wooden waterwheel turned, slapping the water, but when Matthew stepped inside the dim interior of the mill, it was silent, no machinery operating. "Hello?" he called.

"*Ja?* Who is there?" A big man with hair so pale a blond it was near white stepped out from behind some horizontal rollers that Matthew guessed would crush the ripe cane to squeeze the sweet juice from it. Below the rollers were wooden troughs.

"Are you Mr. Bauer?"

"*Ja.* Und you?" The accent was heavily Germanic, barely understandable. Bauer himself was perhaps in his forties, a man who had probably been handsome in a square-jawed, beefy way but was now running to corpulence.

Matthew introduced himself and again explained his errand, attempting to do so matter-of-factly, without hostility. "I hoped you could answer some questions, perhaps show me around."

"Und Herr Landre, he knows you are here?"

Matthew didn't look away from Bauer's flat stare. "I didn't tell him. I'm sure he guessed my intentions."

The very lack of human emotion and expression in those pale blue eyes was chilling. They stayed fixed on Matthew as Bauer thought. At last he grunted. "I show you the mill."

He explained how the waterwheel turned the rollers, and how native workers would feed the cane in. The rollers, four-and-a-half-feet long and twenty-six inches in diameter, weighed about three tons each, he said. The troughs carried the juice to pots where it was boiled before the less valuable molasses was separated from the crystallized sugar. The machine that did the separation, which apparently operated on a centrifugal principle, appeared to be his pride and joy. It had shortened from weeks to minutes the process of separating the molasses and sugar, and produced superior sugar besides.

It had also, Matthew thought grimly, put William Cabe and Edward Landre deeply into debt.

When they emerged from the mill, Bauer completely ignored Puukua. To Matthew he said, "You come up to the house, *ja?*"

Matthew inclined his head. "Thank you."

The interior was no homier than the exterior; no rugs or pictures decorated the walls and bare wooden floors. The furnishings were minimal and masculine, and the front room, at least, was filthy. It reeked of cigar smoke, and ashes overflowed a gourd calabash. Dishes encrusted with dried food teetered on two small tables.

Bauer waved Matthew to a seat, then picked up a box of cigars and proffered it.

"Thank you, but no."

The manager grunted again and lit one up for himself. Acrid smoke increased the reek.

"So. Your questions. Ask."

Ja, there had been trouble with the machinery, he agreed. He had wanted to go to steam-powered, but, *nein*, Cabe and Landre would not hear of it. And so, much went wrong, but they had kept making sugar, when necessary in the old, primitive way, with oxen plodding in a circle to turn vertical rollers. Despite the difficulties, he had done his part; they had shipped a respectable amount of sugar and molasses, though the prices paid for it were abysmal.

Ach, labor was always a problem. The natives were useless. Worse than useless, for one had to employ a *luna*—an overseer—for every ten or so. Since only white men could be trusted as overseers, they must be paid a respectable amount, unlike the workers. The refrain was familiar: The natives were lazy. Bauer seemed not to comprehend why the Hawaiians, once the possessors of an easy, contented life, might not want to perform grueling labor in the cane fields from dawn to dark, though he admitted that for the harder kinds of work he couldn't get white people to go into the fields at all.

And the Chinese, who had been imported in 1852, were proving a disappointment. They were better workers than the natives, he conceded grudgingly, not so likely to put down the tools every time the *luna* turned his back, but they were also quarrelsome and seemingly unhappy.

As Matthew couldn't imagine Bauer noticing any more subtle signs of such a state of mind than a violent rampage, he pressed the matter. Three Chinamen had hanged themselves, the German said in disgust. Here the planters had invested the money to import workers, and these hadn't even completed a year of their commitment before breaking the contract—and in such a way that they couldn't even be hauled before a magistrate, and fined.

Although he couldn't be described as eager, Bauer was co-operative until Matthew began inquiring about the conditions under which the workers lived.

They were paid three dollars a month, as well as receiving food, clothing, and housing, the German said grudgingly.

"One of your overseers spoke of punishing with flogging."

"We must be able to maintain order."

"May I see the workers' housing?" Matthew asked.

Bauer gave him that flat stare. "Why?"

"I want to know how they're treated."

The manager's face flushed dangerously red and he rose to his feet. "That is enough. You must leave now."

Matthew slowly stood, too. "Why?" he asked. "You've been very helpful."

"I've done what I would do for any visitor. Now you tell me how to run the plantation. I won't let you do that. Not even Landre tells me how to treat workers."

Levelly, Matthew said, "When I own this plantation, that will change."

The cold eyes narrowed. "*Ja?* We'll see. Now, you go."

"Very well." On his way out, a flicker of movement caught Matthew's eye. A door had silently opened and a native woman peered out. She was scantily clothed and lushly proportioned, though her skin was scabrous, like that of so many natives. Her dark eyes were wary but curious. What tightened his gut was the discolored swelling that distorted one side of her face.

So, Landre's manager kept a woman here, and treated her no better than he did the field-workers. Matthew looked forward to firing Herr Bauer.

The sky was stained colors Napua had no name for, all shades of orange and pink and yellow and purple. It was magnificent, yet the glances she cast toward the west were anxious ones, for she did not like the night arriving before her business was completed and she could start for home. She had never liked night, dark and secretive; *po* was the time for the gods, day—*ao*—for mankind. And this was not a good night to be out, especially in this place.

In the old stories, this pond was the home of a much-feared *mo'o*, whose lizardlike body was said to be twenty feet long. It was true that she had not been seen in many years, but that might be only because no one had looked. Even in the old days, the *mo'o* were seldom seen, most commonly when a fire was lighted on an altar close to their homes.

The *mo'o* was black, as black as the night soon would be. Would Napua hear the water shiver when the lizard-being slipped out of it? Why had she not brought some *awa* to appease this spirit in her terrible form?

Napua herself shivered and looked back down the lane. Already the sky deepened, and the glow faded as night marched closer. Where was Edward? Had he never intended to meet her at all? And why had he set this place?

In one way she had been relieved by his choice, for it was not impossibly far from the cottage she rented. She had not liked the isolation, but told herself it was only that he didn't want to be seen with her. She would tell him first thing that she had written down all she knew and left it in a place where he would not find it. He would be ruined if what she wrote down was read by others. No, she would be safe; he wouldn't dare touch her.

But she wished he would hurry. The dusk was purple and thick, and she felt the skin crawl on the back of her neck. Perhaps the *oi'o*, the spirit ranks, walked. Napua remembered her father crying out, "I have felt a spirit of the gods." Afterward he had explained that his eyelid had trembled, and thus he knew a ghost was sitting on that spot. Did a ghost sit on her shoulder, breathing softly on the fine hairs on her neck?

She whispered, "O *Akua-kiei!* O *Akua-nalo!* O all you gods who travel on the dark night paths! Come and eat. Give life to me and to my child."

She had made an offering on her altar before she left the cottage. Only a humble one—poi and a portion of the pig she and Kuokoa had eaten for dinner—but it should be enough to appease her *aumakua*. The ghost-gods were not like fire, which never says it has enough.

Nor would she be like that. It wasn't so much she asked for. Edward would be angry after what she had done, but he would see by what she asked for that she wasn't greedy, though her anger could easily have made her so.

He had continued to ignore her notes. Once he had ridden right by her on the street and, though he saw her, didn't stop or speak a word. She'd had only one way of making him acknowledge her: she had chosen one of his enemies and told what she knew.

Of course she chose another *haole;* she didn't really care what happened to either of them, so long as she got justice. Henry Turner had once publicly accused Edward of cheating him on a business deal. He had been a sugar planter until the hard times came. Even then he did better than some. It wasn't until a year ago that he had gone to the government for a loan as all the other planters had done. But he alone was turned down.

Edward had explained it to her at the time. Turner had been told why, but not truthfully: too many other debtors were defaulting on their loans, his land wasn't worth enough as collateral, his mill was too primitive. But really Edward had taken pleasure in ruining a man he didn't like. Sometimes, when he had drunk too much, he liked to talk, and who else dared he tell about the dishonorable things he did?

She knew that Henry Turner still lived in Honolulu, a bitter man who would welcome someone to blame for his ruination. And so she had gone to see him.

It was daytime, but already he was drunk. Still, he had not grabbed her or made lewd remarks. He had showed her to a seat in the grog shop and offered her a drink. He was pathetic, his eyes bloodshot, his hands shaky, his brown hair lank and greasy. Yet she felt sorry for him. She saw in his eyes his misery.

He listened to her in silence. She expected that he would slam his fist on the table or leap to his feet swearing revenge. Instead he had watched her with bleary eyes that she thought when clear would be gray, like the water-laden clouds of Kane that clung to the mountains. At last he asked, in a voice only a little slurred, "Why are you telling me this?"

She answered him honestly. Why shouldn't she?

"So you're using me," Henry Turner mused.

"Yes, but I ask nothing of you."

"No? What if I don't act on what you told me?"

"Then I will go to someone else," Napua said without resentment.

He grunted, not a pleasant sound. "Oh, you won't have to do that. I'll pay Edward Landre a visit, with pleasure. I may beat the tar out of him and do that with pleasure, too."

For the first time, she felt a stirring of remorse, or alarm. She had thought she didn't care what happened to this *haole* any more than she cared what happened to Edward, but that wasn't true. She knew nothing bad about Henry Turner. He was not the one who had committed deceit. What if he got hurt? Would she be responsible?

"You'll be careful?" she asked uneasily.

He laughed, and she saw that he might once have had a good face, before his own *pilikia*. His troubles had worn his face like the *kona* wore down the mountains. Then she heard how bitter was his laugh.

"Careful? Good god, why? So that I can drink myself into an early grave instead? Look at me! There's nothing left that's worth saving."

Selfishly she thought, *But you would save me guilt*, and then was ashamed.

"Perhaps if you went to Dr. Judd, you could get the loan."

"It's too late." His trembling fingers groped for his glass. "I've lost the land now. Nobody would lend me enough to start all over."

"I'm sorry," she whispered.

He looked surprised enough that his eyes almost focused on her face. "I'm sorry for the way the bastard has treated you, too. At least now we both know who to blame, don't we?"

Oh, yes, they knew. And Edward must know what she had done, for three days later, when she checked at Dr. Ford's drugstore on Kaahumanu Street, a note awaited her. He named this time and place, which she had once shown him.

Now he did not arrive. Was her wait in vain? Would she catch no fish in her net tonight?

The lane was narrow, more of a footpath, with the fishpond to one side and, down a small embankment, a thicket of bamboo on the other. The lane curved out of sight in each direction. She wished she could see farther, to know if he was coming. She kept feeling that she wasn't alone, a prickling unease. Napua looked from the still black water of the pond to the deepening shadows at the foot of the lane.

She had almost made up her mind to leave when she heard the steady drum of hoofbeats. So. Napua waited in the middle of the lane, determined to show no fear.

He cantered toward her on a large white horse that shimmered ghostlike in the darkness and the first light of the moon. She thought for a minute he hadn't seen her, and prepared to throw herself to one side. But the rider only mocked her, for at the last second he yanked back on the reins, and the horse pranced to a stop with its steaming muzzle only inches from her face.

Edward—for it was Edward—spoke. "It would seem you've won, this time. Precisely how much do you want?"

She named a figure and he swore. His hand must have tightened on the reins, for the horse bobbed its head and backed up a step or two.

"Greedy bitch!" he snarled and swung his leg over the animal's rump to dismount.

Hastily, Napua said, "I have written down everything I know, and put it in a safe place. It will be found if I don't go back for it."

"So you're smart enough to be scared," he said in a dark voice that added to the prickles down her spine.

"Did you bring money?"

"Nowhere near that much. And if you think—" He broke off. "What was that? Did you hear something?"

Napua stood very still and listened. She, too, had caught a muted beat, like a multitude of footsteps or the rhythm of drums. The undertone was a murmur of voices, many voices. And a whistle. Was it a nose flute?

"We must go!" she cried in alarm. "It is the marchers of the night. They are very dangerous!"

"Don't be absurd!" Edward scoffed, but the horse's ears were flickering, its skin shivering, and it lifted and set down its feet as though anxious to gallop away.

The murmur grew and swelled until she could almost make out the words of the chant. The beat of drums seemed to come from one way, the thunder of four hundred or four thousand feet from the other. Yet the night remained dark and still; her eyes told her they were alone, though her ears told her otherwise.

In panic Napua turned to flee. Let Edward meet the *huaka'i-po* if he wanted. Perhaps the *haole* were safe from the ghosts of Hawaiian warriors and chiefs, but she would not be.

She was checked in midflight by his hand, cruelly tight.

"Oh, no, you're not escaping now! You wanted to talk, and by god we'll talk."

"You don't understand—"

"Oh, I understand—"

The chant was so powerful now that it drowned out the drums. She clapped her hands over her ears, but still she heard the cry, "*O-ia!*" She would be pierced by a spear if among the marchers was no relative to protect her.

"Please! Let me go!"

"What the devil—?"

Something unseen slammed into her back and shoved her off the path. She tumbled over the drop into the thicket of bamboo. It whipped against her face and she fell to her knees. She cried out just as from the lane above her she heard a strangled gasp.

By the time Napua struggled to her feet and backed out of the bamboo, the chant and the footsteps were fading into a whisper. Whimpering, she scrambled on hands and knees up the grassy embankment. The moon rode low and half full, enough to light the white rump of Edward's horse disappearing around the bend. So he had fled—

But no. For on the lane, a dark figure lay still. And when Napua dropped to her knees beside him and reached out a tentative hand, her fingers touched his head and she recoiled from the spongy stickiness.

He had been bludgeoned, and she did not think he was breathing. Already his spirit would be slipping out of the corner of his eye to wander, lost and homeless. Without a doctor or a *kahuna* nearby, how could it be restored?

And if he died, people would think she had killed him.

Six

Anne had intended to move to the Decker household before Nettie's labor commenced, but her reluctance to leave Clara Phillips and her preoccupation with Napua's strange behavior meant she delayed too long. She was summoned in the early morning.

On her arrival, Charles Decker met her at the door. His shirt cuffs were unbuttoned and his cravat untied, attesting to his agitation. "She woke me. She's frightened already and fears the pain is not normal." His look was reproachful. "I wish you had been here to reassure her from the beginning."

She considered reminding him that Clara Phillips had needed her, too, but thought better of it. He was apprehensive, and no wonder, after listening to poor Nettie's fears! "I'm sorry I wasn't here," she said instead, moderately. "I'll go up to her immediately."

Nettie was alone but for a servant, who rose to her feet at the sight of Anne. Anne smiled at the woman and then at her patient.

"How far apart are the pains? Have you timed them?"

Already Nettie's pretty hair was damp with sweat, and she

panted slightly. "Yes, they're perhaps five minutes apart. But, oh, Anne, I don't think I can bear it! When the pain starts, it's as though my hips were being ground between two rocks! Can there be something wrong?" Her voice trembled.

"Let me examine you," Anne said calmly.

She bared Nettie's swollen abdomen and pressed the bell of her stethoscope to the skin, bending over to listen for the baby's heartbeat. She heard it immediately, the quick flutter like a frightened bird's.

Setting down the stethoscope, Anne laid her hands on her patient's belly and began to palpate. Sliding one hand downward, toward the pelvic arch, she felt for the curve of the baby's head. It was there, but not yet pressing into the birth canal.

With apologies, Anne checked to find that Nettie's cervix was not yet fully dilated. Chances were, she had hours ahead before the blessed event.

"Walking might speed matters," Anne told the other woman. "I know the idea seems cruel, but it ought to prove beneficial."

"Walk?" Fretfully, Nettie tossed her head from side to side on the heap of lace-edged pillows. "Oh, I couldn't possibly. Oh . . . oh!" Her voice rose and her hips bucked. "Anne!" she wailed.

Anne felt the muscles contracting under her hand. She rubbed gently and murmured, "Slow, deep breaths. In through the nose, out through the mouth. Yes, just like that. No, keep breathing. See, it's easing away now. You're doing fine."

"I'm not, I'm not! Something is wrong. I know it is!"

Anne explained that it was possible the baby's head was pressing a sensitive location. "Standing up might shift his position," she suggested craftily. "Come, let's try."

Amidst whimpers and complaints from Nettie, Anne eased an arm under her shoulders and prodded and encouraged until the young woman was on her feet, swaying beside the bed.

"Now, take a few steps. I'll be right here. I promise I won't let you fall."

She had her out in the hall when the next contraction struck. Nettie sagged against the plastered wall, rocking a framed oil painting to one side, and splayed her fingers over her belly.

"Remember, breathe deeply," Anne said, holding an arm around her.

When the grip of pain had passed, Nettie opened her eyes. "Why, that wasn't so bad! Oh, bless you. Come, let's walk farther," she said in a tone of determination. "I'll walk until . . . until midnight if I must! I'll do anything to avoid such torment!"

The hours blurred, as Nettie Decker alternately shuffled down the hall and rested upon the high, net-canopied bed. Progress was slow. Anne came to know the pattern of the red Turkey carpet runner in the hall as well as she knew her own face. She kept Nettie's husband informed, although there was little to say. Anne had attended labors that consumed as much as forty-eight hours. She prayed this would not be such.

Once when she stepped into the hall and called for the Hawaiian maid, the young woman asked softly, "The missus— is she dying?"

"Heavens, no!" Anne exclaimed. "She's frightened, and therefore the pain strikes her harder. We must be patient."

The maid, who had introduced herself as Kamiki, asked, "Shall I sit with her?"

"Please. I must speak to Mr. Decker."

She found him in his library. He leaped to his feet at the sight of her, so that he towered over her. Anne's heart leaped, her breath caught in alarm. Even after all these years, she saw instead her father, waited for the heavy weight of his hand. It required all her courage not to shrink back.

Charles Decker couldn't know he was frightening her, she reminded herself. He was not her father. Merely he was a forceful man not accustomed to waiting; he wanted to summon a doctor. "Surely there are means to hasten labor," he said frowning.

She clasped her hands together and summoned her composure. "Yes, but I don't believe they are necessary in this case. Mrs. Decker is bearing up very well. Any drug administered will enter the baby's bloodstream, to what effect we don't know, and I have seen the incautious use of forceps do great damage. The baby's heartbeat is strong, and I'd like to let nature take its course."

The frown did not diminish, but after a moment he gave a curt nod. "If you're wrong . . ."

A threat brought anger to stiffen her backbone. She met his gaze straight on. "The decision is yours. All I can do is give you my professional opinion. I promise you, I won't be offended if you send for a doctor now."

A muscle in his heavy cheek twitched, and then he rubbed a hand across his face. She saw suddenly his weariness, and anxiety. "No, no," he said. "Nettie chose to have you attend her. I must put my faith in you. Only—you will let me know . . . ?"

"When something happens? Of course I will."

Morning drew into afternoon, then early evening; the pains came more intensely, and closer together. Anne rubbed olive oil freely on Nettie's hips and abdomen, then kneaded to loosen muscles that would be required to yield. Light beyond the heavy drapes became shaded with peach and then purple and gray. Nettie sobbed and wailed like hurricane winds through a ship's rigging, as nature's powerful force squeezed her slender, pampered body.

Her cry became surprised when the baby began his descent. Now at last the mother was not helpless, buffeted by the agony inflicted upon her by her own body. Now she could do something useful: push, until her pale face flushed crimson and she grunted with the effort.

Until this point, all had been normal if laggardly. Now, the seconds and minutes slowed to a crawl as Anne waited for the baby's head to crown. Nothing; he was stuck, his mother's hips too narrow, her birth passage too constricting. Anne seized her stethoscope and pressed it to the distorted abdomen. The flutter of a heartbeat sounded faint, weak.

In alarm, she cried, "You must push hard! Here, press your feet against the footboards. Yes, like that. Now push, with all your might!"

For all Nettie's fatigue, she obeyed, her body arching and straining with her immense exertion. Still no head crowned.

Anne stepped back from the bed and signaled Kamiki to her side. In a low, urgent voice, she said, "Find Mr. Decker. Tell him to send for a physician immediately. There must be no delay. Now go!"

The next time she pressed the bell of the stethoscope to Nettie's belly, she heard no heartbeat, however desperately she moved it around and listened.

It was her fault. So confident in her skill, she'd turned away the offer to fetch a physician when one might have done some good. Now she feared it was too late. At most, Dr. Cabe might be able to save Nettie by performing a craniotomy—the dreadful operation in which a crotchet was used to dismember and extract the fetus.

Kamiki burst into the room and Anne hurried to her side.

"I can find Mr. Decker nowhere!" the native woman said in agitation. "He must have gone out. I sent another servant for the doctor. Was that right?"

"Yes, bless you!" Anne looked toward the bed, where her patient lay exhausted in the brief seconds between her futile efforts. "In the meantime, we must do our best."

She laid a clean sheet beneath Nettie's buttocks and used warm compresses to make more elastic the tissue where the baby should emerge. When the next contraction came, Anne pressed on Nettie's belly while Kamiki wrapped her arms around Nettie and held her in a half-sitting position.

"Push!" Anne urged. "As hard as you can. You're doing wonderfully. Again. Oh, keep pushing!"

Was that the baby's head at last? Gently she eased back the tender flesh of the perineum, opening the widening circle. The head crowned and emerged upon a scream from the mother. Creamy vernix pasted the eyes shut. Anne wiped mucus from its nose and mouth, but no cry sounded.

The face was blue and immobile. With the next push, she saw why: the cord was wrapped tightly around the baby's neck.

Too late, she thought again, even as she frantically did all she could to save the child.

"Is it a girl or a boy?" Nettie asked, lifting her head weakly as Anne cut the cord and then breathed desperately into the child's mouth. "Why is it not crying?"

At length Anne had to hand the infant off to Kamiki, who hung it by its heels and slapped its back. Anne delivered the afterbirth and bundled up the bloodied, wet cloths, gently pulling Nettie's gown down to cover her modestly.

The baby remained still and blue. It would not cry, had died before ever it emerged into the world. *My fault*, Anne thought and took Nettie's hand.

"I'm sorry," she began, her voice aching with regret and pity. "Your child is a boy, but he is stillborn. There was nothing that you could have done differently—" Except, perhaps, have allowed a doctor to wrench the child out of the womb before its time with his curving silver instrument. "This doesn't mean you won't bear healthy children." The words quivered. "Oh, Nettie, I am truly sorry."

She expected hysterics, but Nettie only stared blindly up at the net canopy, tears leaking from the corners of her eyes. Anne brushed her hair back from her face but got no response.

"I must go tell your husband, but I'll be right back."

"Where is he?" Nettie asked suddenly, sounding weak but determined. "Let me see him."

Anne understood that it was not her husband she wanted. Kamiki had wrapped the infant in white cloths, and now Anne took him from the native woman and laid him in his mother's arms, where she could cradle him for the first and last time.

She left them together, Kamiki silently crying as she stood beside the bed. Downstairs, Anne found the library quiet and deserted. No servants were about; perhaps they were eating in the kitchen. She wandered until a passage led to an indoor kitchen, rare in this climate. Only the *haole* were stubborn enough to insist on building their houses just as they would have at home, however absurd it was in this climate.

The stove was cold; this part of the house, too, was deserted. Had the Deckers' servants fled Honolulu in a panic over the smallpox, as so many natives were doing? Perhaps Kamiki and whomever she'd sent for a doctor were the only ones left.

But where was Mr. Decker? Had he been called to the store for some kind of emergency? Wouldn't he have let her know he had to go? She'd assumed when Kamiki couldn't find him that he had merely stepped out, perhaps to the privy in the backyard.

Well, he would show up sooner or later. She ought to be grateful for the reprieve. He was sure to blame her for his son's death, as she herself did.

Straightening her shoulders, she started from the kitchen. No sooner had she reentered the dim passage than she heard a door opening behind her. Anne hesitated and glanced back. Charles Decker stepped into the kitchen. As she watched, he quietly closed the door behind himself and latched it.

Dread filled her. She must have made some movement, because his head came up, like that of an animal scenting danger, and she felt the intensity of his gaze.

"Who is it?"

"Anne Cartwright," she said, moving toward him. In the huge kitchen, the squat shapes of chopping blocks, table, and enormous black stove occupied the shadows like silent onlookers.

"You have news?" he asked sharply.

"Yes, I'm afraid so."

"Nettie . . . ?"

"She's fine. But your son . . ." Anne pressed her lips together.

Like distant thunder rumbling high in the Koolau Mountain range, a deeper, more dangerous note entered his voice. "My son?"

She could not evade. "He was born with the cord around his neck. He could not be made to breathe. I'm sorry."

He advanced upon her, thunderclouds driven to spill their fury upon the deserving. "Yet you would not let me send for a doctor!"

Her voice trembled. "The baby's heartbeat was strong then. I had no reason to foresee . . ."

"We trusted you!" he raged. Even in the shadowy lighting, she saw his choleric flush, how tightly his hands were balled into fists as he paced before her. "And you say the child was a boy? A son, at last? Dead, through your incompetence!"

It was not his enraged face, his scathing words that held her straight and silent, but rather the memory of a still, blue face, of tiny hands that would never grasp a mother's finger, a mouth that would never latch onto her breast.

My fault, she thought and at last bowed her head.

It was one of the most wretched nights he had ever passed.

Matthew discovered near dawn that some of his discomfort came from two dogs who curled up on one side of him, in their generosity allotting him a portion of their numerous population of fleas. Equal weight pressed against his other side, and he shoved the dogs away and rolled far enough to discover that he had also shared his mat with a woman! Worse yet, she smelled no better than the dogs.

At least the mosquitoes had vanished with the early morning. They had whined the night through, forcing him to keep an extra shirt pulled over his face despite the muggy warmth of the grass hut. Even so, he itched like the devil, though whether from flea bites or mosquito, he couldn't have said.

Good God, and these people lived like this all the time! They were packed into small huts like peas into a tin. This room couldn't be more than fifteen by twenty feet, and Matthew had counted thirteen inhabitants before they insisted there was space for him. Puukua had slept in another hut, equally overcrowded.

The camp was in an airless gulch surrounded by cane fields. They must carry water here for drinking, which made the sanitation dreadful. Open pits were used for defecation and occasionally covered over. Through Puukua, Matthew had learned that the workers were allowed one day a week to work in taro fields, presumably only because the poi made up most of their diet and thus cost the plantation nothing but the usage of the low, wet land.

When a grinning face appeared in the open doorway, Matthew ran a hand through his hair and managed to smile back. Though these people had little, they'd received him with all the kindness a traveler could wish, sharing their food and mats without hesitation. They had talked, but fearfully; much he had learned of their misery was by implication and what was left unspoken, not from what was actually said. They were afraid of floggings, afraid of losing even this dreadful employment.

The Chinese contract workers were an even worse case, for they were no better than slaves for the five-year term of their employment. Before leaving Honolulu, Matthew had heard a good deal about the Masters' and Servants' Act of 1850. If the indentured men attempted to flee, they could be dragged back to work, where they must then serve not only the original, agreed-upon term, but an additional period twice that of their absence from the plantation. If they violated rules, they could be taken before a justice and jailed or sentenced to hard labor—as if their work in the cane fields was a mere frolic!

Matthew was an abolitionist, and he liked the sound of these contracts no better than he did the idea of one man owning another. The only difference was that the Chinamen were slaves only for the length of their terms—five to ten years. If they could endure that long, they would be free men, unlike the Negroes in the South. In Matthew's opinion, neither institution was right or godly.

He had seen enough to know that, should his case triumph, he would run this plantation differently. He wondered whether his father had agreed to contracting with Chinese laborers. Had his many years in these foreign seas so corrupted his stalwart New England morals that he would willingly become a slave owner?

Though Matthew had secretly circled back to the workers' camp to investigate conditions, he refused this morning to skulk away. If one of the *luna* reported his continued presence, perhaps it would put the fear of God into Bauer. But as fate would have it, Matthew and Puukua met no one on their ride through the cane fields.

They rode in silence, Matthew brooding and Puukua pensive, with none of yesterday's ebullience. Where Matthew's guide was concerned, the effect was probably no more than temporary; he had surely met with racial prejudice before. Though the Sandwich Islands were independent and governed by a native king, the real rulers here were *haoles*, kept barely in check by their rival nationalities. The endless ceremonies conducted in the Honolulu harbor on the occasion of warships arriving and departing—the twenty-one-gun salutes, the dipping of flags, and the receptions—were not motivated by respect for the Hawaiian people, but rather for the strategic value of these dots of land in the midst of the vast Pacific Ocean.

It had rained last night on the Pali, making the steep, zigzagging path muddy and unstable. Sheer cliffs dropped away to one side, and the sound of water falling became a monotonous accompaniment to the clop of the horses' hooves. The ridge extended in both directions, a gray, perpendicular mass that thrust fantastic pinnacles toward the sky.

At the top, the wind buffeted them, so powerfully it felt as if Matthew could lean against it and its force would hold him up. He reined in his horse and gazed back the way he had come, down the dizzying drop toward the green Mokapu Peninsula and the blue brilliance of Kaneohe Bay with the white, lacy line of surf breaking on the coral reef. On the way over, Puukua had told Matthew that from this place, the defeated enemies of King Kamehameha I had leaped to their deaths after being driven here by his army. If Matthew had thought to search the base of the towering cliff, might he find bleached skulls and shattered bones? Or had relatives buried those brave, shamed men?

Matthew's musings did not improve a mood that had become gloomier the farther they came. Impatiently he wrenched his mount's head toward the more gradual descent to the leeward shore.

Now what? he wondered. Cool his heels in Honolulu for weeks or months or years while his lawsuit wended its way through the courts? How would the native judges see him? Landre, at least, was a longtime resident. Matthew might appear as an outsider, an opportunist. Or as a poor loser.

Yet he had always put his faith in justice and the rule of law. Here it might be administered by natives just stumbling out of the Stone Age, but did that mean they were incapable of distinguishing right from wrong, a cheater from his victim? Perhaps they would see more clearly than their supposedly civilized counterparts. Perhaps the Hawaiian courts had not yet acquired the Gordian complexity that made those in the United States so slow to render opinions, and those opinions so likely to be challenged by endless appeals.

And perhaps, he thought sardonically, he would wait those months for a decision, only to have the courts rule in favor of Edward Landre. Then the decision would be his: meekly retire to Boston and rebuild his practice, or stay and fight.

The road wound through thick vegetation—delicate ferns as tall as trees and gnarled hibiscus, a tree with bright yellow flowers that Puukua swore turned red by nightfall. The birds were as gaudy as the flowers, red and yellow and black with yellow pantaloons. Some had peculiarly long, curved beaks, perfectly shaped, Matthew could see, for sipping nectar from the tubular flowers. Seeming to cheer up slightly, Puukua named them: 'i'iwi, 'o'o, and 'apapane, but Matthew couldn't keep them straight. Puukua did say that the feathers from all three had formerly been used in the magnificent feather cloaks and helmets for which the Hawaiians were known.

"I have yet to see an example," Matthew said. "I haven't been to the palace. Does your king wear a feathered cloak?"

No, most often he wore a military-style uniform, according to Puukua, who became subdued thereafter. Perhaps he was consumed by thoughts of his people's former glory.

A memory surfaced in Matthew's mind, strangely vivid considering the elapsed years. His father had written regularly when Matthew was a boy. How he had treasured those letters! They'd had the flavor of a journal, as though Captain Cabe sought to describe everything he saw.

He had written of exotic people and places, China and Tahiti and the bleak tip of the Horn. The boy Matthew had been could see the jungle of Panama, feel the humid malarial air. But most lovingly his father had written of the Sandwich Islands. He had seen them before missionary influence had prevailed, back when the *alii* had been viewed by the common people as gods.

"The chiefs of the highest rank need do nothing to be worshiped," he wrote. "Wherever such a one goes, everyone must fall to the ground in his presence, and woe unto even a child who stays innocently gazing. The natives observe many *kapus*—taboos. The women and men cannot eat together, for example. Those having to do with their chiefs are especially stringent. If a man's shadow falls upon a great chief, or his house, or even an article of his clothing or his bathwater being dumped out, the man is put to death. When the great chief eats, all in his presence must kneel.

"Just yesterday I saw such a chief venture forth from his complex of grass huts. A servant went before him calling out warning, and even the farmers in the taro patches fell face first into the muddy water. It was a miracle that none drowned.

"Another servant carried the *kahili*, made up of white feathers tied atop a staff. The *kahili* is used both to denote status and as a fly brush! Even the chiefs go about half-naked, yet they possess a certain magnificence. The capes and helmets made of thousands of tiny feathers, red and yellow and black, tied to netting in elaborate patterns must excite even European admiration. I doubt Louis XIV of France ever wore so grand a garment!"

Matthew shook his head. How many times must he have read that letter, to remember it so well?

He had kept every one until he reached the brink of manhood and realized that they were all he had of his father. He needed more and in a fit of anger burned them.

Resolutely he put the letters and his father from his mind.

The cool, sharp air of the highlands was becoming warm and heavy as he and Puukua descended into the drier region. The day was unusually hot and still, and Matthew wiped sweat from his face and shifted uncomfortably, his legs chafed by the unfamiliar hours spent in the saddle. He and his guide parted ways in the outskirts of Honolulu, Puukua to return to his family. Matthew paid him and promised to hire him again should he need a guide. "Thank you," he said, holding out his hand.

Very tentatively, the native shook it. Then he flashed a grin. "I good guide. Do laundry, too. You need shirt cleaned."

Matthew glanced ruefully at himself. "Yes, I do. I'll remember that, Puukua. You take care of yourself. Tell everyone you know to get the scratch on their arm."

He sat for a moment, watching the Hawaiian flop along on his scraggly beast. The native women, with their long skirts, rode better than their menfolk.

Shaking his head, Matthew continued down Nuuanu Street, meeting more and more traffic. Ahead he heard the whisper of the surf against the offshore reef. The leaves of coconut and banana palms hung limp in the heat. Ankle-deep dirt from the eroding adobe walls stirred with every clop of his horse's hooves. And it was still only June! What must this climate be like in August?

He had no sooner turned into the yard of the white mission house when Griggs himself hurried toward him.

"Where have you been? I expected you yesterday!"

Surprised, Matthew said, "We spent the night in the workers' camp. I warned you, did I not, that we might linger?"

"Yes, but last night—" He broke off, his narrow pale face troubled. "This morning I heard the news."

Matthew swung off his horse and faced his host. "News? What is it?"

"Edward Landre has been murdered."

Seven

urdered? Edward Landre? Shock momentarily deprived Matthew of voice. He grappled with the idea and at last was able to ask, "How? When?"

"Last night. He was bludgeoned."

"In his own home?"

"No, no, the circumstances were peculiar. He was on a lonely lane in the Nuuanu Valley. Supposedly he was meeting"—there was the briefest of hesitations, then distaste—"the native woman with whom he'd consorted. He had asked her to leave his home a few weeks ago. She apparently wanted money. He'd agreed to meet her face-to-face."

Still stunned, Matthew felt as though they were discussing people he had never met. *Landre*—his enemy—dead? No, it could not be.

"Has she been jailed?" he asked.

"No, though of course she is suspect. But when she discovered his body, she was intelligent enough not to take the money he had brought for her. She ran for assistance; the coins were still in his pocket. She could easily have taken the money and left his body where it lay, with her presence unsuspected. The very fact that, in great distress, she sought help implies innocence on her part."

"Or," Matthew said slowly, remembering her shame and pride, "she was, as you say, intelligent enough to guess that he might have told someone that he was meeting her and why. If she murdered him, she played her hand wisely."

The missionary's mouth puckered as though he had tasted something bitter. "She is indeed an intelligent young woman. What wasted potential!"

"You know her, then?"

"Yes, she was a chief's daughter, a pupil at the Royal School." The memory was clearly unwelcome. "She threw it all away, her education, her prospects, to become the mistress of a wealthy white man. The more fool she."

Matthew nodded toward the barn. "I must untack and feed my horse. Walk with me?"

As Matthew groomed the animal, Griggs told more: of the Hawaiian woman's incoherent story about supernatural beings called Night Marchers, and about how an ancestor of hers among them had saved her life. She knew it must be they; she had heard the chanting and the thunder of their feet.

"In other words, she heard what she expected to hear. The thunder of the marchers' footsteps might have been a horse's hooves," Matthew suggested.

"Yes, so the authorities think, though the constables are mostly native themselves and therefore superstitious. The Hawaiians have countless stories about ghosts. They believe that everyone upon death becomes a ghost for at least a short time. It is such superstitious nonsense that we must struggle to wipe out, before they can see the Light. Even Napua, raised a Christian from age nine or ten, still believes in these ghosts."

"But she saw nothing?"

"No, or so she claims." Griggs took the bridle from Matthew's hand and hung it on an iron hook. "I fear that the authorities will come to question you. I hope you can prove where you were last night."

Matthew closed the stall door behind his horse and turned to face the missionary. "I can," he said steadily. "My guide will vouch for me."

"Ah." Griggs's face showed relief. "Puukua is a good man, if uneducated. So long as you were with him . . ."

"I was."

Matthew was summoned within the hour to see Mrs. Charles Decker. He went immediately, despite his weariness glad for the distraction and interested in meeting Anne Cartwright again.

He'd heard of Decker, an ardent annexationist who was considered one of the cooler heads behind the movement. Perhaps swayed by Griggs and by his liking for men such as Puukua, Matthew was finding himself in sympathy with the Hawaiian people, dying from white men's diseases and under increasing political pressure from those same *haole*. Why should Americans have an inalienable right to snatch these islands from the natives? He was a man of liberal enough tendencies to feel equally sympathetic to the plight of the Indians in the American West; he thought the Hawaiians were a like case, despite the more civilized veneer kept so beautifully polished over relationships between *haole* and native. He expected, thus, to dislike Decker, and was not disappointed, though in fairness he might have felt differently had the merchant not reviled Anne Cartwright with his first words.

"She assured me there was no need for a physician, despite the slowness of my wife's labor. The next thing, I'm told, my son was born dead. 'He could not be made to breathe,' she said, curse her." His voice was vicious.

Matthew glanced up the elegant, curving stairway. He hoped Mrs. Decker's bedroom door didn't stand open so that she could hear her husband. "Such things happen . . ." he began diplomatically.

"My wife is small and delicate. Her difficulties could have been foreseen," the beefy merchant snapped. His face was flushed. "If only she had admitted the limits of her competency . . ."

"Precisely why did you call me now? Is your wife in ill health?"

Decker didn't like being interrupted. His mouth tightened. "Mrs. Decker is sunk in deep melancholy," he said stiffly. "I'm worried about her."

"Ah. Then perhaps I should speak to her."

"Very well." He bit the words off. "This way."

He led Matthew up the staircase and along a carpeted hallway. Stopping in front of a closed door, his hand on the knob, he said rigidly, "I should warn you that Mrs. Cartwright is still here."

"Still here?" Matthew repeated in surprise.

Decker's mouth twisted. "My wife insists on her company."

"I see." Matthew waited, but the merchant still didn't open the door. "Well, then . . ." Matthew prodded.

Decker grimaced and turned the knob.

Within, Anne Cartwright sat in a rocking chair beside a huge, canopied bed. Behind her, sunlight poured in through windows flung open. With no breeze to stir them, sheer curtains hung limply. The vivid orange flowers of the *kou* tree reached to the sill.

At the sight of Decker, Anne's mouth opened in an *O* of surprise, and she started to rise to her feet. Matthew didn't like to see the flicker of fear in her eyes. "Mr. Decker—" Her voice warmed when she saw the man at his heels. "Dr. Cabe."

"Mrs. Cartwright. How do you do?"

Not well, he thought. Though her chestnut hair was neatly confined and her dress tidy, dark shadows marred the pale skin beneath her fine gray eyes.

"I've been better," she said with a glance at her employer. "I suppose Mr. Decker told you—"

"Only a little." He stopped beside the bed. Very likely a pretty woman in better times, Nettie Decker lay against the lace-edged pillows, her face colorless and composed, her eyes gazing blindly forward. Under the covers, her legs were straight, her feet together, and her arms crossed over her chest, as though she had been arranged in her coffin. The comparison chilled him. "Mrs. Decker," he said gently. "I'm Dr. Cabe. Your husband is concerned about you."

Her brown eyes turned to him but stayed disinterested.

Mrs. Cartwright touched her shoulder. "Nettie, will you talk to the doctor?"

"Yes, why not?" Mrs. Decker said, but her voice so lacked human expression, he was not reassured.

"May I examine you?" Matthew asked. Though he saw no sign of fever, his first obligation was to be sure her depressed spirits were not caused by puerperal infection or internal injuries.

"I don't care," the young woman said dully and rolled her head to gaze toward the foot of the bed.

Mrs. Cartwright's high brow crinkled as she studied her patient. After a moment she turned an alarmed look on Matthew. "Nettie—Mrs. Decker—is very modest. I'm surprised—" She checked herself. "Let me ready her."

He understood what she was telling him: the agreement was no more natural than was Mrs. Decker's gaze, which saw past or future but not the present. Perhaps the present was unbearable.

Aware of the patient's husband standing just inside the door, arms crossed and jaw set forbiddingly, Matthew washed his hands and then made his examination as quickly as possible, taking care not to shatter Nettie Decker's sleeping modesty any more than necessary.

When he was finished, he tucked the bedcovers back around her. "Your body is healthy—" Perhaps not the best choice of words. "I'm pleased to see no tearing in the tissues."

Anne Cartwright said nothing.

"The child was stillborn?"

"The cord was around his neck," she said in a stifled voice.

Matthew frowned and turned to Decker. "But you implied the infant's death was the result of your wife's size and some incompetence on Mrs. Cartwright's fault! A cord around the neck is tragic, but an accident of nature. I could have done nothing to prevent it even had I been here."

"A forceps delivery . . ."

"Once the child has strangled, it is generally too late. Using forceps and wrenching a baby out can sometimes tighten the cord, causing more harm than good. Unless the heart was still beating . . ."

Beside him, Anne Cartwright looked troubled. "I heard it stop. If forceps had been used then—"

He forgot the husband of the woman watching him from the bed. Very gently, he said, "It was probably already too late. Had he begun his descent?"

"Barely."

"Then I could not have saved him."

Nettie Decker began to cry, first a trickle of tears down her pale cheeks, then great gulping sobs. Relief flooded the midwife's face before she sank onto the edge of the bed to take the bereaved mother in her arms. Beside the door, a great sigh came from Decker, and he bent his head to disguise the emotions wracking his face.

Decker was the first to speak. Hoarsely he said, "Mrs. Cartwright, I ask your forgiveness. I wanted to believe this could have been prevented."

"I understand," she said softly. Then, "Yes, cry, Nettie, let your anguish out. Of course you're sad. I understand."

Anne's eyes met Matthew's over Nettie's head. For a moment they only looked at each other. He had the uncomfortable feeling she was searching for something in him, some quality he didn't know whether he possessed. It was rare to have a woman gaze so directly, so honestly. He was near the point of looking away for his own comfort when she mouthed the words, "Thank you."

He nodded, feeling stiff and inadequate, although he had undoubtedly done some good here. Anne was right—Nettie needed to cry—that was what had been so unnatural about her. And he was oddly gratified that he'd been able to do something useful for Anne—Mrs. Cartwright. Blast it, why did he want to think of her by her given name?

To his regret, it was Decker who accompanied him to the door. Matthew felt resentful; he would have liked to exchange a few private words with Mrs. Cartwright, if only to tell her he understood her guilt over losing the infant. What doctor or midwife wouldn't feel the same?

He wondered if she knew about Landre's murder. Of course, unless she'd heard the gossip, she would have no way of connecting the crime to Matthew. Had she known Landre? He was curious what she thought of him.

After refusing payment from Decker—after all, he had done very little—Matthew rode home pondering his interest in Anne Cartwright. He supposed it was only that he felt friendless here in Honolulu. They had something in common—both made their livelihood from medical practices of a sort. Neither was missionary or merchant, which put them in the minority here. From her starched white cap to her uncompromising directness, Anne Cartwright was a New Englander as out of place as he felt. Had they been the same sex, he would have liked to be friends with her. As it stood, she would be offended by any approach from him that was not strictly professional.

He realized that he was using the midwife to avoid thinking

about the murder. The moment he thought the word—*murder*—it occupied his thoughts to the exclusion of any others.

Would the authorities have heard about his confrontration with Landre? Had the Hawaiian woman been arrested yet? He pictured the sharp way Landre had reproved her and the dignity and wounded pride of her retreat from the parlor. With a noble heritage, she would not be accustomed to being scorned. If she had attended the Royal School, her parents might have been high chiefs for whom people prostrated themselves. Would her pride be enough to justify murder? Or had she once loved Landre, and her emotions had now twisted into hate?

He tried to picture the scene, the beautiful dark-skinned woman lifting—what? a stick? a rock?—and striking down Landre. Did the authorities know what the weapon had been?

The moment his horse shambled into the yard of the mission house, tension tightened his shoulders and neck. Two horses were tied to the hitching post in the shade, one the typically wretched island beast, the other a reasonably handsome animal. The day's heat was still so great neither did more than flop an ear in his direction. He led his own horse into the barn and unsaddled, turning it loose in the box stall, using the minutes to compose himself.

Matthew entered the house slowly, grateful for the relative cool. Mrs. Griggs met him at the door. In a low voice, she said, "You have callers. They're waiting in the parlor."

"Callers?"

Her mouth became a thin line. "Marshal Parke and a constable."

"Ah." So they had come. "Thank you."

Two men rose from chairs in the parlor the moment he entered. He felt the keenness of their gazes as they assessed him.

"Dr. Cabe?" The speaker was a middle-aged white man, obviously educated.

"Yes?"

"Marshal William Parke. This is one of my constables, Ebenezer Mahaulu. He's inquiring into the murder of our assistant minister of finance, Mr. Edward Landre. I assume you've heard about it."

"Yes, I have." Matthew shook the two men's hands. "What can I do to help you?"

They exchanged a glance. The native constable, a large, muscular man with curly dark hair and fleshy lips, didn't appear eager to take the reins of the conversation. He waited until Parke said uncomfortably, "I apologize for bothering you. There's been a good deal of talk about a fight between you and Mr. Landre. Witnesses claim you threatened him."

"With a lawsuit."

"That wasn't quite how you phrased it. Or perhaps I should say, how your . . . remark was understood."

"I lost my temper and said things I didn't mean."

"I understand how that can happen," the marshal agreed diplomatically. "However it puts us in the position of having to consider you a potential suspect. If you can tell us where you were last night—"

"I am disputing ownership of a plantation at Kaneohe Bay with Mr. Landre. I visited it yesterday and spent the night."

"Someone can vouch for your presence there?"

"My guide. A man named Puukua." Matthew told them how to find the native guide's grass hut on Merchant Street, near the stone church.

The constable nodded and said unexpectedly, "I know him. He is my wife's cousin."

"Then we won't take any more of your time," Parke said. "Thank you for your cooperation, Dr. Cabe. May I say that I hope you take up residence in Honolulu. We need more physicians."

"Thank you," Matthew said, and accompanied them to the door. From the front window he watched them ride away, enveloped by dust that shimmered in a golden cloud, backlit by the sinking sun. He was uneasily aware that they had been serious in their inquiry; they did indeed consider him a suspect. Thank God for Puukua. Who knew whether the plantation workers would be willing to admit to having talked to the *haole* who visited them in secrecy?

Reverend Griggs returned home shortly thereafter and Mrs. Grigggs put the evening meal on the table. Matthew made light of the visit, and conversation centered on the growing threat of smallpox.

"I couldn't find any fresh beef for sale today," Mrs. Griggs said worriedly. "The produce market was nearly deserted. Is the meat safe, do you think?"

"We don't need to worry," Matthew reassured her. "But for those who haven't been vaccinated, I'd be cautious about meat and produce from natives. Until we discover how the disease is spread, it is logical to avoid such direct contact."

Griggs grunted. "The town's markets are filthy kennels! At best they're eyesores, at worst spreaders of disease and death. I've long believed they ought to be regulated. We buy most of our food directly from a decent family of Christian natives with a plot at Ewa. They deliver to us."

Did Christianity equate with cleanliness? Matthew was more concerned about the cesspools under every house, a health hazard even without an epidemic raging through the town, but he didn't consider the topic one for the dinner table.

Servants were fleeing Honolulu in droves, Mrs. Griggs had heard. White families sat down for dinner only to find their cook had left without notice and no one remained to serve.

"The quarantine is useless," the reverend agreed. "We've sent word to missionaries and authorities on the other islands to forbid landings, but who knows how successful such measures will be? If only the natives could be made to understand that it is too late to flee infection; all they do is endanger their families by rushing home."

Mrs. Griggs was kind enough to heat water to provide a lukewarm bath for Matthew that evening. It sufficed, although he thought longingly of the backyard bathhouse belonging to a wealthy merchant. Judd had described it as an enclosure placed atop a stream so that the cool water poured over a seat before flowing freely out the other side.

He slept uneasily. The night was hot and unusually muggy even for summer. He was consumed by images of suffering: the native workers being sliced by cane in the airless fields, lashes driving them on to labor for ten or twelve hours at a stretch; Nettie Decker, arranged on her bed as though ready to die, staring at nothing; the face of Landre's mistress consumed with rage and twisted love as she lifted some shadowy weapon above her head and struck. He'd have sworn he heard the sickening crunch of Landre's head caving in, much like a melon suddenly dropped.

Groaning, Matthew rolled over on the narrow, hard bed.

He felt nearly as wretched come morning as he had the morning before. Matthew washed his face, dressed, and went downstairs but had not even had time to breakfast before a knock came on the front door.

He answered it himself and was somehow unsurprised to find Marshal Parke and Constable Mahaulu on the doorstep. Their expressions were grim.

"What is it?" he asked, his stomach clenching.

Parke said expressionlessly, "I regret to tell you that we were unable to locate Puukua. Much of his family has been stricken by smallpox, and he has apparently fled the island with his daughter. His wife is dead, her sister and husband too ill to answer questions and unlikely to survive. No one knows when he left, but neighbors thought longer ago than yesterday afternoon."

Matthew struggled to draw breath. "But— He said—"

"He said?"

"That he and his family had been vaccinated. He showed me the scratch on his arm."

Parke cleared his throat. "Many of the natives are frightened by the vaccination. They're scratching their own arms."

"Good God." Matthew had not yet taken in the effect of his guide's defection on his own situation. "He may have infected the workers at Kaneohe. And it's my fault."

"Unfortunately that's possible, Dr. Cabe. But at the moment, I must ask whether you can produce another witness to your whereabouts the night before last."

"The plantation workers . . ."

"What about Mr. Bauer, the manager?"

Panic raced through his bloodstream, clouding his thinking. "No. He thought I'd left."

He knew even before he said it how this would be received by his interrogators. Though they didn't so much as look at each other, he could see that he'd sealed his fate.

"I'll send somebody to interview the workers. In the meantime, Dr. Cabe . . ." Parke hesitated, his face sinking into the lugubrious lines of a bloodhound. "I'm afraid I have to arrest you for the murder of Edward Landre."

When she heard that the blond doctor had been arrested, it was as though a great burden had been lifted from Napua's shoulders. She had been so afraid that she was to blame, though she had not struck the blow.

As time had passed, she'd become confused about what she had seen and heard. Could the beat of the marchers' footsteps have been only a horse's hooves? What of the chanting? The *haole* sheriff insisted she had imagined it. Perhaps a bird had been calling, or she'd heard the surf even so far up the valley, or the wind had been whispering through the *ohe*, its chants as ancient as the voices of the ghosts she had imagined. Could it be so?

But what—who?—had pushed her from the path? She could tell that the sheriff didn't believe anybody had. He thought she had heard someone coming and panicked, hiding herself. Perhaps the murderer had thundered upon them from behind and shoved her aside because he didn't wish to kill her, too. He might even have hoped, if he left her alive, that she would be blamed for Edward's death.

But she knew in her heart that she and Edward had been alone on that path when she was struck between the shoulder blades and tumbled into the *ohe*, the bamboo. Was it not possible that an ancestor ghost had seen into the heart of the murderer, thundering toward them on his horse, and hurried to save her, because she was of his blood?

It would be good to know that she had an *aumakua* watching out for her. The *haole* claimed not to believe in ghosts, but Napua thought that really they were uneasy with the idea. They wanted their dead to go straight to Heaven or Hell, not to linger among the living.

It was not ghosts that frightened Napua. It was the thought that by her actions she had set the murderer on Edward. She'd wanted Henry Turner to go to Edward, to let him know that she meant what she said, but she'd given no thought to what might happen. To Henry Turner himself. With Edward dead, that had changed. She remembered their conversation.

I'll pay Edward Landre a visit, with pleasure. I may beat the tar out of him and do that with pleasure, too. And when she had urged him to be careful, he had laughed with such bitterness. *Careful? Good god, why? So that I can drink myself into an early grave in-*

stead? He was a man with nothing to lose. Why not gain his revenge?

Most of all, she remembered how at the end he had said with satisfaction, *At least now we both know who to blame, don't we?*

He knew because she had told him. If he'd committed murder, then she must bear some of the blame.

They would have liked to arrest her, Napua thought, but had come to believe the parts of her story that were acceptable to them. Despite the fact that she had not taken the money from Edward and that she had run for help as quickly as she could, they might have claimed she had done those things to avoid suspicion. But even they had to admit that she would get no more money from a dead man. The small bag of coins Edward had carried to their meeting was to her only a single fish in the thousands that flitted around a coral reef. If she killed him, there would be no more fish to feed Kuokoa. With Edward alive, she could have continued to cast her net.

But now they said that Matthew Cabe was the murderer. She wanted to think that it was so. He, too, had been angry at Edward, and with reason. But how would he have known where to come? That was what bothered her. Henry Turner knew what she intended; he might have followed her, or even read the note she left at the drugstore. Or, incautious in his anger, Edward might have told Turner.

Napua was washing clothes in the pond behind her cottage. She used *haole* soap that was strong and biting, then rubbed the fabric against a smooth rock before rinsing the garments in the stream that tumbled a few feet into the pond. Her son bathed as she worked. He swam like a porpoise already, fearless and graceful. Sometimes she paused to watch him, the sheen of his brown body leaping from the water and submerging again. Always his laughter trailed behind like the song of the whales.

Part of her grieved that now he would forget his father. Another part of her thought this way might be better. Death was less hurtful than disinterest. If Edward had been Hawaiian, Kuokoa might be comforted to think that his father would become his *aumakua*, choosing not to go to Milu, the underworld, but rather to stay near his home to protect his son.

But he was not Hawaiian, and he had not cared about his son even in life. Were *haole* spirits really different from Hawaiian spirits? she wondered. The Reverend Griggs would say Edward had gone to Hell, where he would burn for all eternity. Hell must be like the mouth of Mauna Kea, where Pele trembled between rage and passion. Would she embrace a man such as Edward, or turn him into a stone pillar for the sea to wear down?

What Napua thought was that the *haole* were wrong. The Hawaiians believed a spirit had to have help to find its way to the land of Milu. The dead who were ready to go on must find a *Leina-a-ka-uhane*—a path-for-leaping-by-the-spirit. They were almost always on a bluff looking westward on the ocean. Near the place would be a breadfruit tree where the spirits gathered. From its branches the spirit could leap into the land of the dead, or find other ghosts to help. One of these Quietly-calling-breadfruit-trees was said to be at Kaena Point and another here in the Nuuanu Valley. A Hawaiian spirit would know of those leaping-off places, but would Edward's, or would it wander hopelessly?

He would have no one to place offerings on a secret altar to feed him. His spirit would have to creep through dark places and search for butterflies, spiders, and insects. Napua thought he might be blown here and there, back and forth, with no place to rest because he would have no *aumakua* to help him, no living people to pray for him or to persuade him to come back into his body. He had made too many enemies and no friends. Even the woman he had intended to marry must be angry, once she heard why he was meeting Napua.

She was glad to think of him lost and homeless, feeding on

spiders. It seemed fitting, when he had cast her and his own son out, leaving them homeless. She hoped his spirit was hungry and frightened and that no other ghost helped it find the leaping-off place.

And she hoped that Matthew Cabe had killed him, so that she need feel no guilt to weaken her vindictive anger. She needed that anger, now that she had nothing else.

Napua stood in a narrow space with nothing before and nothing behind. She'd been hiding her fear from Kuokoa, but soon he would have to know that she had no more money to pay for this cottage or buy food. Even if they found a deserted grass hut, still they had to eat. She would have to find work or sell her body. And what kind of work could she do? She quilted, but foreigners did not hire a native to quilt. Mrs. Griggs had taught her how to cook a few dishes, but not enough for her to work as a cook. She spoke English, but who would hire a woman to translate?

Even in her desperation, Napua feared she would not be humble enough to become a servant. Not even the missionaries could teach her humility, and it was the one quality above all others required of a servant.

Once she could have asked Anne for help, but that time was past. It was her own fault that Anne no longer knocked on her door or peered in the windows. Resentful at her treatment by the Griggses, Napua had hidden from her old friend and shushed Kuokoa, who wanted to run gladly to her. Now Napua thought she had been wrong to believe Anne would want to see her lie on the ground and hide her face like the lowest of the *makaainana*. Shamed and hurt, she had wanted to reject everything *haole*.

Now she remembered the times Anne had encouraged her to take pride in the old ways, to hold up her head, to dance the *hulahula* without shame. But it was too late.

The clatter of a horse's hooves in front of the cottage jerked her from her brooding. She signaled to her son.

"You stay here, quietly, while I see who it is."

He nodded, his joy gone as if she had dumped sand on a fire, and she felt a sinking at her inability to keep him safe. What if the sheriff changed his mind and she *was* arrested? What would become of Kuokoa?

She was surprised to see who stood on the porch of her cottage. Herr Bauer, Edward had called the plantation manager. On his occasional visits, she had always felt the small hairs on her neck quiver, as though he were a ghost. Perhaps it was his hair and eyes and skin, so unnaturally pale. But if he were a ghost, he was not *laka*—tame and friendly. She hadn't liked the way he looked at her, but it was hard to say exactly how that was.

Why would he seek her out now? With sudden hope, she wondered if he might have good news. Could Edward have left her something after all?

She stepped from her hiding place behind the pale green *kukui* and said, "Herr Bauer. Are you looking for me?"

He turned with unexpected speed for a man of his size. When he saw her, a smile spread across his thin lips. "Napua," he said in her language. "You're as beautiful as ever. Landre was a lucky man."

"Thank you," she said stiffly and didn't take another step forward. She didn't like the smile any more than she had liked the way those pale eyes always swept over her, like a cold finger of the ocean caressing the sand.

"Are you going to ask me in?" He nodded toward her cottage.

It went against her deepest beliefs not to offer hospitality, but she didn't want to be alone inside with him. She said, "I'm washing clothes in the stream. You can see I'm wet."

"Yes." His gaze lowered to her chest, where damp cotton

clung to her breasts. She was not modest in the way of the missionary women—she had bared her breasts in the hula—but the audience had not looked at them as Herr Bauer did.

She lifted her chin in the way her mother had had of reminding people she was *alii*. "Did you have something to tell me?" Napua asked coolly.

"I came to see if you were well. If I could help."

Had she misread him? The color of his eyes and hair were not something he could change. Perhaps his own people recoiled at his paleness and that was why he hid out at the plantation.

"That's kind of you," she said, beginning to relax.

He stepped off the porch and came toward her. She resisted her instinct to back up. He stopped in front of Napua and lifted a hand, brushing her hair back from her face.

"I've always envied Landre, but he paid me well. I wouldn't try to take what was his. Now you need me, and I can take care of you." The hand wrapped around the back of her neck, like the tentacle of an octopus. "You can even bring your kid. I don't care."

Napua wrenched back. Too late. He grabbed her hair, bringing tears to her eyes, and bent forward, pressing his wet mouth to hers.

"I'll be good to you," he muttered. "Buy you things as pretty as he did."

She struggled uselessly in an iron grip. He must chew tobacco; she could taste the sourness. Anger overrode her fear, and she kicked at his shins. All she did was hurt her toe on his knee-high leather boots.

He put his other hand on her breast and squeezed while he yanked her head to one side so he could bite at her ear. "Pretty," he mumbled.

Still she fought in silence, not wanting to scare Kuokoa. She went for Bauer's face with her fingernails. He howled when she found his eye and ripped at his nose.

He let go of her hair and hit her face with the back of his hand. He ranted guttural words she didn't understand. Before she could cover her face, he hit her again, and she crumpled to her knees, crying out.

She cowered when she heard a thud and a bellow from him. She felt him diving for her and she scrambled to one side. To her astonishment, he fell heavily and didn't rise again.

Wiping the blood from her nose, Napua looked up. Anne Cartwright stood above her, the broken branch from a tree in her hands.

Eight

Was he dead? He lay in a shapeless huddle, much as Edward had. Napua watched as Anne crouched beside him. She, too, saw the slight movement as he breathed.

"Well, I've knocked *him* out," Anne said with unmistakable satisfaction, then added, "Who is he?"

"Herr Bauer," Napua tried to say, but it hurt to speak.

Anne swiveled on her heels to face Napua. "Never mind. Let's get a cold compress on your face. Did he hurt you otherwise?"

Napua shook her head.

Anne wrapped an arm around her and Napua struggled to her feet. Dizziness swept over her but passed, and after a moment she was able to walk. They left Bauer lying like a felled *koa* tree, his face ground into the soil.

"Mama!" Kuokoa exploded from a bush and collided with her. Napua let go of Anne to hug him.

"I hurt my face," she told him in a voice muffled by her swollen mouth but otherwise as cheerful as she could make it, "but the blood is only from my nose. You know how your nose has bled before. For a few days my cheek will be puffy, like sea billows, and perhaps the same color. I'll look silly, and you can laugh at me."

He lifted his face from her belly. "That man—"

"You saw him?"

"I would have hit him, but Mrs. Cartwright did it first." He reached out a shy hand to grip the *haole* woman's fingers.

The midwife smiled at him and said, "You're a brave boy. You'll grow up to be a courageous warrior like your ancestors."

"Yes." He let go of them to swagger toward the pond, where he grabbed a stick. "I'll watch for the man. If he moves, I'll hit him."

"You do that," Anne said, "but stay where we can see you."

She tenderly washed Napua's face and made her lie back in the shade of a breadfruit tree with a cold, wet cloth folded over her cheek and mouth. After a while, she said, "Did I do something to offend you, Napua?"

"No. Oh, no," Napua said in English, trying to rise. Anne's hand on her shoulder pressed her back down. Around the wet cloth, she tried to explain. "I felt angry, humiliated. I didn't want charity."

Quietly, Anne said, "I thought what I offered was friendship."

"I was so angry, I misunderstood what you offered." Napua gazed beseechingly at her. "I'm sorry."

Anne merely nodded, her face averted. Her cheek was plump and soft, the one small curl of hair that had escaped her tight net as delicate and subtly colored as a tree snail. Napua thought how beautiful she could be, if she let her hair down and didn't wear such stiff, confining clothes. It was true that her skin was very white, but if her hair cascaded down her back, it would blaze like fire in the sun, and her eyes made Napua think of the mists cloaking the heights, soft and gray and mysterious. She was round, not skinny like many of the foreign women. Did the *haole* men have such strange tastes?

"Why did you come today?" she asked.

Anne let out a long breath. "To make sure you were all right. I heard about Edward. I was afraid they might try to blame you."

"They've arrested someone else," Napua told her. "That *haole* doctor, Matthew Cabe."

Anne turned sharply, her mouth open like that of a *humuhumu-'ele'ele* fish. "Dr. Cabe? Impossible! They've arrested him? I can't believe he would murder anyone!"

Now Napua did sit up, and Anne didn't even appear to notice. "You know him so well?" Napua asked.

Was that a blush that pinkened her friend's pale cheeks? "Not well, but he's a fine doctor. He's gentle, caring—" She broke off.

"But he blamed Edward for stealing from his father. To avenge dishonor to his family, a man might do much."

Sounding inexplicably distressed, Anne countered, "But one who has chosen to be a physician, to give his life to healing? He might have won in court—"

"Would that have been enough?" Napua asked.

Anne fell silent. After a time she said softly, "I don't know. But I don't believe—" She gave a ragged sigh. "It doesn't matter what I believe, does it?" Emotions dashed across her face. Another sigh followed the first. Finally she squared her shoulders and her eyes met Napua's. "How are *you*, Napua? Was it frightening? Do you grieve?"

Napua looked within herself and told the truth. "I was afraid, but I don't grieve. He did not deserve my sadness."

"No—"

"Mama! Mama!" Kuokoa called from the corner of the cottage. "I think the man is awake. Should I hit him?"

"I'll take care of him." Looking afraid but determined, Anne rose to her feet and hurried toward Napua's son, shaking her dark skirts out as she went. "You watch over your mother."

Napua stayed where she was, gazing up at the glossy split leaves and ripening fruit of the *'ulu* tree and listening to the murmur of Anne speaking. Napua could tell that her friend was afraid of angry men. Some man had hurt her, perhaps her missionary husband, although Napua had never understood how a man could give his life to the salvation of a whole people yet be harsh to his wife. Perhaps it wasn't he; there might have been another man before him.

But Napua also knew the contempt with which Anne would look at the pale *haole* and the scathing tone that would be in her voice. One of the reasons Napua admired her *haole* friend was because she did what she had to even when she was afraid.

It wasn't long before Napua heard the sound of the horse's hooves, and Anne returned. Her face was set in harder lines than usual. "I don't think he'll bother you again," she said.

Napua found she had tears in her eyes, and the words she hadn't meant to say burst out of her. "He may not be able to find me anyway. I must move. I have no money to stay here." Kuokoa dropped his stick, crept over like a frightened puppy, and curled up in her lap, his face solemn but his thin arms comforting.

"Napua." Anne knotted her fingers together. "There are other missionaries. I cannot believe all would reject you as the Reverend Griggs did."

"You're suggesting that I . . . ? No." The tears became hot on her cheeks, and she clutched her son tighter. "No, I cannot. I must find work! I could mend, or clean, or—"

"Was the life so terrible?" Anne asked. "It would be your best chance of marrying, of finding a good man who would value Kuokoa, too."

Still she shook her head. "Even if they took me in, I would meet Reverend Griggs in company, and he would despise me and turn away. No, do not ask it. I cannot."

"Napua." Anne waited until her eyes took command of Napua's. "Will you let any man decide who you are? Will you give him the pleasure of destroying you?"

Napua hadn't thought of it that way. Her mother would have said the same. If Napua met the Reverend Griggs in company, instead of shrinking she could hold her head high, as her mother would have done, and despise him for his cruelty. Perhaps he would slink away in shame, she thought, imagining the scene, shaping it to her satisfaction. Or even beg her forgiveness.

Wavering, she touched her swollen face and said, "I should wait . . ."

Anne shook her head. "No. I'll tell them what happened. I don't believe he'll be back, but I can't be sure, and there'll be others like him. You're a beautiful woman."

A bitter pang pierced Napua's heart, for it was true that there would be other men. They would all think she was looking for someone to replace Edward, and why not? It was natural to fill the hole from which a plant had been removed. And wasn't she the kind of woman they believed her to be? Hadn't she stolen out of the home of good people to give herself to him in return for finery? Even she had trouble sometimes believing she had once loved him.

Gently, Anne said, "I'll help you lay out your clean clothes, and then let's go now."

Napua felt so weak, she let herself be persuaded. This week of terrible events had showed her how alone she was. The missionaries had once been kind. She had thought of them as her family. Was it so bad to go to them for help?

The part she didn't like was that they would want her to turn away from her heritage. They claimed their Jehovah got angry if people believed in other spirits or gods. He must be possessive like Pele, and have a temper like hers.

But would He really know that she secretly thought of her *aumakua*, too, or that she taught her son the old ways, but quietly? She was desperate enough right now to take a chance. Surely He didn't watch each and every person so closely. And if He did and thought to punish her, perhaps her own gods would protect her, if she had been faithfully making offerings to them.

And perhaps, once back in the embrace of the missionary family, the old ways that she'd been remembering more vividly each day would fade again, until they lost their urgency and became no more than a pleasant memory, like childhood games.

She would take her chances.

Just as he had the last time, Kuokoa snuggled in her arms on the ride into Honolulu. It was the same—her nervousness, the grog shops and the familiar buildings, the sound of the surf coming closer—and yet also different, for the markets were almost deserted, with fewer sellers and almost no buyers for the baskets of eggs and the bundles of tobacco and the shimmering fish laid out on *ti* leaves. They passed so many houses with yellow cloths tied out in front, Napua began to look away from them. At one native house, men were loading sick people or bodies, she wasn't sure which, into a wagon. She turned Kuokoa's face into her breast so that he didn't see.

This time they went to the mission compound beyond the stone church. Inside the coral walls, the white-painted buildings had the same air as the missionary wives: proper and severe. Napua felt her heart drumming and the shallowness of her breaths. She was clutching the wagon seat so hard, she had to rub tiny splinters off her fingertips when she released it.

But, oh, this reception was so different! The women welcomed her with embraces and glad words while telling Kuokoa what a fine boy he was and how well he spoke English. The Reverend Taft shook his head in disapproval when he heard how

Reverend Griggs had received her, and quoted, " 'Though I speak with the tongues of men and of angels, and have not charity, I am become as sounding brass, or a tinkling cymbal.' First Corinthians." He smiled at Napua with great kindness. "You are welcome here. I'll speak with Brother Griggs, remind him if need be that 'And now abideth faith, hope, charity, these three; but the greatest of these is charity.' "

In her pride, Napua didn't like to think she was the object of charity, but she knew Reverend Taft meant the word in its richest sense. Hadn't he dedicated his life to a people once strangers to him? When she first came to them, she had been awed to think that when their God commanded they go to a land unimaginably far away to minister to an unknown, pagan people, they had obeyed joyfully, without resentment or fear. Surely the missionaries had more generous hearts than anyone else she knew. She had always believed so, until Reverend Griggs—a man she had once loved and revered—had turned her away so cruelly.

Napua protested when she found out that she and her son were to sleep in Anne's room.

"You may have my room and welcome to it." Anne gave a last smile and soft kiss on the cheek. "All will be well now," she murmured and left before Napua could ask her where she would stay. But someone would know, she thought vaguely, and then she looked over to where her son was gazing in wonder at an open book in the lap of a woman reading him a story. The pages of the book held a fascination greater than the candy he clutched in one hand.

Napua felt a swelling in her chest, like a fishpond filling until the water rose to the top of the embankment and closed her throat. She could not have spoken, so glad was she. *For Kuokoa, I have done the right thing*, she thought. These missionaries would take care of him if something bad happened to her. They would take care of him even if the constable decided she, not the *haole* doctor, had killed Edward and took her to the fort.

No, for her son's sake, she would not regret her choice, whatever the cost.

From the moment the heavy wooden gates of the fort closed, groaning on their massive iron hinges behind him, Matthew was a different man. He'd always been treated with dignity and respect, even admiration. Now he was a prisoner.

He'd become accustomed to the sight of the fort from the outside: its thick coral stone walls, sheathed with more coral, the angular *hau* trees growing directly out of the parapet, the Hawaiian flag flying high. Now the interior spread before him: surrounding an open parade ground of perhaps two acres were barracks and the governor's house and whitewashed stone powder magazines. His gaze went directly to the gallows house, a tiny structure behind the powder magazines. Horror and disbelief filled him. Were he convicted, his life might end there, choked out of him.

Past a sentry, the constable led Matthew through another gate into an enclosure lined by stone cells built into the *makai* wall of the fort. He thrust him into a large one, empty.

In shock, Matthew stood still as shackles were snapped around his ankles, the rusting chain dragging heavy between them.

"I must apologize for these," Marshal Parke said. "We consider the fort none too secure and must take greater measures to hold onto those prisoners accused of a felony. I don't believe you would attempt to escape, Dr. Cabe, but I cannot apply unequal treatment."

Did he expect absolution from Matthew? If so, he was to be disappointed, for Matthew stood silent.

"You have freedom of the yard during the day. You'll find a privy out there. The other prisoners are away at present on work details."

They quietly closed the cell door behind them. Matthew looked around. The room, perhaps eighteen by twenty feet, was empty but for a rush mat rolled up. A single, tiny window let in sunlight and the sound of the sea. Though the bare floor had been swept, the smell of unwashed bodies and urine was overpowering.

With a groan, he stumbled across the cell, sank to the floor, back against the cool wall, and buried his head in his hands. His greatest single emotion was not fear or anger but humiliation. That he, Dr. Matthew Cabe, humanitarian and healer, well-to-do and more often admired than disdained, should be in a filthy hole, shackled like a common criminal, stunned him. How could this have happened? It wasn't possible!

He spent the day sunk in a sort of apathy he had seen but never felt. He didn't once move, just slumped there against the wall. His mind drifted, as though he were half dozing. Sometimes he thought of pleasanter times: dinners with his mother, who had been a gallant woman determined to see the best in every situation; his triumphs as a physician; the woman he had briefly loved, before he saw her slap her Negro maid. Such a small moment, but one that tarnished her. Her copper curls were not as bright thereafter, nor her sparkling green eyes as enchanting.

It was just as well he had never married. Imagine, if he had to write a beloved wife, home in Boston, to tell her he'd been imprisoned for murder!

But why *had* he never married? Though he didn't consider himself vain, he knew many women would have had him, if only he'd offered. He had followed a few into their bedchambers and sported on the soft feather mattresses amidst the lace and perfume. But they were not women he wanted bearing his children.

Children, he thought with a stab of grief, that he might never have now. The Cabe name would die with him, and all because his father had blown his brains out rather than come to his only son for aid.

Matthew remembered the last time he'd seen his father, the stiffness between them, the distance. They were two men brought together by obligation, not affection. Then, he hadn't cared; why should he? William Cabe was a stranger by choice. The sea and exotic ports had lured him from his family. Matthew was indifferent to the regret this man—his father—now expressed. It came too late for his mother and therefore too late for him.

But then when he didn't hear from his father, Matthew eventually stopped by his lodgings. All was silent within, the door barred. He came back the next day, and the next. Eventually he broke a window and found Captain William Cabe slumped over his desk, maggots crawling over what was left of his head. A note, splattered with dried blood, was carefully lined up with the corner of the desk.

Dear Matthew, it said, *I find I have nothing left to live for, and no wish to be a burden to you. Were I younger, I might have the courage to start again, but I'm turned fifty this year, too old for much besides a settled career and a comfortable wife, long cherished. I have thrown away the possibility of both, as well as a closer relationship with you, my only child. Now comes bad news: for my retirement I had counted on income from the sugar plantation in the Sandwich Islands. Just today I received notice it's gone bankrupt. All I invested is lost. Lost. I can scarcely believe it but have not the energy to investigate. What does it matter now?*

All that is left is to say again that, in my own peculiar way, I loved you and your mother greatly. I pray God that some-day you believe my words.

William Cabe had been many things, but he was not a fool-ish man. He would not have invested his wealth without confi-dence. Unfortunately he'd placed that confidence in his partner, Edward Landre.

Dead now, too. But ironically, in his death, he was destroy-ing Matthew.

Blast it, Puukua. If only you hadn't lied about being vaccinated! Was he dead now as well? Dear God, there was death every-where. Mind drifting, Matthew saw the maggots again and imagined them crawling out of Edward Landre's eye sockets, and then Puukua's. Perhaps his own.

Would Marshal Parke bother to send a constable to talk to the workers on the plantation? Would they be afraid to speak out?

He was recalled to his surroundings only when a babble of cheerful voices came muffled through the thick walls. Matthew stumbled to his feet and, dragging the chain, went to the door. It was the women prisoners who had returned, all natives, volup-tuous or even obese, filthy, skin scabrous, but something warm and joyous about them nonetheless. Prostitutes, he supposed, having heard rumors that, although jailed, they slipped out every night to ply their trade. He had even heard it was with the guards' collusion, for how could the women afford to pay their fines if they couldn't work?

To his relief they disappeared into a separate cell, as did the native men who appeared next, wet and seemingly as undis-turbed by their imprisonment as were the women. He had picked up enough Hawaiian for him to gather from snatches of conversation that they had spent the day diving in the harbor for kegs of rum, sunk when a ship's boat overturned.

Last to appear were the foreigners, mostly sailors impris-oned for desertion, drunkenness, or refusal of duty. A dirty, un-shaven, foul-mouthed bunch, they were more resentful of their confinement than were their counterparts. They had been at labor cutting grass for horses and cattle, not a welcome task to seagoing men.

As fifteen or more filed into Matthew's cell, one spotted him, leaning against the wall. "What 'ave we 'ere?" He let out a low whistle. "Lookee, boys. A gentleman."

"And in 'ere with the likes o' us," sneered another.

They crowded around Matthew like street curs circling a pampered pet, accidentally let loose. His apathy vanished in a rush of self-preservation.

"Not a gentleman," he said. "A doctor."

A flurry of obscenities expressed their general disbelief that anyone would jail a physician.

"For what?" someone at last thought to ask.

He let his answer drop like an anchor into a pool of silence. "Murder."

The silence deepened, interrupted only when a British sailor said, "Nah. Can't be. A toff like you—"

"Don't any of you keep your ears open?" asked a wizened sailor who might have been forty. "Town's been abuzz. Dead one is that Landre. Deserved it, from what I heard."

"Yes, he did," Matthew said, "but nonetheless, I didn't kill him. The sole witness to my whereabouts, however, has fled Honolulu in fear of the smallpox, and I was foolish enough to threaten Landre some time ago."

The atmosphere had changed. Men flung themselves into poses of relaxation on the dirt floor. One asked, "You practicing in here, Doc? I got this powerful itch—"

"Hell, my prick's about to fall off," another interrupted.

They competed to supply physical ailments, from the absurd to the serious. But Matthew had to shake his head. "They wouldn't let me bring my medical bag. A scalpel looks too much like a weapon, and they didn't trust me with drugs."

"First time we seen a doctor in here since I come," whined a man too young to be missing several teeth, but rot was undeniably doing its work, for one of his remaining front teeth was blackened. "Don't it figure he wouldn't be no good to us."

"I'm sorry," Matthew said uselessly.

They lost interest in him, or perhaps were kind enough to see that he wanted to be left alone, for they reverted to what he guessed was their usual conversations. The whore on Maunakea Street was compared to one with breasts the size of watermelons who was usually to be found in the lower reaches of Fort Street. There were stories of dangerous times harpooning whales and of captains so foolish they endangered their men, or so cruel they came to suffer accidents beyond the eyes of any who might bear witness.

A guard brought several calabashes full of poi, gray and soft. Matthew's stomach rolled at the thought of dipping his hands in and shoveling the slop into his mouth. The sight of the other hands, some near black with dirt, made him stay where he was.

"Hey, mate," one called. "Only way to get yours is to dig in."

"I'm not hungry," he said, and they laughed.

"You will be soon enough."

They were right about that. By morning his stomach was growling; he hadn't eaten in thirty-six hours. More poi was brought, and he made himself grab handfuls and gobble it, washing it down with water from a communal jug.

Constables wearing crowns on their sleeves and red bands on their caps appeared and roughly hustled the men out.

"We'll be cutting some coral blocks today," one said, and the prisoners groaned.

When Matthew stood, a native constable waved him off. "Not you."

In part he was relieved; his hands were soft, and he wasn't in condition for hard physical labor. Yet he thought he might go mad here by himself, staring at a plastered wall, remembering, thinking, berating himself.

His minister at home would have said that God was punishing him for having taken pleasure in smashing Edward Landre's face, and for losing his temper. The rewards for sin were harsh. But what tore at his gut was his knowledge that half his rage was directed not at Landre but at himself. Landre had stolen from William Cabe, but it was Cabe's own son who failed him in the end. Matthew had wanted to punish himself, so he punished his father's partner instead.

The acid of his guilt had eaten away his self-control, winning him this end.

"Good God, don't feel sorry for yourself!" he exclaimed aloud, letting his head fall back against the stone wall hard enough to hurt. "You wanted the bastard dead, didn't you?"

Oh, yes, his inner voice mocked, but only if it were by someone else's hand. He would never have dirtied his. Look how he quailed from the filth around him!

The day was interminable. He paced for a time, but the irons bit into his ankles and the weight made his long stride a shamble that humiliated him as much as did his confinement. He spread the mat and dozed in the heat of the afternoon. Sometimes he lay staring at the rough beams of the ceiling. Disbelief still somehow cushioned him. This must be a dream, a nightmare. If he slept again it would pass. He would wake to find himself home—no, not home in Boston, but in the narrow bed that had once belonged to the Griggses' boy who now lay in the Kawaiahao churchyard.

He returned to his musings, reconsidered his life. He had been a good physician, he thought, but close scrutiny brought no pride in his personal relationships. How many friends did he really have? Why did he hold himself apart from other men? Did he think he was better than anyone else?

And why no wife? Did he demand too much? Was he foolish to hope for a woman who not only stirred his loins but made him think? Or had he arrogantly dismissed the whole tribe, certain no woman was good enough for him?

He wondered how it would feel to have a woman anxious for him, perhaps petitioning the authorities, visiting to bring him food and clean clothes. He imagined her in front of him. She would scold him for self-pity, remind him that a mistake had been made and it would be remedied. He would be out before he knew it, his wife would tell him.

This wife had a face he knew: Anne Cartwright's. Not beautiful, but composed. The scolding voice had been hers, too. Not at all the kind of woman he would ever have considered marrying, but a comforting kind in these circumstances. He wished she were petitioning for him. Marshal Parke wouldn't be able to pat her hand and send her home; she was far too determined for that.

He did have a visitor that afternoon: the Reverend Griggs, who brought him a warm meat pie and a change of clothes.

The missionary paced the length of the cell, looking around in disgust. "This is absurd!" he declared. "The government is under so much criticism for its handling of the smallpox epidemic, it is determined not to appear incompetent at investigating the murder of one of its own members. And so they rush to throw someone—anyone!—into jail."

His interest sharpened, Matthew said, "You're implying that Dr. Judd—?"

"No, no," Griggs said hastily. "At least . . . who knows? It could be Governor Kekuanaoa, even the marshal himself, although Parke is usually trustworthy. But your arrest is obviously a relief all around. They can point to you and say, 'See? We moved quickly to unmask a vicious murderer, and though he may be a respected foreigner, he is in irons in the fort like any other criminal.' In the meantime, I doubt they look for the true culprit."

"How reassuring."

"Have they said anything to you?"

"Parke assured me he would send a constable to talk to the plantation workers. I've heard nothing more."

Griggs departed soon thereafter, stopping short of offering practical assistance but promising that Matthew would be heard in his prayers. Matthew was left wondering about the relationship between Dr. Judd and the Sandwich Islands Mission. After all, Judd had once been one of them. Despite internal dissension, did they hesitate to criticize him publicly?

Stomach satisfied, Matthew was able to resist the temptation of that evening's poi, but by morning the meat pie was no more than a memory and he perforce dipped his hands into the common pot.

This day was more interminable than the two that had preceded it. He fought his lassitude, his hopelessness, made himself exercise to maintain his strength. This was a nightmare, but it would end: his arrest was an absurdity; he hadn't killed Edward Landre, and he would be released soon. He held on to his belief, to that faith in the justice system. Innocence would be rewarded.

He had another visitor at the end of the day. When he saw Marshal Parke framed by sunlight in the open cell door, Matthew felt sick with hope and terror. Parke would throw aside the irons, offer apologies, a bath. Within minutes, Matthew would walk out of here a vindicated man.

He took a shuffling step forward. Parke stopped and looked expressionlessly at him.

"Constable Mahaulu rode over to Kaneohe Bay. I regret to say that the plantation workers deny having ever seen you."

Matthew felt himself sway. His fantasy had been so real, the shock was too great.

The marshal cleared his throat. "Mahaulu thought they were frightened, however. It may be that they'll change their story."

"And no word of Puukua?" How collected he sounded!

"None."

Knowing how he must look—unshaven, dirty, haggard—still Matthew stood with his head high until Parke was gone. Only then did a groan tear its way from his throat. He let his back slide down the rough wall, uncaring of the damage it did his shirt and welcoming the pain as it scraped his skin.

His cause was lost. He would rot in prison, or die on the gallows, and all because the bitter words had escaped so easily.

I'll see to it that you pay, even if it's with your own life!

Nine

Because Nettie begged, Anne stayed on at the Deckers', but only with the understanding that she would be free to spend her days helping nurse the smallpox victims.

By July the crisis was worsening, the efforts to vaccinate the natives a leaking cork stuck in the mouth of the bottle. Mormon elders attempted to expel smallpox with the laying on of hands and the anointing of oil. They had no more effect than the earlier day of fasting had. The credulous flocked to try any new miracle, particularly once it was discovered that the true miracle—vaccination—did not always take. Those who thought themselves protected sometimes were not. A few people had been exposed to smallpox before they were vaccinated. Or the sea voyage to the Hawaiian Islands was too long; vaccine matter was sometimes found to have lost its efficacy in the months of travel and the extremes of temperature of a trip around the Horn. Desperate orders for replacement had gone out to sources that sent more, which failed. Nor was it always immediately obvious that the vaccine didn't work; the patient sometimes developed a pustule just as he would have if the cowpox had taken, but no immunity was conferred. It was confusing and frightening even to the white population. The failures panicked the natives.

In the early weeks of July alone, Anne's experience of watching the ghastly death from smallpox was repeated ten times, a hundred times. The sight of the swollen bodies, the blinded eyes, the hideous pustules, the rasping breath became commonplace. She wasn't alone in discovering the numbing effect of seeing so much suffering: she heard the wagon drivers talking and knew that they sometimes stopped at a tavern for a drink, leaving their load of corpses outside.

Agonizing over how little she could do, she cooled brows and offered gruel and comfort to those in the pest hospital at Kakaako, just *makai* of the stone church at Kawaiahao. The place reeked of a peculiarly sickening odor, a mixture of the disease itself and death, for bodies were carried out as quickly as the ill were brought in. Twenty and thirty a day were buried at Kakaako in graves only three feet deep.

Exhausted, heartsick, she would drag herself back to the Deckers' mansion on Beretania Street, longing only for a bath and bed. Instead she must spend evenings reaching deeper inside herself for compassion, because Nettie did not quietly mourn and return to her former life. Instead she clung to her melancholy as an armor against facing the future. It was hard to know how much of her grief was for the baby and how much for herself. She was lonely, becoming aware that her husband was old enough to be her father. She hated Honolulu, with its mosquitoes and the merciless sun and the dust swirled by the trade winds. She wanted home, childhood, innocence. She could have none of them.

Anne began to believe that what frightened Nettie most was the possibility of another pregnancy. If she admitted to recovering, she would have to let her husband back into her bed.

"I know he wants me to," she confided to Anne, who would have preferred not to hear such intimate details. They awakened her sympathy, when she would rather feel impatient. —Nettie must be urged to resume her normal life, however unpleasant this one part of it was. But Nettie continued, "Charles is so kind—why, you've seen the flowers and perfume and the dresses! How could I ask for a more considerate husband? But he seems not to mourn James the way I do. He keeps"—her voice broke—"he keeps patting my hand and telling me there will be other babies. How can he ask me to go through that again?"

Anne wanted to say, *Because that is what he married you for: not just to be a beautiful hostess and grace his bed, but to give him sons and daughters to inherit his mercantile empire and carry on his name. Because that is the price you pay for the life you live: you are a woman, and you must bear children.*

But of course she swallowed what Nettie would see as cruelty—what she herself knew to be hypocrisy, considering her own refusal to marry—and murmured, "But he's right, you know; you *will* have other children, and although you won't forget your firstborn, they will console you. His death was cruel mischance. You can't let it keep you from a full life."

Nettie's face crumpled, and she whimpered, "But I'm not ready!"

Thank God, she didn't feel ready to go down each night to dine with her husband, either, for Anne, a guest in their house, would have been compelled to join them rather than taking a tray either in her room or with Nettie each evening. Charles Decker's apologies to Anne had been handsome; she even understood the emotions that had given rise to his rage. But she couldn't forget the hatred that had glittered in his eyes, or the ugly twist to his mouth, or the foul words that he'd flung at her. No matter how much courtesy he offered now, she wasn't comfortable in his presence.

As the days passed, she began to long to return to the mission enclave where she made her home when she wasn't needed elsewhere. It was not a place where she could altogether be herself—it put its own constraints on her—but it was home more than any other. At the moment, however, Napua occupied her room. And Anne must keep reminding herself that Nettie needed her.

She was called to deliver another baby on the Fourth of July. To her enormous relief, this birth was easy, over in a few hours, the newborn girl squalling as cannons boomed to celebrate the American day of independence.

Despite all else that consumed her time and thoughts, Matthew Cabe wasn't forgotten. Anne kept waiting to hear that he'd been released, that evidence had been found to clear him. But the days went by, until he'd been jailed a week, two weeks. At last she asked Dr. Judd, who regularly visited the pest hospital at Kakaako. He told her that Dr. Cabe had had a brief court date, in which Judge Lorrin Andrews, who presided in the cases of foreigners accused of a crime, decided the government had enough evidence to hold him. A trial date was set for August.

"It's a great pity, because we need him desperately. We have so few physicians, and to have one in irons, useless!"

"Haven't I heard that other prisoners have been released to drive the wagons?" Anne asked. She knew that six of the ringleaders of the rioting sailors from last fall were among those laboring among the smallpox victims. It was a measure of the government's desperation that they'd been freed for any reason, considering the actions that had put them in the fort.

The crisis had begun the previous November, 1852, when a sailor, jailed for drunkenness, was killed by a guard. In retaliation, a mob of sailors from the whaling ships burned down the police station at the waterfront. When the fire companies arrived to battle the blaze, the sailors cut their hoses. Several other buildings burned down, and one whaling ship in the harbor caught fire. The mob, increasingly drunken, then marched for the houses of Minister of Public Instruction Richard Armstrong and Dr. Judd himself, failing to find the former. The few who made it as far as Judd's house were turned away at pistol point. Anne remembered the night, lit it seemed by the fires of hell. No one had known where the rioters would turn next. Their drunken shouts had filled the town, and as they paraded down the streets carrying torches, they brought terror with them. Dreadful as the night had been, it could have been worse; if the normal northeast trade winds had been blowing, the whole fleet, packed in the harbor and loaded with whale oil, might have been set ablaze.

Now, in response to her innocently posed question, Dr. Judd agreed, "Yes, they're doing a great service, I can't deny. But a murderer—! That's quite a different matter."

"I doubt Dr. Cabe could secretly slip away from the islands, and he is not the kind of man to choose to spend his life hiding in the hills."

"No, that's true." He frowned thoughtfully. "I'll have to consult the other members of the Health Commission. We could certainly use him . . ."

She said no more, having planted the seed, she hardly knew why. No, that was a lie—she did know. He had rescued her from revilement, if not disgrace; Charles Decker's word would have carried a great deal of weight, she might have lost a portion of her clientele. And she liked Matthew Cabe! She simply couldn't conceive of him brutally bludgeoning another man to death. How must he feel, shackled in irons in a filthy cell so far from home? Had he any friends here in Honolulu to offer support?

The idea of visiting him had edged into her mind shortly after she heard he'd been arrested, but she'd dismissed it. She had to be very careful with her reputation; her livelihood depended on it. What would people think if they heard she'd visited the jail? Unless she were prepared to pull up stakes and return to the States—but she was not.

But would it really be so bad? They'd worked together, he

was a fellow New Englander, he had rescued her from Charles Decker's anger. She'd heard how abysmal were conditions in the jail; if she could go alone to a place like the pest hospital, why not to the *papu*, the fort? A good Christian could do no less, she told herself, and at last decided. She would deal with the missionary disapproval if she must, but her conscience required that she see with her own eyes that Dr. Cabe was well and not in need of anything she could provide.

It was astonishingly easy to enter Ke-Kua-Nohu, Honolulu's fort. She shouldn't have been surprised, because it was reportedly as easy to get out; prisoners were said to wander in and out at will, when guards were napping in the rude shanties erected to protect them from sun and rain. At night the prisoners went over the walls. The sentry at the inner gate seemed amused by her insistence on seeing Dr. Cabe but shrugged indolently, opened the gate, and pointed out his cell.

The jail yard was deserted, but Anne looked around nervously as she crossed it and lifted her skirts so that they wouldn't brush the dusty ground. At the heavy cell door, she hesitated and knocked timidly. Would it be locked? She had a sudden picture of him, emaciated and filthy, shackled to a stone wall. Before she could enlarge on it, the door swung open.

Matthew Cabe appeared, although for a wild instant she didn't recognize him. A reddish beard covered much of his face, his blond hair was shaggy, and he looked dirty and tired as well as irritated. "Good God, civility in this place—" His expression changed. "Anne!"

"I— Good day, Dr. Cabe." How absurdly prim she sounded!

"I must be dreaming you," he said dazedly. "You don't know how many times—"

Her heart gave a peculiar little squeeze. He had dreamed about *her?* No, it couldn't be—perhaps he meant any visitor from what must seem his former life.

"Actually, I'm here in the flesh, Dr. Cabe." She held out a hand and he took it, gripping painfully hard. "You see?"

His eyes cleared, though they remained rimmed with red. "You must think I'm mad," he said.

"No, no. Circumstances—"

He uttered a harsh laugh. "Yes. Circumstances."

She took a deep breath. "I brought you a basket of food. I thought perhaps variety would be lacking here."

He gave that laugh again, and it wrenched at her heart, which seemed to be behaving so unlike its normal, steady self.

"Variety? You could say that." His mouth twisted. "I ought to invite you in, but my present . . . home isn't fit for a lady."

"I . . . I shouldn't stay anyway. I came— I've worried about you—"

His blue eyes took in her face with unnerving intensity. "You are alone, then."

"You haven't had visitors?"

"Only the Reverend Griggs. And my attorney."

"Then you have one." What an idiotic remark!

"Yes."

The conversation seemed stillborn. She winced away from the analogy and said briskly, "Is there anything you lack? Is there anything I can do for you?"

"That's very kind of you, Mrs. Cartwright." She regretted the return to formal tones. "Do you imagine you owe me something?"

"No. Yes." She bit her lip. "Most physicians would have used the opportunity to convince Mr. Decker of the folly of choosing a midwife rather than a doctor. It would have been easy to claim that you could have saved the infant. You were good enough not to do that."

"It was the truth."

"Nonetheless, I do feel an obligation." In avoiding his gaze, her own fell upon his ankles, shackled together. Though she had known he was in irons, she was still shocked. When she swiftly looked back at his face, it was to see his jaw spasm and then a mask descend. He didn't like knowing she felt pity.

"So it's obligation that brought you here," he said expressionlessly.

Her cheeks heated. "I felt it my Christian duty."

Still those eyes devoured her face, as though he memorized it. "And I've been very rude," he said. "No, I don't believe there's anything you can do, Mrs. Cartwright, but I'm grateful for your visit. I have felt very alone."

"Then I'll come back."

"No." He shook his head. "I know what I must look like. Smell like! My company cannot be pleasant."

"I've seen worse—" she began, but he interrupted.

"My case is hopeless, unless a witness is found willing to testify to my whereabouts when Landre was murdered. There are reasons that's unlikely. I don't wish you tarred with the same brush that painted me into the guise of villain."

The words came unbidden. "I don't believe you did it."

He squeezed his eyes shut, and she saw his chest rise and fall with a long breath. His voice had become rougher when he looked at her again and said, "Thank you for that."

In one way Anne was conscious of their surroundings: the stink from the privy, the bare yard, the tops of the masts just visible over the thick wall of the fort. In another way, she felt as though they were alone, surrounded by wavery glass that shut out the world. She wanted to touch him, to lay a hand on his bristly cheek, to feel his heat for a moment, to let him know he wasn't alone. The impulse frightened her and made her take a shaky step backward.

"I— I must go, then."

A muscle twitched in his cheek. "Thank you," he repeated.

"I'm still at the Deckers'. If you do need anything—"

This time, he only nodded.

Anne realized she still held the basket and thrust it at him. "Good-bye," she said and turned away. She walked quickly, blindly, refusing to look back. She was certain she would cry the moment she was out of this place. Perhaps coming had been a dreadful mistake.

With your word as bond, we're prepared to release you." Marshal Parke moved his shoulders uncomfortably. "I can't promise you won't be brought back to the fort when the crisis has passed, should no evidence be found in the meantime to clear you. Of course, you are under no obligation to offer your services. But you are needed desperately."

Matthew tried to quell the hope rising in his chest. When he was no longer needed, he'd stand trial for murder. This was a reprieve they offered, no more. But a surprising one, given the identity of the victim and the political climate.

"The situation is so bad?"

Parke said baldly, "At the pest hospital at Kakaako, forty-two victims were buried yesterday. Thirty-nine the day before. The disease is spreading like wildfire."

"The foreign community?"

"Not more than a case or two. It's the natives who are dying, in unprecedented numbers."

Matthew grunted. His answer hadn't been in doubt. "Very well. I have never denied my services as physician to any man, for any reason. Though I fear there is little enough I can do—"

"The only hope is to vaccinate as many natives as possible, as quickly as can be. Drs. Judd and Rooke and every other physician in this town are working as many hours as is humanly possible, but their efforts are not enough. I'm told you have experience in preparing vaccine matter—"

Matthew nodded.

"Then your help will be invaluable. Let me unlock your irons."

He walked out nearly as dazed as he had been when Anne Cartwright came to see him. Though filthy, Matthew refused the offer of a lift to the Griggses'. He wanted to put one foot in front of the other without the iron biting into his ankles and the chain dragging; he wanted to smell the sea salt and the slaughter yard and the ripening bananas and breadfruit; he wanted to be jostled, to dodge horsemen, to be propositioned by prostitutes. He wanted to savor every moment as a free man.

Today was July 13. He'd been in the jail for sixteen days. His apathy had alternated with rage, which crumbled into numbness and depression and began the cycle over again. He had felt every emotion and been able to act on none of them. He might have lost track of time altogether had he not heard the Fourth of July celebrated. It had been the worst day of all. If only he had never left America!

Now his senses were heightened; he was aware of every smell and sight and sound and texture as he'd never been before.

He strode down Queen Street past merchants' homes and warehouses and thatched huts. Drays lumbered by, giving him a taste of dust, but he didn't mind even that. He expected to draw looks of distaste, but apparently his appearance was no more disreputable than that of the sailors who clogged the port, for he earned hardly a glance.

Had his possessions not been at the missionary's home, Matthew wouldn't have gone there at all. It was time to move to a hotel. A man under suspicion of murder, he was a liability as a guest. The Griggses had been more than generous already; he would accept no more from them.

He did bathe there and eat a midday meal, but despite their protests—not as vehement as they might have been—he packed his trunk and hired a wagon to carry it to the Commercial Hotel on Nuuanu. Good food and a billiards room made the hotel a center for social activity for the ruling class of foreigners in Honolulu. He'd met in passing the proprietor, Henry Macfarlane.

If Matthew's reputation preceded him, the clerk gave no sign of it. He was given a pleasant, well-furnished room with shutters that opened to let in a cooling breeze and a glimpse of the waterfront. The bed was larger and considerably more comfortable than the narrow one that had belonged to a boy now dead. Only thinking back did he realize how that bat and ball had haunted him, reminded him of all those modern medicine couldn't yet save, all those *he* had failed to save. They were ghosts, pale and insubstantial and poignant, mothers who left sobbing children behind, and sometimes the children, too, infants born blue and healthy boys suddenly stricken by terrible abdominal pain and fevers. The faces and causes of death went on and on: epidemics, tumors, accidents, simple childbirth gone wrong. Thank God, here he could sleep without seeing those faces.

Here he was free to be haunted instead by the fate awaiting him: the shackles and the thick walls and the gallows house.

Enough! Impatiently he stood and took a look at himself in the mirror. He needed a haircut, and he was paler than he'd been two weeks before, but otherwise, bathed and shaved and wearing clean clothes, he was himself. The barber could wait, but Matthew had one call to make before he presented himself to Dr. Judd.

It was late afternoon when he knocked on the front door of the Decker mansion. The lanai was shaded by twining vines and perfumed by fragrant flowers. A pretty Hawaiian maid let him in, murmuring that she would see whether the lady was there, and left him in a formal, cluttered parlor that conceded nothing to the tropical climate; velvet curtained the windows and thick, jewel-colored carpets cushioned the floors. The upholstered furniture was overstuffed and fringed, the polished mahogany side tables covered with china ornaments. He felt stifled.

At the soft fall of footsteps in the front hall, Matthew turned to face the doorway. Anne Cartwright appeared, encased in dark calico, her arms white below half sleeves. When she saw him, joy lit her eyes—he couldn't have mistaken her emotion. It elated him beyond reason. No, he had reason enough; she was the only person who believed in his innocence and would be genuinely happy to see him.

"They freed you?" Her cheeks flushed. "Ridiculous question."

"Only temporarily," he said. "Did you have a hand in it?"

"I suggested it only a few days ago. Dr. Judd acted quickly." She stepped farther into the room. "Does it offend your pride to know I'm responsible for your release?"

"Good God, no!" He frowned at the sight of her close up. "You're exhausted. What have you been doing?"

Her dress was limp, and patches of dampness spread beneath her arms. Perspiration beaded her face and neck, and her hair slipped from its pins. Her pleasure at seeing him only thinly disguised the despair that shadowed her gray eyes.

"I've spent the day at one of the hospitals where the smallpox patients are being quarantined." She shuddered. "It's a horrible place. The suffering is indescribable!"

"I've seen it," he said. "Though not in the numbers Parke tells me are dying now. But what were you doing at the hospital? Isn't the Health Commission making use of you in preparing the vaccine matter or at least giving the vaccinations?"

"I don't believe it's occurred to anyone to ask me," she said with a small helpless shrug. "I'm a woman."

"The more fool they." He was scowling at the idiocy of the medical establishment when the idea came to him. Hesitating, he examined it—would she be tainted by any association with him? But surely working together was a different matter than her visiting him in jail. Judd himself had recommended Mrs. Cartwright as an assistant.

"I've never given vaccinations," Anne was saying. "I suppose I could learn—"

He cleared his throat and she paused, her gaze inquiring.

"As you know, I've been released from the fort because my services are needed. I could use an assistant. I'd be grateful if you would consider working with me, although I will understand if you feel doing so would be too awkward, or that any relationship with me would damage your reputation." Aware of how pompous he'd sounded, Matthew quit speaking and waited.

The moment he'd mentioned the word *assistant*, Anne's eyes had opened so wide, he realized he'd startled her. He couldn't help noticing how beautiful those eyes were in her pale face. Her lashes were dark and thick, framing the clear gray with magnificent contrast. Unless it was his imagination, her face had become thinner, too, the angles of her cheekbones and the strength of her jaw more evident in the gentle curve of cheek. Her lips were parted, and he wondered if she'd enjoyed kissing her husband, or whether she had been prudish. If he bent his head now, would her lips stay parted, or would she clamp them in a thin, shocked line?

A tide of pink rose in her cheeks, and Matthew was jolted into an awareness that he was staring at her mouth. God Almighty, what was wrong with him?

"I'm sorry. I was—" What? Hungering for you? Harshly he said, "I'm afraid I was thinking about something else."

Her thick lashes fluttered and the pink crept down her throat. "Oh. For a moment I thought—" She bit her lip. "Gracious. You've . . . taken me by surprise."

"I'm sorry," he said again.

"No. Don't be." Through her obviously acute embarrassment, she met his eyes straight on. "I'd be honored to become your assistant."

Another jolt of elation shot through him. Perhaps that was why he sounded stuffier yet. "Naturally, I'll pay your normal rates."

"You needn't—"

Rather stiffly, he said, "I must insist. The government offered me a stipend. Your pay won't come out of my pocket." He lied without compunction. She had risked her reputation in coming to visit him. This, at least, was a small way he could repay her.

"I didn't meant to suggest that you're in financial straits." How like her to be blunt. "Only that I didn't expect recompense. I've volunteered my services at Kakaako. And what do I have to spend money on? My needs are simple."

"A home of your own?"

A fleeting look of sadness crossed her face. "Someday, perhaps. For now"—she had herself in hand again—"for now, my evenings are taken up by Mrs. Decker." Anne nodded toward the doorway, beyond which the stairs rose to the second story. "She is still abed."

"Abed?" he said surprised. "There was nothing wrong with her."

"Nothing but grief." She sighed. "And reluctance to begin another pregnancy."

"Ah." He'd seen it before. "Is her husband, uh, courting her?" Anne—Mrs. Cartwright—seemed unaware of any awkwardness in discussing a subject not usually mentioned in polite company.

"Yes." Her brow crinkled in a way that made him want to smooth it out with his fingertips. "But thus far his efforts are to no avail. She is genuinely frightened."

Seeing again the exhaustion that had drawn purple circles

beneath Anne Cartwright's eyes, Matthew said with a hint of impatience, "Surely this is her husband's concern."

"Yes, but he professes to want me to stay also, and she clings to me so desperately. And . . . they don't mind my working elsewhere during the day." She didn't say what he knew to be true—that she had no real home awaiting her return, anyway.

"Well, then, shall I call for you in the morning, once I know where Dr. Judd intends to send us?"

Now she seemed unable to meet his eyes. "Do you have a carriage? I do own a cart and pony, if that wouldn't be beneath your dignity."

"Dignity?" The harshness reentered his voice. "I have none left. Your cart and pony would be splendid, Mrs. Cartwright. Just as you are. I don't think I adequately thanked you—"

"Please." Her hand on his arm stopped him as surely as did her grave eyes. "No thanks. I felt . . . an affinity for you. We're both strangers here, in a way. That's all."

Had she read more of his thoughts than he'd guessed and was issuing a warning? This was hardly the time to ask whether she thought there could be more between them. He must be mad to be speculating about her as a woman, and about why she had never remarried. For god's sake, he was a man facing the gallows!

Stiffly, Matthew inclined his head, accepting that for now she wanted no suggestion of greater intimacy—and he had no right to make such a suggestion. "Very well," he agreed. "Until tomorrow."

Outside he mounted his horse, turning its head toward the waterfront, where the government building stood. He would look there first for Dr. Judd and discover what his reception would be.

They began the next morning. The days blurred that first week. If Anne had been tired before, it was nothing to the bone-deep

exhaustion that mercifully numbed her to the death that surrounded them.

She thought sometimes that the entire Hawaiian race would
be eradicated. Once she had heard an old man say, "Death by
Hawaiians takes a few at a time; death by foreigners takes many."
This time, it might take all.

They could not vaccinate the natives fast enough. The drug-
stores didn't have enough imported vaccine matter. Collecting
pus from the arms of those already vaccinated for use on others took patience and care. Dr. Judd had once said that they had
on hand in Honolulu the very best of vaccine matter taken from
babies with white skin, but in truth there were so few healthy
people *to* vaccinate, they must take risks—specifically, vaccine
matter from those less assuredly healthy.

If they vaccinated a man with the safer cowpox matter,
waited six to eight days until a pustule formed on his arm and
ripened, then removed pus to vaccinate other people, they were
taking the chance that he had in fact been infected first with
smallpox, and that they were passing on the dread disease itself
rather than the more benign cowpox that offered equal immunity. The pustules looked so similar.

And so many of the natives carried other diseases. If they
took pus from the arm of a man with scabrous skin, they might
be giving the healthy his venereal disease as well as the more
beneficial effect.

Disagreement was rampant. How long until a pustule was
ripe? How large a quantity was required to impart immunity to
the patient? Dr. Cabe insisted that only tiny amounts were
needed; others among the physicians made large wounds with
their lancets in the arms of the frightened natives and used
much greater quantities of the limited vaccine matter.

There was even an absurd argument about vaccination with
cowpox versus the ancient practice of inoculation with a mild
strain of smallpox itself. Common sense won, thank God, for

there was no mild strain in Hawaii; virtually every native who was infected died. Either the smallpox itself was particularly lethal or the Hawaiians unusually vulnerable. The latter seemed more likely—after all, hardly a white man caught the disease in this year of 1853. But the reason scarcely mattered. The result of inoculating the natives with smallpox would likely have been death, as surely as if nothing at all were done.

Anne had half expected that her role would be to hand Dr. Cabe instruments and fetch and carry. Instead he trained her as quickly as possible to collect the pus from the round, raised pustules on the arms of those previously vaccinated, store it in phials, and to do the vaccinations herself—or do them arm to arm. They worked side by side, a man and a woman, an experience that was for her without precedence. He asked for help, rather than demanding; he waited patiently for her attention when she was already engaged. And he insisted, despite her protests, on paying her what seemed an absurd amount, though she guessed that he lied about receiving a stipend from the treasury.

In addition to participating in the massive effort to vaccinate natives, Dr. Cabe took charge of a quarantine hospital at Waikiki. It was there that they saw the devastating effects of the epidemic: the rows of disfigured corpses laid out for burial, the horribly foetid smell, the patients in a state of living putrescence, faces unrecognizable beneath the clusters of perfectly round raised pustules, as though their skin bubbled in some grotesque cauldron.

Dr. Cabe insisted on cleanliness, light, and air. He had thatch removed from the sides of the structure so that a breeze could blow through. They worked frantically to cool the fevers. Yet nothing helped, for smallpox attacked the organs and throat as well as the skin. They died, the Hawaiians, in numbers that increased by the day.

The situation was so desperate, the resulting task so grisly, that notices were posted on every street corner: "Whereas much difficulty is found in procuring aid to bury the dead, the Royal Commissioners of the Public Health hereby give notice that all able-bodied men, if recovered from the Small Pox, or already completely exposed thereto, are liable to be called on to render assistance in burying the dead, without remuneration. Any person so called on, refusing to assist, shall be liable to a fine, not exceeding twenty-five dollars, or imprisonment not exceeding six months."

They had little contact with the other four or five physicians working as urgently to halt the spread of the disease. Anne didn't know and hadn't the courage to ask whether Dr. Cabe was encountering dislike or disapproval from the foreign element in Honolulu. She knew that the natives were grateful to him; more than once, women and men alike clutched his hand and said fervently, "You have the heart of a chief."

Anne thought the same. One way he showed his kindness was by insisting without fail that they stop for a stroll at midday. Mornings were spent at the hospital, afternoons in town vaccinating natives. For the two of them to maintain their own health, Dr. Cabe declared, they must find time to eat and exercise their bodies. She suspected his concern was for her rather than himself but didn't argue; the half hour each day was too precious. She was cleansed by the breeze off the brilliant blue water, soothed by the rhythm of the surf, cooled by the bars of shade cast by the grove of coconut trees. Death lost its hold on her; she could bend and sift the pale hot sand through her fingers and remember better times. She supposed they conversed, but it made no particular impression on her. What did was his undemanding presence, the vitality he unthinkingly radiated, his understanding. It was the scenes that were peculiarly Hawaiian that lingered: the sight of dolphins leaping from the glittering water, or a group of young men riding the waves on long, heavy boards, their shouts and laughter an antidote to her aching heart.

Then the cart would rattle into Honolulu, she would see the first strip of yellow calico hanging limply before a brown thatched hut, speaking of the horror within, and the stink of death would fill her nostrils again. Yet she had something to cling to: hot sand and quiet words and dolphins playing.

At night she fought to hold onto those images, rather than the ones of death, but it was hard, for Nettie's grief recalled not only the blue-tinged face of the baby who would never breathe but the horribly disfigured ones of the children she saw each day. If it was torment for her, how must it feel for Dr. Cabe, who had to be thinking about his own end, should he be convicted of Landre's murder? In her dreams, the blue face sometimes became his, the cord around the neck a rope, and she would wake shuddering.

It was during one of these waking episodes that she wondered: was anybody truly giving an honest effort to discovering who had killed Edward Landre? What if Dr. Cabe did produce a witness who placed him elsewhere at the time of the murder? Would suspicion revert to Napua?

Staring into the darkness, for the first time Anne really considered the basic question. If not Napua, and not Matthew Cabe, who *had* killed Landre? What had he—or she—gained by his death? Was the murderer somebody whom Anne knew?

Ten

I can tell you this: I'll lose my shirt if the whaling ships go elsewhere come fall. And I'd lay money on the fact that every one of you is in the same straits." The words, though muffled by the closed parlor door, were still clear to Anne, as was the murmur of agreement that followed.

Surprise penetrated her weariness. Rather than continue upstairs, she paused with her hand on the balustrade and gazed at the door. It sounded as though a dozen men or more were meeting here.

Another voice, rougher, said, "I blame King Judd for this disaster! More should have been done."

"That excuse for a government is negligent!" another speaker chimed in belligerently. "In their usual bungling way, they waited too long to act. Judd doesn't give a damn about the whaling season. Hell, he'd rather the captains stayed away, to protect the virtue of his heathens. God Almighty, the man doesn't give a damn about what's good for this town!"

In astonishment and anger, Anne removed her foot from the stair and faced the door. How dare they blame Dr. Judd for the epidemic! As though a one of them had done anything useful!

At last she recognized a voice: Charles Decker's. "My shelves are groaning with inventory. I can't hold out a year. I'm told that on Maui, effective measures have been taken. The natives have been instructed to drive canoes away and not let them land. The grass houses, garments, and personal effects of all those exposed to smallpox have been burned. Dr. Baldwin began vaccinating as soon as he was warned. As a result, their cases are in the dozens rather than the thousands. If we don't do something soon, the whaling ships will go to Lahaina instead of Honolulu this winter. I suggest we consider what measures we can take."

"Get rid of Judd and Armstrong!" With shock, Anne realized that she knew this impassioned speaker as well: George Lathrop, the physician who had diagnosed the first smallpox cases in May. He had been quarrelsome almost from the beginning, resentful perhaps because *he* hadn't been appointed to the three-member Royal Commission of Health.

Amidst the tumult of agreement, she couldn't make out everything said. Still alone in the dim hall, Anne tiptoed closer to the parlor door. She wanted to hear precisely what they did plan.

For now at least, their actions weren't to be drastic. Public meetings had been held the past two evenings, with the intention of considering what further measures might be taken to halt the epidemic. Apparently some of the men here tonight had denounced the government ministers at this evening's meeting but had been silenced.

"We'll call another meeting for tomorrow night, and this time *we* will shape the agenda!" one declared and was noisily seconded.

They would form resolutions to be forwarded to the government. "We'll set the stage," Decker said, his voice rich and self-satisfied, "for greater things. This government cannot hold out long. The king is a drunkard who would just as soon abdicate. Once we get rid of Judd, the whole flimsy structure will come tumbling down."

The notion apparently pleased his listeners, for one of them shouted, "A toast to prosperity!"

"To annexation!"

"To Judd's downfall!"

When it became apparent that they had decided all that would be decided tonight, Anne slipped away, upstairs. She would hate to be caught eavesdropping by any of the servants, even Kamiki. Who knew how loyal she would be to her employer?

Troubled, Anne lay abed that night trying to decide what she ought to do with her knowledge of what was planned. Although well aware of the cries for annexation of the Sandwich Islands to the United States, she had paid little attention to the rumblings of political discontent. Heaven knew, she shouldn't be surprised that smallpox had brought in its wake greater troubles.

Honolulu existed solely as a whaling port; the money poured into it during the early spring and fall was its prosperity. One season without ships refitting, revictualling, barrels of sperm oil unloading and reloading for transport to New England, sailors pouring their share of the catch into whores and liquor—one year, and the merchants and chandlers and shipping agents and grog shop owners would go broke. It was now July 19; if the town was not free of smallpox by the beginning of October, economic collapse might follow on the heels of the epidemic.

It did no good to blame God for the disaster, but *someone* must be held culpable. Who else but Gerrit Judd, already resented for his efforts to keep the king sober and his subjects more so than suited the foreigners who would profit on the sale of liquor?

No—she was being too charitable. The merchants meeting

tonight weren't hunting for someone to blame for their misfortune; they intended to *use* the misfortune to bring down a good man who cared more for the well-being of the natives than he did for commerce, who had fought for years to keep the Hawaiian kingdom independent.

But she'd heard nothing that hadn't been expressed, more venomously, in the *Weekly Argus*. If meetings were held, common sense could be aired as well as the opinion of the antimissionary faction. And what harm would resolutions do?

Only a few days before, on July 15, the town had been abuzz about a letter published in the *Polynesian*. Signed by "a Physician," the letter criticized government apathy and expressed much the same sentiments she was hearing now: the town would be ruined if it was not ready to receive the fall whaling fleet. Why would the government not act more efficiently? One of the men here must have written it, perhaps Dr. Lathrop.

It might even be that he was genuine in his concern, yet she had the feeling tonight's gathering portended more dangerous actions than those openly discussed. These were men who had long chafed under the authority of a government made up of natives and their missionary advisers. They saw an opportunity and were prepared to seize it.

She would wait, Anne decided, see what came of tomorrow night's meeting.

In the end, the *Polynesian* reported that out of all three meetings had come seven resolutions, forwarded to the Privy Council. Their contents were practical and innocent enough, as reported in the newspaper: the public demanded that contaminated houses be burned, vaccination improved, and that volunteer leaders be appointed to take charge of preventative measures in each district in Honolulu. But of course the July 20 meeting had gone further. A Council of Thirteen appointed itself to circulate petitions calling for the dismissal of Dr. Gerrit Judd and Richard Armstrong, Minister of Public Instruction and another of the missionaries who had resigned from the Sandwich Island Mission to gain greater influence over the natives through the government. They had been negligent, the Council of Thirteen trumpeted. The two former missionaries were also cordially hated for their moral stands, but that wasn't mentioned. Having heard what she had, Anne knew that the ringleaders were moved by revenge and bitterness: here was a chance to pay back for old grudges. Among the members of the Council of Thirteen, of course, were Dr. George Lathrop and Charles Decker.

Anne remembered what Richard Armstrong's wife had once said: "We all rejoiced to have pious, principled men come here as merchants, but, oh, their example has been infinitely worse than the infidel, because they have disgraced our cause."

Anne might still have said nothing to anybody had she not been enraged by the accusation that many vaccinations had failed because the Health Commission had allowed "amateurs" to give them. She was brooding about the critics' perfidy several days later, when she and Dr. Cabe made their usual stop along the road from Waikiki. He tied the pony to a palm tree and held up his hand to help her down from the cart.

"Which way today?" he asked.

"It doesn't matter. Whatever you choose."

He offered an arm and a sharp glance. "Something troubles you."

He directed their steps away from the ocean today. Inland was a lily pond, reflecting the sky. Beneath the coconut palms that rimmed the pond was a carpet of lush green grass, which swept toward the pale beach and ocean. Anne caught only glimpses; the surf was veiled by the ferny growth of *kiawe* trees. As they strolled on the bank of the pond, the skinny trunks of the palms around them curved drunkenly this way and that, their rich green fronds poking upward while the old dry fronds hung ready to fall. When she tilted her head back, Anne could see the ripe coconuts clustered high above. This grove belonged to the king, she knew; his ancestors had surfed off this beach.

She could feel Matthew's gaze on her face. "It's these attacks on the government," she confessed. "How dare they imply that I and others like me are to blame for failed vaccinations!"

"They don't blame *you*," Matthew said dryly. "It's merely one more dart thrown at Dr. Judd. I doubt Drs. Lathrop and New-comb believe their own propaganda, but the bulk of the population will swallow any slander, as helpless as they feel against the smallpox."

She was silent for a moment, frowning. At length, the words tumbled out. "I don't know what's come of these petitions presented to the government—"

"I believe the Privy Council has a committee deliberating on the contents."

She nodded unhappily. "You know Charles Decker has joined the Council of Thirteen. One night I overheard something—" Flustered, she stopped. "Perhaps I shouldn't speak of it to you. You can't be in sympathy with the government—"

"Because of my own troubles, you mean?" He gazed straight ahead, his voice wry. "I hold myself responsible, not Parke or the government. Good God, if I'd kept my mouth shut—!"

"The fault lies in the mouth," she murmured.

He lifted an eyebrow.

"The Hawaiians have any number of sayings concerning the importance of speaking cautiously. That's one of them. Another is: 'Life is in the mouth; death is in the mouth.' " She'd spoken without thinking and then was aghast at her lack of tact. The possibility of his own death must be constantly on his mind.

"In other words, I could harm or help myself by my choice of words."

She snatched a peek at his face. "Yes."

Matthew grunted. "The fault undeniably lies in my mouth. Not to mention my fist. I recognize my own culpability. I hope I'm not prejudiced against the government."

She nodded, still reluctant. Matthew was probably indifferent to Hawaiian politics. It was a miracle that he cared enough for the natives to work twelve-hour days, when his trial for murder had only been postponed. But to whom else could she speak? Why was it that she couldn't altogether share the convictions and sentiments of the missionary community, who ought to be her best friends? *Had* she any real friends besides Napua? Was it her fault?

Well, she needed only a sympathetic ear, and it might be that her worries would be a welcome distraction to Dr. Cabe.

"You've heard how bitterly the government is attacked for 'inefficiency.' I overheard some of what was said at a meeting at the Deckers'. The Council of Thirteen masquerades as the representatives of concerned citizens who want to carry out improvements, but in reality they hope to bring down the government. These resolutions and . . . and petitions are only the first step. Even bringing about the dismissal of Dr. Judd and Mr. Armstrong is not an end in itself; they hope the king will be weakened without their stalwart service."

"With annexation by the United States as their goal."

"Yes. Perhaps." She frowned, recognizing her own uneasiness. "I don't know. Wouldn't annexation imply statehood for Hawaii, and thus citizenship for the natives? I can't imagine Decker and his compatriots agreeing to stand on equal footing with the Hawaiians."

"He might consider equal footing better than the current status of foreigners, forced to pledge their allegiance to the king," Matthew suggested.

She made a face. "I doubt that *he* has. Except that I know he owns large parts of Honolulu, and in theory any foreigner must take the oath of allegiance to become a property owner."

"There are ways around anything." The distaste in Matthew's voice made her suspect that he was speaking of matters personal to him.

"I suppose so," she agreed. She reached out to run her fingers over the rough texture of the trunk of a palm tree. "What else could they have in mind?"

"A republic, with themselves as the government?"

Shocked, Anne stopped and swung to face him. "Are there rumors?"

"I'm presently staying at the Commercial Hotel. I've heard . . . conversations."

When he didn't go on, she demanded, "What else?"

"They imagine having things to their own liking for a few years, then selling the islands to the highest bidder, preferably the United States."

"But . . . that makes them traitors!"

"To whom? To King Kamehameha III? Not if they haven't taken the oaths. To the United States, whose interest in the Sandwich Islands appears to consist entirely of preventing them from falling into the hands of England and France?"

She resented his reasonable tone. "This council—you don't think Hawaiians have cause to be frightened by their ambitions?"

"Why should they? Talk is not necessarily followed by deeds. I of all people know that!" He offered his arm; she ignored it, and he raised his brows. His tone became patient to the point of sounding patronizing. "They have taken no action beyond those any responsible resident might consider his duty. It's true that the government—and perhaps Dr. Judd—must take some responsibility for the epidemic. They should have begun vaccinating the natives sooner, certainly in February when there was the first scare, if not long before that. It was inevitable smallpox would arrive in a port as busy as this! Yet they hid their heads in the sand, until it was too late."

Aghast, she said, "You're in sympathy with the Council of Thirteen."

Matthew Cabe's face hardened. "And why not? They're my fellow countrymen. They're right that the ministers bungled matters. As a physician, I must speak out. Nor can I respect a government anxious to accuse me unjustly of murder, merely so they can proclaim nonexistent efficiency!"

Somehow she had backed up against the tree trunk. "You said you were not prejudiced . . ."

His mouth twisted. "It would appear I lied."

She whispered, "Then . . . I was foolish to confide in you."

"No." His hand came out to grip hers. "I hope you know I would never betray any confidence of yours. And need we agree on every issue to have a discussion? I have no reason to feel sympathy or loyalty to a king I've never met; because I don't disagree with the little said or done thus far by the Council of Thirteen doesn't mean I will rise on their behalf should they foment revolt. You can trust me."

Her heart fluttered oddly and she couldn't meet his intense blue eyes. How had this conversation become one about their relationship? Why did the touch of his hand affect her so profoundly? And—trust him? He asked the impossible; she had never, could never, trust a man.

"No!" The word burst from Anne, surprising even her. She tugged at her hand.

"What?" A frown formed between his brows and he sounded startled.

"Would you release my hand?"

"Release . . . ?" He glanced down, as though confused, and promptly let her go. "I'm sorry. I didn't realize . . ."

"You were hurting me," Anne lied, flexing her fingers.

He made a sound—could it be a groan? "That's the last thing on earth I want to do," Matthew said, his voice rough.

What could he mean? She knew only that he was frightening her. How else to explain her dizziness, her disordered breathing, her urge to break into tears?

"It was nothing—" she began hastily.

"If I hurt you, it wasn't *nothing*." He spoke so tenderly, she panicked.

"We ought to go." Anne sidled away, her upper arm scraping the rough palm trunk. "We'll be late."

Still he searched her face with that peculiar intensity, penetrating her veneer of calm. "I've upset you."

"No!" She closed her eyes, drew a deep breath, moderated her voice. "No. It's . . . the situation. This is my home. I've grown to love the Hawaiian people. I can't bear to think that greed will result in these islands being stolen from their rightful owners. If I can do anything to prevent such an end, I will."

Matthew's mouth tightened, but he said, "Then go to Judd. Warn him."

"I doubt I'll tell him anything he doesn't already know."

"Probably not. He's no fool. He knows his enemies. But he may not realize their goal goes beyond annexation."

"Do you think they're serious?"

"Yes. Although how competent, I can't say. I gather this won't be the first time the government has faced a challenge."

They began to stroll again, returning to the cart. The sound of the surf intensified. To their right was the endless stretch of pale sand and the curve of blue ocean beyond. A triangle of white sail was visible on the horizon. Closer in, a double canoe skimmed the water. Glimpsed through the trees was the Roman nose of Diamond Head. All so familiar, Anne could pretend nothing out of the way had happened, that Dr. Matthew Cabe had not looked at her as though her opinion alone mattered to him.

"No, of course not." Her voice sounded only a little high,

breathless. She was grateful for the mundane topic of history. "The French and English have taken turns seizing the fort and threatening to sack the town. We've had two recent scares, the first perhaps a year and a half ago, when some California vigilantes arrived with the professed intention of 'revolutionizing the government of his Kanaka majesty.' Of course nothing came of either attempt; there weren't enough men, and we had warning. I suppose they were encouraged by the ringleaders here to believe all the white men in Honolulu would rise to support them, while in fact many support the king and are content with things the way they are. Even those who complain might be excused for not throwing in their lot with some goldfield ruffians."

"Were they arrested?"

She wrinkled her nose. "Less exciting than that. Most went home again. I believe a few were arrested for rifling the mailbags on the voyage out to destroy letters warning of their purpose. I imagine they've long since served out any jail terms."

They'd arrived at the cart, where the pony placidly chewed on long grass in the shade. Matthew helped Anne up, somewhat to her discomfiture—usually she was unconscious of such courtesies, but today the touch of his large hands was a reminder of the earlier intimacy.

As much to distract herself as him, once he'd taken up the reins and was urging the reluctant pony to amble forward, Anne continued, rather in the way of the teacher she'd once been. "A few of the current Council of Thirteen have been involved in earlier schemes to overthrow the government. Charles Decker is one who was greatly embarrassed just this spring when an anonymous letter in the *Polynesian* exposed his plans. He actively encouraged the second batch of California filibusterers. Their arrival was supposed to be a secret, but someone with inside knowledge wrote the newspaper all the details, so the government was already drilling troops yet again and the royal family knew better than to give audience to their leader, a man named

Andrew McLynn. Despite the alarm the first time around, the second attempt was actually the more frightening of the two, because it wasn't preceded by rumors. Had it not been for the letter in the *Polynesian*, the ship full of filibusterers would have come as a complete surprise. Decker vehemently denied it, but according to the letter writer, this Andrew McLynn was prepared to assassinate Prince Liholiho, whose influence is known to be all that keeps the king from stepping down, weary of his responsibility. And of course the prince prefers the English to Americans, so when *he* becomes king, annexation to the U.S. will be unlikely."

"Did anybody ever find out who wrote the letter?"

"No, and I suspect it wasn't for lack of trying. Decker in particular was furious. Loud talk about annexation is one thing; going so far as to bring in a small army from California with the intent of seizing the government is another matter altogether. The suggestion that assassination was part of the scheme was especially scandalous. His reputation as a respectable businessman was damaged; he's not received at the court, and I doubt that any Hawaiians, or the more loyal foreigners, would frequent his store. Unfortunately the whaling captains don't care. If anything, they were in sympathy. They resent the government's efforts to regulate liquor and morality. There are constant clashes."

"I heard about the sailors burning down the police station."

"Yes, that wasn't long after the first incident. On that occasion," she added, "the *Game Cock* was the ship that carried the Californians to Honolulu. Appropriate name, don't you think?"

The conversation lapsed into the commonplace thereafter, and at Dr. Ford's drugstore they found a long line of natives awaiting vaccination. Anne worried that the precaution came too late for them. Since it was at least a week, and more commonly two, after exposure before the smallpox rash appeared, many of these people were probably already infected. How could they not be, when so many had been nursing sick relatives, perhaps buried them beneath the dirt floors of their thatch huts or in the yards? Wagon drivers had reported finding corpses that to all appearances had been shallowly buried but unearthed by dogs or rooting pigs.

But the horror must end somewhere, she reminded herself, and every person who could be saved was hope for the future. Anne fastened on that belief as she used her lancet to make wounds and then carefully mixed pus with the blood before cleaning the lancet in the chlorinated lime solution and moving on to the next in line.

She and Matthew were just replacing the phials and surgical instruments in their velvet-lined cases and discussing the next day's plans when a Hawaiian policeman approached, apparently having walked over from the courthouse. Glancing at Matthew, Anne saw how his eyes narrowed and his shoulders tensed.

"Constable Mahaulu." Matthew's voice gave nothing away.

"Dr. Cabe." The constable's broad, fleshy face was equally expressionless. "I have news for you."

"Yes?" Matthew asked guardedly.

"A witness has come forward, a worker on the plantation at Kaneohe. He says he and the others were frightened to admit they talked to you. They're still frightened of this Bauer, the manager, although now they're confused, too, because they know there will be a new owner. He says if it's you, they'll all be eager to say they spoke to you."

Tightly, Matthew said, "And you, of course, interpret that to mean that they'll say anything once I'm the one paying them."

The constable inclined his head. "It is possible."

Matthew was silent for a moment. Anne saw an almost imperceptible movement as he rotated his shoulders to release tension. Then he grunted. "Their lives are wretched. If I were they, I, too, would say anything to please my employer."

Was it her imagination that Mahaulu's face softened, as though he was disarmed by Matthew's agreement?

"You see why I'm cautious," the constable said. "But this one man, he says he doesn't want to work at the plantation anymore. He says his family has claimed a *kuleana* Ewa way and they don't need what he earns, so he is free to speak the truth now."

"But you don't believe him."

A flicker showed in Mahaulu's dark eyes. His voice stayed impassive. "For now, I believe him. When I was over there asking about you, I said nothing about Puukua. But this one, he told about your guide. He says your guide talked for you, that you didn't know Hawaiian."

Anne let out a breath she hadn't realized she was holding. Did this mean suspicion had turned away from Matthew?

As expressionlessly, Matthew agreed, "That's true."

"This man. His name is Huki," Mahaulu said as though casually, but his eyes were sharp. "Do you remember him?"

Matthew met his stare. "No. Should I?"

"You will please not leave Honolulu."

"But within it, I'm a free man?" The doctor's voice was ironic.

"Yes," Mahaulu agreed, "but I will not forget you, in case I find that you made another trip over the Pali, or sent someone to offer this Huki money for his word."

"I didn't."

"The wrongdoer does not tell on himself."

"Don't you know an honest man when you see one?"

"Yes," said Mahaulu. "I think I do." Then he nodded. "Good day, Dr. Cabe. Miss."

Frowning, Anne watched him walk away. She wanted to dislike him but found she couldn't. He seemed to her an honest man himself, one genuinely trying to find a murderer.

Looking back at Matthew—when had she begun to think of

him by his Christian name?—she saw that he still stared after the native constable. She couldn't read the expression on his lean face, which unaccountably disturbed her. These past weeks, she'd begun to feel as though she knew his thoughts before he expressed them. They'd worked together as smoothly as two gears inside a watch— No! she corrected herself. More like a farmer and his mule, who were in tandem only for a few hours, not permanently, as were the gears. For in fact she knew no more about what had formed Matthew Cabe, about his secret thoughts, than he did about her life or the few dreams she allowed herself.

We're strangers, Anne thought, and snapped shut a mahogany instrument case. She found she didn't want to look at Dr. Cabe again; she was as frightened now by the distance she felt between them as she'd earlier been by the tenderness in his voice and the insistence in his hands. She remembered thinking weeks ago that he was a dangerous man. What she hadn't known was that he was dangerous to her.

However comforting the missionary embrace, Napua soon knew that she could no longer return it unreservedly, with her heart as well as her mind. More than ever she belonged nowhere, was not even sure what she was. And if she was confused, what would become of her son, for was not the child an echo of the one from whom he learned? What did she teach Kuokoa? To become like the shifting sand of Punahoa, remaking himself constantly as his mother did?

She saw him looking anxiously at her sometimes, as though he felt her worry. She always smiled and teased him from his anxiety. If he was washing, she told him he was a descendant of Lohi'au—very slow. He would giggle and splash and let her tickle him into forgetting what he had guessed of his mother's troubled thoughts.

She wore the clothes that pleased the missionaries and slept in the bed that belonged to them and ate their food and prayed in the stone church, and all the while she felt a hardness inside that made her friendly face a lie. She was made ashamed by the way she pretended, and by the weakness that kept her here, because it was easy and safe. She was sea lettuce, she told herself with contempt, swayed by the tide. First it washed her this way, then that, and each time she went with it, as though she had no strength to set her own course.

But what was her course? She tried to imagine what life she would choose if free to do so, but was left more confused than ever. Always she had wanted most the kind of love that was like a wreath that never withered through the summers and the winters. When she had slipped away to go to Edward Landre, she'd thought that that was what she would have. But she had been so terribly wrong, now she was like a fish that had once taken a hook and was afraid to take another.

A home of her own was something she wanted. At last she made that her goal. Only inside her own walls could she raise her son as she'd been raised rather than in the stricter way of the missionaries.

They hired her to teach at a school for Hawaiian and *hapa-haole* children like Kuokoa. At last, a kind of work for which she was trained! Napua thought she was a good teacher; she'd learned patience from her son, even as she'd taught it. The same way she teased him worked on the other children, and she found them eager to learn. The salary was small, but included the use of a horse. It was enough, she decided, when she and Kuokoa could also eat the banana and breadfruit that grew in the yard of the cottage. And so they moved back, though each day they rode into Honolulu double on the bony back of the sad animal that was considered good enough for an unimportant teacher.

The schoolhouse was in little better condition than the

horse. It was thatched with *pili* grass, much of which had been eaten away by the stray cattle that sometimes shook their long sharp horns at the children and frightened them. Inside were only mats, not chairs or tables, and half a dozen children had to share each slate and book. She learned quickly to make them take turns with the books, or else the same ones always claimed them and the others learned to read, if at all, upside down, peering hopefully at the pages.

The lessons were in Hawaiian, as were the books; when the missionaries first came, they'd settled on an alphabet of seventeen English letters and begun to translate the Bible and useful tracts into Hawaiian. Napua took pride in her language, and she preferred it to English. But she had come to think it was wrong that so few Hawaiians were taught to speak or read English. The missionary teachers showed maps and talked about the world beyond the dark blue ocean of Kane. Yet the books translated into Hawaiian were limited. The lack built a wall around the imagination of those who could not read another language. Also, it seemed to her that most business and government was conducted in English or French, which kept the Hawaiians at a disadvantage. Was this intentional? she wondered.

But when she tentatively suggested adding an English class, the Reverend Taft was adamant.

"It would only confuse your students, who struggle to master reading. They can learn more quickly when it is their own language they decipher."

Quietly, she said, "I learned both languages."

He smiled kindly. "Yes, but you had exceptional ability and were of the *alii*. The rulers obviously must speak English, but is it necessary for the masses?"

Once she would have agreed, either out of pride in her own superiority or meekness before his wisdom, but she'd changed. "Yes, I think it is," she said. "Foreigners take advantage of my people in business deals. You know it is true. Look how few Hawaiians are left owning land! And what of the government? It is no longer the chiefs alone who rule; now we have a legislature. I've read in the newspapers of the fights because the Hawaiian and *haole* legislators can't speak to each other. Who loses? I think it must be the Hawaiian people."

"You presume to cure such problems by teaching English to children?" He didn't ask as someone who truly wants to know, but rather as someone who is humoring a foolish one.

"Those children will grow up."

Annoyance edged his voice. "I'm sorry, my dear, but the minister of public instruction sets our curriculum. I'll mention your suggestion to him."

What could she do but shrug and teach what she was told to teach? But she thought the decision was wrong, belittling, suggesting that the Hawaiian people were children themselves, capable of taking only small steps while clinging to the hands of the missionaries. Did the Reverend Taft think that, if he let go, Hawaiians could do no more than crawl? Napua knew it was not so. She had made mistakes—who would not, in this confusing new world?—but she could walk upright and hold her head high. Many of the Hawaiians did speak English. Some of the legislators did, she knew; they refused to use a foreign language out of anger that the foreigners would not try to learn *their* language, for was not the kingdom Hawaiian?

Yet she could not harbor too much anger at the missionaries, for they did what they believed right, and they had given their lives to her people. They had showed the other foreigners that the Hawaiians could be educated and converted to Christianity. Napua had heard it said that fewer Hawaiians were illiterate than Americans. Several Hawaiian-language newspapers appeared weekly. The missionaries had taught the native people how to earn the respect of the *haole*, so that the kingdom could stay independent. And they were kind to her, out of generosity rather than duty, for they owed her nothing, and she was unimportant.

Yet still it felt to her as though they offered one hand to help the Hawaiians rise to their feet and walk, while using their other hand to push them back down so that they must crawl.

At night, and in moments when she was alone, she tried to peer through the mist to see ahead of her, but it veiled any landfall from her and kept her confused, tossing on the sea that might sweep her farther from land.

Today she refused to let herself squint into the grayness. Instead, because she had just been paid, Napua planned a stop at the market. The children were gone for the day; she had heard their laughter receding. As she straightened the books and slates and prepared to go home, she pictured the red, juicy bite of watermelon. Yes, she would buy one, if any were available. These days, so little was for sale in the native markets. Food must be rotting in the fields, with so many ill or dead. Her classes were half empty. She only hoped it was not death alone that left the mats unrolled. Surely many of the students had fled Honolulu and would return when the pestilence passed.

A throat cleared in the doorway of the classroom brought her head up in startlement. A strange man stood there. No—she recognized him. The blond doctor, who had been arrested for Edward's murder. She had known he was out of jail, but she hadn't expected to see him. What did he want with her?

She shrank back in her chair, and he said quickly, "Don't be frightened. I came— Miss, uh . . ."

"Napua," she said. "Napua Kanakanui."

"Miss Kanakanui." He stepped into the classroom, his movements cautious, as though he expected her to leap to her feet and scream. "My name is Matthew Cabe. We . . . met once."

"We were not introduced." Bitterness tinged her voice.

"No. I thought him very rude."

"He was ashamed. He wanted me, but it embarrassed him when other foreigners knew that he kept me. To him, I was sugarcane—sweet to taste, but then to be tossed aside."

He nodded, this *haole* with his golden hair and blue eyes, like sunlight and ocean. He was tall and stronger looking than most white men; she thought he would have the muscles to paddle a canoe long distances. She could see why Anne's cheeks became warm when she thought of him; he must be a man who always had women about him, like a rock clung to by barnacles.

Alarm flared in her. What if he was another Herr Bauer and thought she was a flying fish eager to leap into his hands? But when she searched his face, she saw no light in his eyes for her. No, it must be something else that brought him.

She stood. "What do you want?" Better to find out.

"I understand you have a son. Landre's."

Puzzled, she said, "That's true. He's four years old." She didn't add that he was outside playing.

Dr. Cabe didn't move. Looking as stiff and expressionless as a wooden idol, he said, "Are you aware that I was arrested for Landre's murder?"

"Yes."

"I'm officially no longer a suspect. A witness has come forward to testify that I couldn't have killed him. Landre and I were disputing ownership of a sugar plantation at Kaneohe Bay. I was there, looking the place over."

She grappled with the news. "But if you didn't—"

One of his bushy, dark gold brows rose. "That's the question, isn't it?"

Was the murder her fault after all, then? *Think about it later,* she told herself, pushing down the fear. *Not now, when those sharp eyes are watching you.* She lifted her chin. "Is that why you're here? To ask me what I know?"

"No." He reached up and tugged at his cravat, looking as though he didn't know what else to do with his hands. "I'm here because the courts have awarded me temporary control of the sugar plantation, while they decide whose it rightfully is."

"And you think I'll fight you for it."

"No," he said again, surprising her. "The plantation was originally owned half and half by my father and Landre. His half should belong now to his son."

She gaped at him. As though in a dream, she heard the *pili* grass rustle and turned her head to see Kuokoa peering through the thatching. He gave her a mischievous grin and disappeared. When she looked back at the *haole* doctor, it was to see that his gaze had followed hers.

"Your son?"

Caution made her want to lie, but she was too staggered by what he'd just said. "I . . . yes." She felt short of air. Was this a cruel trick, meant to tempt her into some mistake?

"Ah. I met him on the way in. He's to make sure my horse isn't stolen."

"He likes horses." Napua felt as though her voice were coming from someone else. It was distant, muffled. The mist swirled around her again, gray and insubstantial, but deceiving the eyes.

Sounding formal, he said, "I'd like you, as his guardian, to accept half the income from the plantation and use it on his behalf."

"You want to give me money?" Was it possible?

"Yes." His eyes were so direct, it was as though they had burned a hole through the mist, letting her glimpse clear skies. "I have no right to Landre's part. So far as I can determine, your son is his only issue."

She should snatch what he offered. But some part of her— the foolish part that had believed Edward Landre's soft words— felt she must match his generosity with honesty.

"We weren't married." Why did she still feel such shame?

"I'll wager he promised you marriage. But it makes no difference. The boy is Edward Landre's son. Morally, I cannot take what should be his."

"He . . . Edward . . . did not intend to provide for Kuokoa." Again her cheeks were suffused with shame—shame, she saw now, because she had let herself be deceived by a poisonous concoction made of *'auhuhu*, for so Edward had been. Why had she been blind to his true nature?

Dr. Cabe's blue eyes flashed. "He was a cad and a scoundrel! So long as I have the disposition of part of his estate, I'll act in the way any decent man should." He stopped, cleared his throat. "Provided you will accept."

For all Napua's pride and consciousness of her heritage, she began to weep. Silently, but tears ran down her face.

"Yes," she whispered. "Yes. I accept. Gratefully."

Eleven

Half in anger, half in amusement, Matthew tossed aside a note, written in an elaborate hand on heavy ivory paper, cordially inviting him to dine and dance the following evening at the home of a wealthy British merchant. It joined a heap of other invitations on the bureau. How extraordinary, he thought cynically, that the cream of society should suddenly have noticed his existence. He had, of course, been invisible while under suspicion of murder. Now he was not only an eligible bachelor, he was a cause célèbre—further evidence of the government's incompetence.

In the next two weeks, he had his choice of attending the Royal Hawaiian Theater, an evening musical society, an amateur theatrical production of *As You Like It*, and a shipboard ball on a visiting French man-of-war, as well as an array of dinner parties. Most were invitations he would not have received had he still been staying with the Reverend Griggs; the missionaries officially disapproved of theater and dancing. With the Griggses, Matthew had once attended an evening gathering of the ladies' sewing society, more of a social occasion than one seriously devoted to stitchery. On the stroke of nine o'clock, the sanctimonious portion of the company rose and took their departure. Even before they were out the door, the floor was being cleared for dancing. There had been many a scandalized murmur, for Dr. Judd's daughters stayed behind and were seen dancing.

Matthew would have preferred to ignore these invitations; he didn't care to dance himself and had no interest in flirting with a bevy of young ladies. He despised those who could party gaily, unconscious of the numbers of dead and dying. By nightfall he was exhausted as much by a feeling of helplessness as he was from his work among the stricken. Nor did he like the feeling that he was being used for a political end.

Yet he was becoming curious about Hawaiian politics. Anne's passionate convictions had awakened his own interest. Were the members of the Council of Thirteen solid citizens justifiably outraged at governmental abuses, or were they self-serving villains, as she believed? Where did the other American residents in Honolulu stand?

He'd seen the petitions supposedly signed by vast numbers of the king's subjects and at present being studied by the privy council. The king had surrounded himself with "pernicious councillors," these petitions declared. "Their inefficiency and misdeeds may be artfully conceal'd from your Majesty, but their selfish cupidity, political imbecility, and malfeasance in office are well known, and grievously felt by your people." The signatories called for the dismissal of Judd and Armstrong. Matthew had glanced at the petition presented for his signature and been disturbed by the numbers of native names all written in the same hand and accompanied only by a mark. How easy it would be to manufacture names—and how difficult to verify the existence of the transient natives.

But more than curiosity moved him. Constable Mahaulu had made it plain that Matthew was still potentially a suspect in Landre's murder, even if the confirmation of his alibi meant the

investigation must also look elsewhere. He would not be jailed
when the epidemic had run its course—unless the government
was so desperate to "solve" the crime that Mahaulu—or Parke—
decided the plantation worker had lied in return for a bribe. No,
Matthew didn't dare assume he was safe; so long as he was told
not to leave Honolulu, the possibility yet existed that he would
be jailed again, or held for trial.

How competent was the investigation? Mahaulu might be
effective with the natives, but he'd find doors slammed in his
face in the foreign quarters of town. Matthew wondered if even
Marshal William Parke was in a position to move in Landre's
social circles. Chances were, that's where his enemies would be
found. Until the one enemy willing to murder out of hate, or
for gain, or revenge, was ferreted out, Matthew would be
trapped here, not free to sail home to Boston. Who had better
motive for hunting down that enemy? Weary or not, he would
accept invitations.

The following evening, the American consul, Mr. Angel,
called for Matthew in his carriage. By the time the carriage disgorged them at the waterfront, the tropical sun was melting like
candle wax into the great arch of sea, spreading pools of gold
and purple and orange. Children splashed in the water beneath
the pier, their laughter drifting up. A boat waited to carry the
guests out to the French warship *La Forte*. Along with several
ladies in rustling silk and gentlemen in black tie, Matthew and
Angel stepped down into the boat, which shoved away from the
dock to cut silently through the darkening water toward the bulk
of the man-of-war.

The USS *Portsmouth* was also in port, and its boat full of officers in full dress was already boarding *La Forte*. Only the
British Navy was missing, although their country was represented by their consul General Miller and his wife. Of course,
the French consul, Monsieur Louis Emile Perrin, was greeting
guests as they came over the side, his charm in full evidence.

The quarterdeck of *La Forte* had been transformed astonishingly. Brightly colored flags of a dozen or more nations enclosed it. Covered by cushions and flags, gun slides made seats around an open dance floor. Above, a chandelier had been contrived of bayonets lashed to an iron hoop, candles fitted into the holes. Room had been left on the poop deck for the musicians. Lanterns, some already lit, hung from the rigging. A supper room had been set up in the officers' quarters, red baize spread as a carpet over the ladders and passages.

Matthew circulated, chatting easily with officers of the United States and French navies as well as Honolulu merchants and consuls from half a dozen nations. He had been there for some time when he was struck by the fact that not a single Hawaiian was among the guests. Interesting, considering that many of these men were counted among the loyalists. Of course, it was presumably the French who had issued the invitations—

The thought was cut off when he realized that also lacking were the avowed annexationists and rebels. No, the French had reason to dislike the idea of the Hawaiian Islands becoming a chunk of U.S. soil; they would hardly drink toasts with the ringleaders of the movement.

And toasts *were* drunk. Champagne was so plentiful, most men held both a bottle and a fluted glass, so that they could frequently fill one from the other and avoid dry throats. Matthew sipped gingerly from his glass; he was not a drinker, but preferred to avoid offending his hosts.

Several white men from government circles were among the guests, including the minister of foreign affairs, Robert Crichton Wyllie. A native of Scotland, he was a debonair bachelor known for charming the ladies while becoming entangled with none. Being independently wealthy put him above some of the finagling for more generous salaries or bonuses in the form of land that had tainted the reputation of others. Matthew had heard that his relationship with Judd was none too good, dating back some years to a conflict over a thousand dollars Judd considered due to him from the treasury but which Wyllie had blocked. Worse yet, Wyllie had reputedly discovered that Dr. Judd paid bribes to get information against a previous United States commissioner and open enemy of the cabinet. Judd was not a gentleman, Wyllie had announced in outrage. In retaliation Judd refused to interpret during cabinet meetings for Wyllie, who spoke no Hawaiian.

Yet they must have cooperated when it was most important, for they were the two linchpins of the kingdom, which had endured through a number of crises in the past ten years. Partly out of curiosity, Matthew took care to place himself in Wyllie's path, so that as if by accident they came face-to-face. Matthew found himself looking down at the much shorter Scotsman.

Wyllie's bearded face immediately assumed a regretful mien. In a rich Scottish burr, he declared, "You can only be Dr. Cabe. I've heard a great deal about your heroic deeds in this dreadful epidemic. And being wrongfully jailed for a crime you didn't commit! I wonder that you were generous enough to answer our call when we needed you!"

Matthew lifted a brow. "Ah, but it wasn't *you* who needed me. I consider the natives to be innocent parties."

Wyllie raised his champagne glass in a salute, his gray eyes amiable. "I gather you're joking. But my gratitude is extended sincerely."

"As were my services." Matthew smiled. "Is Dr. Judd here tonight?"

"No, no! Thank God. He's a cold water man, you know. He'd be raving about iniquity and damnation, which might spoil the bouquet of this very fine champagne. It survived the rigors of the voyage nicely, don't you think?"

"Indeed, although I'm no expert." Matthew hesitated, then chose a direct approach. "Were you well acquainted with Edward Landre?"

"He was a protégé of Judd's." The minister grimaced. "Weren't we all, once upon a time? I've never known anyone to have such a talent for incensing even those who call themselves friends."

"Landre and he had a falling-out?"

"Oh, I don't know." It seemed to Matthew that Wyllie was being deliberately vague. "They argued, but then who wouldn't when he had to rub against Judd day after day?"

"You've heard of my problems with Landre?"

"I've little influence on the courts, but if I can be of any help . . . ?" Wyllie waited courteously.

"Thank you, but I shall let my case be heard on its own merits." Next to the elegant Scotsman, Matthew felt blockish and stiff, but he was not here to curry favors. Rather, he persisted. "Do you know who might have been Landre's friends?"

Wyllie appeared amused. "Damned if I know whether he had any! For a charming fellow, he had something of a reputation for havey-cavey business deals. Very smooth; nothing that could be proved, or he'd have been shot down some dark night." Abruptly he seemed to hear himself. His mouth tightened. "Never cared for him. I questioned his honor."

"I won't argue," Matthew said softly.

Wyllie's gaze rested on Matthew's face. "No, I don't suppose you would. I meant what I said about speaking to anybody who might help your cause. You have only to send a note around."

"Thank you."

The cabinet minister drifted away, but Matthew found another man had taken his place. Balding, but with the full beard and coarse hair on his fingers that seemed to go with the loss of hair on the head, he was nattily dressed in gray with a figured peacock green waistcoat and an elaborately folded cravat.

"You ask about friends," he said. "I considered myself as much. Name's Gordon. Heywood Gordon. Landre was to marry my daughter."

Matthew raised his brows. "You were not aware that he'd already formed a . . . connection?"

Gordon curled his lip. "You mean some native woman? Don't most red-blooded men, in the absence of choicer ladies?"

"White."

"Aye." He shrugged. "Landre was frank about her. I told him so long as she was gone before the wedding, I didn't give a damn. Isabelle might've been a little more sensitive, but you know young ladies."

"You had no hesitation about entrusting your daughter to a man who'd throw another woman and his own son out on the street for no better reason than that he'd tired of them?"

He'd earned an incredulous stare. "You're suggesting he should have married his whore? Or that he should be condemned for bedding her? For God's sake, Doctor, look around you! There's probably not a man here hasn't tumbled some darkie and given her a few coins. That's all the natives want. Hell, you try to keep 'em away from the sailors to protect their morals, and what do they do? Slip away once night falls and swim right out to the ships! They like the tumbling, and they like the coins. But Landre was through with that. He was important in government and he needed a wife like my daughter. He satisfied me as to his intentions. Don't know that I like your implication that I didn't make a sound judgment."

In the interests of learning more, Matthew ignored his instinctive repugnance and choked back his usual frankness. "Forgive me," he said, inclining his head. "I didn't know Landre well. You understand that he and I were at loggerheads, which perhaps colored my impression."

Gordon shook his head. "Must have been a mistake. Damn smart businessman, Landre. His touch was golden! Every dealing I've had with him, we both made a tidy profit. Why the devil would he bother to cheat you out of a few fields of cane? Price sugar is, it's hardly worth cultivating."

Matthew's anger and disgust won. "He may have made a tidy profit recently, but his original stake came from that plantation. And I have no doubt whatsoever that he used his position in government to cut my father out. If I were your daughter, I'd be counting my blessings."

Watching Gordon stalk away, Matthew reflected that he hadn't made a friend there. Well, who the devil cared? he thought scowling. He wasn't going to learn anything useful about Landre from a man who'd viewed him as the golden goose. Heywood Gordon wasn't likely to have roasted that goose.

The musicians were playing a sprightly Spanish dance, and couples crowded the floor. The women were elegantly gowned in silk taffetas and satins flounced and edged with lace that exposed white throats, shoulders, and bosoms. Their skirts were enormous bells that swirled and swished gracefully as they twirled to the music. Pretty ringlets bobbed, and Matthew had more than a few young ladies smile shyly as they were escorted by. But his mood seemed to be perpetually dark these days, shadowed by the fort and the gallows house and the horror of mass graves. Tonight's guests seemed impervious to the devastating effect of the epidemic, except insofar as it inconvenienced them.

Matthew turned to the railing and frowned at the dark horizon. A full moon had risen, turning the surf breaking beyond the reef into filigree silver. The gaiety aboard ship must be heard all across the harbor. The other ships were hulks in the darkness, their masts and rigging like spiderwebs cast by the night, intricate black designs against a sky strewn with stars, unnaturally brilliant in this tropical sky. Night here was as magnificent as the fiery sunsets, making Matthew feel small and his problems insignificant. But death on such a large scale—surely God had noted the suffering and cared, though these good churchgoers did not.

Matthew made himself turn from the rail and sip his champagne, which tasted sour to him, although the bubbles produced a pleasant sensation. He circulated some more, ladies' skirts brushing his legs as he made his way slowly to the supper room. A lavish spread included everything from a whole pig—presumably a bow to the Hawaiian luau—to dishes of strawberries and cream, puddings and cakes, watermelon cut in glistening red balls, scones, and cheeses. The array was staggering, and greedily received.

Matthew spoke to half a dozen more men who'd known Landre well. From none did he receive a sense that they'd been intimate friends, but a surprising number had respected a man he knew as a liar and cheat. Landre had done good work for the kingdom, all agreed; despite the pull of his commercial ventures, he'd been loyal to His Majesty and "King" Judd.

"Wasn't popular among the more rabid annexationists," commented a merchant. "More than one considered him a traitor to his country."

"Nobody's yet murdered Judd or Armstrong," Matthew pointed out. "If that were the motive, surely they'd be more likely targets."

"Unless there was a special reason— But damned if I can think of one."

Matthew departed with the first boatload, feeling he'd learned all he could. In truth, he was left with a picture of Landre that didn't jibe with the man he detested. Why *had* Landre supported the *Kanaka* government? Was he capable of any kind of idealism? Or had he viewed the independence of the Hawaiian kingdom as an advantage to some of his ventures? But which ones? Those merchants with whom he'd invested seemed unlikely murderers. No, Matthew suspected the answer lay farther in the past, back before Edward Landre had developed the golden touch. Back when he'd had to cheat and steal to save himself from penury.

Or else it involved a woman scorned, one who was capable of holding her head high and lying about ancestor-ghosts and the chant of the Night Marchers. Frowning, Matthew found it sat ill with him to think of Napua Kanakanui, a beautiful, delicate woman, taking his place at the gallows. However, if she had indeed murdered her lover, Matthew wasn't so chivalrous as to take the rope around his neck in *her* place. To avoid that unpleasant possibility, it might be wise, he thought, to hear her story himself. Perhaps she would be less wary with him than she'd been with the constabulary, reveal something she hadn't meant to.

To this point, he'd attended services at the Bethel, where the Reverend Damon preached in English. On this Sunday in early August, hoping to encounter Napua, Matthew followed the ringing of the bells to Kawaiahao, the coral stone church. He joined the stream of natives in their Sunday best, taking his place in a pew near the front just as a murmur ran through the crowd.

"What is it?" Matthew asked the Hawaiian gentleman beside him, who like many others had brought a long-necked calabash with a hole in its side—a serviceable spittoon, Matthew had discovered quickly.

His smile revealed several missing teeth, the others stained yellow by tobacco. "King Kamehameha," he said, followed by more in his own language.

Matthew craned his neck. Proceeding down the aisle was a handsome, dark-skinned, mustachioed man in full dress uniform. On his arm was a somewhat corpulent but pleasant-appearing woman, presumably the queen. They smiled graciously at their subjects, passing within an arm's reach of Matthew before taking their places in a pew backed by a window draped in rich crimson and orange satin—presumably held for them. His Majesty had not recently appeared in public, Matthew had been told; an infirmity was the official excuse, but drunkenness was what was whispered behind closed doors.

Throughout his reign, King Kamehameha III alternated periods of sobriety with binges, usually brought about by difficult times and decisions he preferred not to make. Perhaps his appearance here today suggested that he had made a decision. In favor of abdicating and signing a treaty of annexation? Or was he showing himself to his subjects to remind them that the kingdom still existed, and he was at the helm?

The minister rose and implored the divine blessing in an invocation. Matthew had met him briefly; the Reverend Mr. Clark was a kindly man who had pastoral charge here. Unfortunately, his voice was not sufficient to carry with conviction throughout the huge church. Those in the galleries had to strain their ears to catch his wisdom. As he preached in Hawaiian, Matthew understood almost nothing and was able to scan the crowd in hopes of spotting Napua Kanakanui without the distraction of following a service. He looked for Anne Cartwright as well; he had not seen her at the Bethel on previous Sundays and had assumed she worshiped here. He'd never thought to ask. How odd that both women were absent. Well, perhaps they'd gone to the adobe-walled, thatch-roofed church in the north end of town, where the Reverend Mr. Smith presided.

The choir rose then to sing a hymn, king and queen with them to contribute fine singing voices. It was peculiar to listen to familiar tunes accompanied by strange, indecipherable words.

Though His Majesty was a handsome man, solid and dignified, Matthew was disappointed in the royal presence. Childishly so, he supposed ruefully. He wanted the king in his father's letters, the divine personage held in awe and fear, robed in *malo* and cape, barbaric and splendid, escorted by *kahili* bearers. In European costume, His Majesty King Kamehameha III was merely a dark-skinned, middle-aged gentleman.

At length the Reverend Clark rose again and began his discourse. It lasted nearly an hour, by Matthew's pocket watch. The benediction came as a welcome relief to him, although the natives listened attentively. The crowd rose, but nobody filed out until the king and queen had passed, smiling and nodding again. His Majesty's dark, intelligent gaze met Matthew's; the slight inclination of his head seemed intended for him. Did he know of the American doctor, suspected of murdering His Majesty's assistant minister of finance?

Matthew borrowed a horse at the livery stable and rode, as he had every Sabbath since his release from the fort, to make his rounds at the Waikiki quarantine hospital. Sunday was the one day of the week he'd insisted all along that Anne take off, for her health. The place stank of disease and death, and half a dozen sailors caught deserting ship were digging graves, but not a single new case had been brought in today. The epidemic was not done, he thought, but perhaps the impact of mass vaccinations had finally slowed its destructive swath.

Gently closing the swollen eyelids of yet another victim whose suffering had ended, Matthew railed at his own ignorance and at God for allowing it. If only they knew how smallpox originated or passed from one victim to another!

Some believed that the miasma created by rotting corpses must be responsible. Yet too often that explanation didn't suffice. Clearly the living passed this and other infectious diseases in ways not understood. Until they were, how could they be combatted? Quarantine, when successfully carried out, was the only defense, and look how difficult it was to carry out, and how dismally it often failed. Puerperal fever, which had so often proved fatal in women after childbirth, was greatly reduced when the attending physician and housekeeper maintained standards of scrupulous cleanliness. Yet cleanliness alone did not prevent the onset of killers such as smallpox and cholera.

Matthew watched two sailors carry out the dead man, then looked around. What little that could be done for the patients was being done: gruel spooned into their mouths and their fevers cooled with damp cloths. He was not urgently needed. If he came back later, he decided, he could take a few hours to call on Napua Kanakanui. It was selfish, perhaps, when death walked so much closer to the natives groaning pitifully as they awaited its touch. But selfish a physician must occasionally be, even when he was not suspected of murder! Else how could he do what he must, or live with what he saw?

He found the Reverend Smith at the missionary enclave. He didn't know whether Napua had been in church that morning.

"I don't recall seeing her," he admitted, sounding troubled. But then his face cleared. "She must have gone to Kawaiahao."

Matthew chose not to correct him.

"Ah, well, the worshippers will have long since gone home." At Matthew's request, the missionary directed him to her cottage in the Nuuanu Valley.

Matthew made the journey on horseback at a leisurely pace. The sun baked down on his head as he traversed the barren lower slopes of the hills, once forested with *ti* plants, he'd been told, but now denuded by the cattle and the need for firewood. He was thankful for the cooler air as the road rose from town. The valley was bounded on each side by ridges in which lava rocks and grass were intermingled. Eventually he topped a green hill and could look back at the Punchbowl, that peculiar volcanic remnant that dominated Honolulu and served as a battlement topped with cannons.

From here even the stone church looked tiny; the ships in the harbor were mere children's toys, far too minute to face the vastness of the Pacific. Today the curve of the horizon was indistinct, with a hazy meeting of the vault of blue sky and the ocean of blue water.

He hadn't reached as far as Judd's Sweet Home when he found a lane turning off the road at a clump of banana trees that met Smith's description. His horse snatched at a mouthful of rich, green grass and meandered in the direction he suggested.

He passed one imposing house wrapped in lanais and surrounded by cool stands of bamboo and flowering shrubs. Beyond, the lane narrowed and became insignificant, dipping beneath a shoulder of exposed, crumbling lava rock. The whisper of running water led him on until he abruptly came in sight of a small white cottage with a neat front porch. An enormous breadfruit tree towered behind its peaked roof, and a silvergreen *kukui* with round green fruits ripening enveloped one corner. Just beyond the cottage a stream briefly appeared and then vanished in a shrubby tangle. The whisper had sharpened to a murmur distinct enough to suggest a small waterfall nearby.

Anne's cart and pony stood in the shade of a tree fern, Matthew was mildly annoyed to see. He wanted her stubbornness for himself, not as an obstacle. She wouldn't like him interrogating her friend.

Still, he tied his horse beside her stocky pony and stepped up onto the porch. His knock went unanswered. Peering in the front window, he saw a room dominated by a quilting frame. The quilt in it was like none he'd ever seen, filled with sinuous shapes in red against a white background. But the chairs stood against the walls, not at all as though two women had been interrupted at their quilting or had ever intended to work. Without much hope, he knocked again. Still no one responded.

Well, perhaps they were out back. The sound of running water suggested an idyllic spot for picnicking.

Even before he rounded the *kukui* tree, Matthew heard the singing. Women's voices, high and clear, intertwined with the melody of the stream and played against it, as though it were an instrument. The words were Hawaiian, the tune simple, even monotonous, and yet stirring. Intrigued he pushed aside a branch and saw the small waterfall, splashing over a drop the height of a man into a lovely pool fringed by shimmering tree ferns and broad-leaved greenery beaded with droplets.

A boy, brown and naked but for a loincloth, sat cross-legged on the grass. He was laughing and clapping, looking at a point beyond Matthew's view.

Matthew took another step and felt as though a fist had slammed into his gut.

Anne Cartwright was hula dancing.

So was Napua, of course, but he barely saw her. He couldn't take his eyes off Anne, scarcely recognizable as the prim widow of a missionary. She'd loosed her hair, and, beneath a crown of some shiny green leaves, it tumbled over her shoulders and breasts. Thick and glossy, her tresses had the shimmer and rich grain of fine pecan wood, golden brown with fiery highlights. That glorious hair alone changed her, softened her, made her more womanly. But she hadn't stopped there.

Unless he was greatly mistaken, she wore only her shift under a skirt thick-bunched at her waist. The thin white cotton left exposed her neck and milk white shoulders, soft and rounded, and the voluptuous swell of her breasts above the embroidered neckline. And the skirt, red and voluminous, ended halfway down her calves, which were bare, as were her feet. He'd never known the mere sight of a woman's feet could be erotic. Perhaps it was the way she curled her pink toes in the grass, as though taking sensual pleasure in her childlike freedom.

Stunned, he dragged his gaze back up the length of her body. She moved with such innocent abandon, her hips swiveling in a way his body recognized, although he doubted she had any such intention. Her white arms were raised to the sky, which lifted her generous breasts and pressed them against the fine cotton. Had it not been for the flower lei she wore about her shoulders, he would have been able to see her nipples.

Anne Cartwright was a woman in her full glory, not slender and delicate, but sensuous and wanton. With jolting passion, Matthew wished she were dancing for him, that they were alone, that she would glide toward him on her bare feet, hold out her soft arms . . .

He must have moved, for her head turned just then and she saw him. In a heartbeat, the dreamy look on her face vanished, to be replaced by shock and horror.

God might just as well have struck her with a bolt of lightning. In her foolish rebellion, she had all but begged for His anger, prancing out here in this indecent costume, and on Sunday, too.

On a wave of nausea, Anne stood stock still and closed her eyes, hoping desperately that she had imagined seeing Dr. Matthew Cabe standing half-concealed by shrubbery, that when she opened her eyes he would be gone. But, no— He was there still, and seemed frozen in shock. Shock, and something more. It must be repugnance she saw in his eyes, and no wonder.

With a gasp, she snatched at her skirt, whirled, and fled for the cottage. But not even Napua's bedroom proved a refuge, for when Anne closed the door behind her and began tearing off her skirt, Matthew's voice floated through the open window.

It sounded odd. Rusty. "I've upset Mrs. Cartwright."

"*Haole* women all seem determined to hide themselves inside their clothes like crabs in the sand. Why is that?" Napua's puzzled question was as clear as his halting response.

"We believe in modesty—"

Napua made a disgusted noise in her throat. "And why is it a virtue to feel shame about your body? Did not God make man in His own form?"

"Women are made to entice men—"

"So women must suffer the torment of whalebone corsets and layers of clothing despite the heat, because men are *weak*?"

Another time, Napua's indignation would have made Anne smile. Now she was too busy tugging up her corset and pulling the strings to tighten it until it squeezed what breath she had left from her. Her heart was beating so hard, it deafened her. She missed his response, and Napua's next comment.

In despair, Anne knew she couldn't blame anyone—this had been her own idea. Oh, the price she would pay for her longing for freedom! She could never look him in the face again, never see admiration for her in his eyes. He could ruin her, although at the moment that seemed scarcely worse than knowing the full force of Matthew Cabe's revulsion.

His voice came to her again, stiff, even stuffy. "*I* do not make up society's rules! Kindly don't berate *me*, as though it were my sole aim in life to repress Mrs. Cartwright! Good God, that's the last thing I'd do!"

In the act of dropping her dress over her head, Anne frowned. What did he mean? He had used similar words before—claimed that hurting her was the last thing he wanted to do. If it was true, she thought slowly, perhaps he wouldn't tell anyone what he'd seen today. Perhaps, at least, he would give her that much.

She had to untangle the lei from her dress. The crushed petals released their fragrance, reminding her of the garland of maile leaves about her hair. When she lifted her arms to remove the wreath, her hair didn't seem to want to relinquish it; long strands clung, and in her upset she tore several from her scalp. Tears sprang to her eyes. Blinking them back, she dropped the lei and the circlet of maile onto the vivid red pool on the floor formed by the *pau* skirt. Sinking onto the edge of the bed, she let the tears fall.

Oh, how glorious she had felt when Napua helped her dress for the hula! She'd protested removing her dress and corset, letting down her hair—after all, the cottage wasn't so hidden that Herr Bauer hadn't found it, but as Napua pointed out, he hadn't come back, and no other man had come calling. Why would anyone interrupt their privacy on a Sunday afternoon?

Anne had still been arguing when her friend tugged her over in front of the mirror. Stunned, she could only stand and gaze at her reflection while Napua wrapped her with the stiff *pau* made of tapa, the beaten bark used since ancient times by Hawaiians. She seldom looked at herself in a mirror any longer than it took to be sure her hair was neat and her collar straight. Why linger, when there was no pleasure to be found in scrutinizing a round face that a kindly observer would have described as ordinary? Men—and other women—admired dainty waists and golden hair and china blue eyes, not brown hair, gray eyes, and a determinedly plump figure that not even the sturdiest corset could mold into a twenty-inch waist. She was plain, had long since resigned herself to that fact.

Until today, when she'd seen with a thrill of hope that, freed from corset and practical fabrics and a severe hairstyle that became her face not at all, she could be pretty. Or perhaps she had soaked in the Hawaiian way of viewing the world, which included admiring statuesque women. Why, *they* would think she was proportioned just as a woman ought to be. And so she'd let herself be persuaded to step outside with her feet and arms and shoulders bare, to let the air stir over her skin like the shadow of a caress, the spray from the waterfall cool her like a bath, the grass gently tickle her toes. She'd felt so different, so free. Her inhibitions had melted away and she knew no shame at all in swinging her hips and lifting her arms and chanting Pele's story as Napua taught it to her.

> From Kahiki came the woman, Pele,
> From the land of Pola-pola,
> From the red cloud of Kane,
> Cloud blazing in the heavens,
> Fiery cloud-pile in Kahiki.

She'd felt the story flow through her, take her over.

Fly little *i'-ao*, O fly
With the breeze Koolau!
Look at the rain-mist fly!
Leap with the cataract, leap!
Plunge, now here, now there!
Feet foremost, head foremost;
Leap with a glance and a glide!
Kauna opens the dance; you win.
Rise, Hiiaka, arise!

So carefree, so foolish! Now shame burned in Anne's belly and she understood for the first time how a woman could let her life be ruined for a few minutes of glory.

At last she wiped away the tears and reached for her brush. In no time she had dragged her hair back in its usual knot, almost grateful for the pain as she stabbed in the hairpins. Composed again, pale, she gazed at herself in the mirror and saw the woman she had always been and always would be: so plain, she might as well be invisible.

Something twisted in her chest, but she ignored the wrench. Drawing in a deep breath, she left the room. She must face him sooner or later. Why not sooner?

She'd known from the murmured sound of Napua's voice and the occasional gruff reply that he was still here. They were sitting on the grass beside the pool, their backs to her. Kuokoa's frolics in the water must have drowned out the sound of her approach, for she was almost upon them when Matthew suddenly turned his head and their eyes met.

Heat flooded her cheeks, but she held her head high and stopped a few feet from him. She scarcely noticed Napua's silent retreat.

Voice constricted, Anne said, "Dr. Cabe, thank you for staying. I should explain— You've been so kind—"

Suddenly he was scowling up at her, his dark gold brows

meeting. "Kind? What nonsense is this? You've been that rare blessing in a medical man's life, a useful assistant. I've taken shameless advantage of you, with no regard for your reputation or other obligations. You owe me nothing! Certainly not an explanation of what you do with your free time!"

She gaped at him. "But— Aren't you shocked?"

He rose to his feet, his gaze holding hers. "Enthralled, rather." His voice had become huskier. "You're intrigued by the Hawaiian way of life and wanted to try their dance. I've been curious myself about the hula. I thought it was beautiful."

"I . . . I'm clumsy. Napua—"

"You have a natural grace. Letting your hair down suits you."

So hot was her face now, had it been nighttime she would surely glow, like coals left uncovered! Anne said falteringly, "You do not think the hula is *depraved?* Or my conduct unseemly?"

"I cannot judge the hula from such a brief glimpse. What I saw made me want—" He stopped so abruptly, she wondered, particularly when his cheeks darkened. After a moment, he cleared his throat. "I wouldn't presume to judge your conduct."

Anne nibbled on her lower lip. "You . . . you won't tell anyone?"

His face softened. "Need you ask?"

She never cried, and now tears threatened again. She shook her head and blinked hard. "No. Thank you."

He reached out a hand and touched her cheek with his knuckles, the softest of brushes. "Anne . . ."

Her throat closed and she stumbled backward. He frowned and stepped closer again.

Panic swamped her gratitude. "Why . . . why are you pursuing me? I am no different than I was."

"But I see you differently. My eyes are unveiled."

Her spine stiffened. "You don't presume to judge my conduct, but you now see me as a loose woman? How dare you!"

His hand dropped to his side, and he glowered at her. "As a loose—? Devil take it, woman—" His throat worked, as though he were strangling on the words he wanted to say. At last he roared, "Can't a man kiss a decent woman?"

Kiss? Shocked to her core, Anne stared at him. He still thought her a decent woman, and he wanted to *kiss* her?

"I don't understand," she said stupidly.

"That is all too obvious!" Matthew snapped. He added icily, "Forgive me, madam, it was not my intention to alarm you."

"Alarm me?" Hearing herself, she almost groaned. Oh, what was wrong with her? He must think she was an imbecile!

With chilling formality, he said, "I believe it would be a relief to both of us if I were to take my leave. I only hope I haven't made it impossible for us to work together."

He was leaving. She ought to be thanking God. Instead, her mind stumbled over the very logical question of why he had come in the first place.

"But . . . did you need me? Is there an emergency? Must you perform surgery?"

A flush darkened his cheekbones again. "No. No, nothing like that. In fact—" He hesitated. "I was not here looking for you at all. Rather, I was calling on Miss Kanakanui."

Dumbfounded, she stared at him. Why in her conceit had she assumed his interest was in her? Perhaps he had brought Napua more money. Or—

The possibility that came to her was so horrifying, it opened her eyes wide and brought a gasp to her lips. Surely he didn't think he'd *bought* Napua with his money! After all, his generosity paid her rent and put food on her table. Many men would assume she owed him in return. Was Dr. Matthew Cabe no better than Edward Landre or *Herr* Bauer?

She'd often been told her face was expressive. It must be so, because Matthew said grimly, "You're determined to think the worst of me, aren't you? Was your husband such a saint, no man compares?"

"A saint?" She couldn't help but laugh, although the sound was harsh and not at all amused. "No. He was no saint. What does he have to do with anything?"

His eyes narrowed. "Perhaps nothing. Good God, Anne— Mrs. Cartwright! Do you really think so little of me you believe I'd try to kiss you even as I'm luring your friend into my grasp?"

Her face burned again. She seemed fated today to make a fool of herself in every way possible. "No," she whispered. "I'm sorry. It's only that others have tried to take Edward's place with Napua. Can you forgive me?"

He didn't answer. Instead his gaze went past her. Immediately his face set in expressionless lines.

Anne turned slowly. Napua and Constable Mahaulu came toward them across the grass. Looking anxious, Kuokoa trailed behind.

"Dr. Cabe," Mahaulu said, bending his head. "How convenient—and interesting—that you're here. I came to speak to Napua about the murder, but perhaps you, too, could give me some time."

"Certainly," Matthew said in a remote voice, and Anne knew she was forgotten.

Twelve

Brooding, Matthew had to conclude that he'd been extraordinarily clumsy, both in his courting and his investigating. He'd never flirted with Anne before, so it wasn't unreasonable for her to suspect his motives considering that he'd just come upon her half-naked, doing a heathen dance. He thought he'd succeeded in reassuring her; why the devil hadn't he left well enough alone then and chosen a later moment to hint at his romantic interest?

He ought to have left well enough alone where Landre's Hawaiian mistress was concerned, too. He'd snatched at the brief time when Anne was inside the cottage changing to question Napua about Landre's murder. He had no doubt he'd offended her as well and found out nothing.

It wouldn't surprise him if the Deckers' maid slammed the door in his face this morning on Anne Cartwright's orders. He'd escorted her home last evening on horseback, after Constable Mahaulu was done with him and Napua. Every time Matthew had tried to converse with Anne on the winding way down the Nuuanu Valley, she had managed to slow or speed her plump pony and foil him. Her "Thank you" and "Good evening" had been pleasant but distant. He had absolutely no idea whether she considered their association at an end.

It wasn't as though she couldn't assist smallpox victims in other ways. The two of them had been vaccinating fewer every day; the rest of the population had already been stricken or died—or fled Oahu altogether. He believed the epidemic must be on the wane. In another few weeks, he would have found himself back in irons in the fort if the plantation worker hadn't come forward. How could he argue if Anne decided to nurse victims in a different hospital, or to go back to her midwifery practice?

He turned his horse loose in a box stall in the Deckers' stable, just as he'd done every morning this past month, then went to the kitchen door. The maid who answered it smiled.

"Dr. Cabe. Mrs. Cartwright said to tell you she'll be right down."

Anne appeared almost immediately. She lowered her eyes as she came across the stone floor, and pink tinged her cheeks. Matthew was perturbed to see that she had donned a dark, long-sleeved, high-necked gown today despite the heat, and that her hair was scraped back so tightly it stretched her skin at her temples and must hurt abominably. Was the severity of her costume a way to scourge herself, or was she hoping that he would forget what she'd looked like with her hair tumbling around her bare white shoulders?

If it were the latter, he thought somewhat grimly, she could bury her hope; her creamy skin, magnificent hair, and lush curves would haunt his nights for the foreseeable future.

At the door, her gaze stole to his. Sounding shy, she said, "Good morning. Where do we go today?"

Relief flooded him. "Waikiki first. This afternoon we'll leave the vaccinations to others. I have several patients ill from different causes to see. If you wouldn't mind accompanying me—" He paused.

"Of course not," she said briskly. "Kalakona, good day. Make sure Mrs. Decker has a choice of fruits when you take up her tray. I worry she isn't eating enough."

Underway in her cart, Matthew inquired as to Nettie Decker's health. Personally he thought she needed a good kick in the bustle, but he sensed Anne sympathized with her. She must, or else how could she bear Nettie's self-pity despite her own exhaustion from long days caring for those who truly needed her? Which made him wonder again about Anne's history. Had she miscarried or lost a child also?

Sounding very like her usual, collected self—Matthew might have believed her genuinely composed had she not been so careful to gaze anywhere but at him—Anne said, "I believe Mr. Decker's blandishments are near to achieving the desired effect.

"She actually went down to dinner last night. Perhaps it was good for her that I wasn't there. I begin to think the time has come for my departure. When I'm available, she leans on me. However, she's quite capable of standing on her own two feet."

"Where will you go?" he asked quietly.

"Oh, the Tafts keep a room for me, when they haven't a guest. It's where Napua stayed, you know."

"Does it feel like home?"

Her lashes—long and thick, he saw now—fluttered down to conceal her expression. "Not precisely. But then, I have no responsibilities, either, which is not to be sneered at! The Tafts are remarkably understanding about my coming and going and occasional odd hours."

He sensed the loneliness behind this speech. Or perhaps he only wanted to believe it was there, that she would like a home and husband and children of her own. Matthew intended merely to nod. To his shock, he heard himself saying, "You must surely have received proposals of marriage since your husband's death. Haven't you been tempted by any?"

Her voice was icy calm. "No. I am content as a widow."

Matthew understood that he had just been warned off. What he was determined to discover was why. No woman had yet found his person offensive, and he and Anne clearly had many interests in common. Why was she so intent on discouraging him?

Given her tone, and yesterday's debacle, he reined in his impatience—or did he feel wounded pride?—and remarked in a conversational way, "It would appear that the authorities have no new suspects in Landre's death. I dislike their renewed interest in me, given my taste of jail life." They were just then passing the high wall of the fort. Were Anne looking, his glance might have given away too much. Just last night he had awakened gasping, hands tearing at his throat, feeling the rope biting through skin and flesh to crush his windpipe. Although rationally he had known he was still a suspect, emotionally he had convinced himself that he would never again see the inside of Ke-Kua-Nohu, whose crumbling walls reared over him now. But the constable's renewed questioning had shaken him. A mild way to phrase his renewed terror! He knew one thing: he'd prefer not to have that dream again.

Deliberately he looked around, anywhere but at the fort behind them. The waterfront bustled; early morning was the best time of day for a ship to enter the harbor, before the wind set in a contrary direction, so already large double canoes were towing in a whaler that appeared battle-scarred. Drays collected, and the great wooden doors on the stone storehouses had been flung open. The trade winds brought the scent of the sea, fishy but nowhere near as unpleasant as the stench of the slaughter yard.

He'd been wise to change the topic, though he had chosen an uncomfortable one for him. Anne's brow crinkled and she turned to him as naturally as though no new constraint had entered their relationship. Almost fervently, she agreed, "Yes, it frightened me, the way the constable questioned Napua. He seemed not to believe a word she said! Was he the same with you?"

"Unfortunately, yes."

"What did he ask you?"

Matthew grunted and snapped the pony's reins. "Nothing I haven't answered a dozen times before! On how many occasions Landre and I met; what we said; why I punched him; where I was and what I was doing the night he was murdered."

She looked fully at him for the first time, her beautiful eyes wide and innocently inquiring. "Why *did* you punch him? When I heard about the incident, I couldn't believe it was really you. Forgive me, but you're so . . . controlled. An act so impulsive and passionate seems unlike you."

Frowning ahead, where he caught glimpses of Diamond Head beyond the roofs and treetops, Matthew said, "I've never done anything like it in my life. I suppose I was already angry— I had just that day discovered the truth about his dealings with my father—and then he seemed to goad me. I'd almost think he *wanted* me to assault him, but why?"

"To make you look in the wrong, perhaps," she suggested. "Any judge, having heard you'd attacked Mr. Landre, would be less likely to be sympathetic to your cause."

"That may be." He was silent for a moment. Gruffly, Matthew said, "I was almost immediately ashamed of myself, but too late."

Her voice was soft and sympathetic. "You must have loved your father very much."

"Loved him?" He laughed, an ugly sound. "I came closer to hating him! As a child, I think I did hate him, when I wasn't desperately wishing for him to come home. He all but abandoned my mother and me. Oh, he sent money, but I didn't see him above half a dozen times in the first eighteen years of my life and then for no more than a week or so at each visit. I knew other boys whose fathers were whaling captains, but they at least stayed home for a few months between voyages. Mine always had his eyes trained on the sea, though he had just walked in the door." Every word leached bitterness, a child's sense of loss stored too long, like wine become acid. He was shocked to have revealed so much.

Anne laid a gentle hand on his arm. "I'm sorry."

"No need," he said brusquely. "It was long ago; I'm an adult now. I'm merely explaining my lack of filial devotion. No, I'm here in Hawaii, I suppose, out of guilt rather than love. Three years ago my father gave up whaling, left the management of the plantation to Landre, and sailed for home. He regretted his neglect of us, he said, but he came too late for my mother, who had died a few months before. I had no interest in playing the part of a grateful son whose father has been restored to him. I hurt him, I think; I know that when he got word that the plantation was lost to pay the debt, and with it his investment and any hope of income, he killed himself rather than depend on me for his support."

Anne gave a small gasp but after a moment said stoutly, "Then he gave up on you far too easily."

"Or perhaps he understood me too well." Matthew's voice grated. "I suspect I would have rejoiced in seeing his fall. Oh, I'd have given him an income, but it would have been bitter fruit, plucked from a son determined to punish his father."

Anne was silent; perhaps, he thought unhappily, he had convinced her to despise him. But no—for she did speak at last, thoughtfully.

"No wonder you hated Edward Landre. Because of him, you had no chance to forgive your father."

He turned his head to stare at her. The truth of her words sank in. Perhaps in his heart he'd always intended to forgive his father; he'd only wanted him to suffer first.

Matthew made a ragged sound. "Is it only men who blunder along in their anger with no understanding of its roots?"

Anne smiled at him, very kindly. "Men aren't taught to examine their feelings. Why, they aren't supposed to have feelings! At least, none more subtle than duty and pride."

"We're simple creatures," Matthew suggested.

Her smile became merry. "Well, so you'd like to believe!" Then her gaze fell on the hospital, just ahead, and sadness stole over her. Already a stench no wind could cleanse drifted to his nostrils, and like her he fell silent.

During their noon walk, Matthew decided to probe a little more. Mahaulu had reluctantly consented to let Anne be present when he questioned Napua, but he had firmly expelled Matthew, who was determined to know what had been said.

Anne walked beside him near the water's edge. The sun shone mercilessly, and this morning's breeze had died. Despite the ocean only steps away, the air was hot and still. Sweat dampened the dark cotton of her gown and her face was flushed from the heat. Her narrow boots persisted in sinking into the damp, hard-packed sand, and her struggles made her hotter and more disgruntled by the moment. She scowled and grimaced and let out impatient puffs of breath. Yet it was she who had insisted she wanted to stroll on the beach.

Finally, lifting her skirt and dodging a finger of incoming foam, she burst out, "Oh, I wish—!"

"That you could go barefoot?"

He could no longer tell if her cheeks were red from discomfort or embarrassment. Her attempt to sound cool and snippy came closer to wistful. "Sir, please don't remind me."

"Is it so very bad to long for things that we took for granted as children?" Matthew asked. "I confess, I wouldn't mind feeling this sand on my own toes." He bent and let the water wash over his hand. It was astonishingly warm, accustomed as he was to a cold ocean.

Behind him, Anne heaved a heartfelt sigh. "I so envy the Hawaiians! Is modesty truly such a virtue?"

"Your friend Napua asked the same the other day."

"Did she?" Anne kicked savagely at a hillock of broken shells. "Sometimes I'm tempted to dye my hair and go live in some distant village where nobody will mind if I frolic in the water or stroll about half unclothed! There. I confess it! I detest these petticoats and skirts and—" She choked off the next item on her list.

"Your corset?"

"Especially my corset," she said defiantly. "What is wrong with our bodies as God designed them? If Eve had the courage to eat the apple, surely she would have refused to wear some absurd thing that stole her breath from her!"

Matthew had a vivid recollection of Anne Cartwright dancing—of the swell of breasts and soft white flesh and bare toes. "Nothing whatsoever is wrong with women's bodies the way God designed them," he said with feeling. "As a physician, I'd like nothing better than to see every corset burned! They damage women's health and are an abomination when used to try to conceal pregnancy. And this gown—" He took Anne by the arms and turned her to face him. "Look how uncomfortable you are in this heat. Why the devil can't you wear something loose that would allow the circulation of air?"

She gazed up at him, wide eyed, no trace of the nervousness on her face that he was used to seeing when he got too close to her. Breathlessly she said, "Because nothing is worse than to be seen 'going native.' We're here to set an example, not relax our standards."

He glanced up, where a large white bird with black-edged wings and red feet passed overhead with powerful wing-beats. "However absurd those standards in a different climate?"

She wrinkled her nose in the way that so charmed him. "I sometimes wonder about our insistence on reproducing New England here. Our houses and clothes and menus are grossly unsuitable, yet we cling to them however much we suffer! The truth is, it's not in the missionary nature to be flexible."

"Convictions strong enough to bring a man or woman halfway around the world to minister to savages must be rigid indeed. Is it any wonder those beliefs must be constantly upheld?"

"Oh, yes," she said, and he heard pain and anger in her voice, "they must uphold their standards for the world. How else to conceal what goes on in private?"

"What do you mean?"

Her startled gaze flew to his. Her mouth opened—and closed. She gave her head a small shake. "I fear I'm being cynical. Don't listen to me." Already she was retreating. It seemed she'd finally noticed how close she stood to him, and that his hands still rested lightly on her upper arms, for she twisted away, forcing him to let her go.

With regret he felt the distance that had opened between them, but he was smart enough not to attempt to close it. *Not yet*, he told himself. *Wait until she's lowered her guard again.* But why did she need to be on her guard? Who had taught her it was necessary? The missionary husband who was *not* a saint?

"But I enjoy listening to you," he said quietly. Before she could take flight, he added, both to distract and because he wanted to know, "Can you tell me without betraying a confidence whether your friend Napua was able to help Constable Mahaulu? Had she remembered anything new about the murder?"

"I don't believe she's remembered anything new," Anne said, rather carefully, he thought, and with a peculiar emphasis on *remembered*.

He tried to be patient. "But she chose to tell him something new?"

"Yes. It . . . well, it may apply to the murder, or it may not. She hesitated to accuse anyone unjustly . . ."

He read between the lines and said shrewdly, "So she knew

of another enemy and told Mahaulu. Well, that might at least take some of the heat from us."

"From you," Anne said. She lifted her skirts. "Shall we start back?"

"Certainly," he agreed, "so long as you tell me what you know as we walk."

Her chin lifted, as he might have predicted it would. "And if I choose not to?"

"Why in God's name keep Landre's secrets?" he asked, puzzled.

"This one involves Napua as well. In a way. That is, she feels a responsibility—" Anne stopped struggling through the sand. "You might think this casts Napua in a bad light. But you must understand—"

His patience shattered. "How can I, if you don't tell me?"

She flinched. "Please don't shout at me."

With a jerky motion he turned away to stare ahead. A flock of small brown birds took off in unison from the beach, wheeled in the air, and settled farther away, where they went back to scuttling after the waves. "I apologize," he said stiffly.

"I just . . . don't want you to judge Napua."

"Blast it, how can I—!" He let out a long breath. "There I go again. It would seem I owe you another apology."

"No, I'm frustrating you. But not deliberately, I promise you! It's just—" Anne resumed walking again, which kept her head bent as she fought the soft stuff that wanted to swallow her narrow, high-heeled boots. She seemed not to notice the foamy tip of a wave that lapped at her soles, then hissed as it was sucked back into the ocean. Her voice was troubled. "You know that Napua lived with Edward Landre for some years, and that they had a son together."

He agreed that he did, and she told him more history: Landre had thrown Napua out with no more than a handful of change. When she sought financial support for herself and their son, Landre refused. When she persisted, he ignored her existence. At length, in desperation, Napua had resorted to blackmail, although Anne Cartwright phrased it somewhat more delicately. Apparently Landre had been careless about what he said in front of Napua; she knew a good deal of his business, and much of it was unsavory. She threatened to tell others what she knew; still he ignored her, so she'd made good on her threat by explaining to a former sugar planter named Henry Turner the cause of his otherwise inexplicable problems: Landre. Turner in a rage had presumably confronted Landre, who promptly agreed to meet Napua and had brought a bagful of coin.

"So she's afraid this Turner is the murderer," Matthew said.

"Yes, and you can see why she feels a sense of responsibility."

He grunted. "She thinks Turner followed Landre that night?"

"Or somehow found out about their meeting."

"Possible, I suppose. Turner had better have a damned good alibi."

"Yes."

Matthew was already frowning. "She explained all this to Mahaulu."

"Well . . . More or less." He understood the note of constraint in her voice.

"She didn't want to tell everything else she knew about Landre. So she lied about her motives in going to Turner. But why? Does she intend to use her knowledge to blackmail others?"

"Of course not!" Anne exclaimed indignantly. "She would never do such a thing! Edward Landre was different. He *owed* her."

"I'll concede as much."

As though he hadn't spoken, she swept on passionately, "You see, you are judging her, just as I feared! You have no idea how powerless a woman is. Napua had no place to turn and used the one weapon in her grasp. Is that so terrible?"

He'd unwittingly tapped a depth of emotion that seemed out of proportion to his mildly phrased question. Was she only defending her friend? Or had Anne, too, known how powerless a woman alone was? She'd presumably had someplace to turn; the missionary community hadn't abandoned her, though he thought it odd that she hadn't gone home once her husband died. Had they lacked the means to pay her way? Or had she no real home awaiting her there? She was as alone and dependent on herself as any woman he had ever known, but he felt more admiration than pity. Her weapon had not been blackmail, at least. She'd had marketable skills and developed them to a degree unusual in a woman.

"No," he said, meeting her eyes. "It's not so terrible. Landre deserved any weapon she could use against him that didn't kill."

"What she fears," Anne said unhappily, "is that hers did."

"Turner."

"Yes."

"We can only wait and see. Mahaulu is a capable fellow. If Turner has no alibi, he'll be in irons by nightfall." Matthew was buoyed by hope. Might the answer be so easy? Until now, he hadn't known how the weight of anxiety pressed him down. He offered his arm. "May I suggest we walk under the trees, where the going isn't so difficult?"

Her struggle was evident on her face; it ended in a rueful glance. "Until the day when I run away to that remote village and throw off the shackles of civilization, I suppose I'd better stay off the beach."

"You needn't run away to throw off the shackles, you know. Perhaps some midnight we should sneak down here and frolic in the waves." With a sweeping gesture he took in the surf and the salty air and the hot sand.

"You know perfectly well that I can't do any such thing," she reproved him, her voice prim. But he saw the longing on her face and was satisfied.

For now.

The moon was fat and full tonight. Its reflection floated in the dark pool as though the moon itself swam there. Napua sat cross-legged on the grass beneath the breadfruit tree and frowned into a night that should have soothed her.

Mahaulu hadn't wanted to believe a word she said. And why should he, she thought, when she was telling him only part of the truth? He hadn't accused her of lying, but she'd known he was thinking it.

Had he talked to Henry Turner yet? She didn't know what to hope from that meeting. Turner might lie and claim not to know her or have heard what Edward did. Or he might admit it and be able to prove he was elsewhere the night Edward died. And then what?

She should have told the constable about the other things she knew, the other harsh words she'd heard, the other secrets whispered in her hearing. Why didn't I? she wondered in puzzlement. She had no reason to protect Edward's memory; she felt contempt now, not love.

Perhaps it was the others she sought to protect, those caught in Edward's sticky webs. Why not keep their secrets? she asked herself defensively. Why be one who stirs up still waters?

"Why?" she asked aloud, her voice startling the night. "Because one might be a murderer, that's why!"

No, the truth was, shame had kept her quiet; she hadn't wanted to admit that she had intended blackmail. She'd claimed to have gone to Henry Turner out of anger at Edward, and because she thought what he'd done was wrong. But she was a fool to let shame be stronger than her fear of imprisonment. More than a fool. Did she want Kuokoa raised by the missionaries, as she had been?

"Mama?" Her son's voice came timidly from the darkness behind her. "Who are you talking to?"

"Myself. Come." She held out an arm. "Sit with me."

He crept out of the shadows and snuggled at her side.

"I thought you were asleep."

"I couldn't," he said simply.

They sat in silence for a time. His warm body comforted her, and with an effort Napua put aside her troubles. "Let's lie down and look up at the moon," she suggested. "I'll tell you a story."

Wriggling with delight, he pillowed his head on her arm when she stretched out on the grass.

Napua began, "Once there was a mother with a large family of children and a lazy husband. Weary of providing for them alone, she sought a home on the sun. But when she tried to go up to it, she became too hot. Then she tried to make a home on a star, but the others twinkled and she thought they were laughing at her troubles. At last, when the full moon rose, she changed her children into gourds and traveled up a rainbow toward the moon. Her husband saw her and snatched at her ankle, but her foot slipped off like a lizard's tail. So Lono—for that was her name—climbed to the moon and remained there. See the shadows, round like gourds?"

Napua pointed, and Kuokoa whispered, "Yes, I see them."

"There is Lono and her cluster of gourd vessels." If only she could run away from her troubles as Lono had done!

He gazed in silence for a long while. At last her son's voice came softly to her ears. "Do the children mind being gourds?"

She remembered wondering the same, picturing her body altering until it was round and smooth and hard like the gourds her mother stored food in. The idea had been upsetting.

"I don't know," she admitted. "But perhaps they aren't so different from you. After all, you were born an empty vessel, and slowly you are being filled with much that is worthwhile and some that is useless and even a little that is poisonous. One day you'll be full, and some may even slop out so that you can't recover it. In old age, cracks appear in the gourd, and more of what you know is lost, until at last in death the gourd cracks open and what you are spills out, for it no longer needs walls to hold itself together."

"And then you are a ghost."

"So our people always believed. In church they say the soul that is left goes to Heaven."

"And then the tears fall and the clouds weep," he said contentedly.

"If you were much loved."

The clouds hadn't wept when his father's body had been laid to rest in the *haole* way in the cemetery, marked by a handsome stone. That day the hot wind would have dried up any tears before they could fall. But she doubted any mourners there had cried. Certainly not the heavens.

But her son didn't ask about his father, a fact that both saddened her and made her grateful. In his heart, Kuokoa had no father, which wasn't right. The branches grow because of the trunk, and it might confuse him not to see whether he was *'ohi'a* or *kukui* or *lauhala*. What kind of leaves would he spread to catch the sun? What kind of seeds would he set? She must make sure his roots had a strong grip and teach him to bend in the wind. But unlike the *haole*, the Hawaiians believed in letting their children grow up a little wild, not cultivated too carefully. If Kuokoa was to make a tall tree that stood above the others, she must not stunt his growth for fear that he wouldn't find open sky when the time came.

"Let's go in to sleep," she said softly and discovered when his head lolled against her arm that she had only to carry him to bed.

It was hard the next day to keep her mind on her teaching.

She had the feeling one does in the stillness before a storm, when the earth holds its breath. Surely the constable would tell her what he found out from Henry Turner! It must be Mahaulu she expected to see every time she raised her head from the circle of children who listened to her read.

But the day crept on; the sun reached its height when the shadow retreats into the body and then began its descent, and still the police constable didn't come. At last Napua let the children go for the day. Laughing and calling, they scampered out. Only Kuokoa lingered, waiting for his mother.

Napua tidied up, as was her habit. Leaving Kúokoa turning the pages of a book, she went to the doorway of the thatched building and shaded her eyes against the brilliant sunlight. The school stood on a small hill, at the foot of which were rich green taro fields and, beyond, ancient fishponds. Thickets of *hau* and *kukui* and *ohe* offered shade to the children when they played at midday. Now the yard was deserted but for her horse, dozing in the shade and twitching his ears at flies.

She was starting to turn back into the schoolhouse when a flicker of movement in the *hau* caught her eye. Was one of the children hiding, perhaps reluctant to go home for some reason?

The thought had scarcely formed when she saw the spark of fire and then heard the roar of thunder. Something rustled the *pili* thatch inches from her head.

But it couldn't be lightning, the sky was clear, she thought in confusion. She struggled for understanding in the way one struggles to wade through a muddy taro patch that clutches at one's feet.

But comprehension came, or she might not have lived, for even as she saw another spit of flame she was diving for the dirt floor inside the dim interior of the schoolhouse.

Someone was shooting at her.

"Kuokoa!" she screamed. "Down! Get down!"

Thirteen

Crawling on her hands and knees, Napua reached Kuokoa, snatched him up, and scrabbled behind the table that was the room's one piece of furniture.

Now what? Would someone who'd tried to shoot her without being seen dare to walk in here to finish what he'd begun?

Did *she* dare push through the thatching and run? Or would the danger be greater in the open?

If I have any aumakua, she prayed, *please help me now.*

Kuokoa trembled in her arms. "Mama, what's wrong?"

"Hush," she whispered. "Somebody was shooting a gun."

She couldn't take her eyes off the doorway. If someone came through it—

Kuokoa, too, would die, she thought, a cold like the depths of the ocean gripping her heart. They couldn't wait.

The thatching was thin in back. She made a big enough opening to stick her head through. Silence. Nothing moved.

"You first," she whispered. "Wait for me."

He crept through and crouched against the back wall of the school. Napua had to wriggle like a fish to squeeze between the crosspieces to which the *pili* grass was tied. Once outside, she hurriedly pushed it back together to hide their escape hole.

Where to go now? Movement caught her eye, and her heart leaped sickeningly. But then a great rush of relief washed through her, for an owl, *pueo*, swooped low over the grass and settled in a clump of *kukui*. There she could just make out the owl's soft, mottled brown and white. He must be leading her; she'd heard stories of owls acting as special protectors to those in danger.

"Let's run to the *ohe*," she murmured. Still nothing but the owl moved; no sound came to her ears. Did the gunman crouch in the *hau* out front, waiting? Did he hope he'd shot her and she lay dead just inside the schoolhouse? Or had he fled?

Crouching, she and Kuokoa ran, Napua shielding her son with her body. The softly rustling leaves of the bamboo seemed to speak of their arrival, and she wanted to beg them for silence. But when she peered out, still no one had rounded the building.

"Now to that clump of *kukui*," she told Kuokoa. He nodded and they ran again. Just as they arrived, the owl rose in a hushed beat of wings and left them.

"Thank you," she whispered.

From here Napua could see their horse's tail, swishing back and forth, oh so normal, as though she'd dreamed these last frightening minutes. But the *hau* where the gunman had hidden was on the other side of the school building.

The minutes crept by. The sun sank toward the sea. She didn't know whether to be afraid of the approaching darkness or grateful for its shelter. They couldn't stay here forever. If only someone would come.

A brief rain swept in from the uplands, the gentle kind that would set the *lehua* to swaying but only dampened Napua's hair.

"Mama, I'm hungry," Kuokoa whimpered.

"You've been a brave boy," she said. "Soon I'll go see if the man is gone."

If only the horse weren't tied, he might have wandered their way! But she'd been afraid he would stray too far, and so each morning Kuokoa staked him out and each noon moved him.

"Mama, someone is coming!"

With a quick gesture, she silenced him and listened. A horse's hooves clopped somewhere in the distance. Was the gunman leaving? But no, it seemed to her the sound approached rather than receded. The lane ended at the schoolhouse; who would come at this time of day?

She prayed wordlessly, whether to her own gods or to Jehovah she couldn't have said. The horseman must be right in front of the school now, perhaps dismounting.

Not Anne. Please don't let it be Anne. Napua didn't know why the man had shot at her, but mightn't he shoot Anne, too? He must be crazy; what other explanation could there be?

And then a man appeared around the school, silhouetted dark against the fiery sky. Napua pressed a hand over Kuokoa's mouth and held her breath.

"Napua! Are you here?" he called, and her breath whooshed out in a sob. It was the constable, that Mahaulu. She had never thought she would be so glad to see him.

"Yes!" She rose to her feet and pushed out of the *kukui*, which whipped at her as though resentful of the use she had put it to. "We're here!"

He strode toward them. "Is something wrong?"

"Did you see anyone?" she cried even before she reached him. "Did you meet anyone on the lane?"

"Nobody. Why?"

"Somebody tried to shoot me," she said baldly.

He listened in silence as she told her story. He walked over to the clump of *hau*, then came back without comment and fingered the wood door frame, scarred by the second bullet.

"It's getting too dark to find the bullets," he said. "I'll come back in the morning." He laid a hand on Kuokoa's shoulder. "Did you hear the shots?"

Napua stiffened as she realized that Mahaulu was expressing doubt about her tale, but she let Kuokoa answer.

Shyly he said, "I heard thunder, but the sky is clear."

The constable grunted. Brows heavy and drawn together, he looked at her. "Do you know who it was?"

"How would I?"

"We sometimes know our enemies."

"I have no enemies!" she cried.

He grunted again. "But the gallbladder has burst; the yellow color is spreading."

It was true; someone must have harbored hate that had now burst out, but why for her?

"It must have to do with Edward's death," she said, as much to herself as to him. "Perhaps the murderer is afraid I saw him."

"Perhaps. But why wait so long?" the constable asked, logically enough. "Why not kill you before you had a chance to tell someone everything you saw?"

The answer came to her: *because the murderer is not afraid of what I saw, but what I know.*

But again, why wait so long?

"I saw nobody," she said.

"The one who shot at you, he is ruthless, with the hands of a gale. You'd be foolish to paddle your canoe into the gale."

She looked back at him expressionlessly. "I am not foolish."

"Good." He nodded toward her horse. "I'll escort you home."

Part of her wanted to tell him she didn't need him; the other part, the sensible part, was grateful for his company. "Thank you," she said. "Kuokoa, will you get our horse?"

Her son gladly ran to fetch the placid animal. As soon as he was out of earshot, Napua asked, "Did you find that *haole* Henry Turner?"

"Yes." She could no longer make out his thoughts on his face, but Mahaulu sounded disgusted. "Even in the morning, he was drenched by the water from the rain clouds. It was hard to talk to him."

She nodded. "When I saw him, he was drinking, too. He didn't seem to care if he lived or died."

Mahaulu shrugged. "He cared enough to tell me where he was that night. Others confirmed his story. He didn't kill Edward Landre."

Hope rose in her chest like a bubble to the surface of the water. "You're sure?"

"I'm sure. You thought he'd done it?"

"I was afraid—" She broke off. "I shouldn't have told him what Edward did. I knew he'd be angry. Then when I saw Edward, dead—"

"Why did you wait to tell me about Turner?"

"I was ashamed," she said simply. "Once my anger died, only ashes were left."

"So it usually is."

On a spurt of resentment, she wondered if he was always so emotionless, so stone-hearted. Had he never felt fury great enough to cause him to say what he shouldn't, or to strike out?

He boosted her onto the horse, and her son behind her, then mounted his own. They spoke little on the ride. Napua let Mahaulu search her house before he left. She didn't like knowing that he was in her bedroom, seeing the heaps of clothes in rich fabrics that Edward had given her. Mahaulu wouldn't know that she never wore them.

He left, saying only, "Lock the doors and latch the windows. You must be careful now. If he knows where you teach, he knows where you live."

She hadn't yet thought so far; the cottage had felt like her sanctuary. But the constable was right. Here, she was afraid. Kuokoa wanted to swim, but she wouldn't let him. It was hot in the house with the windows closed. She tensed at every sound and sat beside his bed after he was asleep. She must find somewhere else to live, Napua decided. In the morning they would leave by a different route than they'd ever taken before, and not come back until it was safe.

Awakened at dawn, Kuokoa followed her instructions without argument. They packed their most important possessions into two baskets, then slipped out the back door. Napua lifted the boy onto their horse, then took the reins and led the animal up a narrow trail from the pool. The way was difficult; branches whipped at her face and snagged her skirts. By the time the Nuuanu Pali road came in sight, she was scratched and tired.

Now they had to wait until someone came along so they wouldn't be alone on the road. Standing well back, out of sight, Napua let a lone horseman pass. A large group would be best.

The sun rose and flies buzzed annoyingly around her face. They, like mosquitoes, rats, and fleas, had arrived on ships with the *haole*. The mosquitoes had come not so long ago, in 1827, it was said, when sailors from a whaling ship dumped barrels of stagnant water into a stream. Trying to imagine Oahu without flies and mosquitoes, Napua wondered if the *haole* had other evils to loose on the islands. Was smallpox the last?

A cloud of dust rolled down the road toward Napua and Kuokoa's hiding place. From it came the lowing of cattle and the shouts of herders. Napua waited until they had passed, perhaps twenty cows, several calves, and two native men on foot. Then she used a lava outcropping to mount with Kuokoa in front of her and guided the horse out behind the herd.

"Hide your face in my gown," Napua told her son. She could only half-close her eyes and endure as the dust enveloped them in a gritty red shroud. For her purposes, it was perfect; if

the gunman hid along the road waiting for them, he'd be unlikely to see them until they'd passed. Besides, it was her hope
that he wouldn't shoot when there were witnesses.

The herdsmen tried twice to let her pass, crowding the cattle to one side of the road, but Napua hung back and waved
them on. Their shrugs indicated they thought she was crazy, but
finally they ignored her.

She didn't turn off until Beretania Street, well into town. The
cattle must be destined for the waterfront, either the slaughterhouse or to be loaded into pens onboard a ship. This part of
Honolulu was mostly residential, and the streets were deserted
so early in the morning. Napua kicked the horse into a trot,
clinging to its mane with one hand, her other encircling Kuokoa.

In the stable-yard behind the Decker mansion, she shook off
as much dust as she could manage, then knocked on the kitchen
door.

"I've come to see Mrs. Cartwright," Napua told the servant
who answered the door.

The Chinese houseboy looked her up and down and said,
"Wait there. I'll find out if she can see you."

"My name is—" But the door slammed shut, cutting off her
words.

The wait seemed very long. Long enough for her to wonder where she could go if Anne couldn't help. The Tafts had disapproved of Napua's returning alone with her young son to the
cottage. She hated to admit they'd been right and she wrong.
She supposed they would take her in again, and kindly, but then
what? How long would she have to stay?

She had no family, of course, but there were Hawaiians in
high places, classmates of hers from the Royal School, who
would surely extend their hospitality if she asked for it. What
Hawaiian wouldn't? Napua had never asked, because she felt as
if she had shamed her station by living with a *haole* instead of
using her education and position for the benefit of her people.

The door opened suddenly and Anne appeared. Her expression of inquiry changed in a heartbeat. "Napua! Is something wrong?"

Napua hated to be so near tears. "Yes. Someone tried to kill me yesterday."

"Kill you?" Anne repeated in alarm. "How— No, don't tell me yet. Come in."

"Kuokoa is here," Napua said, waving to where he sat docilely on the dusty horse.

Both women turned their head at the sound of hoofbeats rounding the house.

"And here comes Matthew." Anne corrected herself quickly. "Dr. Cabe." Her voice held an odd note, as though she were both glad and sorry about his arrival.

"Have you time?" Napua asked. "I could come back, or—"

Anne gave her a reproving look. "Don't be absurd."

Dr. Cabe dismounted and stopped briefly to speak to Kuokoa; then he led his horse to the steps. His sharp blue eyes saw beyond Napua's dust to her distress. "What is it?" he asked.

"She hasn't told me yet," Anne said. "Why don't you all come in—" She frowned. "No, that's probably not a good idea. What about the stable?"

The American doctor led both horses. Inside the shadowy, cool structure, a dapple gray with a pretty head poked a nose over the half door of a stall and whickered softly. Matthew patted his muzzle and turned his own mount loose in a box stall. He lifted Kuokoa down and wrapped the reins of Napua's homely animal around a sturdy post.

The women seated themselves on bags of grain. Kuokoa sat at Napua's feet. The doctor propped one shoulder against the rough boards of a stall. The two *haole* gazed expectantly at Napua.

She glanced around, feeling safe in the dim confines of the barn. Daylight slanted, golden and dusty, through cracks in the walls and the open double doorway. It was warm and still in here but for the quiet sounds of horses moving in their stalls. Even the sweet smells of hay and grain and manure were reassuring.

She told Anne and Dr. Cabe about the gunman outside the schoolhouse, and about how she and her son had hidden until Mahaulu came. "He says if the man can find me there, he can find where I live," she concluded. "I think I must hide for a while."

"Of course you must!" Anne agreed. "But where?"

"She can't hide forever," Dr. Cabe said. "Napua, could this assault be unrelated to Landre's death?"

She spread her hands. "I can't think of any reason someone would want me dead. Perhaps it was a crazy man."

Nobody commented. They didn't have to. She knew how unlikely it was that she would be chosen by chance so soon after Edward's murder.

The doctor didn't look away from her face. His skepticism showed in his penetrating gaze. "You didn't see anything?"

"No!" Napua jumped to her feet, sending her son tumbling onto the hard-packed earth floor. Her hands curled into fists, and she glared at him. "Why doesn't anybody believe me?"

Anne reached up and took her hand. "It isn't that he doesn't believe you—"

He interrupted, voice pitiless. "If somebody is trying to kill you, there's a reason. And I think you know what it is."

She held her head high and glared at him, *alii* contemptuous of a commoner, but he only waited, those strange blue eyes stripping her of pretense. For he was right, just as Mahaulu had been. She did know—or guessed.

Her pride seeped out, like water from a container not worthy enough. She sagged back onto the feed bag and held out a hand for Kuokoa, who scooted back against her leg.

"I'm sorry." Napua bit her lip and picked bits of straw off

her son's shirt. "Truly, I saw nothing. If the murderer thought I had, surely he would have killed me then. Why wait?"

"What about Henry Turner?" Anne asked.

"Constable Mahaulu says Turner couldn't have murdered Edward. And I know nothing bad about him. The shame was on Edward's part, not his."

The doctor didn't say anything, only watched her. A horse's hoof clunked against the board wall behind Napua's back. She took a deep breath and blurted, "When I lived with Edward, I heard things meant to be secrets. Perhaps someone guesses that."

Slowly the *haole* doctor straightened. "But *how* would they guess? Were you caught with your ear pressed to the door, or loitering in the hall? And devil take it, you departed Landre's house weeks ago. Why is somebody afraid of you now?"

It was Anne who said unexpectedly, "The *how* must have to do with Henry Turner. Until you told Constable Mahaulu what you knew about Edward's dealings with him, nobody had any reason to suspect you had any intimate acquaintance with his business. But the fact that you knew so much about how he had cheated Turner might have led someone to wonder what else you had overheard, or Edward had told you."

"What would be interesting," Dr. Cabe remarked, "is to find out who Mahaulu told about your story. And who *they* told."

"Yes," Anne agreed, "and I don't see why we can't ask him."

"Napua?" Dr. Cabe looked at her.

She frowned. "Mahaulu thinks I killed Edward."

The *haole*'s mouth twisted. "When he isn't thinking I'm the murderer."

"Well, let's ask him anyway," Anne said. "But I suggest that we quit assuming he'll solve the crime. If he's too busy concentrating on you two, he won't look elsewhere."

Dryly, Dr. Cabe said, "Do you intend to correct his assumptions?

Her eyes flashed. "No. I suggest we find the murderer ourselves."

Napua turned her head to stare at her friend, who sat with her back as straight as a cliff, her hands folded on her lap and her face stubborn.

"Are you mad? Napua's already a target!" Dr. Cabe snapped. He was glowering at Anne. "Do you propose to make yourself one as well?"

Anne's chin lifted just a little higher. "Do *you* want to hang for a crime you didn't commit? I won't let Napua be arrested or murdered because I was afraid to help her. And you must concede I'm in a position to talk to people neither of you can. I speak Hawaiian; I'm received everywhere; I have friends even at court." She glanced at Napua. "You remember when I nursed Makalika?" Napua nodded, and Anne continued. "Because of Edward, you would be looked upon with suspicion by the chiefs who think Hawaiians should rule Hawaii. They wouldn't talk to Dr. Cabe at all."

The doctor frowned. "Why would Napua not be welcomed? One of Landre's few virtues was his loyalty to the kingdom. I'm told that even Prince Liholiho concedes that Hawaiians need foreign advisers until they are themselves educated and well traveled enough to deal on equal footing with other nations. Wouldn't those foreigners who have taken the oath of allegiance and served the government well be respected by all the chiefs?"

Napua's voice shook. "But he was not loyal. I heard him once. He was scheming with the annexationists to overthrow the king."

She felt as though she'd lanced a boil; this secret, of all, had most festered under her skin. Knowing his treachery and not speaking of it had been like a poison made of 'auhuhu that had eaten at her innards until she wondered that her heart still beat and her stomach still digested food. She should have left him then and gone to one of the chiefs. Perhaps Kaipoleimanu, who was a distant cousin of her mother's. But taking such a step would have meant admitting how foolish she'd been, how blind. She had told herself they wouldn't succeed, that others would discover their plans as well. After all, no matter how much one covers a steaming *imu*, the smoke will rise. But that was an excuse, and she knew it and despised herself.

They were staring at her with shock. "Annexationists?" Anne echoed. "But . . . why?"

"I heard him say that it was money. If Hawaii became part of the United States, his investments would prosper. Those were his words."

"So he was spying on the government?"

"Yes," she said stolidly. "He told them what happened at cabinet meetings. At least, he did once. He was careful; I think, if they failed, he didn't want anyone to know he had helped them. I only overheard two conversations. The second one was angry; I thought he might have been discovered, because he was shouting that he hadn't done something. Written a letter, I think. I don't know. But then nothing happened, so either they believed him or the argument was about something else."

"When was this argument?" Dr. Cabe asked, seeming to forget he didn't think they should look for the murderer themselves.

"Not so long ago. This spring, I think."

"Before I came?"

She cast her mind back. "Yes. Not long before."

Anne leaned forward. "So he was murdered only a few weeks later . . ."

Napua saw the fierceness of the frown the doctor leveled at Anne. "It's true that you're in a position to investigate people I can't. People Mahaulu can't, for that matter. But I won't have you put in danger."

"No one will suspect me."

"When you ask questions, you'll be careful to make them sound innocent."

"Of course," she agreed tranquilly.

"Very well." He still didn't look happy, but he must have seen that her determination would crumble no more quickly than did the Pali. "Napua," he said, "we'd better get you tucked away somewhere safe. The *Polynesian* lists houses for rent. I'll rent a small one, and you and your son will stay out of sight there."

"But I must go to work," she protested. "The children will come for lessons."

"I'll take your place today," Anne suggested. "Dr. Cabe, can you make do without me?"

"I'll manage," he agreed. "Napua, you stay here while I find a house. After I've taken you there, I'll let Mahaulu know where you are. I think you'd better tell him what you've told us."

Reluctantly she nodded.

"And I'll leave it to you to find out who he told about Turner."

Again she nodded.

"But before we part, tell us everything you know, Napua."

She glanced down at her son's bent head. Anne's gaze followed hers.

Anne rose to her feet. "Kuokoa, would you like to see some kittens that were born only a week ago? If you're gentle, I don't think the mother would mind if you touch them."

He looked up hopefully. "Mama?"

"What a good idea," she said smiling.

The kittens were in the last stall. Anne left him settled happily there. When she returned, Napua cast her mind back. She told them everything she remembered: every snippet of conversation, every shouted threat, every drunken confession. Her shame increased as she talked. Truly she had been swirled about by the eddying waters, made dizzy until she no longer knew right and wrong. Else why had she stayed with Edward?

When she was done, the doctor said, "I believe I'll cultivate the annexationists. It shouldn't be hard; they've made overtures to me already."

Anne nodded. "And I'll concentrate on the chiefs. If they found out what he was up to, they would have felt betrayed."

Napua said unwillingly, "Kaipoleimanu disliked Edward. What happened was a long time ago, but if Kaipoleimanu found out Edward was using his office to steal Hawaii's independence, he would have been angry."

"You're saying he's capable of murder?"

"He is a proud man," Napua admitted. "His temper rises easily."

"Worth checking out, then," the doctor said. "Except for the fact that I can't think of any good reason he'd have to try to kill you."

"It's occurred to me," Anne said, "that the two assaults might *be* separate. Herr Bauer is just the kind of man who'd want revenge for being bested."

The two women looked at each other, Napua in consternation. She hadn't thought of the ghostlike *haole*. "But then," she pointed out, "it would be *you* he'd be after."

"Anne?" Dr. Cabe growled. "Bested? What the devil are you talking about?"

Anne wrenched her gaze away from Napua's. "Do you know Bauer, Landre's plantation manager? Oh, I suppose you do. Well, he tried to rape Napua, and I hit him over the head with a tree branch." She gave a sniff of satisfaction. "I would have sworn he was too humiliated to come back."

"He had a native woman living with him at Kaneohe," the doctor said frowning. "She had bruises on her face. He obviously doesn't like being thwarted."

Napua didn't know the word *thwarted*, but she understood the concept. Even among the Hawaiians there were brutish men like that, who took pleasure in beating a woman.

Anne said strongly, "Why don't you set Mahaulu on Bauer?"

"The fine for what he did is only fifty dollars. He could pay that easily," Napua said.

"He should be tossed in the fort for six months!" Anne seemed to savor the thought. She let out a huff of breath. "But Mahaulu could at least find out where Bauer was yesterday."

"I'll ask him," Napua agreed.

"Well, then." Anne stood. "Shall we get started?"

"I know I'm going to be sorry," Dr. Cabe muttered. He gave Anne a peculiarly piercing look. "Anne . . . Be careful."

Her smile was soft and bashful. "You, too. Find a safe place for Napua."

He gave a brusque nod. "Where's the school? I'll come out there before the children go home at the end of the day."

"I'll tell you how to find it," Napua said.

His scowl didn't lessen, but he nodded. "Then let's get on with it."

If only she could call on the Griggses without awkwardness! But of course that was now impossible. Anne frowned over the problem as she opened her basket and laid out the bits and pieces of her noontime meal. The children shrieked outside, running off their pent-up energy from a morning of docility.

Of course, the seeds of her suspicion had been planted by the same scene that alienated her from Reverend Griggs.

She hadn't liked to mention that suspicion, even to Napua. She'd tried to dismiss the memories of half-understood moments that had crept into her night thoughts, the wondering that refused to leave her alone.

Soon after she began seriously considering who might have

hated Edward Landre enough to kill him, she'd thought of the Reverend Ambrose Griggs. Napua, with her pleasing appearance, quick intelligence, and regal manner, had been his protégé, his pride, evidence that his work was not in vain.

The missionaries all despaired when they lost a prized student who rejected their teachings, but Anne remembered again his reaction when they discovered that Napua had gone to Landre. Even then it had seemed out of proportion and uncharacteristic.

But she had always assumed that if Napua repented she would be welcomed back, both in the church and in the home of the Griggses. They had truly loved her, Anne had believed. Until she brought Napua there that day, and Reverend Griggs turned her away with such bitter triumph, as though he had longed for a time when he could strike a lethal blow at her.

Did a loving father let a wound inflicted by his daughter suppurate until anguish became enmity and spilled out to spread its bitterness? Such malice more often grew from soured love between man and woman, in Anne's experience. She had reason to hate both her father and her husband, but if she could choose between the two, she would rather see John Cartwright burn in hell. Her feelings for her father were too complex: understanding vied with bitter resentment. She knew the disappointments that made him what he was. He had been harsh, merciless; but mixed with her memories of being whipped or belittled were others when he was kinder, or at least didn't strike her either with hand or vicious tongue when she expected it. So children must always remember their parents, she suspected, and parents their children, even in households where love was not acknowledged: good with the bad, tenderness with the barbarous. Families were a stew that had been slow-cooking for so long, the tastes blended together until one couldn't be separated from another.

With men and women who met and loved as adults, a feeling of betrayal wasn't leavened by a lifetime that created understanding if not sympathy. The tastes were sharp and distinct: passion, anger, possessiveness, duty, and hatred. One supplanted the other, with no sauce of memories to sweeten the bitterness.

It was not that Anne thought Napua and the Reverend Griggs had ever had a liaison. She couldn't imagine that Napua had thought of the missionary as anything but mentor and father figure. Or that he had consciously thought of her as anything but daughter and pupil.

But he had been a very *fond* father, almost indecently eager with the hugs and gentle kisses considered suitable. It was the way he'd touched Napua that Anne found herself remembering: how often he had smoothed her hair, caressed her cheek, felt it necessary to guide her through a crowd. When Anne recalled those days, the Reverend Griggs always seemed to have his hands on Napua.

And he'd been curiously possessive as well. He took the credit for Napua's achievements and the duty of chiding her for her failures. She seldom spent time with the other young Hawaiians of her class; her free days belonged to the Griggses. She lived as though she were a *haole* daughter of the missionaries, not a young chiefess being trained in godly ways.

The question was, had the Reverend Griggs hated the man who casually seduced Napua enough to kill him? Might he have been goaded into such drastic action by the news that Landre had abandoned Napua? And, finally, had turning Napua away not been enough to assuage his own bitterness at being rejected by her? Was killing the only way to quiet the torment of a love that the missionary, a married man, stern in his morality, could never accept?

Or, Anne reflected ruefully, was she imagining emotions never felt? And how could she find out the truth?

Fourteen

Anne packed away the remnants of her noon meal—little enough, for she seemed able to eat no matter how troubled she was. Not even a brutal wedding night had spoiled her appetite; then she had eaten for comfort. Her mind worked better when she was eating, and why not eat? She'd been plump from girlhood, never sought after by the boys. Even then she had been torn between natural longings and the revulsion inspired by what she had guessed of her parents' marriage. She'd heard her father's grunts, his voice raised in anger, the nightly creak of the bed and her mother's muffled sobs afterward. But she'd convinced herself that not all men were like her father. John Cartwright seemed kindly, scholarly rather than physical. How she had let appearances deceive her! Her own marriage had ripped the veil from the remaining mysteries between man and woman. She only wished they had stayed veiled forever.

The thought led to another as the children filed into the schoolhouse, giggling and whispering. The truth of the Reverend Griggs's feelings for Napua could stay veiled, so long as Anne could discover his whereabouts on the night Edward Landre was murdered—and yesterday, when someone had tried to kill Napua. Perhaps Anne wouldn't have to talk to him at all. Who knew better his habits, and any break with them, than his wife?

She kept quiet about her intentions when Matthew arrived at the schoolhouse and escorted her to the Smiths', where she was promised for dinner. He told her that he'd found a cozy house on King Street where he thought Napua would be safe.

"We were careful going there. I can't believe we were followed. She did speak to Mahaulu, by the way; unfortunately he told any number of people about Henry Turner, which leaves us without any obvious leads to pursue. I fear that he thinks the scene was a ruse to deflect his suspicion of her."

Anne adroitly avoided answering his queries about her own plans; she had a suspicion he wouldn't let her make a move alone if he had advance notice of her intentions. Satisfied by her assurance that she would spend the night with the Smiths, he left her at the neat frame house behind the walls of the mission station.

Always the wallflower in large gatherings, Anne didn't normally look forward to the monthly Sewing Society meeting, which was to be that evening, but now she seized on it eagerly. The professed purpose of the group was to aid the sick and destitute stranded on these shores, but in fact the society was more of an excuse for a social gathering than one with serious goals.

Generally by nine o'clock the carpets were rolled up and a volunteer found to play the pianoforte so that the company could dance. Before that happened, the missionary portion of the company took their leave. Anne, of course, had never publicly danced nor ever told anyone that she wished she could. Sometimes couples were already twirling around the floor before she and the missionary wives and daughters were out the front door. Some of her glances back had been wistful; dancing must surely be the one time any woman would wish to be in a man's arms.

She had vague memories of herself as a child dancing with her mother, twirling, dipping, laughing. Her mother would hum tunes that sounded nothing like the Sabbath hymns. They were gay and sprightly, compelling her feet to move, as a fresh spring morning made even the cart horse prance. Then one day her father had discovered them. Her mother had gone quietly when he took her arm and hauled her into the bedroom. When she came out, her face was white, her eyes downcast, her movements slow and painful. They had never danced again.

Such memories came more and more often these days. New emotions must be recalling old ones, confusion and hurt and the rare moments of joy. Why did her bad memories seem so much sharper than the good ones? Anne wondered, troubled. She saw with great clarity the expression her mother had worn in the presence of her husband; but her mother's laughing face would not come clear in her mind. Anne could just hear the fading laughter, as one caught a faint scent and then lost it.

"Mrs. Cartwright, how do you do?"

Anne wrenched herself from her abstraction to greet her hostess. She chided herself to quit brooding. She had a new life here, in the Hawaiian Islands. Her escape was a miracle. She should rejoice in it rather than dwell on the past she'd turned her back on.

Unfortunately on these occasions the conversation was usually as dull as the dancing was lively, in Anne's estimation. Tonight was much as always, she saw, looking around; perhaps forty guests, nearly half men, gathered at the home of a British merchant whose wife was particularly fond of dancing. The ladies were presently piecing bed quilts, which would be sold to raise money for the Seamen's Home Society. Anne was relieved to spot Mrs. Griggs, but not the reverend; although she wouldn't avoid him or back down when they met, she thought she might learn more from Lydia Griggs without her husband's disapproving eye on them.

Better yet, beside her was an empty chair. Anne hurried across the room, bypassing clusters of guests, and set down her sewing basket on a small table beside the wing chair.

"Good evening, Lydia."

Lydia looked up from her stitching and her eyes widened. She summoned a smile that appeared forced. "Anne. I've been hoping to speak to you. That day when you came by, I know Mr. Griggs sounded harsh. Please try to understand."

"There's no need—" Anne tried to say, but Lydia swept on.

"He says I forgive too easily, that people must suffer the consequences of their choices. I . . . I believe he was affected by Napua's plea, as I was"—her voice trembled—"but he is stronger minded than I am. He . . . he doesn't hold your softheartedness against you, you know."

"How kind of him," Anne said ironically. Scarcely seeing the pieces, she laid out a quilt block on her lap. She was piercing a Bear's Paw quilt in tan and red. "The Reverend Taft said he would speak to him."

"He did, and I'm afraid relations between them are strained. They already disagreed on several points at the general meeting." She sighed. "Reverend Taft is willing to baptize anyone. He hasn't yet learned to be critical of the natives' sincerity. In the first rush of enthusiasm, they all think they're ready, but of course they backslide, just as children do." She carefully snipped a thread. "You may recall his argument with my husband, which became somewhat heated. Perhaps someone else would have been a better choice to speak to my husband."

"*I* had no choice in the matter, nor was it my idea!" Anne said, refusing to feel guilty because she might have caused distress to a man who could not find forgiveness in his heart. "The Reverend Taft felt the reminder was timely."

Anne threaded her needle; a sidelong glance took in Lydia Griggs's flushed cheeks and unusually large stitches, hurriedly taken. Yet Anne refused to apologize when the fault was not hers. The two women sewed in silence for several minutes. Around them others chattered; the gossip and laughter blurred into meaningless sound to Anne.

Lydia suddenly let the fabric drop into her lap. Her eyes, beseeching, met Anne's. "I didn't agree with him," she whispered.

Anne reached out and took her hand. "I know," she said, squeezing. "I saw how glad you were to see her, and how distressed you were by your husband's decision. You must abide by it; I understand."

"Is she . . . well? Safe?"

"Yes." Anne smiled gently. "You needn't worry. I believe you'd like her very much, now that she's a woman rather than a girl. Her son is a joy to her, and with good reason."

Lydia momentarily closed her eyes; she pressed trembling lips together. "Thank you," she said shakily.

"I've done nothing—"

"But forgive me." Shame was mixed with the sadness on Lydia Griggs's face.

"If anyone needs it—"

"He's a good man." She spoke urgently. "You must believe that! I think . . . I think Napua hurt his pride unbearably. And who among us has no weakness?"

Images paraded before Anne's inner eye: herself committing gluttony, dancing the hula (and on Sunday!), envying women like Nettie, who sometimes seemed to her to have everything.

"Not I," she admitted.

"Then you'll forgive him as well?"

The trap was of her own design. "Has he asked for my forgiveness?"

"No, but I know he wants it."

Lydia seemed serenely certain that her husband had suffered

the same heartache she had. What would she think if she knew Anne suspected him of murder?

Well, the sooner Anne could dismiss her suspicion, the sooner she could cleanse her conscience.

"Perhaps," she suggested gently, "forgiveness should come from Napua. Do you think he'll change his mind?"

Lydia laid down her sewing again. "I don't know." Her face contorted, but she breathed deeply and held back the tears. "He takes pride in arriving at firm decisions and upholding them. I think he regrets this one. But admitting a fault is not easy for him."

"No." The conversation made Anne grateful, not for the first time, that death had released her from bondage to John Cartwright. For she would have become like Lydia Griggs, a woman who must always accept her husband's judgments, however idiotic or inhumane, who must go where he went, bow her head before his anger and be grateful for his kindness or mercy. Anne might be lonely sometimes, but at least she existed in her own right; she had a will and a conscience and freedom of choice. She'd be mad to exchange all that for the comfort of belonging to a man, for the chance to have children.

Her fingers had stayed busy as they spoke. Now she let a few minutes lapse before she commented, "I'm so glad a witness has come forward to clear Dr. Cabe of suspicion in Mr. Landre's murder. How much simpler if he'd been with you that evening! Did you expect him?"

"We weren't certain," Lydia said. She laid down two pieces, red and white, and picked up two more. "Mr. Griggs was out, but I prepared dinner enough to feed Dr. Cabe if he returned. He was bound to be hungry after his long ride."

How to ask where Reverend Griggs had been without sounding intolerably nosy? Anne affected surprise. "Your husband wasn't searching for him, was he?"

Lydia glanced up, eyes wide. "Heavens, no! He'd let us know

he might be delayed. No, no, Mr. Griggs was at a meeting. I believe it had to do with plans for the Fourth of July celebration."

"I see," Anne said noncommittally. Fortunately, Lydia didn't ask what she saw. Anne knotted her thread and cut it, meanwhile wracking her brain for a way of asking about the Reverend Griggs's whereabouts yesterday afternoon. "The sunset was particularly lovely yesterday," she ventured.

"Was it?"

"Didn't you see it?"

Lydia gave her an odd look. "Our house faces *mauka*."

"Oh. So it does." Anne's smile was weak. "So you were home."

"Well, of course I was. Where should I have been?"

"Nowhere. Cooking, of course." Hastily she added, "I've been staying at the Charles Decker home, you know. They have a French chef. I begin to long for cooking such as yours."

"Why, thank you."

"I hope your husband appreciates your meals." She sounded like an idiot!

Lydia's brow crinkled. "Well, I hope—" She stopped and fixed a doubting look on Anne. "Are you trying to say something?"

"I . . ." Anne took a deep breath. "Yes. Was Reverend Griggs home yesterday afternoon and early evening? I . . . I thought I saw him, and the knowledge has been disturbing me ever since. I've been telling myself I was mistaken."

Lydia's back stiffened and her sewing fell to her lap again. "Whatever can you mean?"

"Oh, it's no doubt absurd. If he was home . . ."

She saw immediately by Lydia's expression that he hadn't been. "Can you tell me where he was?"

"The epidemic—" Lydia swallowed. "He . . . he was giving comfort . . ."

Bracingly, Anne said, "Then that's undoubtedly the explanation for where I saw him. Forgive me. I've upset you. It was foolish of me to jump to a conclusion so out of character for the man I knew."

Lydia stared at her in shock and outrage. "You thought— A grog shop? Or . . ." Her voice rose. "Not a prostitute?"

What a dreadful thing to have implied! And she had done so knowing she would cause distress! Anne had to remind herself of Napua's danger; if she must trample on other people's sensibilities to uncover the murderer, then that was what she'd do. Nonetheless with genuine contrition she apologized. "I shouldn't have said anything. Forgive me."

"How could you think—!"

"I . . . I suppose in my heart I didn't . . ."

Lydia snatched up her sewing and thrust it into the basket beside her chair. She rose to her feet and said in a terrible voice, "How dare you? I counted you a friend!"

Anne stabbed her finger with the needle. The pain gave her an excuse for the tears that welled in her eyes as she watched the woman who had been so kind to her hurry away. She had few enough friends, and she had just lost one.

Lost a friend, and not learned enough either to accuse or absolve the Reverend Griggs of two dreadful crimes.

The news that Judd had resigned from the Royal Commission of Health on August 22 was certain to cause a good deal of whispering at the levee held only days later by His Majesty at the Iolani Palace. Surely none, however, would dare speak openly of the turmoil in the privy council, which had voted nearly a week ago by the narrowest of margins to dismiss both Gerrit Judd as minister of finance and Richard Armstrong as minister of public education. Both had refused to surrender their posts; Judd had offered the merest sop by resigning from the Commission of Health. Would he commit the folly of appearing here tonight? Anne wondered. The size of the crowd indicated that many hoped for fireworks.

The palace, with its hipped roof and colonnaded lanais, was brilliantly lighted for the evening reception. Escorted by Matthew, Anne arrived at about eight. The borrowed coach disgorged them, and they strolled through the gardens led by sprightly music from a band playing on the veranda. Anne slipped into the state bedroom to lay her bonnet on the bed, a magnificently carved monstrosity trimmed in damask and covered by Chinese satin.

Matthew waited in the hall. Anne had become accustomed to seeing him, and although he always affected her, she was rarely struck dumb by the sight of him. Tonight she saw him before he saw her; he stood a little apart from the gaily dressed crowd, his narrowed gaze moving restlessly over it. She knew that, like her, he had begun seeing a murderer behind every face, had begun to speculate about everyone's motives.

He wore black tonight with a white linen shirt and cravat. His hair had been bleached by the sun to a blond as pale as Waikiki sand, while his face was tanned to bronze. Tall and athletic, elegantly dressed and assured, he was a god, not the stern, sometimes stuffy, sometimes irascible doctor she knew. Her reaction was partly physical, the kind of absurd response a young woman has to a handsome man, the longing for she knew not what. But Anne also had a moment of terror because she was so glad to see him, had come to depend on him, to dream of his rare smiles, to think of him as friend. How had she dared? How did she dare go to him now and lay her hand on his arm and say, "Have you seen anyone of interest?"

But she did exactly that, and he smiled, slow and warm.

"Mrs. Cartwright, you're beautiful tonight."

Anne glanced ruefully down at her dark silk gown and then glanced around. Oh, to wear fabric the color of the skirt that swished into the reception room! A rich green, it would have brought out the fiery highlights in her hair and made her skin creamy. She would have liked some lace, or fashionably puffed sleeves, or even a flounce or two, except that flounces would have made her look like a cake with too much icing.

There she went again! she reproved herself, wanting to be what she wasn't. She was better off as she was, in plain dark gray, with her hair pulled back as tightly as ever and her cheeks unrouged. Unattractive to men, she was free of their domination.

As she looked around, Matthew murmured, "I haven't seen Dr. Judd, if that's what you mean. Which doesn't surprise me; he would be a fool to antagonize the king, and he's anything but that."

"He wouldn't have survived in politics as long as he has if he weren't adroit at managing the king and chiefs," she agreed. "If he plays his cards right, His Majesty may yet support him."

They entered the reception room to find it crowded with a group of young Hawaiian *alii* who had attended the Royal School, including the pretty Emma Rooke, a *hapahaole* daughter of Hawaiian chiefs and granddaughter of John Young, Kamehameha the Great's English adviser. She asked after Napua, and Anne was able to reassure her. Napua was unwilling to approach these old friends, but Anne thought her mistaken about their feelings. Hawaiians had never been judgmental about sexual matters. They seemed genuinely indifferent to race. White skin, brown, or yellow, what difference did it make? They intermarried happily: witness Emma Rooke, who was reputedly being courted by Prince Liholiho himself. Part white, she might become queen one day. Yet because Napua had *not* married, she was ashamed. Or perhaps she was ashamed of her foolishness in trusting a man as evil as Edward Landre.

Liholiho greeted Anne with respect and Matthew with the wary courtesy he offered to most foreigners these days. Of all the powerful men in the kingdom, this one, little more than a boy, was the greatest threat to the hopes of the annexationists.

If he were ever to place the crown on his head, Anne believed
Hawaiians would see a resurgence of their culture and a reduc-
tion in the role played in the government by foreigners. He had
been heard to say bitterly that the Hawaiian war god Kukail-
imoku, "Ku-Island-Snatcher," could learn lessons from the
Americans, who were so eager to snatch what was not theirs.
Had Charles Decker's scheme worked and Liholiho been as-
sassinated, the loss to the kingdom would have been great
indeed. The king was too weary and confused by alcohol to continue without a strong presence to give him hope for the future.

The prince was a slight, handsome youth with wavy dark
hair, exceptionally large, bright eyes, and an ease of manner and
sophistication that often surprised Europeans. "Dr. Cabe," he
said pleasantly, "you've done fine work among the ill. This nation must be grateful to you."

"I've done no more than any physician would, Your Majesty,
but I thank you for the commendation."

"You're modest." His English was fluent and held the strains
of New England, thanks to his tutors. "Tell me, do you intend
to stay in Hawaii?"

"I'm afraid not," Matthew said, just as courteously. "I hope
to settle an injustice in your courts and then return to my medical practice in Boston."

"Ah. A pity." Yet he didn't sound as though he really meant
it. "Well, enjoy yourselves, Dr. Cabe, Mrs. Cartwright."

In a low voice, Matthew said, "Was it my imagination, or
am I not popular with Liholiho?"

"I believe he fears all foreigners," Anne told him. "He sees
what a threat Americans in particular are to the future of his
kingdom and to his chances of ever becoming king. He attempts to influence his uncle against them. I suspect he'd be delighted to be rid of Dr. Judd."

"Who has done much to protect this kingdom."

"But who holds a good deal of power. If he departs the cabinet, that will leave a vacuum, and Prince Liholiho could step into it."

Matthew's blue eyes surveyed her with some surprise. "You're well informed. I should have realized you would be."

"I read the newspapers, including the Hawaiian-language ones. Should I not, because I'm a woman?"

He took her arm and steered her out of the path of a very large Hawaiian chiefess, who took up the space of three normal-sized people. "Have you read of the Seneca Falls manifesto?" he inquired.

"Indeed I have!" Anne said with spirit. "And subscribe to it. Would you dispute its tenets?"

He held up his hands defensively, his eyes smiling. "No, no! I have long believed that many evils spring from the fact that women cannot hold property in their own names before widowhood. They are left helpless, dependent entirely on the generosity of their fathers and husbands. If all men were generous, the system might work, but of course they aren't. No, you have my support."

"Even to the point of voting for women's suffrage?"

"Why not?" Matthew seemed to be enjoying her militant posture and the challenge in her voice. "You are better informed and have more common sense than most men I know. I don't believe gender determines fitness for self-government."

"Then you're unusual." She admitted it grudgingly, though she oughtn't be surprised, not after the respect he had given her as his assistant. "Fortunately we're ahead in some respects here in Hawaii; girls are receiving equal education, at least, and many of the chiefesses hold great power and wealth. Yet I fear that will change as the natives learn to admire the same virtues that Americans and Europeans prefer in a woman." Longtime anger at the injustices lent acid to her voice. "Or do I mean weaknesses?"

"You're bitter," he said with what sounded like surprise and interest. "Have you received such ill treatment from men?"

"Must one have been abused to take a stand for her sex?"

"No, but with such fervency—" He broke off. "I believe we're being summoned to His Majesty's side."

In fact, they had been waiting their turn, for the king was surrounded by a crush of guests. Kamehameha III held court at one end of the large room furnished with sofas and lounges and chairs around the perimeter and brightly lit by chandeliers suspended from the ceiling. In the center stood a table of native koa wood, richly colored and grained. Arrayed on it were gifts from foreign kings and presidents.

Dressed in a Windsor uniform, the king was a handsome man of genial countenance, easy in his manner although he avoided speaking English in such company. Tonight his face appeared puffy and his eyes bloodshot. He had a tendency to lurch between alcoholic binges and strict, cold-water sobriety. He disappeared for weeks at a time. Publicly he was said to be "ill." Privately everyone knew the truth. Between the epidemic and the crisis in his privy council, he'd been under a good deal of pressure lately. It would not be unusual for him to respond by drinking heavily. The entire nation feared for his health.

Usually one of the ministers stood at his side to translate. This evening a chief who sat on the privy council took that role, the very man they had most hoped to see tonight: Kaipoleimanu.

He was a young man, another of the generation educated so carefully by the missionaries at the Royal School. They had succeeded in some respects: their pupils were learned and well read. They were also resentful of the very missionaries who had so altered their lives.

His father, dead in the measles epidemic of 1848, had been one of the principal chiefs on Maui. Kaipoleimanu, bred to rule, had unhesitatingly accepted all represented by the *kahili*, the feathered staff carried to honor and warn of the presence of a high chief. More than Prince Liholiho or even the king, Kaipoleimanu looked the part of ancient Hawaiian *alii*, large both in girth and height, though not obese. His features were less finely cut; he did not mimic foreign styles, like having a small mustache, as both the king and his heir did. Anne envisioned Kaipoleimanu easily in *malo* and helmet, a warrior and chief.

Yet, Anne thought, perhaps he'd had too much responsibility too young; Kaipoleimanu was both proud and as humorless and stern as the missionaries who had shaped him. How he would have hated to see in himself the mirror image of them, for he now attended the Catholic church and openly opposed the policies of *"na makua o ka pono"*—the fathers of righteousness. He was known to support a troupe of hula dancers, who performed frequently at his homes here in Honolulu and in Lahaina. Thus did he defy the ban that had not quite become law but was nearly as effective.

For that Anne admired him. For the hatred that ate at his soul and caused him to support nearly any cause or legislation that would undermine missionary influence, she despised him. The French, who sought to open the islands to the free import of their wines and brandy, with his support frequently attacked the high import duty and the laws that forbade selling liquor to natives. In the early years of white influence, the effect of liquor on the Hawaiians had been devastating, yet Kaipoleimanu would sacrifice his own people to his bitterness.

It was his wife Anne had nursed after a miscarriage. Great affection appeared to exist between Kaipoleimanu and Makalika. Now his aloof expression warmed when he saw Anne.

"Mrs. Cartwright." Like Liholiho, Kaipoleimanu spoke fluent English. "How good to see you."

She curtsied. "Chief. Your Majesty. May I present Dr. Matthew Cabe?"

Both men studied the American doctor. The king held out

a hand. He spoke in Hawaiian; the chief translated. "How do you do? His Majesty regrets the unpleasantness you suffered in the fort. We are not a barbaric country."

"Such mistakes happen in the United States as well," Matthew said. "I don't consider my incarceration a black mark against the Hawaiian kingdom."

Kaipoleimanu translated, listened to the king, and said, "His Majesty is grateful. He hopes you'll enjoy yourself this evening."

It was clearly a dismissal; they thanked King Kamehameha and retreated, although not before Kaipoleimanu said quickly, "Mrs. Cartwright, might I have a word with you later? When I'm free?"

"Of course," she agreed. "I believe we'll look for refreshments now."

"Certainly," he said and turned back to the next guests who were greeting His Majesty.

Matthew gripped Anne's arm and drew her toward the doorway. "What does *he* want?"

"I don't know," she admitted. "But that will give me a chance to talk to him."

"Not alone."

She stopped. "Why ever not? Do you think he'll attack me here in the palace?"

Matthew scowled. "There must be some dark corners out in the grounds."

"Murder in the king's billiards room?"

He didn't like her frivolity. "Blast it, *somebody* has committed murder!"

"You know," she said mildly, "if Kaipoleimanu wanted to murder a man—or woman—he would be unlikely to do the deed himself. He would send a flunky to do the job."

"Which makes it harder to eliminate him as a suspect."

"Nearly impossible," she agreed. "But we have to try."

His dark gold brows met, giving him a fierce mien. "I won't let you out of my sight."

"Might your guardianship extend to procuring me a glass of lemonade?" Anne inquired tartly.

He gripped her arm and led—or did she mean hauled?—her across the hall into the sitting room, where a table held pitchers of lemonade and plates of cake. "Wait here," he ordered and returned in a moment with a glass, giving her an approving nod when he saw that she hadn't moved an inch.

Anne ruefully recalled the brief fantasy in which she'd seen him as a golden god. He'd succeeded in reminding her that he was a typical man: impatient, masterful, and exceedingly irritating. Well, not altogether typical—he did, after all, support women's suffrage, and he was willing to believe a woman might be competent outside the home. But still, he felt the need for physical mastery.

Her instincts had been right; she ought to do her sleuthing *without* advance notice to Dr. Matthew Cabe.

Not too long afterward, Kaipoleimanu appeared in the doorway, obviously searching the room. When he spotted Anne, he made his way to her side. He inclined his head dismissively toward Matthew and eased Anne away, although he made no move to lure her out of the palace into the shadows behind some shrubbery.

"I believe my wife is expecting a child again," he said in a low voice. "Would you see her?"

"Of course." Anne glanced around, but no one was eavesdropping. "Is she having difficulties?"

"No, not yet, but we fear—" His Adam's apple bobbed. "You understand."

"Yes. I'll come tomorrow, if that's convenient."

He didn't move, but she felt him relax. "Thank you," he said quietly.

"It will have to be afternoon. I'm teaching at the Ewa school in Napua's place at present. She had an . . . unpleasant experience there the other day."

His expression was only puzzled. "Unpleasant? What do you mean?"

"It's . . . not something we'd like known." Ought she tell him? Would she learn anything from his reaction, or was he already too practiced in disguising his true emotions and thoughts?

His nostrils flared. "I know much that the world does not."

He considered her caution an insult. Anne bit her lip and nodded. "She was attacked."

"Attacked?" Alarm and something more calculating flared in his dark eyes. "In the schoolhouse? How could such a thing happen?"

"With a gun. A man tried to shoot her."

"She was not hurt?"

"Only frightened."

"Did she see this man?" He spoke urgently, which was to his credit. A guilty man was more likely to try to sound as though he asked out of the merest curiosity. An innocent man would be angry that women were not safe, and perhaps he'd been fond of Napua; Anne wasn't sure. She'd have to ask Napua what kind of relationship they'd had.

Oh, how tempted she was to lie, to frighten him if the gunman was one of his retainers! Yet all she would do was put Napua in greater danger yet. They might eventually get desperate enough to bait a trap, but surely not yet.

"Unfortunately not," she admitted. "Of course, she's frightened now."

"And should be." He frowned, his dark, strong-featured face brooding. "Perhaps she should join my household. I doubt anyone would dare attack her there."

"That's kind of you," Anne said. "I'll tell her of your offer. I believe she's found a place to hide."

"She would be welcome," he said. "Until tomorrow, Mrs. Cartwright."

Disquieted, Anne watched him make his way across the room greeting guests, smiling, answering brief questions, but in short order slipping out of the room. Was he returning to the king's side? she wondered. Or had something she said reminded him of urgent business? Business like finding Napua, in order to kill her.

I am so bored!" Feeling childish but desperate, Napua gazed beseechingly at Anne. "I can't bear it!"

"It will only be for a short time," Anne promised for the fourth—or was it the fortieth?—time. It was the morning after the levee, and Napua had been in hiding for ten days already. The walls of her house had begun to look as thick to her as the walls of Ke-Kua-Nohu. "Kuokoa, is he bored, too?" Anne asked.

Napua laughed a little, at herself. "He is more content than I! He has me all to himself."

The two women were preparing a meal in the cookhouse out back. Most Hawaiian houses had separate kitchens. In this climate, an oven or stove would have uncomfortably heated a house. Besides, traditionally the natives had lived not so much in a hut as in a complex of huts: it had been *kapu*, forbidden, for husband and wife to eat together or for their food to be prepared together. Thus the husband cooked his own meal in one building, his wife's in another; the man had his own eating house, the woman hers. Though they now ate together, some of the old ways had lingered. Napua thought it would have been better if the men still did all the cooking!

Tonight, Anne and Napua had baked taro in the *imu*, oven, and now Anne peeled it as Napua pounded it into poi. The cookhouse, a small thatched building, was uncomfortably warm, with no windows and only one door, as was typical of a native house.

"Tell me about your day," Napua said eagerly. Anne was still teaching for her as well as visiting several women in the early stages of their pregnancies. Anne had told both the Reverend Smith and the children that Napua was ill. He'd willingly accepted Anne as a substitute for the present.

"Um . . . I saw Makalika again. She's very anxious. I'd be reminded of Nettie Decker, except that Makalika has reason. She's miscarried twice before. Everything looks good so far, but I've suggested for the next month or so, when the danger is greatest, that she rest as much as possible. Of course, Kaipoleimanu will do anything for her! She now does nothing but lounge on her mats, eating, with a woman waving a fan to keep her cool. She'll no doubt become as round as a gourd!"

"*I* was as round as a gourd before I had Kuokoa," Napua pointed out, amused.

"And as firm. Makalika is soft already."

"But beautiful."

An odd, wistful look crossed Anne's face. "I envy her for being admired. If only *haole* men admired statuesque women."

"But you always say you don't want to marry."

She had seen her friend shudder at the idea, which she didn't understand. Love gave life within; although she was wary now, she had also discovered how cold were the nights without a man. Anne had been married; didn't she miss the hot fire within the body?

Tonight she said only, "I don't," but her words lacked their usual conviction, and she frowned as though hearing herself. Napua was no fool; she had seen the way Anne looked at the American doctor. There was a saying: love is like the slippery moss on the sand of Mahamoku. Napua thought that Anne was about to discover how slippery the moss was; she was falling in love without even knowing it.

Napua was smiling to herself when the door crashed shut behind her, plunging the interior into near darkness. Her heart leaped and she turned with a start. Anne bumped into her as she did the same.

"Kuokoa?" Napua called, her voice quivering just a little bit. Her son had been asleep in the house when she came out; had he woken and decided to play a trick on his mother?

She heard no giggle, hesitated, then took the steps to the door. Napua reached to open it just as something thudded against it from outside. Her heart bounded into her throat and she jumped back.

"Who is it?" she cried.

Beside her, Anne shoved against the heavy door. "Help me!"

Napua threw her weight against it, too, but it wouldn't budge. They were trapped. But why?

A horrifying answer came to her. "Kuokoa!" Napua screamed. "What if he—" Anne's hand over her mouth stopped her words.

"He might hear you," she whispered. "He may not know Kuokoa is here."

Drawing in a sobbing breath, Napua choked on the smoke. Was their food burning? She swung around to stare at the *imu*, but realized she had taken the last taro out. At the same moment, she heard the crackle of flames.

A gasp told her Anne had understood, too. The murderer was going to burn them alive.

Fifteen

L ie down on the floor!" Anne cried. "There's less smoke there."

Terror gripped Napua, but also a cold practicality. They must get out. Quickly. She'd once seen the fiery conflagration when a thatched church burned. In the blink of an eye, a heartbeat, it was a roaring inferno.

She fell to the earth floor and crawled to the wall. Digging her fingers into the *pili* grass thatching, she tried to rip it away.

But the cookhouse was newly constructed, the crosspieces only inches apart and the thatching thick and tight. It was not like the schoolhouse, which had been grazed upon by cattle and weakened by rain and winds. Napua turned to look frantically around.

"We must find something to chop with!"

"The ax is outside." Already, Anne was reaching for a knife, although she doubled over coughing, so thick was the smoke becoming. "Try this."

Napua snatched it and slashed at the thatching. The knife slid through and got stuck. She wrenched it out and tried again.

But the slits she was making were tiny, and the knife only gouged the branches used as crosspieces.

The crackle was becoming a roar, and the first flames licked through the side wall. The heat baking her back, Napua renewed her attack on the crosspiece. When it cracked, Anne kicked out. The branch splintered, and Anne began yanking at the *pili* grass even as Napua slashed at the cross branch just above.

They might have squeezed a hand out now. Sweat streamed down both their faces and they choked as the fire with a whoosh leaped up to the roof.

Making a strangled sound, Anne crumpled to the floor. Napua could do nothing for her. She cried hot tears as she struggled to make an opening that would never be large enough in time. Darkness was closing over her, too, misting her vision. *Oh, Kuokoa!* she mourned. *Who will take care of you?*

The door opened. Daylight flooded her just before fire sprang for the air. She fell to the floor.

A hand on her arm was tugging at her. "Out, out!"

Her voice croaked. "My friend."

"Go!"

She crawled, feeling the flames sear her hair. Outside she collapsed on her face, then scrambled forward to escape the heat towering above her like Pele's wrath.

Behind her the cookhouse crashed inward.

"Anne!" Napua wailed, lifting her head. A man with blackened face and hands stumbled to his knees beside her and gently laid Anne's unconscious body beside Napua.

With her naked hands, Napua beat out a flame snatching hungrily at Anne's skirt. She saw that her own skin was covered with soot, as was Anne's face. She bent down and heard her friend's shallow breaths. Anne would live, then, if her spirit found its way back into her body.

Napua lifted her eyes to the man who kneeled above Anne. Even through the pungent smell of smoke she smelled liquor. He was so dirty it was hard to recognize him, but she knew those red-rimmed eyes. Eyes she had once thought kind.

Henry Turner had saved their lives. But how? Where was the murderer?

A wave of fear so strong it might have been nausea swept over Napua. Had he set the fire and then saved them, too, for some mysterious purpose?

I saw the fire," Kuokoa whispered. He sneaked a shy look at the circle of adults. "I saw a man running away."

"What did he look like?" Matthew asked.

The boy squirmed; finally he murmured in Hawaiian to his mother, who said, "He doesn't know. The man was dressed in black and wore a hat. Kuokoa thinks he was *haole*, but he isn't sure."

Matthew grunted and glanced at Henry Turner, who was now cleaned up and sobered by the experience and the passing hour or more.

Matthew himself had arrived shortly after the cookhouse collapsed. He'd been passing nearby when he saw the thick black column of smoke. Sickness gripped him when he realized the source had to be Napua's, or very near. He'd galloped as though the Night Marchers themselves were at his heels, chanting and waving their spears. God! What he had felt when he saw Anne, lying on the grass, so still, her eyes closed— He drew a ragged breath.

"Then what?" Matthew prodded the boy.

"I tried to pull the bar from the door, but I couldn't. So I ran for help. This man"—he gestured shyly—"he was riding down the street on his horse. When I asked, he came with me."

Napua glanced at Turner, then asked Kuokoa something in the native language. He replied volubly. She relaxed as he spoke and at last gave Turner a breathtaking smile. "If it had not been for you—"

His cheeks darkened above the stubble. "Any man would've done the same, ma'am."

"You put yourself in danger. The roof could have collapsed on you as well as us."

In his Texan drawl, he denied any heroism. Napua argued; Matthew finally turned his head to where Anne sat silently beside him. Rage kicked in his belly, as it did every time he saw her blistered hands and singed hair. She had nearly died, would have died if it weren't for Henry Turner. Matthew hadn't known how powerful his feelings for her were until he'd nearly lost her.

Gritting his teeth, he asked in a low voice that sounded harsh, "What did she ask him?"

Anne looked vaguely at him and blinked. She had been like that ever since he'd scooped her up in his arms and carried her into the house. Shock, he diagnosed. After washing up—Anne now wore one of Napua's loose-fitting, Mother Hubbard–style gowns—they'd settled in the front room of the small house, having commandeered every chair in the place. Anne had scarcely said a word since. She would normally have been self-conscious, at least, about letting her hair dry in the company of two men. She must be unaware of how the wet strands had dampened the cotton of her gown, making it cling to her back and breasts.

"Him? Oh. Kuokoa. Um." She checked to be sure Turner wouldn't hear her and said in a low voice, "She asked whether he could have been the one who set the fire. Kuokoa says not. He isn't dressed the same. Kuokoa thinks the villain was bigger, too. And he says Mr. Turner was coming from the opposite direction on horseback."

"A genuine hero, then." Matthew studied the other man more carefully. Shorter and stockier than Matthew, he was softening a little around the waist. He might once have been handsome, before he'd ruined himself with drunkenness. Now his face was puffy, his eyes bloodshot, his two days' growth of beard grizzled. He'd been drunk when he came, filthy and stinking. Yet he had willingly crawled inside a burning building to rescue two women, one of whom he had no cause to love. A decent man still lurked inside the shell of Henry Turner.

Landre, Matthew thought grimly, had a good deal to answer for.

Matthew interrupted brusquely. "Were you passing by chance?"

A muscle jerked in Turner's cheek. After a moment, he looked down at his hands, spread open on his thighs. "No," he said. "I was coming here."

"Here?" Napua echoed. Her huge dark eyes held puzzlement and even hurt. "But . . . why?"

Matthew heard the rasping breath Turner dragged in before he lifted his head. His mouth twisted. "I'm ashamed of myself, ma'am, but the truth is, I was peeved that you'd given my name to that constable. I told myself you'd killed Landre and were doing your damned"—he cleared his throat—"your best to see that I hanged for it. I got liquored up this afternoon, and after I brooded on it for a while, I resolved to come out here and give you a piece of my mind."

Matthew found himself on his feet. "How the devil did you find her?"

"Find her?" He looked puzzled. "Why shouldn't I have?"

Napua, Matthew, and Anne exchanged glances.

"Because," Napua said softly, "this is not the first time someone has tried to kill me."

Matthew fixed a hard gaze on Turner's face. "She's only been at this house for a week, and she's stayed inside. We've taken care not to be followed when we come."

"I saw her the other day. I was passing—by chance, that time.

The boy ran out to see a passing herd of horses. He started to open the gate, and . . . Miss Kanakanui hurried out and led him back in. I thought nothing of it."

"Except that seeing her is what set you to brooding."

Turner was an honest man. "Yes."

Matthew looked at Napua.

She nodded. "It's true. I thought Kuokoa would be trampled if he got out into the street."

"Devil take it!" Matthew sat down heavily. "Did the whole world happen to be parading by just then?"

"Or," Anne said quietly, "did Mr. Turner tell anyone he'd seen Napua?"

They all turned their heads. Turner ran a hand over his chin. "No. I won't deny I was drunk, but . . . no." He grimaced. "I'm not a sociable man. I drink alone."

"You're sure?"

He made no effort to avoid Matthew's eyes. "Yes."

"Blast it, then how—?"

"One of us must have been followed," Anne said. She sounded sharper; she was thinking again, and worrying. "Which means that Napua's assailant knew whom to follow to find her."

"And therefore knows us."

"Yes."

The thought was sobering. No, disturbing. Yet hardly a surprise. Frowning, Matthew said, "I suppose we can be sure Napua was the target."

"Considering the previous attempt on her life, and the fact that this is her home, I think we can be safe in thinking that. Besides"—Anne made a face—"why would anyone want to kill me?"

"Herr Bauer might," Napua pointed out. "Or . . . Reverend Griggs was very angry at you."

"I have it from his wife that he doesn't hold my softheartedness against me," Anne said dryly.

"Sanctimonious . . ." Matthew muttered.

"Indeed," she said crisply. She felt for dampness in her hair, still seemingly unconscious of the intimacy of the scene. Her gaze went to her friend. "Napua, you must move again. Perhaps you should take Kaipoleimanu up on his offer."

Fear looked out of Napua's eyes, large and dark. "Even if he means to protect me, would I be truly safe there?"

Anne turned to Matthew. But unexpectedly, it was Turner who spoke up. Matthew had almost forgotten the other man was still there.

"P'raps she should leave Oahu. If she slipped away on an interisland schooner, no one would be the wiser."

Wearing an arrested expression, Napua said, "Yes, but where would I go?"

"I could . . ." He cleared his throat. "I'd be pleased to escort Miss Napua to Maui. My plantation in the Hana District has gone to wrack and ruin, but the house still stands. She could stay there."

Hating the necessity of being suspicious, still Matthew wondered: a genuine hero? Or had Turner something else in mind?

Napua gave him a cool glance. "Why would you do this for me?"

"Because that son of a—" He wiped his brow and swallowed the profanity. "That villain Landre shouldn't be allowed to win. He may have ruined me, but if I can keep him from ruining you, too, I'll have some satisfaction."

Matthew didn't try to hide his incredulity. "You would disrupt your life for a woman you scarcely know?"

Turner gave a grunt that might have been intended to express amusement, although real humor was completely lacking in his face. "My life? I have no life. I'm a drunkard and a wastrel. I don't make this offer for her." He jerked his head toward Napua. "I make it for myself. I'd like to think I am still capable of doing one worthwhile thing."

Matthew was unexpectedly moved by this emotionless narrative. Henry Turner sounded sincere—and his offer was invaluable, if it—if *he*—could be trusted.

Anne said something in Hawaiian to Napua.

Turner cleared his throat again. "I should tell you that I speak the language."

Matthew hadn't known skin as dusky as Napua's could blush, but her cheeks bloomed with rose. "Then you understood earlier, when I asked Kuokoa about you? About whether you could have set the fire?"

"Aye." Turner sat straight in his chair, as grim as a man facing an execution. "I wasn't insulted, and I understood your reasons for asking. If I'd said something, you would have been embarrassed."

As she obviously was now, but she only let out a breathy sigh and nodded before ducking her head shyly.

"You were a sugar planter?" Matthew asked abruptly.

"Yes." A muscle in his cheek twitched. "Not a successful one, as it turned out."

"Did any survive without being shored up by loans?"

"Probably not," the other man admitted. "When prices sank so low, there was no way to make growing cane profitable. Yet I still believe it will be."

Out of curiosity, Matthew asked, "Do you know Bauer?"

"Aye." His face tightened.

"Is he competent, do you think?"

"Yes."

Matthew read the undertone. "But a bastard?"

"That, too."

"Tell me," Matthew asked, "what do you think of the contracts with the Chinese laborers?"

"I don't care for 'em," Turner said. "It's not that I have anything against Chinamen. But I don't believe in slavery. My abolitionist stands are part of the reason I left home. P'raps if the contracts could be made fairer . . ." He shrugged.

"Any chance you'd consider managing another man's plantation?"

"Yours?" As he thought it over, Turner's face worked, until he looked like nothing so much as a man trying to swallow a cumbersome and unpalatable bite. Apparently he got it down rather than choking on it, for at last he nodded. Once. "Aye. I'd consider it."

"Good." Matthew smiled at him. "We'll talk about it when you've returned from taking Napua and her son to safety. Assuming"—he turned courteously to her—"she's agreeable."

She'd been listening with avid attention to the conversation. Her lack of hesitation now suggested that she'd been coming to her own conclusions.

"Yes," she said. "I think I must go. My son has seen this man who tried to kill us. If he saw Kuokoa . . ." She shivered. "If Mr. Turner would be so kind, I can't refuse."

Matthew stood. "Then we have only to find when the next boat leaves for Maui."

The sun beat down ferociously onto the deck of the schooner, which pitched into a trough of the sea then rose out only to fall into the next. The duck sails flapped, unable to catch a breeze.

Napua sat cross-legged under an awning of tapa, breathing through her mouth so as not to smell the bilge water. Mr. Turner was at the rail, vomiting up what little his stomach might still hold. She was uncertain whether he suffered from seasickness, or the lack of liquor.

Traveling conditions were not pleasant: the schooner was so crowded, sailors had to walk the gunwale to go bow to stern. Mr. Turner was the only white man on board, but natives of all classes were packed like hogs in a pen. They'd brought their dogs, chickens, pet pigs, and even horses. Horned cattle were kept in a small area of the deck, where they lowed incessantly and scented the close, hot air with manure. Black flies swelled in annoying clouds. Napua had never seen or felt fleas so thick, or cockroaches so large. Even the rats that scuttled from heaps of lumber down hatches were monstrously sized and frighteningly bold.

Yet there was a generosity of spirit among the passengers that she liked. Laughter blended with Christian hymns and the voices of playing children. The hungry were welcome to share poi from their neighbors' calabashes. When Mr. Turner turned from the rail and picked his way back to Napua, a minor chief from Maui whom he apparently knew offered him a drink of *awa*, the Hawaiian's fermented liquor.

Intense longing passed over the *haole*'s face, but he shook his head. "No, thank you."

Napua studied him carefully when he stumbled down beside her. He looked ill, and had been short-tempered. No wonder; he must feel as though his stomach had been wrenched inside out. He'd refused to touch a drop of liquor since their departure four days before and had been sober when he met her at the wharf. She wasn't sure whether he'd promised Matthew to stay that way, or whether he'd made a vow to himself. Either way, the decision was costing him. She respected a man capable of such self-discipline. Nor would she judge him for his drunkenness; there was an old saying: "Only the mists know the storm that caused the streams to swell." She wasn't close enough to Henry Turner to know the reasons for his problems, beyond the wrong done to him by Edward.

Scowling he said, "Do you suppose the captain has any idea where we are?"

"With no wind, does it matter?"

"I suppose not." He glanced around. "Where's Kuokoa?"

"There." She pointed. "He found another boy his age." At

the moment the two were playing *loulou*, a game in which they hooked fingers together and then pulled to see who could last the longest without letting go or straightening his finger.

Mr. Turner's kindness to Kuokoa was one thing that softened her feelings for him. He had snapped at her a few times but never at the boy. He had even showed Kuokoa several new ways of working the string in *hei*, cat's cradle, and had told him some stories from his days as a harpooner on a whaling ship.

"I've made this passage before in three days. Of all trips to take so cursed long!"

"It's the season." She sounded as though she were apologizing, as though she had a hand in the weather!

"I've begun to think this is what hell will be like," he said gloomily. "Becalmed on an endless ocean with suffocating heat, I'll spend eternity being eaten by fleas and bitten by these *blasted* flies—" He slapped viciously at one. "And meantime everyone around us is unfailingly cheerful! And you! Why aren't you impatient?"

Napua spread her hands. "Bananas don't fruit in a single day. Why waste passion on something that can't be changed?"

He gave her a look of active dislike. "I suppose you're used to this wretched way of traveling."

"Were the grog shops paradise?"

"*Christ!*" he exploded. "At least there I could dull my misery!"

"You could here, too. You've been offered *awa*."

"I swore I'd keep you safe."

"I *am* safe," she said softly. "Knowing that makes it easy to be patient. I didn't like to think of Kuokoa alone—" She stopped.

He touched her hand with his rough one, then pulled back as though embarrassed by his own tenderness. He spoke gruffly. "He won't be."

"Tell me about your sugar plantation."

His gaze turned from her to the sea. "It's on the slope above Hana. One of the most beautiful places on this earth." Eyes unfocused, pain on his face, he talked about the land closest to his heart: about the volcano Haleakala, wreathed in mist above; about the bay, where the waters were the most intense shades of blue and green; about red-faced Ka'uiki, the hill where Maui himself pushed the sky up, so that the clouds never touch it.

"Not far away are dozens of falls and pools, and the black sand beaches. Your hair sometimes reminds me of the black sand when it's wet." He gave her a startled look, as though he hadn't meant to say so much. Perhaps he was embarrassed, and that was why his voice became harsh. "But I've lost my lease on the fields, and the house and small piece of land I own are worthless. I'd never have gone back if it weren't for you."

"I'm sorry," she whispered.

His mouth twisted. "Perhaps I can sell it while we're there."

"But if it's your dream—"

"I've drowned any dreams." He swallowed, and she saw that his face was green again. "If this damn ship would just quit rolling—"

A moment later he was leaning over the rail again. Pity might have taken her to his side but for the fact that she knew he would so detest being the object of it. Pride was not a bad thing; she respected him for that, too.

If only the wind would rise and fill the sails!

Her wishes did no good. For that entire day, the schooner tossed helplessly in the waves, making no headway. Only as evening came did Napua see clouds, which fishermen called "the eyes of the wind" because they showed the wind's direction. Long strings of them, like flowers on leis, took on the colors of the sun when it set. Any chiefess would have been admired had she worn the heaps of leis in orange and purple and golden.

Soon the breeze ruffled the canvas and stirred against

Napua's hot skin. She lifted her face gratefully to the coolness.

Beside her Mr. Turner slumped in a half-doze from which he jerked and moaned every few minutes. His face was either burned by the sun or flushed from the heat, because it was very red. Sweat soaked his shirt and even his trousers, as though his body were wringing itself out. She didn't think it could be good for him to lose so much moisture, especially since water might have to be rationed if the voyage took too long.

She touched his arm. "The wind. Feel it. The wind is blowing at last."

Of course the *Lahaina* had to beat against the wind, but at least the rigging creaked and hissed and they could feel they were making progress. Napua took out a calabash of pale pink *poi* and she and Kuokoa ate, although Mr. Turner recoiled from it. She insisted he take sips of water, however warm and stale it was. He seemed not to mind her speaking to him as she did to Kuokoa. Perhaps no one had cared enough to tell him what to do in a long while.

She slept at last, right there on the deck. Mr. Turner had reserved them two berths in the cabin, but below decks the heat and suffocation were unbearable. Here at least she could breath and see beyond two feet in front of her face.

During the night she woke to the shouts of the captain and crew and the howl of the wind through the rigging. With a gasp she sat up, startled to discover that her head had been pillowed on a man's shoulder. Cries of alarm came from all around her, as the ship slid down the black face of a wave and slammed into the next before groaning and dragging itself up. Oh, yes, the wind had found them. Perhaps too many prayers had been answered all at once.

Blindly she reached out for Kuokoa, to find him curled tightly against her, head under his arms. She could tell from his rigid muscles that he was already awake and cringing in terror. In all his years, he'd never been out on the ocean; on those rare occasions when Edward traveled among the islands, he left them behind. Once she'd had family at Hilo, Hawaii, which she remembered visiting as a young child. In her grief, she hadn't written to them when her mother died; she didn't know if they still lived or not. At least Kuokoa swam well, but she should have found some way for him to become more familiar with the sea.

On her other side, she felt the stirring as Mr. Turner awakened. She was glad he had slept long enough for her to scoot away. She wondered what he would think if he knew how her body had curled into his in sleep.

"Now what?" he shouted over the wind. "Are we in trouble?"

"I don't know," she yelled into his ear. She held Kuokoa tightly, so that he didn't tumble away when the deck became a *pali*, with them clinging to the top. It was near pitch darkness; she could feel but not see the waves poised above the tiny schooner. When Mr. Turner's arm came around her shoulder, she was grateful for his warmth and nearness. If he hadn't come on this journey, oh, how alone she would have felt!

They huddled there throughout the night, listening to the wind and the shouts, and praying, but silently, for words were snatched away. At some time, Kuokoa relaxed into sleep, but, like a mother dog with her puppies, Napua stayed watchful. Beside her, she felt Mr. Turner's wakefulness. Each time the deck pitched, he moved to brace them. When waves hurled their cold spray over the ship, he used his body to protect her and Kuokoa.

The storm died gradually; the waves became hills instead of cliffs, and then only steep slopes. Dawn pearled the sky and the clouds scudded away, like cowards who had been taunting a chief under the cover of darkness and ran away with daylight.

The schooner must have blown too far north to see the island of Molokai. Like Mr. Turner, Napua hoped the captain could navigate. The one time she felt uneasy on the ocean was when she was out of sight of land. Could one sail and sail and never see the green of land again?

By midday the sun gnashed its teeth, making it very hot on the packed deck. At least the wind continued to fill the sails. The world began to seem very tiny, the deck of this ship all that existed, afloat in the vast blue sea. The tedium might have been unendurable otherwise, but as it was, Kuokoa played quietly with other children, his usual boundless energy absent. Napua sometimes read aloud, for she had brought a volume of a *haole* man's plays with her.

The words written by this Shakespeare were sometimes incomprehensible, but sometimes beautiful. He made his home, England, sound a little like her own: a beautiful green isle on which people quarreled and loved and often did foolish things. Shakespeare, Napua thought, wrote *meles* the equal of any Hawaiian master. She had never been to a play; the missionaries disapproved of them, and Edward hadn't taken her to public entertainments. She would have liked to see the story of *Romeo and Juliet* or *The Tempest* on the stage.

When she read aloud, Kuokoa quickly became bored, but Napua noticed that Mr. Turner listened. Sometimes she thought the words made him remember other places and people. Seeing his sadness made her wonder about his life before he took to the sea as a whaler. Did he have a wife in America, even children? Was that why he knew what would please a small boy?

For herself, she was strangely contented. There was food enough for weeks, if need be, and now that the wind blew, she wasn't worried about water. Many casks were yet untapped. For now, this little world was enough. Here she didn't have to worry about who she was, or what way she ought to take. She had no more dreams in which she tried to peer through the mist. She wasn't surprised, that day right after the storm, to see a rainbow arching above the sea. She felt as though it were a sign to her alone.

By the sixth day, Mr. Turner had begun to eat again, and he no longer stumbled to the rail every time the ship shuddered and rolled. A beard grew dark and wiry on his jaw, the silver hairs mixed in it shining in the sunlight. It scratched her cheek sometimes at night, when she curled too near. Yet she had ceased to be embarrassed by their closeness. It felt right.

She was too wary to think about love. But food could be cooked in the embers, Napua reminded herself; there was no need to light a big fire. Nights had been so lonely; she liked having a man's shoulder solid beneath her head, his breath playing with her hair, his arm heavy on her breasts. She liked the heat within that his touch awakened. Why not enjoy it?

Of course, she could enjoy it no more than she already did as long as they were on the schooner. So, although she had been contented, her heart lifted when on the seventh day a new shout was raised, and she, too, saw the purple silhouette of mountains on the horizon, one low, the other immense. Haleakala! By nightfall, they'd be dropping anchor. And then she would see what came.

Matthew bowed. "Mrs. Cartwright, could I persuade you to take a walk with me?"

August was drawing to a close now. Nearly a week ago Anne had been replaced in the schoolroom by a missionary's wife. At last all the sick fit into the quarantine hospital, and far fewer new cases of smallpox were being diagnosed. Seeing that the need was less, she had asked to be released from her obligation to Matthew. Instead she was nursing the only son of a Chinese shop owner. Innocently playing in the waves, the boy had been swept away from shore by an undertow. Pulled out by a native fisherman, the child had contracted pneumonia.

Now that Anne wasn't working with Matthew, he couldn't with propriety just snatch her up and take her away without manufacturing an emergency that required her assistance. So, hat in hand, he had called on her at the Reverend Taft's after church services on Sunday and was begging for the pleasure of her company.

Mrs. Taft smiled benevolently: "It is a lovely day, Anne. Why don't you go?"

Anne gave him a look of inquiry. He tried to return it with one fraught with significance. Apparently he succeeded, because she rose to her feet. "Thank you, Dr. Cabe. That sounds pleasant."

Outside she waited until they'd strolled under the trees to the gate in the coral block wall around the mission compound. Then she burst out, "Oh, how I've wondered what was happening! Tell me, have you heard from Napua or Mr. Turner?"

"No, no; depending on the winds they might not even have reached Hana yet."

"But you spoke to Constable Mahaulu?"

His face tightened. "Sooner than I anticipated. He called on me to ask his questions yet again."

"But—why?"

"Because he doesn't believe the answers. It would seem that the plantation worker who came forward to support my story has disappeared, died, or fled; Mahaulu doesn't know. All he knows is that the *kuleana* north of town is deserted. The constable isn't yet prepared to say that Huki—that was his name—lied, but I can tell he's thinking it."

Recalling the interview was enough to make him break out in sweat. Yesterday, Matthew had imagined that he was being followed but convinced himself he was developing paranoia. The razor edge to Mahaulu's questions, his expression of open suspicion had been enough to bring on that blasted dream again. Before dawn Matthew had awakened groaning and thrashing, desperately sucking in air. As a result, he was less than well rested—and quite certain that he had not imagined yesterday's surveillance. Blast it, what did Mahaulu think that he'd do? Revisit the scene of his crime?

His face must have shown too much of his perturbation, for Anne was gazing worriedly at him. He rubbed an unconscious hand over his throat and said with deceptive calm, "Our friend the constable was somewhat less than pleased to be told that Napua had fled. He inspected the burned cookhouse, however, and upon being assured that he could lay his hands on her if need be, gave his belated blessing to her flight." Perhaps, Matthew thought privately, because he was again convinced that the *haole* doctor was the murderer. What did it matter if Napua was out of reach?

The natives they passed on the dusty street were dressed in their best, though they often had bare brown feet beneath the decorous gown or, in the case of the men, the dark trousers. The ladies were bedecked in flowers: leis about their neck, narrower circlets of vivid flowers around their shining dark heads. Their chatter was gay, their greetings joyous. The women seemed to possess a natural grace that gave them a flowing walk Matthew admired. He couldn't help comparing his surroundings to the far more restrained, proper Sunday afternoon scenes back in Boston. The Hawaiians, with their warm welcome and easygoing approach to life, were growing on him.

Anne's thoughts apparently didn't parallel his more pleasant ones, because, sounding combative, she surprised him by demanding, "With Napua safe, are we to give up now?"

Sardonically he said, "With my own neck dangerously close to a noose, I have no intention of doing any such thing. However, I would be just as happy if you would."

"I'm too stubborn to resign."

"Or too nosy," he muttered.

She gave him a sidelong, mischievous smile that tweaked his heart. "Surely, Dr. Cabe, you don't expect me to admit to such an unworthy motive?"

The words he so longed to say formed themselves. But his tongue felt thick, clumsy, and—blast it!—he and Anne were coming upon a family who smiled sunnily and called, "Aloha!"

In the flurry of greetings, his moment was lost, assuming it had been the right one to begin with. What business had he broaching any such subject, with the death sentence yet hanging over him? Yet he would have spoken if they hadn't been interrupted.

A carriage rattled by; he steered Anne into the grounds of the Kawaiahao Church, foursquare and solid, a part of New England although constructed out of alien materials.

His frustration made his voice abrupt. "Reverend Griggs did indeed attend that meeting to plan the Fourth of July celebration. We can safely cross him off our list."

"Oh." She breathed the word softly and, he thought, thankfully. "You're certain?"

"Yes."

"I confess I'm glad. More for Mrs. Griggs's sake than for his. She suffered so with the loss of Napua and then her son."

"I didn't like the idea myself," Matthew admitted. "The Griggses were kind to me. I've been unable to discover any more about Kaipoleimanu, but it's hard to seriously imagine him attacking Napua. And why the devil would he bother with Landre? Why not just expose him as a traitor? Wouldn't the resulting outrage have been more satisfying to a man like Kaipoleimanu, and better for his cause, than a secret crime?"

"You'd think so, wouldn't you?" Anne sounded as dissatisfied as he felt. "But surely only a madman commits murder, and how can we guess how he thinks?"

"But is Kaipoleimanu a madman?"

Anne paused beside a crooked *hau* in full bloom, its heart-shaped leaves forming a dappled canopy that turned the light to a mysterious golden green and partially screened them from the churchyard. Great crinkled flowers of yellow shading into the orange of afternoon peeked between the leaves. She turned slowly to face him.

One part of Matthew's mind noted how unflattering was the severe hairstyle, how uncomfortably pinched her waist was, how *plain* that face. Yet another part of him saw her intelligence, her magnificent gray eyes, her milk-white skin. How did she keep it that way, in the tropical sun? Despite himself, his gaze lowered. No, the crisp fabric of her gown couldn't disguise the swell of lush breasts. He knew them to be as white. He knew how they swayed when unconfined.

He was vaguely aware that she spoke.

"I refuse to give up, but what on earth can we do—" A pink as rich as the dawn sky swept over Anne Cartwright's cheeks. "I— Is something wrong?"

"Wrong?" His voice sounded odd. Perhaps that was because his heart was pounding so cursed loud. "No. Nothing's wrong. I, er, was about to ask you something."

She gazed at him with perplexity. "Yes? What is it?"

Feeling as though he were stepping off the Nuuanu Pali, Matthew asked, "Mrs. Cartwright, will you marry me?"

Sixteen

Anne stared in shock. Had Dr. Matthew Cabe just asked her to marry him? Was it possible?

Dear God, it was, for he continued. "Have I taken you by surprise? Please, just listen to me for a minute."

How could she listen when her pulse was hammering in her ears and her mind seemed to be spinning dizzily? She couldn't look away from his face. How could a man so handsome be asking her to marry him? *Why* was he asking?

"I don't know how you feel about me," he said quietly. "I flatter myself that at the very least we're friends, which is surely a sound basis for marriage. As my wife, you would gain advantages over your present life. You could have your own home and no longer be dependent on others. Although I'm not a wealthy man, I can support you well. I trust we would have children someday. I know that you'd be a magnificent mother."

Herself, a mother. As she grappled with the idea, a shaft of longing pierced her womb with a pleasure sweeter than any she'd ever felt.

"I don't understand. What advantage is there to *you?*"

"To me?" A frown crossed his broad, golden brow. "What do you mean?"

It hurt to ask, but she must. "Why do you want to marry me?"

"Surely you know, you've guessed." The glow in his eyes mesmerized her. "We have a good deal in common. I don't believe I've ever enjoyed a woman's company so much. I discovered last week, when I came so close to losing you, that I love you."

His gaze lowered, caressed her body. When it touched upon her breasts as palpably as a graze of his fingertips, she recoiled. *He wanted her.*

Her husband had wanted her, too, although he'd hated his own weakness. Still staring at Matthew, she saw her husband instead. He had just yanked closed the curtain that screened their berth from the tiny cabin, which they shared with three other couples on the long voyage. In the feeble light of the candle that hung in a bracket on the wall, his eyes reflected a strange glitter that, with the terror born of their short marriage, she recognized as passion. His face was contorted with distaste and anger because she, a woman, had tempted him.

She'd already changed to her high-necked flannel nightgown. Without a word, John Cartwright had wrenched it up above her breasts and positioned himself between her knees. He unbuttoned his breeches, freeing his sexual organ, a great swollen thing far too large for her narrow passage. Even then, she'd known vaguely that if he would let her body soften, ready itself, her duty would have been less painful. But he gave her no chance, only battered his way inside her, smothering her cries of pain with a wet mouth, squeezing her breasts until the agony equaled that between her legs. Over and over, he'd grunted and rammed his way into her until she felt his spasm, heard the whistling exhalation that was triumph and disgust mixed.

Within moments, he had rolled off of her to the edge of the

bunk. There he lay rigid, his whisper knife-sharp. "God in heaven, have I done Thy will? My flesh is but weak, and the whore Thou hast bound to me works her wiles. If I am not to touch her, but send me a sign."

She'd closed her eyes; they stung with salty tears. Her breasts would have huge, ugly bruises the next day; thank God she didn't have to dress in front of the other women. Her insides felt scraped raw; there would be blood on the sheets, as though she were a virgin, though this had been the sixth time he had taken her. How he despised her, come morning! She would be safe for several days. Four or five, perhaps. And then she would notice him watching her, his eyes feverish. There was never any tenderness, any stolen kisses. It would only be like that night—he'd come to bed and use her body, loathing her and himself the whole while. If she whispered a protest, he would strike her, always where the resulting bruise couldn't be seen.

Only once had she dared do anything but lie still with tears seeping out of her eyes after the blow fell. She hunched away, sought to protect herself, struck his arm aside. All she'd done was enrage him. "It is my right to chastise you!" he told her over and over again as more blows fell. She'd learned to accept what he did to her, as her mother must have accepted what her father did. She had foolishly chosen her fate and must live with her decision.

Would it ever be any different? If only they had some privacy, could she talk to him? But the voyage would take months! She often looked at the serene faces of the other missionary wives and wondered whether their husbands took them as brutally. Was she the only one who was learning to hate the man she had married so hastily, in the belief that he was her last chance for happiness and children?

"Mrs. Cartwright—Anne." The husky voice parted the thick veil that separated past and present. Her eyes flew open, and she saw that he—no, not John Cartwright, but Dr. Matthew Cabe—

was bending forward, his eyes now fixed on her mouth. He intended to kiss her. To grind his teeth against her lips until she tasted blood, to smother her cries for help—

"No!" Blindly she retreated, until her back came up against a long branch of the *hau*, and the leaves trembled. "No! Don't touch me!"

"Anne!" Matthew stopped several feet away. "What is it? Why are you frightened?"

The tears were real. They burned in her eyes. Her breath came in gasps, and she clutched her skirt as though to run.

"I won't hurt you. I won't touch you, if you don't wish it. I promise." His face was a blur, only the vivid blue of his eyes in focus. She felt his distress, heard the gentleness in his voice.

In horror, she realized how dreadfully she was behaving. What must he think? He was a good man. He'd asked her to marry him. She ought to have been flattered, even if she didn't choose to accept. Instead she'd reacted as though he were Herr Bauer, come to rape her. Or was there a difference? Did some men only cloak their brutal natures in gentility?

"I . . ." Her throat felt thick. "I'm sorry. I . . ." What excuse could she give?

Matthew's face tightened. "Your husband caused your terror, didn't he? That's what you meant, when you spoke of the missionaries concealing what goes on in private. What did he do to you?"

In a faint whisper, she said, "Nothing that he wasn't lawfully permitted to do—"

"A man can lawfully beat his wife to death. Did he beat you?"

"Not often. Only when I angered him—"

"And what was your crime?" His demand could not be avoided.

She made herself lift her chin and meet his eyes. "I cannot speak of it. Perhaps to another woman, the way he . . . touched me would not have seemed so bad. Women must endure as much all the time. I shouldn't have protested—" She gave a ragged sigh. "But, it would seem I'm not made for marriage."

His voice became rougher, yet also, curiously, softer. "You think the act of man and woman coming together must always be terrible. In fact, it is often pleasurable, and not just to the man. Your husband was a fool. Give yourself another chance."

"Why should I?" The words she'd spoken so often to herself came easily. "So that I can give up my will, my possessions, even my life, into your keeping? You say I wouldn't have to be dependent on anyone, but of course I would be on you. No, thank you, Dr. Cabe, but I must decline your offer."

"You dislike me."

Shocked to an awareness that her own turmoil had led her to hurt him, Anne shook her head. "No. Oh, no! Please! It's not true. I . . . I've treasured the chance to work with you, your friendship. Have I destroyed it?"

His mouth twisted. "If anyone has, it was I. I knew I risked that, when I asked."

"I must ask your forgiveness," she said unhappily. "I wish, oh how I wish, I could say yes and become your wife! My head knows it's possible to find contentment in marriage, but my heart is too frightened to try. I pray you'll understand. My refusal is not because of some . . . some lack in you, you see. It's me."

"Then perhaps there's hope for me." He didn't take a step toward her, but she felt him looming nonetheless, a predator sensing weakness.

"No! Please believe me," she cried. "I cannot marry. I won't change my mind."

"But you do not dislike me," he said. She sensed how carefully he was phrasing what was, after all, a question. "It's only that you fear the more intimate acts between man and wife."

A blush warmed her cheeks, and for the first time she realized that they were talking about something that unmarried men and women did not discuss. Yet she had raised the subject, wanting him to understand that she might have cared for him and been willing to endure her wifely duty were she not scarred by her father's cruelty and her husband's hatred. "Yes, I suppose," she faltered.

"Then might I ask one favor of you?"

"A favor?" she echoed warily.

"Could I kiss you? Just once? Not for myself, but for you. I promise to be gentle, and to release you the second you ask it. I want only the chance to show you that a man's touch need not be fearsome."

The dreadful thing was that she was tempted. She wouldn't think about John Cartwright, wouldn't picture his lips drawn back from his teeth as he used her body as though she were in truth a whore and he a married man detesting himself and her because he broke his vows. Just this once, couldn't she let herself know what other women felt when a handsome man stole a kiss?

"I don't want you to think I might change my mind—"

He smiled, and her heart gave a peculiar, uncomfortable lurch. "If I think any such thing, it will be my own fault," he pointed out.

"I . . . I should not . . ." There was nowhere for her to escape. Her back was against the crooked lower branch of the *hau*. Or was she merely excusing the fact that she made no effort to evade him when he took one long stride forward and tilted her chin up with a gentle hand.

"It can be pleasant," he murmured and bent his head.

Anne waited for terror to spurt through her, but astonishingly she felt nothing but curiosity and—oh, a sort of ache that lodged between her legs, a little like that she felt when she imagined herself bearing a child. She saw his mouth descend until she could make out individual, shaven whiskers on his hard jaw, felt the whisper of his breath on her lips just before he touched them with his own. How could she be frightened then, when his mouth was so gentle? Really, it felt warm against hers, soft, a caress like a fragrant breeze wrapping around her. She sighed and lifted a hand to his chest, where she felt his heart hammer beneath her palm. She relaxed enough so that her lips parted; she shivered to realize that she could feel his open mouth as well. He had drank in her sigh, as she drank in his. For an instant she imagined that his tongue had touched her lips, as though he licked at a sweet. What if it slipped into her mouth? She was swaying toward him even as the first flicker of panic registered.

The large hand that had lifted her chin was now closed around the back of her neck; his other hand gripped her upper arm, so close she felt it brush her breast. The mouth that pressed hers was suddenly not Matthew Cabe's, but her husband's. He had loved and despised her breasts. She couldn't bear it if he grabbed them and squeezed. She would cry out! She would—

Trembling, she stood alone. Matthew had released her and backed up. They stared at each other across the shade-dappled space that separated them. She saw the look in his eyes and knew that letting her go had not been easy for him. But he'd kept his promise. He hadn't hurt her. The kiss had even been . . . pleasant. Wasn't that the word he'd used?

"Was that so dreadful?" he asked huskily.

"No. Of course not."

"Good." He offered an arm. "Can we, perhaps, continue as friends?"

Friends? she thought in despair. How could they? But, oh, she didn't want to lose him!

The next instant she thought in shock, *Lose?* They'd been colleagues of a sort, acquaintances, perhaps friends. But the only way she could claim him was marriage. Had a secret part of her truly been thinking of him in such terms? She couldn't think now. Later—

Hesitantly she stepped away from the tree, extended a hand, laid it on his arm. "Thank you," she said. "I'd like that very much."

Charles Decker rose to his feet, wineglass in hand. "A toast!"

"A toast, a toast!" Other voices took up the cry, faces turned expectantly toward the man tacitly acknowledged as leader of the annexationist/republican forces. Matthew was dining with half a dozen members of the Committee of Thirteen at the Commercial Hotel. He had a sense of unreality. Today was September 4. In another month the whaling ships would be arriving to refit. He'd never thought to see them. When he'd come in May, he had expected to be departing Honolulu by now. He had then declared a lack of interest, if only to himself, in Hawaiian politics. Now he was deeply enmeshed.

"To Dr. Judd," Decker declared, smiling when he was roundly booed. "Ah, but you haven't heard the latest. It seems the lifelong proponent of independence for the nigger kingdom is our brother, in truth. I have it on reliable word that he submitted to the king a proposal that would have a certain Mr. Alfred Benson of New York *buying* the Hawaiian Islands for a price of five million dollars."

Babble broke out. Matthew ignored it, though in this company he took care to hide his perturbation. Dr. Judd, prepared to sell out the islands he had defended so long? What would be their fate? Did this proposal guarantee statehood? Yet how could it, without the agreement of the United States Congress? Could Decker have been misinformed?

"Hah!" Lathrop tossed back his wine. "Shall we invite him to join us?"

"Did the king throw him out on his ear?" asked Elijah Freeman, Matthew's acquaintance from the shipboard passage around the Horn last spring.

"His Kanaka Majesty would have been too drunk," Dr. Newcomb said with contempt. Contempt that Matthew couldn't like, considering the doctor was supporting the proliquor interests here in the islands. He, like most of the white men, was indifferent to the fact that the natives seemed to have no more resistance to powerful spirits than they'd had to smallpox or measles.

John Mott Smith, a dentist, asked, "Can we make use of his change of conscience?"

Decker grinned wolfishly. "No need. He'll be out before a week has passed! No one has quite dared give him the last push, when he still had the support and friendship of the king, but he has unwisely demolished both. Word has it that the ministers will all be required to turn in their portfolios. Only Judd's will not be returned to him."

Cheers erupted. The evening became a celebration, which Matthew amiably joined although he didn't pretend to share their politics.

He had let it be known that he was sympathetic but neutral. "I don't know whether I'll be staying in the islands or not," he had frankly told Dr. Newcomb, whom it had seemed most natural to approach. "Your concerns are primarily economic; why should I share them?"

"Because you, too, have an economic stake in these islands!" Newcomb declared. "With Landre gone, the plantation will be yours. Think of the profit to be made if the U.S. tariffs go down!"

Looking thoughtful required no effort. It was true that he'd welcome a lowering of the tariff, which would make Hawaiian sugar more competitive. He'd accepted the invitation to this evening's gathering with only a small show of reluctance.

And it would seem his act had succeeded, for as the committee members collected their hats and prepared to depart in jovial spirits, Charles Decker himself drew Matthew aside and said quietly, "Walk with me?"

"The exercise would do me good," Matthew agreed.

They had been dining in a private room. As he and Decker passed the main dining room to leave the hotel, Matthew's eyes met those of another man. Marshal Parke, alone at a table. Had he overheard some of the toasts? The Committee of Thirteen were clumsy conspirators.

Or was Parke watching for Matthew, in place of his constable?

He didn't rise, only inclined his head. Matthew did the same, chilled by the reminder of their few meetings.

The evening was fine, more pleasant than had been the hot, dry, windy day. Matthew tried to shrug off his uneasiness. A chance encounter had been inevitable in a town this size. Parke might not even know that Mahaulu was still pressing him. And blast it, they could prove nothing!

Nonetheless he would feel better if Huki or Puukua reappeared, as they might now that smallpox was declining. A few cases were still diagnosed each week, but the number decreased precipitately. By October and the advent of the whaling fleet, Honolulu should be free of the scourge.

He almost looked forward to the rainy season, despite the resulting influx of sailors and the fact that the streets must become little better than pig wallows when wet. Clearly he wouldn't be departing as he'd planned unless he was willing to stow aboard a ship or find a sympathetic captain who would help him make his escape undiscovered, abandoning his claim to the sugar plantation and Anne Cartwright.

He might have been tempted; even now he was unpleasantly aware of the bulk of the fort squatting above the harbor just as Constable Mahaulu's suspicions hovered over him. But he couldn't bring himself to believe that Anne had given her final answer.

Despite her refusal, he still had hopes. How could he not, after feeling her hand on his heart, having her lips part for his, after hearing her cry, "I wish, oh how I wish, I could say yes and become your wife!"

It was almost a pity her husband was already dead, Matthew reflected. Angry as he'd been at Landre, he'd never felt the desire to commit murder until now. John Cartwright had not just frightened his wife. He'd hurt her. Matthew wanted to believe time and care were all that was needed to convince her that marriage wouldn't be so terrible, but he couldn't be certain. If he pressed too hard, he'd scare her. If he kept his hands off her, her scars would never heal. They needed touching, soothing, kisses.

Time, and kisses. Neither so much to ask. Tilting his head back, Matthew gazed up at the brilliant canopy of stars, so much brighter than he had ever seen them, just as nightfall came so much earlier than it did at home in late summer. Seasons weren't clearly noted here, close enough to the equator so that days didn't lengthen and shorten with the seasons. He realized to his surprise that he was growing accustomed to Honolulu, to the friendly, colorful, mild-tempered natives, to this tropical climate, even to the vitriolic approach to politics taken by the foreigners marooned here by choice or need. No, a winter here wouldn't be so bad if only Landre's murderer was arrested and tried. No, not bad at all, not if it meant sailing for home next year with his rights to the sugar plantation secured and Anne at his side as his wife.

He and Decker had walked in silence a distance down Beretania Street. An occasional carriage rumbled past. Decker exchanged greetings with a horseman who looked curiously at Matthew. Trying not to be obvious, he glanced over his shoulder several times to see if any other pedestrians chanced to take the same route. A native hung well back—did he wear the armband of the police force? But, no, he turned at the next street corner, and Matthew relaxed.

The night air was faintly perfumed, the hushed sound of the surf ever present. They had left behind the businesses and were passing only houses, set well back from the street and surrounded by gardens, when Decker said at last, "I'm sorry to hear you say you intend to return to the States. You're just the kind of man we need here in the Sandwich Islands. You have education and ability. You could go far."

"I have a well-established practice in Boston."

"I was not speaking of medicine, but of politics. You can practice as a physician anywhere, but how many opportunities will you have to affect the destiny of a nation?"

Decker had the qualities of a fine orator; his voice rang with powerful convictions calculated to stir his listener.

Matthew considered himself tone-deaf to oratory. A sermon that brought everyone around him to tears left him unmoved. Ideas excited him, not their presentation.

So he only inquired, "And if my ambitions don't lead me that way?"

"How can they not?" the other man declared expansively. "Think of the good you could do, compared to your present limited scope. How many lives might you have saved in the smallpox epidemic, had you been in a position to make decisions! Surely the notion of having such power is seductive."

It certainly was to some men, but politics had never called to Matthew. He had no desire to be either cursed or admired by people he had never met. Government ran on compromise, but he detested the idea of moral compromise. However he pretended to sound doubtful.

"Forgive me, Mr. Decker, but why are you exerting yourself to recruit me? The committee includes at least two physicians already; by my profession, I contribute nothing new. And I'm not altogether in sympathy with some of your views. I must confess, for example, that I don't automatically regard the natives with contempt, as it seemed to me tonight's company did."

"I don't regard them with contempt; far from it." Decker spoke quickly, persuasively. "I believe only that they are not ready to govern a nation entering the modern age. The time will come when they're prepared for equal citizenship, but we make a mistake to hasten it. No, I'm no bigot, Dr. Cabe, but rather a man of practicality. I'm a businessman, first and foremost, but I cannot prosper when the government deliberately undermines the economic health of the kingdom because it is run by missionaries more interested in saving souls than in developing a treasury or encouraging commercial enterprise.

"Why you?" he continued. "I must speak frankly, in the hopes that you will keep confidential what I say."

At last he began to interest Matthew, who somewhat childishly crossed his fingers behind his back as he said, "You may depend on me, at least that far."

Decker stopped, his hand on the wrought-iron gate in front of his house. "Splendid! You'll come in for a brandy?"

"Thank you."

In Charles Decker's library, Matthew settled into a leather chair, brandy snifter in hand. His host paced from his handsome koa wood desk to a wall of bookcases and back. He was not a reader, Matthew diagnosed; as much shelf space was taken up by objets d'art as by books, and the titles were too obviously those an educated man was expected to own, rather than the eclectic collection of someone whose interests led him in genuine exploration. The ambience of the room was used by the merchant as a frame to his portrait: the richness of the carpet and woods, the golden lamplight, the hints at his intelligence and education. Here was not a common clerk who had risen to prosperity, suggested this library; its owner was a well-to-do man born to his station. Matthew rather suspected the room lied.

Decker stopped and faced Matthew. He swirled the brandy in his glass and looked somber. "I must tell you first that, although I'm not opposed to annexation, I don't believe its time has come. The United States is too reluctant to antagonize

Britain and France, and the American public too unwilling to accept dark-skinned natives as full citizens."

This expression of opinion was not the surprise to Matthew that Decker had apparently imagined it would be. Matthew raised his brows. "Has revolution been your goal all along?"

"I have always considered it a possibility." Decker rocked back on his heels. "One of several. Why not face the facts? The Hawaiians are dying. We'll soon outnumber them and dilute their race through interbreeding. The islands are too strategically important for us to allow sentimentality to influence their future. Seized in a strong hand and ruled with common sense, the Sandwich Islands can have a golden future! But my vision of that future means I must think not only about the transitional stage, but about setting up a new government. That will require men of your ability."

Matthew opened his mouth to speak, but Decker lifted one hand. "Wait. Hear me out." He paced for a moment, stopped again. "You see, I am well aware that even some members of the Committee of Thirteen have not the wisdom or leadership to be ministers of government. Dr. Lathrop is a good physician; I'm inclined to think he ought to stick to his profession. Mr. Blair is a lawyer, but I fear not a good one. He hopes for a republic in the belief that it will be a stage for him to star upon, but I believe he would find himself unable even to produce a decent monologue. Dr. Newcomb is far too excitable. And thus it goes. Too many white men are here because they were failures wherever they came from. You are an exception."

"You don't know me well," Matthew said.

Decker gave a small, satisfied smile. "But I'm impressed by what I do know of you. Your medical knowledge and skill are superior. You are blunt-speaking, but cautious. You proceeded intelligently in your campaign against Edward Landre, but for the one slip, which I think may be excused. He had a way of exciting passions."

"I understand that Landre flirted with annexation."

Decker went still for a moment. "You're one of the few to know that."

"But you knew as well," Matthew observed.

His host contemplated him dispassionately. Matthew could all but see the wheels turning as Decker wondered what he knew. "Yes," the other man said at last. "I was his contact. He could have been a great help to us had he lived."

"In what way?"

Decker gave a half laugh and tossed down a deep swallow of brandy. "I suppose it's obvious enough that he passed on the subjects of discussion in cabinet meetings. I like to be well informed. He understood that."

"Did he intend to come out publicly on your side?"

"I'd promised him a place in the new government. I believe he was able. But we'd talked only a few times, so who knows what would have come of it? Ah, well." He shrugged. "We're on the brink of success now. Shall we drink to it?"

"Why not?" Matthew said easily. He hadn't learned a great deal, but he would, if he earned Charles Decker's trust. That might not be possible, for Matthew wasn't willing to get too deep into their schemes, but it might be enough to flirt with the idea of joining them. Who knows—they might persuade him, or he might in the end betray them to Kamehameha III's government.

Apparently he had time, like it or not. He would have to see a murderer step into the gallows house before he would be a free man again. But he wouldn't go, in any case; not until Anne Cartwright came with him.

"To success," he said, lifting his glass, and swallowed.

It was true. Dr. Gerrit Judd was out. On September 5, the king reappointed every minister except Judd. The portfolio of minister of finance was offered to the former United States consul, Elisha H. Allen.

In front of the Honolulu courthouse, the Committee of Thirteen gathered to orchestrate a celebration. Matthew stood in the crowd and watched Dr. Newcomb preside as Lathrop, J. D. Blair, and the dentist, John Mott Smith, among others, presented resolutions trumpeting the end of the "malignant tyranny" of Judd. The "delightful influences of liberty, free conscience, and independent action" had triumphed, they declared. Smiling, Charles Decker hovered in the background.

Two evenings later, Matthew called on Anne at the home of the missionaries. An uneasy group had gathered—or, perhaps, huddled together—in defense against outside events. Guns and cannons exploded throughout the town, and torches turned the sky orange.

Mrs. Taft clutched her shawl and gazed with frightened eyes out the window. "It reminds me of the night the sailors rioted and burned the police station."

Others moved to reassure her. No one noticed when Matthew and Anne slipped out.

"I must see for myself," she said fiercely, and he acceded to her wishes.

They didn't have to walk far. The torchlight parade had made its way through the town to the palace, where a huge crowd gathered under banners to listen to orators. Guns and fireworks went off all around the crowd, but most in it were too far on the road to drunkenness to fear for their safety.

"The new cabinet has called for an immediate investigation of the treasury accounts!" Blair told the masses. "We shall soon discover how mad and self-serving was the system set up by the tyrant overthrown this week by the will of the people!"

"Self-serving?" Anne said bitterly. "Do you know that years ago a chief offered Dr. Judd the whole of the Manoa Valley? If he had accepted, he would be a wealthy man, but his principles led him to refuse. Why would he have done that, if all he wanted was to feather his own nest, as these . . . these fools would have us believe?"

Her fingers bit into his arm. He laid his free hand over hers. "I think that perhaps it is not *what* Dr. Judd has done that brought his downfall, but how he did it. He can console himself that he has survived a long career and done a great deal of good."

He felt her sigh. "Shall we go?"

King Street was deserted beyond the parade route. Anne walked quickly and in silence so that he had to hasten to stay with her. Behind them, the shouting voices and pop of gunfire became muffled. King intersected with Merchant, and then they turned down Mission Lane and into the gate. The small golden squares of windows from the tall, plain house scarcely penetrated the darkness. The temptation to take advantage of the opportunity she'd given him was irresistible.

In the dark shadow of a tree, Matthew stopped Anne. He couldn't see her face, but he felt her reluctance. "Don't be afraid," he whispered and bent his head without giving her time to think. His lips found her cheek. Her quickened breath led him to her mouth. For a moment she stood marble still and unresponsive beneath his touch, but just before he despaired and let her go, her mouth began to soften, her body to lean toward him.

Matthew fought the rush of passion, kept the kiss gentle and undemanding. His hand still covered hers on his arm; although his fingers tightened, he made no effort to take her into his arms. She was like a bird, tempted onto his fingers, but trembling with fright. She would fly away if he tried to trap her.

He ended the kiss before she could. He felt her staring up at him in the darkness, heard the long breath she drew in.

"Unfair," she accused.

"Why not repeat a pleasant experience?" he asked lightly.

"You don't believe me, do you?"

"That you won't change your mind?" She said nothing. "I don't want to believe you," he said. "Will you be angry if I try to persuade you to alter your decision?"

"I suppose"—still she sounded breathless—"that it depends on your methods."

"And was this one so repugnant?"

"No." Yet she was unhappy. "No, of course not." Now she was trying to persuade herself.

"Shall we go in?"

"*I'll* go in. Perhaps this would be a good time for you to say good night, Dr. Cabe."

"I'm being sent away," he said with the first real amusement he had felt in days. The fact that she felt it necessary to flee from him seemed a hopeful sign to Matthew. Or was he indulging in wishful thinking, and in truth she was frightened?

"Yes," she said firmly.

"Then may I claim a good night kiss?"

"Incorrigible!" She actually laughed. "You're a determined man, aren't you?"

"Couldn't you have guessed as much?"

"You wouldn't have come to Hawaii if you weren't. What you must bear in mind, Dr. Cabe, is that I, too, left my home behind and sailed halfway around the world. Unlike you, *I* am determined enough to stay."

"I have not left yet," he said. He lifted her hand to his mouth and kissed it. "Good night, Mrs. Cartwright."

"Good night, Dr. Cabe." He loved the soft, flustered sound of her voice and the breeze she created when she whirled and hurried away. He waited until he saw her pass inside the lighted doorway, then began his long stroll back to the hotel.

He was well satisfied with his evening, although less and less liking Charles Decker's brand of "success."

Seventeen

Napua awakened. The instant of wondering where she was passed quickly, and when she opened her eyes she saw what she expected to see: the small bare interior of Henry Turner's house above Hana. The furniture that hadn't been built-in was gone; probably when he left the fields to the weeds, people thought he wasn't coming back and took everything that might be useful. But yesterday she and the *haole* had cleaned, so that the mouse nests and the dust were gone. The missionary's wife had promised to bring them some chairs and a table, although Napua thought they wouldn't come free; she would want to know whether they lived in sin, and she would expect them to come to church on Sunday.

Napua eased away from her sleeping son. Slipping out of her bed, she saw that Henry Turner's place on the floor was deserted, his blankets thrown carelessly aside. On silent feet, she went to the door.

She expected to find him on the porch, stretching as he watched the sun rise. Instead he stood near the corner of the house, head thrown back and shoulders held stiffly, looking toward the deserted building that had housed his mill. Iron tracks led from it, up the slope through the grass and the cane grown wild. Trolleys must have carried the harvested cane to the mill. He'd told her, gruffly, that the mill had been disassembled and the machinery sold. His lease had expired. With one great sweep of wind, all was gone, lost to him.

His face showed that he was remembering, perhaps seeing the fields not as they were now but as they'd been, waving with ripening sugarcane, stripped of dead leaves, well weeded. Perhaps when he closed his eyes he saw the giant rollers turning in the mill, squeezing the sweet liquid from the cane.

He never knew she was there. His look of longing made her heart ache, and she turned away. Did it hurt more, she wondered, to see the land unused, or would it have been worse if the plantation had been green and prosperous under someone else's ownership?

Napua went silently back inside and stirred up the fire in the iron cookstove.

At breakfast she suggested they climb Ka'uiki, the odd steep hill guarding the bay. Not only would the view be magnificent, but it was the home of many legends.

Henry Turner began shaking his head before she finished. He had done his part cleaning but otherwise had kept to himself the past two days, since they arrived in Hana and he looked over the grass-choked land that had made up his sugar plantation.

"Please come," Napua said softly, and Kuokoa turned pleading dark eyes on the *haole*.

Perhaps because of her son's silent plea, he growled, "Why not? I have nothing else to do."

She let pass the implied insult; she had just seen his pain.

In midmorning, they set off. As they walked, the breeze stirred her long black hair. She gazed dreamily down the long slope of golden grass to the bay and Ka'uiki above it.

"Did you know," Napua began in her storytelling voice,

"that near here is where the Hawaiian Islands were born?"

Kuokoa took her hand. "Why here, Mama?"

"Maui himself baited a magic fishhook with feathers from 'alae, the mudhen that brought fire to the people. He and his three brothers paddled to a certain place in the ocean, and then Maui let the hook fall into the water. When it became stuck to the vast, unbroken bottom of the sea, Maui ordered his brothers to paddle as hard as they could. 'Don't look back!' he told them.

"But though his mother had warned him against it, he had taken into his canoe a harmless-looking gourd to bail with. Just as the land emerged from the sea at the end of the fishing line, a beautiful woman stepped out of the gourd and seated herself behind the brothers. One brother became so curious, he turned to see her, and because he had looked, the land shattered into pieces.

"Maui's magic fishhook was called *Manai-ka-lani*, 'Made Fast to the Heavens.' At night, the line can still be seen as a trail of stars that follows the path of the sun."

Kuokoa frowned. "Why didn't he listen to his mother?"

How young he was! Napua hid her smile and said gravely, "He was foolish enough to set aside the teachings of a parent."

Her son's mind, quick as a *kihikihi* among the coral, had already darted to the next thought. "If there were no islands, where did Maui launch his canoe from?"

"Perhaps Tahiti," Napua suggested.

He nodded, satisfied, and tugged at her hand. "Let's go. Can we? I want to see where Maui pushed up the sky."

From behind her, Henry Turner said, "You know that he is supposed to have created Ka'uiki itself, as well."

Napua gave him a warm smile over her shoulder. "This land is like a quilt he stitched. You can feel him when you run your fingers over it. Perhaps his bones are even hidden here somewhere."

"What story?" Kuokoa demanded, predictably.

"I'll tell you when we're on top of the hill," Napua said firmly. "Aren't you the one who is ready to go?"

He tugged away and, laughing, ran down the gentle slope toward the church spire and cluster of rooftops that made up Hana. Napua let him go. He would come to no harm here. Unlike Lahaina and Honolulu, where the whaling ships wintered, Hana was still small, a place where there were more ghosts of famous chiefs and gods than living people. Few *haole* had yet come here; most of the houses were still thatched.

They followed a trail that headed directly down the slope to the sound end of the village, soon catching up with Kuokoa, who had detoured to stalk a pair of nene, the black-headed geese that sometimes sounded like cows out in the grass.

Napua was surprised when Kuokoa dropped back to walk beside the *haole*. Her son was quiet for as long as he could bear it. At last she heard him ask shyly, "Do you surf?"

"I don't swim well enough," Henry answered. "Wish I did. You?"

"The boards are too heavy. I will when I'm older," Kuokoa answered confidently.

They walked in silence for a distance. Amused, Napua waited for more words to burst forth. She often teased her son by telling him that he was a crow, a loud-voiced bird. He was happiest when talking.

He didn't disappoint her. "Look!" he said. "Why do the waves stop so far out?"

Henry gave a bark of laughter. "There's a story to explain it, of course."

"Tell me," her son begged, enthralled.

She almost told him not to bother Mr. Turner, but held her tongue. He had laughed, hadn't he? He needed help coming out of his shell. Perhaps Kuokoa would tug just enough. It surprised her that this *haole* had listened to the Hawaiian tales. But perhaps she shouldn't be. He had learned the language, too, when few *haole* but for missionaries bothered.

"The way I heard it, a chief from Tahiti wanted to go surfing, but the waves hereabout weren't big enough for him. He marched off to a *heiau* and asked the gods for something a little more spectacular. Well, they obliged, and he swam out with his surfboard."

"Did he fall off?" Kuokoa asked eagerly. Napua sneaked a glance back to see that he had trustingly taken Henry Turner's hand. The *haole* had an odd look on his face, as though he'd tried his first bite of poi and wasn't sure he liked it. But he didn't pull away, and he continued with his story as though telling it were an everyday event.

"Now, son, legends aren't usually told about chiefs who do things as unheroic as fall off their surfboards. No, in this case two village girls had fallen madly in love with him. Guess they were having some kind of beauty contest, because they dropped their drawers—actually, their *pa'u*—until they stood buck naked, there on the beach. When that chief caught sight of them, he stopped dead right where he was, which happened to be on top of his board riding a wave in. The wave stopped with him. To this day, that's as far as the surf goes."

Her son giggled, although he probably had understood only partially. She had made sure he learned English to please his father, but she could tell he was forgetting it already, since his lessons had been in Hawaiian and she used their own language with him. Usually, like today, her son and the *haole* used his own language.

Ka'uiki Hill was famous as a fortified refuge during the many wars fought over Hana. If Napua had imagined a stroll up it, she'd been foolish. The trail scrabbled along the edge of steep cliffs through bunch grass and exposed red lava. Dr. Judd insisted that, despite the romantic story about Ka'uiki's creation, it was an ancient cinder cone, like Punchbowl and Diamond Head. If so, Pele was probably angry that someone else had stolen the credit!

On top, it seemed the world opened at their feet. The early morning rain—*noenoe uakea o Hana*, the white rain of Hana—had already come and gone even before they'd risen that morning. But other clouds had gathered, shrouded Haleakala, the volcano, and cast shadows over the upper slopes and out on the sea. Through an opening in the cloud cover, the sun bathed the town and bay in golden light.

Napua turned slowly, looking down sea-battered cliffs to white waves shattering on rocks far below. On most sides, it would be impossible to scale the hill. She could see why the ancients had felt safe here even when under attack. Their greatest danger had been having their supply of fresh water cut off.

She wished that this were a day when the *akule* were running. What a thing it would be to see from such a height the great schools of mullet entering the harbor! But three days ago, she and Kuokoa and Henry Turner had just missed the *hukilau*, the day of fishing that involved the whole village. It happened almost weekly, Henry said. Kuokoa would enjoy wading into the water and helping haul in the nets in exchange for a share of the catch.

Signs of old fortifications could be seen everywhere, although it had been a hundred years since Ka'uiki had been used for anything but a watchtower. From here Captain Cook's white sails had been spotted. A whole fleet of canoes went out to meet him. Right here, off Ka'uiki, Kamehameha himself had boarded Cook's ship for the first time. And it was from here that a *kilo i'a*, a fish spotter, would signal the village when the *akule* next ran.

Of course, as they ate the guava and poi Napua had carried in a basket, Kuokoa insisted on the story of Ka'uiki's creation at Maui's hands.

The first part came easily, for it was about the love of a parent. Napua told how Maui had named his daughter Noenoe Ua Kea O Hana for the misty rains of Hana, often accompanied by rainbows. As the years passed, Noenoe grew into a beauty as magnificent as the sunlight meeting the raindrops over the bay. She loved the sea and swam as well as the dolphins that played there.

Each day on her way to the shore she passed a pool of clear water, never looking toward it, for she had been warned that it was inhabited by Menehune, the old race of tiny beings capable of mischief and cruelty. But one night she returned late, when the moon silvered the night, and in passing the pool, she heard laughter. She could not resist looking. Hundreds of Menehune danced and dove and played in the water.

A handsome youth suddenly appeared before her. He promised to help her, for she had broken the law of the Menehune by looking upon them.

Though she had never met him, she knew who the youth was. The Menehune had a foster son named Ka'uiki, who had come to them on the waves, a gift from Kanaloa, the sea god.

Here Napua found herself growing self-conscious. What did Henry Turner think of the old stories and the Hawaiian gods? He'd solemnly explained why the surf stopped short of the shore, but that was not quite the same as a love story about the daughter of a half-man, half-god. Did he believe in love? Would he keep silent for the child's sake, or would he mock her?

"Noenoe fell in love with Ka'uiki the moment she laid eyes upon him," Napua said, carefully looking only at her son and not at the *haole*, as though she were in as great a danger as Noenoe looking upon the Menehune. "Ka'uiki loved her as well. He led her safely away, and they began to meet each night. They would marry, they decided, and have children together.

"But they were discovered by Maui, who told his daughter their love could not be. 'Ka'uiki is *kapu*,' he said. 'He is of the sea, and to the sea he must return someday.'

"But he saw such pain in his daughter's eyes, Maui thought of a way that the lovers need not be separated. He changed Ka'uiki into a high hill. His beloved daughter, Maui changed into the misty, gentle rains for which she was named. To this day, Noenoe clings to Ka'uiki, caressing its high cliffs."

Napua waited apprehensively for the man who lounged on the grass, head propped on his hand, to say something. She should have known he wouldn't have a chance. Always, Kuokoa had to quibble.

"If Noenoe loves him so much," he said in dissatisfaction, "where is she now?"

Henry Turner gave another short, sharp laugh. "Even people who love each other need to be apart sometimes. Keeps 'em fresh."

"Ka'uiki doesn't look fresh," her annoying son pointed out. "I think he must be getting old."

"You can love even when the blossom withers," Napua said gently.

"*I* wouldn't want to be turned into rock because of a girl!" Kuokoa declared.

"Little boys always say that," Henry Turner told him. "But they change their tune when they grow up."

"*I* won't!"

"Look at it this way," the *haole* suggested. "If Ka'uiki hadn't loved Noenoe, his bones would be dried by now. Instead, legends are told about him."

Kuokoa scrunched up his small face. "I'd like legends told about me because I'm a great warrior. Not because of a girl."

Henry Turner's smiling eyes met Napua's. "Romance is wasted on him."

"You don't think it's silly?" she heard herself ask.

The smile was gone from his eyes, but they were still kind, as she remembered thinking they were the first time she met him. Sadness hid inside them, too.

"There's not much to live for," he said. "A man's land is one of those things." He didn't turn his head, but she knew that for an instant he saw not her, but rather the fields of rich green cane. "Love is about the only other."

"Yes." She spoke just above a whisper. "We Hawaiians say that love gives life within."

He grunted, and she didn't know if the sound was meant to be a laugh. "Maybe that's why I sometimes wonder if I'm dead and I just don't know it."

"You would know if you had let down your weariness."

He released a long sigh. "I've been too drunk to notice anything."

"Not too drunk to save my life."

"That's the only thing that gives me hope." He made that sound again, and this time she heard the despair in it. "Right now, ma'am, you're the fishline hauling me off the bottom."

"I have been worse things." She glanced around and alarm made her eyes widen. "Where is Kuokoa? Did you see him go?"

"No." In one move, the *haole* was on his feet. His voice changed. "There he is. I believe he's under siege, and we're the enemy."

She spotted her young son at the same moment. He crouched behind the rubble of old fortifications, peering out at them with bright dark eyes.

"Either that," Henry remarked, "or he's being chivalrous enough to give us some privacy."

"Privacy?" Her heart began to beat harder and her cheeks to warm. "Why would he think—?"

"Hell, maybe he likes me."

Or maybe, Napua thought, *Kuokoa has seen into my heart.* "I'm sorry," she faltered.

"Sorry?" Mouth twisted, he met her eyes. "Lady, I just wish your boy were right about what we both wanted."

Napua gaped at the *haole*. Did she dare assume from his words that he felt the embers of a hot fire stir inside when he looked upon her, as she did when she looked upon him?

First joy, then confusion, rose in her. Was he like Edward and Herr Bauer and most of the other *haole* men, who wanted a native woman only until they could find one of their own kind? But now was not the time to ask him any of the questions that crowded her mind. Already her son was scrambling over the tumbled-down wall and running toward them. She would wait until she was alone with the *haole*—with Henry.

In the meantime, she must think, and try to understand why she always wanted a foreign man and not a Hawaiian. That Mahaulu had looked at her as though he thought her beautiful, but she had felt nothing for him. Was she truly so confused about who and what she was? Were these stirrings for another *haole* something of which she should be ashamed?

Yes, it would not be a bad thing to take some time and think before she spoke to Henry.

Anne gently moved her hands over the swell of Makalika's abdomen. The young woman lay still on the heap of mats, her dark eyes fixed anxiously on Anne's face.

At last Anne sank back on her heels. "All seems to be well thus far. I can hear your baby's heartbeat through my stethoscope."

"His heart beats? Already?" She looked stunned.

"Oh, yes!" Anne smiled. "Quickly, like a bird's. He is no larger than a baby bird yet."

"He?"

"Or she."

Seemingly unembarrassed by her nakedness, Makalika rested her own hands over her pregnant belly. "Would it be better if on Sundays we went to the stone church? My husband, he chooses Our Lady of Peace not from piety, I think, but from resentment. Will the prayers of *na makua o ka pono* be stronger?"

"You are wise," Anne said. "I, too, believe Kaipoleimanu attends the Catholic church to defy the fathers of righteousness. But I also don't believe God would take this infant from you because you don't worship in the right church. When it is known that you are pregnant again, the missionaries, too, will pray for your health and the safe birth of your child."

Makalika's hand seized Anne's with surprising strength. Her dark eyes pleaded. "Would you ask Reverend Griggs to visit me? My husband might be angry, but right now he will deny me nothing."

"I'll ask." Anne squeezed her hand. "Continue to rest for another few weeks. Don't overeat." This last was a useless command; Makalika must weigh 250 pounds. She was not as large as some of the famous chiefesses, like Ka'ahumanu, King Kamehameha's third wife who became *kuhina nui*, the kingdom's premier. But by *haole* standards she was undeniably obese, if still graceful on those rare occasions when she was on her feet.

"My husband waits for you outside. If I say everything is well, he won't believe me. He has faith in you."

"I'll visit next week." Impulsively, Anne bent to kiss her soft cheek. "Don't worry."

"How can I help it?" Makalika asked softly.

Indeed, Kaipoleimanu paced outside the grass building, one of several set in the old way around a central courtyard. He might worship in the Catholic church, but this chief was a man proud of his own people's traditions and not anxious to grasp for all the *haole* offered.

"Makalika is doing well," Anne reassured him. "I believe we are past the most dangerous time."

"This is the longest she has gone."

"The baby's heart beats strongly."

His dark face convulsed, and she thought for a horrified moment that he might cry. But he stiffened and breathed deeply. In English he said, "I'm grateful that you're willing to attend my wife, Mrs. Cartwright."

"Why wouldn't I be?" she asked in surprise.

"I oppose annexation." His voice had no inflection, and he stared past her shoulder. "It must sometimes look as though I oppose your countrymen."

Don't you? she wanted to ask. But she knew she would do more good by gaining his gratitude than by challenging him. "Childbirth is the same for all women, whatever their nationality. We're all sisters."

He gave a jerky nod and at last, with seeming reluctance, his eyes met hers. "Napua. She is safe?"

"Yes."

"I would foster her son, if something happens to her."

"You're kind. She worries about him, since she has no family."

"I don't want to know where she is. It's better if no one knows."

Anne studied him in puzzlement. "Yes. I think that's true."

He held himself like a soldier at attention, stiffly, shoulders back. "If I can help . . ."

"Thank you."

He nodded and she knew herself dismissed. Obviously, Anne reflected on the way home, he had heard about the second attempt on Napua's life and her subsequent flight. Not surprising, since Constable Mahaulu was informed. Still, the conversation struck her as peculiar. Why had he made such a point of not asking where Napua was? Wouldn't it have been less awkward not to mention her at all, or simply to say, "Tell Napua she has only to call on me for help"?

Or, Anne thought wryly, were her suspicions becoming too convoluted? He couldn't possibly know she had considered him a possible murderer.

The truth was, she found it harder and harder to fit him into the role. Landre's murder was brutal and secretive, as were the attacks on Napua. Kaipoleimanu might, in Anne's estimation, be pigheaded, but he was usually open in his defiance of the missionary edicts. And when she considered his tenderness toward his wife and their unborn child, she found it difficult to imagine him attacking a woman, and one he had known well at that.

Yet, if not Kaipoleimanu and not the Reverend Griggs, who *had* killed Edward Landre? And why must Napua die, too? She had told everything she knew, and none of it had pointed at a logical suspect.

Very well. Either she knew something she hadn't guessed was a secret, or the murderer thought himself recognized, either in the act or earlier, when meeting furtively with Landre.

Chickens flapped across the road in front of her, followed by a grinning, naked boy whose scabbed pocks showed him to be one of the rare natives to survive the pestilence. Once they were out of the way, Anne snapped the reins to hurry her pony, who was dawdling along between the traces. He laid his ears back but otherwise ignored her. The heat and dust were stronger arguments than any she could offer. Anne scarcely noticed, her thoughts moving on.

No, meeting together was hardly a crime. Unless they shouldn't know each other. A rabid annexationist, for example? No, that still made no sense. Landre might have wanted to hide that connection, but why would the annexationist be embarrassed by it? And to the point of murder? Absurd!

Well, perhaps an argument. Anne frowned. Napua had mentioned overhearing one, but hadn't known who the other man was.

Anne wished she could discuss her reasoning with Matthew, but she hadn't seen him in a week, not since that second kiss. They had resumed their former lives, and she now felt the loneliness of hers. Had she been mad to turn down his offer of marriage? Mightn't it have been worth suffering the torment of the marriage bed to have his companionship and children of her own? His kisses even made her wonder if the marriage bed had to bring nothing but torment. It was a duty few women seemed to welcome, but perhaps, if the man was gentle, it needn't be so terrible.

By the time she arrived back at the missionary compound, dusk was settling with the startling suddenness she had never quite become used to. Anne unhitched the pony from the cart and led him into the stable. In the act of unbuckling the harness, she leaned her head against the pony's warm, steaming back. Despair squeezed her chest. If only Dr. Matthew Cabe had never come into her life! She'd been happy. Well, content, anyway, she amended, determined to be ruthlessly honest with herself. Oh, why had he made her want what she'd long ago resigned herself to not having?

She slipped unseen into her tiny cupboard of a bedroom at the back of the house. There she regained her composure as she gave herself a sponge bath and rebraided her hair. Peering into the small, wavery mirror, she saw no trace of her inner turmoil. No, the woman who looked calmly back at her was plain, well groomed, and serene. Contented with her life, Anne thought ironically.

Her serenity suffered a painful jolt when she entered the dining room to find that, along with a visiting ship's captain, Dr. Cabe was a dinner guest. He smiled at her with such warmth, her heart contracted as though it sought to become less vulnerable.

Amid the flurry of introductions and greetings, only a slight breathlessness sounded in her voice. "Dr. Cabe. How pleasant to see you."

He lowered his voice. "I hoped you wouldn't be out this evening. We haven't spoken in some time."

Would he give her a chance to reconsider? Did she dare? But his presence renewed her fear. It was easier to imagine enduring the sexual act when she wasn't within two feet of the man who would be forcing his way into her body. The breadth of his shoulders and the strength of his outstretched hand brought her a waking vision: he was rearing over her in the darkness, roughly separating her legs, his hands on her breasts. Pain would stab her, and afterward there would be burning inside her, where he'd been. No! She couldn't do it. Night after night! No.

She shook her head hard. "I . . . I'm sorry."

He raised a brow. "What?"

Her eyes widened and hot color swept over her cheeks. Oh, Lord, she'd spoken as though he had asked again and she were refusing! What must he think?

"I . . . that is . . . I'm sorry, I thought you'd said something?"

Creases formed between his brows. "No. Mrs. Cartwright, will you walk with me after dinner?"

"Have you news?" she asked eagerly.

"I'm afraid not."

"Then . . ." Anne took a deep breath. "I must plead weariness. Perhaps another time." Deliberately she turned away.

Captain Ellsworth was delighted to make her acquaintance. He talked endlessly of his wife, home in New Bedford, and the pleasure of conversing with a genteel white woman who reminded him of his Emily. Having heard so much about Mrs. Ellsworth, Anne wasn't sure she ought to feel flattered, but he gave her an excuse to ignore Dr. Cabe, who was forced to make conversation with Mrs. Taft on his other side.

Since the men neither smoked nor drank liquor, they followed the ladies into the parlor after dinner. Anne's intention of making her excuses was forgotten when Captain Ellsworth settled himself on the sofa and remarked, "I dined last night with General Miller and Mr. Wyllie. Both are convinced that the most earnest efforts have failed to make the natives a truly moral and Christian people. General Miller insists that, though they wear long faces on Sunday, in fact the *kanaka* have no more respect for honesty, chastity, and truth than they ever did."

Hotly, Anne said, "I wonder what General Miller really knows of the Hawaiians. Other than some native servants and his dealings with the king, the general has managed to insulate himself quite well from the Hawaiian population."

"What evidence did he offer for his opinions?" the Reverend Taft demanded. The pugnacity sat oddly on a round face designed to match his sweet temper. At the moment, even the crown of his balding head was flushed red.

Captain Ellsworth crossed his legs and gazed about with faint surprise, as though he hadn't realized how inflammatory his comment would be in this company. "He swears he knows a native deacon who gave up his own daughter to prostitution."

"Even if the story is true," Anne said, "it is unlikely to be as simple as it sounds. Perhaps he consented to give her to a man he considered decent to save her from less savory hands. And it's an unfortunate fact that white men still seem to the Hawaiians to have godlike properties. I believe the women hope to absorb *mana*"—she glanced at the captain—"that is, divine strength, from the white men. They flock to them rather than to men of their own race because our superior technology has convinced them that we're greater beings, as they always believed their *alii* were favored over the commoners."

"Which might explain a lack of chastity." The captain's tone suggested he found the explanation less than compelling. "But do you find the natives possess any kind of conscience in regard to lying and stealing?"

To her surprise, Matthew said, "I have the impression they lie and steal no more often than do the foreign residents. You must admit that, excepting the missionaries and some principled men"—he inclined his head, as though willing to extend his description to the present company—"the *haole* in Honolulu set a poor example."

"But the Hawaiians are taught the moral virtues," Captain Ellsworth insisted, "and are fortunate enough to have men like Reverend Taft to provide a living example. Yet however much they might pretend to abhor dancing or a glass of wine, still the *kanaka* think nothing of cheating or committing adultery. Even Mr. Wyllie, who has given his life to these people, was forced to reluctantly agree that their hearts remain corrupt."

Anne ground her teeth. After a hasty glance at her, Mrs. Taft intervened. Her gentle answer kept the conversation from degenerating into one unsuitable to a social occasion. And what was the use, anyway? Captain Ellsworth was expressing common sentiments. Like most of his kind, he didn't want to see the dark-skinned natives as men and women no different from his neighbors in New Bedford.

Anne waited for a pause, then rose to her feet. "If you'll excuse me, I believe I'll retire."

Matthew rose, too, lazily unfolding himself. "Ah, but Mrs. Cartwright, you promised to take a stroll with me. I was greatly looking forward to it."

Anne looked at him with astonishment. He half smiled, sure of her response. He might have won if his eyes had begged her pardon, but that smirk, his confidence, infuriated her.

"Then I must apologize," she said coolly. "I'm afraid I don't recall that particular promise, and I'm very tired." She gave a general, vague smile. "Captain Ellsworth, I hope you soon have a chance to return to Mrs. Ellsworth. Good night, everyone."

Although she didn't look at Matthew again, she felt the waves of frustration radiating from him. But what could he say? With the others, he murmured, "Good night."

Past the kitchen, hers was the only bedroom down the long, narrow hall. On one side were two storerooms; the back door led to the yard and stable. This part of the house was an after-thought, an addition when the mission outgrew the original frame house and when several families had made their home here. Now only the Tafts were in residence, and their two sons had both sailed home to New England to complete their educations.

Anne hadn't lied; she was tired. In her bedroom, she went straight to her bureau and began pulling pins from the knot at her nape. She unplaited the braid and, with a sigh of relief, plunged her fingers into her hair to massage her scalp.

At the knock on her door, she nearly groaned. Had Reverend Taft sent his wife to chide her for being uncivil to their guests? But she was only another guest and could do nothing but call, "Come in."

The door swung inward, and Matthew Cabe filled the opening. His swift gaze took in the room, lit by candlelight: bare wood floor, unpapered walls, a narrow rope bed. A child's bedroom, or a nun's cell. But it was as near to hers as she had, which fueled her outrage. "What do you want?"

His blue eyes pinned her. "Why did you turn me down?"

"I told you why I wouldn't marry—"

He made an impatient gesture. "Why wouldn't you walk with me? Did I frighten you so much the last time?"

Back straight and head high, she said, "Is it impossible to believe that I really was tired? You said you had no news."

His mouth compressed. "And you didn't want to encourage me to think you might change your mind."

She said nothing. He took a step toward her. His voice roughened. "You're as beautiful as I remembered you with your hair down."

Anne sucked in a breath. Some pleasurable sensation quivered in her belly. He truly thought her beautiful?

"You should leave," she said shakily.

"You agreed that the kiss wasn't so bad."

She couldn't say, *A kiss is only the beginning. It's the rest that frightens me.*

"You can't accept my answer?"

"No!" Raw emotion darkened his eyes. "Blast it, why won't you give me a chance? Not all men are the bastards your husband was!"

Near to tears, Anne fought to control the tremble of her mouth. "How can any woman trust a man?"

She regretted the words the moment she spoke them. Seeing Matthew Cabe's open shock, she squeezed her fingers together. "I shouldn't have said that. I'm sorry. Please . . . please leave."

His chest rose and fell, and he looked away from her for a moment. When he faced her again, his mouth had thinned. "Apparently we were not the friends I thought us. But, before I go, I'd like to understand your bitterness."

Why not once be honest? He had treated her with unusual respect, and deserved as much. Anne took a deep breath and straightened her shoulders. "Very well." She heard herself as though from a distance. "My father spoke most fluently with the back of his hand. He never gave me an affectionate word in his life. I don't believe he ever gave my mother one. Women are like . . . sows or milk cows. Useful, but hardly the object of tenderness. I know that he beat her, though he did it behind closed door. I know, too, that she found her . . . marital duties unpleasant. My mother died after a long illness when I was fifteen. I believe she was happy to go. He was impatient even while she was sick. He was certain that, if she had enough fortitude, she could rise from her bed and take over the household again!

"If I committed any minor transgression, he considered that I'd earned a blow. But that wasn't the worst part. He'd punish me by not speaking to me for days or even weeks. Our farm was isolated. Most people don't understand what it is to feel alone. I married the first man who asked me because I wanted to escape my father. Mr. Cartwright offered a distinct advantage: he was taking me so far from home, I would never have to see Father again. Mr. Cartwright wore a courteous mask; I thought him kind, at least. I knew the missionary board had suggested he marry, which explained the hasty courtship. I didn't know they had required him to take a wife. He despised women. Because I'm a woman, my husband called me a whore and treated me like one."

"But other men—"

"Which ones?" She felt icy, gripped by a cold certainty that she was driving him away, no longer sure that was what she wanted to do but committed to painful honesty. "The Reverend Griggs? His wife loved Napua like a daughter, but she can't offer help or even a sympathetic word. She's afraid to defy her husband, you see. Reverend Taft? Mrs. Taft mourns every day for her sons, but her husband insisted they be sent back to New England to school, and so they went. She won't see them for years, if ever again. When I deliver babies, I often hear tales from women who fear their husbands. If not his advances, I'm told, she lives in dread of his commands. Women suffer much at the hands of men. And you wonder at my bitterness."

Expression bleak, Matthew said, "I cannot deny there's truth in what you say. But happy marriages exist; many men love their wives and treat them with affection and esteem. You have closed your eyes to such relationships."

"I think they must be rare."

"Perhaps," he admitted. "But you know me well. Do you really believe I'll turn into an ogre only because I have become your legal master?"

"No." Of course he was right. "I've never thought that. But I was sadly mistaken in the man I chose to marry. How can I trust my judgment?"

"You have faith in God, although He has not revealed Himself to you."

"And so I should have faith in you?" Her half-laugh turned into something nearer a sob. "Oh, I wish I could!"

Matthew took a step toward her. "Is it only the consummation of the marriage you fear?"

She could no longer meet his eyes, which searched hers so intensely she imagined he saw even her heart and mind. Cheeks flushed, she stared down at the planked floor. Voice nearly inaudible, she confessed, "I suppose that's my greatest fear."

"Then what if we put it to the test? What if we consummate our relationship before we are married? That way you'll know if you can bear it or not. You won't be trapped. You risk only one fleeting experience. It can be no worse than what you've already lived through."

Shock brought her gaze flying to his. "You are suggesting—"

"Yes." He faced her, looking grim rather than amorous. "It is ungentlemanly of me, but I can think of no other solution. Unlike you, I have faith that I can prove we are meant to be together. Rather than lose you altogether, I am willing to wager that you will not only find the act nothing to be feared, but actually pleasant. You're a courageous woman, Anne. Be brave now."

Her candles were burning down, the shadows in the corners growing. The room seemed to have shrunk. Matthew dominated it with his sheer bulk and vitality. Despite herself, she stole a glance at her narrow, hard bed. Did he actually intend—? Now? Here?

"Why not?" he challenged. "I said good night and departed, returning unseen through the back door. Are we likely to be interrupted?"

Interrupted. Oh, God. He did mean it. "You must be mad! If we were discovered, I'd lose my home, my friends—"

"*Are* we likely to be discovered?"

"Any risk is too great!"

"Is it?" His voice was now low and husky. "You're a courageous woman, Anne Cartwright. Is this risk so much greater than others you've taken?"

Was it? In truth, the only times she could recall either of the Tafts knocking on her bedroom door was when she was being summoned to attend a childbirth.

Shock brought a small gasp to her lips. She couldn't possibly be thinking of agreeing, could she? Of cooperating in her own ravishment?

"You ask too much," she whispered.

"Do I?" Another step and he stood just in front of her. "Is it so much, considering what we have to gain?"

"What if . . ." Oh, she sounded pathetic! "What if you want me only for tonight?"

His hands framed her face, lifted her chin so that she couldn't evade his gaze. Roughly he asked, "Do you believe that?"

"No—" Suddenly she couldn't breathe. His mouth was so close, his thumbs tracing patterns on the tender skin of her throat. Was she afraid?

But she couldn't think, either. Sensations washed over her, feelings she didn't understand. She actually wanted—wanted!—him to kiss her.

His mouth descended, brushed hers, teased, nibbled. She was both shocked and excited to feel his teeth nip her lip. Anne gripped his shoulders and whimpered. This must be what other women felt, what brought a flush to their cheeks when young men lured them into a private drive after church or a breath of fresh air during the Sewing Society. She'd never been pretty enough to tempt a man. Never been kissed, except for the painful way John Cartwright had ground his mouth against hers. That was nothing like this, nothing like—

Matthew's tongue slid into her mouth, stroked hers, came back to do it again. She gasped and stiffened. In a voice oddly thickened, he whispered, "This is part of it. Be brave."

Brave? Her head swam. Already he was kissing her again, his tongue against hers, and it seemed she liked it, for heat spread through her veins like warm honey, thick and slow and sweet. Anne knew with one part of her mind that he was unbuttoning her gown. Cool evening air touched her shoulders, and she lifted heavy eyelids to find that he was cupping her breasts through her shift.

"Beautiful," he murmured huskily. "Damnation, why do women wear so much?"

"To keep things like this from happening." Her voice sounded no more natural than did his.

"How the devil do you get this corset off?"

"It unlaces." As if in a dream, she turned her back to show him. Fingers fumbling at the knot, he moved his open mouth hotly against her bowed neck. Anne heard herself make a sound in her throat like a cat's purr. She stretched, arched a body that ached for something more—

A knock sounded loud on the door. Now terror lanced through her, but too late, for the door was swinging inward.

"I saw the light and knew you were still awake—" Mary Taft's breath left her in a hiss. In that terrible moment, Anne saw the wanton picture she must make: the bodice of her gown around her waist, shift pushed from one white shoulder and breast, a man lifting his mouth from her neck.

Anne couldn't seem to move. The Reverend Taft's wife lifted her candle as though she couldn't believe her eyes. Her voice sliced the silence. "Those who live in this house are committed to serving the Lord, not . . . not fornicating! How dare you?"

Eighteen

The long walnut table, set with fine china and silver, shimmered with reflected light from the crystal chandelier. Masculine laughter muted the ladies' murmured conversation as servants brought in chilled tomato soup. Only Matthew hadn't taken his seat.

"I have an announcement," he said, picking up a wineglass and waiting for everyone's attention. When he had it, he smiled at Anne. "Mrs. Cartwright has agreed to marry me."

The dinner party was taking place at the Deckers' a week after that dreadful night. Now that Anne was Matthew's affianced wife, the Tafts had deemed it suitable for her to accompany him to such social occasions. The other guests this evening were Drs. Newcomb and Lathrop and a Mr. Freeman and his wife.

Nettie jumped to her feet in a rustle of silk and hurried around the table to hug Anne. "Oh, how wonderful! I know you'll be as blissfully happy as I am."

"A toast to the happy couple!" Charles Decker declared, rising, too. Wine was drunk, congratulations tendered and received. Anne kept up a smiling front; she only hoped Matthew didn't realize how artificial her manner was.

That horrible evening when they were discovered, he had spoken up immediately to the Reverend Taft's wife, ironically using the same words as tonight. "Mrs. Cartwright has agreed to marry me. I'm the most fortunate of men. I only hope she'll forgive me for letting my . . . impatience sweep us away. Blame me, not Anne. Despite her brief marriage, I fear she's too innocent to know what was happening."

Her blushes as she covered herself must have given credence to his excuse. Neither blushes nor excuse was sufficient to exonerate her in the eyes of a missionary or his wife.

Anne was saved only because Matthew had agreed to marry her. The Tafts hadn't asked her to leave, although she was no longer treated as the member of the family she'd always felt herself to be. A coolness had entered their manner, a hint of censure. She'd violated their trust unforgivably.

Of course, she was trapped. If she refused to marry Matthew, she'd be ostracized by the pious portion of the foreign community. She would have opened herself to indecent offers from men who now doffed their hats for her. She had Hawaiian friends who would have taken her in, but for how long? Few were in a position to employ her. The panicky thoughts had stumbled over each other, becoming tangled, but no amount of unknotting would change the truth: she must marry Matthew Cabe.

In the days since, her emotions had pitched as wildly as a ship in a vicious squall. Sometimes she was nearly resigned to her future, numb, if not quite at peace; other times she bitterly blamed him, certain he'd known precisely what would happen that night; and other times yet, she despised herself, convinced that on some level she must have *wanted* matters to be taken out of her hands. Did she long to marry him but hadn't the courage to admit it? Well, at best she'd been foolish. She deserved her fate as his wife, whatever that was to be.

She'd been unable to express any of her feelings to him. When Matthew called on her the next morning and they were permitted a private meeting in the parlor, he had come straight to her and taken her hands.

"I'm sorry. My dear, I'm so sorry."

Unsmiling, she'd faced him. "Yes. I'm sure you are."

His eyes searched hers. "You know I want to marry you."

"It would seem you're to have your wish." Her voice trembled and she took a deep breath. "I can think of no way out. If you're certain . . . ?"

"I'm certain," Matthew said frowning. "But you—are you wishing me to Hades? I don't like the idea of forcing you to the altar."

Oh, how she tried to keep the acid from her voice. "Have you any better ideas?"

"No. Damnation." His hands curled into fists at his side. "I swear I'll be gentle! You have nothing to fear from me. Say that you believe me."

Around the lump in her throat, Anne said, "I believe you wouldn't deliberately hurt me."

He uttered a profanity that made her stare. "Would you prefer I didn't touch you? That we deferred the wedding night?" Hope blossomed in her chest, but she said stiffly, "I can't ask that of you. It's my fault as much as yours that we're in this position. In any case," she lowered her gaze, "I do look forward to having children."

"I'm glad you look forward to something I can offer." His dry tone brought her gaze back to his. A muscle in his cheek jerked. "Anne—" He cleared his throat. "You know the possibility still exists that I'll be arrested again for Landre's murder, even hang for it."

Alarm poked its way through her self-absorption. "No—"

"Yes." His mouth had a grim set. "Under normal circumstances, I wouldn't have asked a woman to marry me when my own future was so uncertain. But I flatter myself that you'd be better off as my widow than you are now. I'll leave you reasonably well provided for. You can have a home of your own, at least. My greatest fear is that you might become pregnant—" He drew in a ragged breath. "I don't like to think of you raising a child alone. Perhaps it would be just as well if we did postpone intimacies that might lead to such an end."

She saw how rigidly he held himself. Did he dread her eager agreement? Well, then, she would relieve him.

"No." She pressed her lips together. "If . . . if I were to lose you, I wouldn't remarry. A son or daughter would be the greatest legacy I could hope for." There—she had thought it again— if she were to *lose* him— Did she truly feel as if her life would be poorer without him?

He stood completely still for a moment. At last he gave a jerky nod. "Then so be it. Mrs. Cartwright," he bowed, "will you do me the honor of becoming my wife?"

"Yes, thank you," she said, as prim as he had sounded formal. And—dear heaven!—she had been nearly glad to say it.

But that same formality had shaped their relationship since, despite all that had come before. Somehow they'd become strangers. They had attended several functions together, and Matthew was invariably courteous. He seldom left her side, and he at least pretended to convincing warmth for the benefit of others. But he hadn't kissed her again, and in those rare moments completely alone, both remained silent.

Now, at the Deckers', Anne was relieved when talk turned from her engagement to recent events. Her relief was short-lived, however, for Mr. Freeman, having imbibed several glasses of wine, said loudly, "So being jailed for Landre's murder changed your mind about affairs here, eh, Doctor? No wonder you've pulled up a chair to this table rather than King Judd's."

Anne must have stirred, because Matthew's large hand suddenly gripped her thigh in silent warning.

His voice had an edge. "Although I'm not a man to hold grudges, I must confess that in this case I may make an exception."

Freeman shook his balding head in disgust. "Ridiculous that the government can't even solve this crime, the murder of one of its own!"

Matthew gave a last, cautionary squeeze to Anne's limb before removing his hand. "In all fairness," he drawled, "a crime without witnesses can be difficult to solve. I was over at Kaneohe, myself, and as you've perhaps heard, a plantation worker came forward to confirm my story. But by the time he did so, weeks had gone by. Memories fade. If anyone did see something, by then he or she would have forgotten. As an illustration, I doubt any of you can remember where you were that night."

How clever! Anne thought in silent admiration. One couldn't just ask someone where he was when a murder had been committed. But Matthew had overcome that difficulty. Silence now would appear odd.

Charles Decker raised a glass as though in salute. His mouth twisted into a smile, although his eyes were heavy lidded and unreadable. "In fact, you'd be wrong, Doctor. I remember that night all too well. Edward Landre was murdered the very night my son was born, and died." He inclined his head apologetically at Nettie, who had made a small sound of distress. "It was an eventful night in this house. I believe I wore a path in the carpet outside Mrs. Decker's bedroom, pacing the hall."

Yes, but he was nowhere to be found when Kamiki went hunting for him, Anne remembered, troubled. And some time later—as much as two or three hours later—when she herself had sought him, he'd been coming in through the kitchen door, wearing his coat. It had almost seemed, she thought, frowning, that there was something furtive in the way he slipped into the dark kitchen. She had been too agitated to think about it then. But now that she *was* thinking, she couldn't help also recalling the peculiar absence of servants. At the time, she'd assumed most had fled Honolulu and the epidemic. But she was certain that the next day a full staff had been at work. Why would Charles Decker have given them that of all nights off?

She very nearly was imprudent enough to say, *But I know you went out that night.* Common sense came to her rescue. Either he had nothing to do with Landre's murder, in which case she would sound very rude, or he *was* a murderer, in which case . . . Well, she didn't like to think.

She blinked suddenly and realized that she was looking directly at him, some of her brooding very likely showing on her face, and that *he* was looking right back at her, his eyes narrowed. For a moment she felt dizzy and unpleasantly helpless, rather like a monk seal being circled by a shark. But of course that image was ridiculous; she had good reason not to like Charles Decker, but that didn't make him a murderer. It was true that Matthew had discovered a connection between Decker and Landre, but the two men had been allies, perhaps even friends.

Dr. Newcomb was speculating about his own whereabouts that night, although in truth he didn't remember, or pretended not to. Anne managed to summon a smile for Mr. Decker before she placed in her mouth a forkful of something tasteless. When she stole a glance at her host, he was speaking gently to his wife, whose face was averted. By the time the ladies left the gentlemen for a time, Anne had nearly forgotten her absurd suspicion.

But not altogether. In the chaise she would have mentioned it, had Matthew not looked so remote, his face closed to her. They scarcely spoke as the carriage rumbled through dark streets. Once, she thought with a sinking heart, she had at least been his confidante; now she was—what? The woman he claimed to want to marry. But did he really? Or had her reluctance cooled his ardor?

Of all her fears, this one was the most frightening. To become a cherished wife was one thing, to become an unwanted one another. What if he dragged her back to Boston with him, only to shut her out as he was doing tonight? What if they were no longer friends?

All punctilious courtesy, he escorted her to the doorstep. "Good night, Anne." Did he truly sound tender, or did she only long to believe that he felt so?

"Matthew—"

He laid a finger on her lips. "Don't worry. I shall do my best to make you happy."

She nodded dumbly, unable to ask whether he loved her, unable to say, *Something tonight made me think, made me wonder—*

"Good night." He was gone, springing agilely into the chaise and whipping up the horses, apparently with no thought of kissing her, of courting her the way he once had.

Anne sighed and went within.

Mary Taft had waited up for her. She sat in the parlor, head bent over her stitchery. The top of an album quilt, made for the wife of a missionary returning to the States for the sake of her health, pooled at her feet.

If her expression had been sympathetic when she glanced up, Anne might have been tempted to spill out some of her troubles. With Napua gone, to whom else could she talk? But Mary lifted her chin, mouth pinched, and said distantly, "Did you drop the bolt? Good, then I believe I'll retire." She folded the quilt top in a basket and swept out, only making sure Anne had a candle first.

Anne made her way down the hall to her room, feeling bitterly alone. There she set the candle down on the commode and went to the window, flinging it open to the fragrant night air. She tried, and failed, to remember what Boston smelled like from her brief visits, the last awaiting passage to the Sandwich Islands. Nor, when she closed her eyes and tried to imagine herself standing at her bedroom window on the farm where she had grown up, could she remember breathing in the air with pleasure, thinking, Ah, that scent is the rotting maple leaves and that the fallow earth, there the pigs and manure behind the barn, and that the bread baked this morning. That time was too distant, too deliberately expunged from her memory. Perhaps at least in the fall and winter it had been too cold for smells to rise from the chill earth.

She sighed and turned to bed, leaving the window open. How had it happened, despite all her vows, that she would be sailing away from her tropical home, returning to a city within miles of her father's farm? Would she have to see him?

Shuddering, she blew out the candle. Never! She would not go home, like a dutiful daughter, any more than she would visit John Cartwright's grave to say good-bye.

Her sleep was restless. The third or fourth time she came awake, Anne nearly groaned. At least in slumber, she found respite from her desperate thoughts.

But this time, just as she was preparing to burrow deeper beneath her quilt, like a groundhog shutting out the weak winter sunlight so that he could hibernate, she heard a creak of the floorboards.

Anne quit breathing. She knew the spot, between her window and the commode, and made a habit of avoiding it. Someone had just stepped there and now stood frozen only a few feet from her bed. She lay on her stomach, face toward the wall. Could she turn her head unseen? But her eyes, just opened, would be unable to make out anything in the darkness.

I should scream, she thought, but what if no one was there at all? A nightmare—she could claim to have suffered a nightmare. But she couldn't scream until she breathed, and now she was afraid she must drag in an audible gasp of air.

The floorboard creaked again, another footstep fell hard, as though he had abandoned caution. She felt the rush toward her and shoved herself upward, to her knees.

The dark shape blotted out the window. She saw an arm raised—oh, God, a knife!—and screamed, a long undulating cry of terror and rage.

The knife descended, tore through her nightgown, but she'd flung herself away, and if it sliced flesh as well, she didn't know it. Even as she scrabbled away, she screamed and screamed.

Muffled by ceiling and walls, a voice shouted her name. Feet thundered overhead, down the stairs. Too far away. She dove off the foot of the bed, knocked against her attacker's legs. He staggered, cursing. She ought to know the voice, but had never heard such ugly words.

Her scream was no more than a hoarse sob now, as she evaded each thrust of the knife. In the pitch darkness, it was chance, luck, the whisper of a breeze as the knife stabbed. Blind, she had become deaf, too, to anything but her sobbing breaths and his rasping ones.

The assault had gone on forever when suddenly he checked, then spun and dashed for the window. Her door was flung open, and in the blaze of whale-oil light the Reverend Taft appeared with a club in one hand, the other lifting the lantern. The fringe of graying dark hair around his bald pate stuck up in little tufts, silversword rising from the lava, she thought wildly. He saw, as she did, the black figure clambering out the window.

"Catch him!" she cried.

But his was not the soul of a warrior. He hesitated, an indecisive gaze swinging from her to the window.

"Outside!" she gasped and tried to struggle to her feet.

"He'll be long gone," the reverend said. "Do you know this man?"

Oh, Lord. Hysterically she realized that he thought she had

welcomed another man into her bedroom. She pressed her hands to her wet cheeks. "No. He tried to kill me."

He frowned sternly down at her, crouched on the floor. "He?"

"You don't believe me." This time she did stand, and he sucked in an appalled breath. Following his stare, she looked down at herself.

Her white cotton nightgown was rent in several places, baring stripes of white flesh beaded with red. Blood red.

She swayed and, with an exclamation, Reverend Taft dropped the makeshift weapon and caught her with one hand, steering her to the bed. "Mrs. Taft!" he bellowed.

Wearing her nightgown and cap, his wife was already in the doorway. "Dear God, save us!" she breathed.

"You stay with Mrs. Cartwright while I ride for the doctor," he ordered.

Anne quit fingering the strips of cloth and lifted her head. "Dr. Cabe," Anne said. "It must be Dr. Cabe."

"He shouldn't see you like this—" Even in the lantern light, his flush was apparent. Either it had occurred to him that *somebody* must see her like this, or that Dr. Cabe had already seen a good deal too much of her. "Yes, very well," he agreed hastily.

Before he went, he closed and fastened the bedroom window and checked the other downstairs windows and doors. His wife barred the front door behind him before hurrying back to Anne, who still sat in a dreamlike state, marveling that she felt nothing from the cuts. Though none looked deep to her, no worse than a cat's scratch, still they ought to sting.

Mary brought a quilt to wrap around her shoulders and after a time a bowl of hot water that she used to gently sponge the scratches clean. She cooed and clucked all the while, so like her old self that Anne's eyes did sting. With her brown hair, gently touched with gray, loose around her face, she was pretty and motherly. It was possible to imagine her as a young bride.

"Mary," Anne said to her friend's bent head, "I'm frightened of marriage."

Mary Taft sat back, hazel eyes round with astonishment. "Frightened of *marriage?* Not of . . . this monster?"

"Of him, too, of course." She'd begun to cry, weak tears that seeped out against her will. "But most of all, I'm afraid of the marriage bed." There. She had said it.

"But . . . you've been married!"

"Yes." Anne cried all the harder.

"Ah." The corners of Mary's mouth tucked in disapprovingly. "He wasn't kind."

"No. I think he despised women. Our marriage . . . it was sudden, he had to have a wife, and I thought the life he had chosen noble. I hardly *knew* him."

Mary began dabbing again at the deepest of Anne's cuts. "So it was for many of us. But, my dear, it needn't be unpleasant. In fact, such closeness with your husband can be joyful, something that helps carry you through hard times." Her cheeks were rosy, but she concluded simply, "Such a union is blessed by our Lord God, you know."

Anne tried to smile through her tears. "Thank you. I haven't had the courage to ask others. I have begun to dread—"

She was interrupted. "Yes, well, you needn't." The lines of middle age in Mary's forehead deepened as she looked up. "I thought— That night—"

Anne knew she must be blushing, too. "I— Oh, I suppose I was testing myself. He . . . he pressed me for an answer, and I thought, if he kisses me I'll know if I can bear his caresses. And then . . ." She frowned.

"You quit thinking."

"Yes," she said in astonishment. "I only felt."

"Then you have your answer, don't you?"

"Do I?"

Mary smiled kindly. "Trust in God and your husband. And," she rose to her feet, "that is very likely Dr. Cabe now."

Anne waited docilely while Mrs. Taft went to answer the pounding on the front door. In seconds, Matthew appeared in Anne's bedroom. In this light, his eyes looked nearly black as his gaze swept comprehensively over her.

His voice was raw. "Oh, my love—"

He had never called her that.

"I am . . . merely scratched," she said shakily.

"By the grace of God." Matthew knelt in front of her and set down his medical bag. His hands shook and he curled them into fists. "May I see?"

Her eyes met Mary's over his head. Taking a deep breath, Anne shyly parted the quilt.

Matthew sucked in a breath. After a moment, he said in an eerily calm voice. "I shall rend him limb from limb."

The Reverend Taft, who stood in the doorway, did not, Anne noticed, speak about Christian forgiveness.

"We must discover who he is first," Anne pointed out.

Hand still trembling noticeably, Matthew cleansed a six-inch-long cut on her upper leg, then opened his bag and produced a phial of ointment. "This will sting."

"It . . . it already does." How odd that she hadn't noticed!

Only when he was done did Matthew look her in the face again. His jaw was bunched and his eyes blazed. "Did you recognize him?"

Anne shook her head. "No. How could I? It was so dark! If I hadn't awakened . . ." Her heart constricted.

"Did he make a sound?"

She pointed. "He stepped . . . just there. The floor creaked. If he had not come straight to the bed—"

How tightly he held her hands! "But he did. Now you must tell me everything you remember. Did he speak? Had you a sense of his size? Strength?"

"Only that he was larger than I am. And he cursed me. In English."

"Will you repeat the words?"

She looked to the Reverend Taft, who nodded silently. The words were so foul, she faltered, but Matthew only listened with a slight frown between his brows.

"That doesn't sound like a sailor."

"No." She listened to the way she had just echoed even her attacker's intonation. "No, his accents were more those of an educated man."

Behind Matthew, Mary burst out, "What can this mean? Why would someone break into our house to try to kill you? I don't understand!"

"There are . . . things I have not told you," Anne said with difficulty.

Voice cool, Reverend Taft said, "Then I believe it is time you do. May I suggest you change, Mrs. Cartwright, and we await you in the parlor?"

It seemed absurd to dress in the middle of the night; Mary, after all, wore only a long nightgown and cap. With Mary's help, Anne changed to a second, heavier nightgown, flung a shawl about her shoulders, and they rejoined the men. The scene was odd—the dark house, the two men waiting in the silent parlor with only candles lit, flickering from the movement as the women found seats.

Matthew told most of the story: the attempts to kill Napua, their suspicions, the questions they had asked. When he mentioned the Reverend Griggs, the Tafts exchanged a glance but said nothing.

At the end, Matthew said, "But what could have incited tonight's attack? That's what I don't understand. He took a risk to break in here. We've assumed it was Napua who threatened him. So why you?"

Anne folded her hands on her lap. "I may be wrong—oh, so

dreadfully wrong!—but I remembered something last night, and I believe that Mr. Decker saw that I had."

"Charles Decker?" Matthew echoed sharply. "What do you mean?"

"It was you who suggested that nobody would remember where they were the night of Landre's murder. Mr. Decker claimed that he did—he was walking the hall outside his wife's bedroom." To the Tafts, Anne added, "That was the night she lost her baby." Looking to Matthew again, she said, "But in fact, he was nowhere to be found for an interval! It might easily have been two hours, perhaps even three. Time ran together, you see. He intended for no one to see him leave or return, I think, because most of the servants were gone. Given the night off, I suppose; they were back the next day."

"Given the night off, when his wife was in childbirth?" Mary sounded incredulous.

Matthew rose and began to pace. "In that length of time, Decker could easily have made it there and back, if he knew Landre was meeting Napua and where."

"Mr. Decker has admitted that they were associates. Perhaps they were more, friends, even," Anne suggested. "Mr. Landre might have confided in him about what he would have seen as Napua's greed."

Face reflecting intense frustration, Matthew swung around. "Yes, blast it, but why would he have killed him? Particularly if they were still friends?"

Though this was their home, the Tafts sat silent now, side by side on a straight-backed settee. No wonder if they were shocked!

"I don't know!" Anne cried. "Perhaps they competed for . . . oh, a business deal, or a woman, or . . ." Ideas failed her.

"You've seen Decker with his wife. Do you really believe he would be interested in another woman?"

"No," Anne admitted. "Although she was, well, less appealing when she was with child, and afterward she stayed abed for weeks . . ." Blushing furiously, Anne couldn't look at the reverend or his wife.

Matthew grunted with dissatisfaction. "Business— Yes, I suppose it's possible." He took another turn around the room. "But not likely. No, it was politics that bound them. Could Landre have changed his mind, wanted to withdraw from their secret compact?"

"But why kill over that?" Anne asked. "Either way, Mr. Decker would lose Mr. Landre's inside information. He might regret that but surely not to the point of a murderous rage. And Mr. Decker's affiliation with the annexationist—and revolutionary—forces is well known! So what if Mr. Landre spoke out?"

"To murder," the Reverend Taft contributed unexpectedly, although perhaps his understanding of human motivations should not be unexpected from a man who heard his parishioners' greatest regrets, "a man must feel wronged, or threatened. If Edward Landre was no threat to Charles Decker, might he have wronged him?"

"He was handsome and charming." Matthew's brooding gaze captured Anne's. "Could he have wooed Nettie? Good Lord, what if Decker discovered the son he expected to be born that night was not his, but Edward Landre's?"

Anne shook her head reluctantly. "No. I believe that Nettie truly loves her husband, despite the years that separate them. And remember, her husband's relationship with Mr. Landre was secret. They would not have been meeting socially. How would Nettie have encountered him?"

Matthew grunted again. "True enough. Well, what then? Or are we looking in the wrong direction again?"

After a moment of silence, the Reverend Taft cleared his throat. "We're agreed that Landre's conduct has never been above reproach. What if Decker discovered something about him, as you did, that exposed an untruth he'd told? For example, what if he lied about what happened at a cabinet meeting? Decker might have discovered what really happened from another source."

"Or," Anne said slowly, "what if Mr. Landre told someone else what he'd learned from secret meetings of the committee? Could he have been traitorous to *both* sides?"

Matthew faced them, his expression arrested. "You know, the one thing that's bothered me about Landre was his loyal and efficient service to the kingdom. It was out of character for him. I kept asking myself what was in it for him. He never did anything without adequate return. As you say, perhaps he played both sides of the field until he decided where his advantage lay, then betrayed the losing side."

"Yes!" Anne cried. "To Dr. Judd, perhaps? Mr. Landre could have claimed that he was playing spy, his loyalty entirely given to the crown. It would be like him to curry favor. Would Dr. Judd tell us?"

"I think he might. I shall certainly ask him." Matthew began to pace again, fresh energy quickening his steps. "But is the act of betrayal enough by itself to justify murder? Or did Landre pass on something so potentially damaging that he had to be silenced?"

"Or punished," Anne said quietly.

The Reverend Taft took his wife's hand. "You need not look far to find an occasion when Charles Decker failed at a scheme."

"And," Anne straightened, "was publicly humiliated."

Matthew looked wolfish, a predator tasting his kill. "Refresh my memory."

"You recall my telling you about the brief scare we had during the winter of 1851–52 when a ship arrived from San Francisco loaded with restless young men who reputedly planned to overthrow His Majesty, with the assistance of compatriots here in Honolulu. Well, those compatriots were never discovered, if they existed at all. The attempt was really absurd, in part because rumors sailed faster than the *Game Cock*, and troops were drilling by the time they arrived.

"But this spring a second shipload of filibusterers arrived from California, and this time no rumors presaged their coming. Only a week before their ship reached Honolulu, a letter was published anonymously in the *Polynesian*, detailing the plan and its participants. The mastermind was Charles Decker, who was greatly embarrassed. No, more than that. Had the government been able to prove that he conspired to assassinate Prince Liholiho, as the letter writer claimed, I believe his store and property would have been seized and Decker himself tried for the crime, or at least expelled from the islands. But the author of the letter did not come forward, and both Decker and the supposed assassin denied the charges, so in the end it dwindled into merely another scandal. In fact, Decker was ridiculed in the press for thinking that one hundred men could overthrow the government. Perhaps he hated to be the object of ridicule as much as anything. He is not a man who would like to feel foolish."

The Reverend Taft nodded. "Most people made light of the whole affair at the time, and with good reason. England and France and the United States would surely not have accepted such blatant thievery."

"But Decker has similar ideas now," Matthew said frowning.

The reverend grimaced. "Yes, but I fear the political climate has changed somewhat, at least in the United States. Pressure for annexation is growing; an independent republic might be seen at home as merely a step on the way to the islands becoming American property. And if England or France attempted to reverse the results of the revolution, the United States might step in to protect *its* interests. Or so, I suppose, Mr. Decker believes. Perhaps he is even in communication with the U.S. Commissioner."

"Who must wish him to Hades!" Matthew commented.

"Perhaps not," the reverend suggested. "He keeps continual pressure on His Majesty's government, which increases the likelihood of the king's agreeing to annexation in order to save the islands from violent revolution. Rumor has it that a new U.S. commissioner is even now on his way here, with a mandate to negotiate the transfer of sovereignty."

"For which Decker might find himself rewarded," Matthew commented with distaste.

"Yes." Reverend Taft's face hardened in an expression unlike his usual one of benevolence. "He ridicules the Iolani Palace, but I doubt he'd turn down the chance to become the first governor to take his office there."

"No." Matthew ran his fingers through his hair, disordering it to give his countenance the look of a wild man. "So Landre was not necessarily a threat to Decker's present plans. Rather, Decker somehow discovered that his supposed conspirator had upset his previous apple cart, and he was unwilling to let the knowledge rest with no more than angry words."

"Though he may have started with those, which Napua overheard," Anne interjected.

"Very likely," Matthew agreed. His eyes commanded Anne's. "You know him best. Do you think him capable of a murderous rage?"

She bit her lip, thinking on the one hand of the charming merchant who had—with the exception of the one occasion—treated her with great civility, even when it must sometimes have seemed as though she encouraged his wife to act the part of invalid. She thought, too, of Nettie, who respected her husband and spoke of his unfailing kindness. Poor Nettie, who might already be pregnant again! But in the end, Anne could not evade her memory of the encounter in the kitchen, when she'd told Charles Decker that his newborn son had died. She saw again the way he stalked toward her, hands curled into fists. Remembering his choleric flush, the fury in his voice, and his willingness—eagerness!—to lay blame for the tragedy, she could not doubt that he was capable of hatred that great.

"Yes," she said, reluctant despite all. "I fear so. Worse yet, I remember him telling me about how you had struck Mr. Landre and threatened his life. At the time I was a little shocked by his delight. Now"—she took a deep breath—"now I think that he made his decision then. He believed he could safely commit murder, knowing well that you would be blamed for it."

Matthew's jaw flexed, but he sounded cold and detached. "Then let us make our plans. We will flush him out of hiding."

Nineteen

In the end, a simple bribe did the trick. The *Polynesian* was officially unwilling to disclose the names of its correspondents, many of whom wrote under pseudonyms for good reason, given their inflammatory prose. It was Anne who tentatively suggested bribery, although she clearly expected Matthew to have moral scruples. He thought bribery a small sin compared to murder.

The newspaper offices were located, like those of its rivals, on Merchant Street, sometimes called Printer's Row. Matthew marched in and loudly demanded answers, which he was refused. Within an hour of his visit to the newspaper office, he received a note. The signer thought he could help. "Be behind the offices tonight at 10:00 P.M." concluded the message in large awkward script.

When Matthew arrived at the head of the alley, the Seamen's Bethel bell in its wooden belfry was ringing for the last time, announcing the closing of saloons and dance halls and ordering sailors back to their ships. The traffic on the streets made Matthew's presence unremarkable. Despite the lantern he lifted before him, he didn't like the look of the blackness gaping from the alley, but he stepped in nonetheless. He hadn't gone ten feet when behind him, a rough-textured voice muttered, "I remember the letter ye asked about. Set the type meself, from handwritten sheets."

Matthew turned slowly, so as not to alarm his informant. The other man stood behind the circle of light cast by the lantern. He was only a dark shape.

"Indeed," Matthew said, "and are you aware of the identity of the author?"

"Aye." The man coughed. " 'Course, I'm sworn to silence, I am."

"Would a hundred dollars loosen your tongue?"

"T'other gent paid me—" He stopped abruptly.

Matthew didn't let his face reveal the triumph he felt. "Two hundred dollars if you tell me who the other gent is, too."

"Lemme see the money."

Matthew lifted the lantern higher, showing in his outstretched hand a bundle of greenbacks. The other man took a step forward, his eyes fixed on the money, and in the flickering light Matthew recognized his face from the visit to the *Polynesian* offices.

He withdrew the money. "Tell me."

"Landre," the newspaper employee whispered. "Edward Landre. Ye're the one what was supposed to have killed him, aren't ye?"

"They let me out of jail."

"Then why does ye care—?"

"Does it matter?" Matthew gave his answer a harsh edge.

"Nah. 'Course not." The dark figure shuffled his feet. "Charles Decker was t'other one wanted to know. Runs a store down on Fort Street—"

"I know him." Matthew hesitated. "Was he surprised to hear that the author was Landre?"

"Him? Not likely. Or he didn't show it. No saying with one like him."

"He's smooth," Matthew agreed. "One last question. When did you tell him?"

In the darkness, he made out a shrug. "Few weeks after the letter came out. Someone told me he'd been asking. I . . . Well, I thought he might give me a little something for the information, so I went to him."

"I'm sure he was grateful," Matthew said dryly.

"Aye." The man edged closer. "If there's nothing else—?"

"No. Nothing. Thank you."

His informant snatched the money from Matthew's hand and, without another word, vanished. Matthew heard a scrabbling sound at the head of the alley and knew himself to be alone.

The long walk back to his hotel gave him opportunity to mull over what he had learned. At last they had an answer that made sense. Charles Decker had reason to hate the murdered man; the timing of his discovery fit with the timing of the crime itself; and he'd had opportunity to commit the act—had even lied about his whereabouts that evening.

After confronting Landre with his knowledge, Decker must have found out that Napua had been home. Perhaps as he left, he'd seen her skirt swish around a corner, or he'd spotted her in a window as Matthew had. How dismayed he would have been to realize he might have been overheard! From that moment on, Napua's life had been in danger. So why hadn't he killed her when he bludgeoned Landre? The night had been dark. Had he not seen her? She claimed to have been pushed off the lane. Who had pushed her, if not the murderer? Landre, in a last noble act? Or an ancestor ghost, as she believed?

Decker, of course, had seen Anne's knowledge in her eyes the other night. He'd wasted no time in deciding *she* must be eliminated.

Matthew's visit to Dr. Judd had produced no results. The former finance minister and missionary insisted he was ignorant of Landre's flirtation with the annexation movement. Landre had not been sent by his superiors to infiltrate the conspirators.

Despite the lack of confirmation from that source, Matthew had no doubt they had found the murderer. How to prove his guilt for a court of law was another matter. Matthew was coldly determined to do so, although he was not unaware of the irony in his hunting down a man who had done something he, in his heart, would have liked to do. *God help me*, Matthew thought, *had Decker stopped at the one crime, however heinous, I might have been tempted to let it go. If ever a man deserved to die, it was Edward Landre.*

Thank God he had been saved from such a hideous moral and emotional decision. For Charles Decker had also involved Matthew by choosing him as scapegoat. And then he had viciously assaulted two women. He would have murdered both, only because their existence threatened his own safety.

For that, Matthew had every intention of seeing to it that Decker's neck snapped in the gallows house.

Napua lay in bed listening to the soft patter of the morning rain on the roof and savoring the trusting warmth of Kuokoa's skinny body curved against hers. Awake, he was all angles and jutting bones—an elbow in her belly when she hugged him, a sharp point of shoulder in her side when she walked with an arm around him. But in sleep, that same body remembered infancy and tried to mold itself to fit hers, an instinctive grope backward for the beginning. She needed to treasure such remembrances, for he grew so fast. And who knew if she would ever have another child?

As though the rain had washed away the last tendrils of sleep-mist, Napua became more aware of her surroundings. The floor creaked, the door whispered on its hinges. She opened her eyes to find Henry's pallet empty and the front door standing a little ajar, letting her see the pearl gray of the damp morning light.

Napua pressed a tender kiss to her son's temple and then arose herself. She crossed the room quietly. He must have left the door open so as not to make any more noise than necessary. She thought he might have gone to the privy, but if that had been his intention, he had decided to wait until *noenoe uakea o Hana* had ceased to caress the earth, for he sat on the porch step, leaning back against the railing, and watched the misty rain.

She hugged a quilt from the bed around herself, feeling as bashful as *'o'opu*, the shy fish of Kawainui. "Good morning."

His head turned and his eyes traveled swiftly over her. "Good morning. Is Kuokoa awake?"

"That one?" Her laugh was soft, loving. "Not him! He would like to sleep all day like a chief who is afraid to go abroad for fear he will be touched by the shadow of someone who does not see him coming!"

Henry smiled at her reference to the old days, when it was *kapu* for commoners to touch or cast a shadow on any part of the chief or his possessions. "The boy acts as if he thinks he's a chief, or will be, anyway. I mean that in the best way. Considering how his father neglected him, you've done a fine job."

"Thank you." Napua hesitated, then went to sit on the step beside him. She held out one hand beyond the overhang of the roof and felt the dampness of the morning rain kiss her skin. "You are good to him," she said.

He was staring now toward the mist-swathed bay. "I like him."

Napua wrapped her arms around her knees and studied his profile. He had a large nose. It was noble, she thought; in old age, it might even grow fierce. The puffiness around his eyes was less now, although he was still not a man whose looks drew women's eyes. She didn't mind. She'd had such a man and been foolish enough to think she alone would be enough for him.

"Have you been happy, these weeks with us?" she asked, surprising herself as much as him, although she had meant somehow to discover how he felt about her. But it had proved hard to ask; she had let days pass. Chances slipped by, for she was not as bold as she would like to be. But she could see that he had not gone back to drinking *haole* liquor or even *awa*, and she thought it must be for her sake, or her son's.

He didn't move or look at her, but a quiver ran through him, as if a harpoon had pierced his flesh. "Yes," he said roughly. "These have been good weeks."

She nodded and squeezed her knees harder. They sat in silence, watching the edge of the rain pass until damp sky melded with the swell of ocean. Only to Ka'uiki, as the story promised, did the mist still cling.

Why him? Napua asked herself again, and still had no answer. Because he was here? Because he was *haole* and therefore more powerful than Hawaiians? Because he was kind and could be trusted?

"And you?" Henry asked at last in a low voice. "Are you content?"

"Yes," she said dreamily. "Why shouldn't I be?"

"Because you have something better to compare it with. Landre gave you everything."

"Not everything." Anger strengthened her voice. "Not love. How could I be happy?"

"He was a fool."

"I think *I* was the fool."

"He had you and he let you go."

Her heart soared, and yet she must argue. "You don't know me so well."

"I know you."

How she wished she were brave enough to ask, *Would* you

let me go? But her mouth would not speak the words; her courage failed her.

Henry spoke abruptly. "What do you plan for the future?"

"The future?" She stared at him.

"When the danger to you is past."

She made herself look away. Would she ever be safe again in Honolulu? She found she didn't much care, so long as the murderer didn't seek her here. But her contentment here also made her feel guilty. It would be wrong if Mahaulu arrested the *haole* doctor again. And Anne—was she well? Had she understood yet what she felt for Dr. Cabe?

Napua sighed over her worries. "I do not know. Perhaps go back to Honolulu." Inside the quilt, she shrugged. "Perhaps not. I like it here. It's good for Kuokoa."

"You would not be bored?"

"No." Napua rose and faced him, her toes curling against the rough plank porch. The air was sweet, washed clean, the morning pink and gold. "I can see why you grieve for what you had here."

He, too, rose slowly. She felt dizzy, which frightened her. Was she to be swirled about again, until she no longer knew right and wrong? But it seemed to her that even if she did not, Henry Turner did. He was like a rock standing in the sea. It did not move no matter how the water eddied. Perhaps it was that steadiness that drew her to him.

Gruffly he said, "I've come to think that I might start again, if I had a reason."

"There are many reasons."

"I can think of only one," he said.

She smiled tenderly, joyously. "Can you name this reason?"

"I have no right." He took a step closer. "Am *I* a fool, Napua?"

"No," she whispered. "Oh, no. Tonight—"

"Tonight what, Mama?" her son asked from the doorway.

Napua could not look away from Henry Turner's eyes, the color of green-dark Nuuanu Valley seen through the clear gray of a rain shower.

"Tonight," she said, her eyes promising what her lips could not, "I shall dance the hula for Mr. Turner. I think he has never seen it done the way it should be."

"Can I watch, too?"

"No. This hula is for night, and you will be in bed."

Henry clasped her hand in his. Looking down at their joined hands, she felt the embers stir. Even sun darkened, his skin was lighter than her own. Beneath the clothes, his body would be pale. He would rise over her like sea foam over a black sand beach, white over dark, man over woman, in a rhythm as ancient and timeless as the ocean's pulse.

"Tonight," she whispered.

At first when Napua danced, it was like always; *she* was no longer there. Her prayers to Làka, the goddess of hula, were answered, for her body became *ohi'a*'s flame flower, beloved of forest birds, or *pupu-kani-oe*, the voice of land shells, or the sweep of the river. She was the water of Kane.

> Yonder, at sea, on the ocean,
> In the driving rain,
> In the heavenly bow,
> In the piled-up mist-wraith,
> In the bloodred rainfall,
> In the ghost-pale cloud-form;
> There is the water of Kane.

But gradually she returned to herself, so that she alone danced, a woman for her man. Facing him across the fire, night at her back, Napua moved with the *oli* that she sang. Her hips undulated, her fingertips chased the sparks. Defying the mission teachings, she wore the stiff *pa'u* about her hips, anklets of shellwork, and lei around her neck and encircling her hair, which hung loose down her back. Her bare breasts, red-brown in the firelight, swayed at her gentle, provocative movements.

> I long for one soul-deep gaze,
> One night of precious communion;
> Such a flower wilts not in the cold—
> Cold without, a tumult within.
> What bliss, if we two were together!

Henry Turner sat transfixed. Napua felt her power and his weakness for her. A woman needed sometimes to redress the balance. There was a saying: "A woman is like a yellowed banana leaf that tears when one pokes at it." But Hawaiian women had their own kind of strength; else why had Kamehameha himself created the office of *kuhina nui*, or premier, and given it to a woman?

Only by slow steps did Napua make her way around the fire. Henry stood, and she danced so close that she brushed him as she moved. She had never danced an erotic hula before; back when her *kumu hula* had taught her, she was only a child, and then the missionaries forbade dancing at all. Edward had not liked to think of her as Hawaiian or chiefess. Would Henry Turner feel the same?

The firelight tricked the eye into thinking he was tall and strong. The bones in his face showed prominently, his nose a great beak, his cheeks cast into relief by shadows. He looked at her as though he found her beautiful. His fingers worked into fists, the tendons standing out, as if he strained to keep his hands from her. She gently bumped against his hips and felt him swell like the sea at high tide, rising to slam against the shore. She was the lava rock—Pele incarnate—and he would slide into her like the cool ocean into a lava tube. She had an image of spume bursting into the air from a blowhole.

> The mat bends under your form.
> The thirsty wind, it still rages,
> Appeased not with her whole body.

She came to a stop, trembling, in front of him. The fire crackled and sank into itself, the blaze sinking to glowing embers.

"I want you," he said hoarsely. But his hands stayed at his sides.

"Is that bad?" she whispered.

"I'd like to think of myself as an honorable man."

Anger—or was it fear?—tightened her throat. "And honorable *haole* men don't bed heathens? Is that it?"

He jerked. "No. That's not what I meant! It's just that after that bastard Landre, I'm afraid to take advantage of you. You deserve better."

"And what is better?" she asked bitterly, close to tears.

"A wedding ring."

Her heart stilled, then burned with a sudden cramp of pain. "But who will give me one now? I have a bastard son. In your *haole* eyes, I'm ruined."

"Ruined?" At last he lifted a hand, brushed a tear from her cheek. "You're the most beautiful woman I've ever seen. You're kind and gentle and loving. Sometimes I envy Kuokoa, the way you talk to him and hold him. I've never had anything like that—"

Her own pain was forgotten at the sight of his. "Only come to me, and I'll hold you."

"I'm afraid to." His voice cracked. "I want more than your body tonight. I want children with you. I want to see you grow old. I want to keep looking into your eyes until I don't need to see the bottom of a liquor bottle again."

"I don't understand."

"Will you marry me?"

Now she trembled anew. "*He* asked me that, too, but he never meant it. Once I gave him myself, he was like the morning glory vine, twisting this way and that, always out of my reach."

A grimness she had never heard entered Henry's voice. "I may have sunk low, but not that low. I won't take offense, since I understand you have good reason not to trust men. That's why I can't touch you. My body is near to screaming at me to kiss you, but I won't lay my hands on you until you're my wife, right and proper."

Napua gaped at him.

He harumphed. "If you'll have me, that is."

Tears gushed forth. "Kuokoa?"

"I'd be proud to look on him as my son."

"You are certain?" she asked tremulously. "You wish to marry *me?* There are people who will look down on you for it."

His throat worked. "Damn them. I wanted to marry you the minute I set eyes on you. But I didn't—don't—have a thing to offer you."

Through her tears, her smile dawned. "Even a little taro green is delicious when love is present. I want nothing more."

A shower of sparks let her see the anxiety on his face. "I've thought of taking Matthew Cabe up on his suggestion that I manage his plantation at Kaneohe on Oahu."

"I can be happy anywhere," she said softly.

"Then—" His chest rose and fell. "Shall we speak to the Reverend Whittlesey tomorrow?"

"Yes." Her tears were like rain falling, washing away the bitterness. "May I kiss you, Henry Turner?"

He gave a choked laugh. "How can I say no?"

Napua stood on tiptoe and laid her hands on his hard, scratchy cheeks. Lovingly, she pressed her mouth to his until she felt a groan begin deep within his chest. Then, laughing, Napua backed away. "I must not tempt you."

"Tonight's hula wasn't meant to tempt me?"

"Well . . ." She smiled.

"But you won't succeed." There was that grimness again. "I love you, Napua Kanakanui. But I won't make you mine until you're my wife. I want your trust as much as I want your body."

"I think," she said gravely, shaking her hair over her shoulders until it covered her breasts, "that you are a fine man, Henry Turner." *You may not be handsome or rich*— she wouldn't say that. "This time," she said, "I think I am not a fool."

Twenty

"No. Absolutely not!" Matthew glowered at Anne across the Tafts' parlor.

"But we must catch him," she pointed out reasonably. This conference was taking place the next morning, in the light of day. Her cuts, scabbing over, might be hidden from his view, but he had not forgotten them. "How else can we lure him into a trap?"

Constable Mahaulu nodded. "Mrs. Cartwright need not actually be there. So long as Mr. Decker *thinks* she is . . ."

"What if he comes after her some other time, when we're not expecting it?"

"He may try that, anyway," Anne said. "This way, we might control *when* he comes."

Matthew scowled. "I don't like it."

"It will not work unless you cooperate," Mahaulu said. "Only you can speak to him without him wondering."

"Anne won't be in her room?"

"It might be better if I was—" At the warning look from the native constable, she subsided.

"Better for Decker, so he can succeed in his object,"

Matthew growled. As was his wont, he paced the narrow room before squaring his shoulders and accepting the unpalatable. "Very well. I'll speak to him."

He left to make an appointment to meet Decker only after repeated promises that Anne would not be left alone, even for a moment. She was to see Makalika this morning, but Mrs. Taft promised she would go, as well, and that they would travel in a closed carriage. "And with the ladies' aid meeting tonight, he'll get nowhere near her."

Matthew would have liked to be alone with her himself, but he could see that that was an opportunity unlikely to be offered him. He wanted to hold her— But she was unlikely to be soothed by *his* arms, he reminded himself caustically. He wasn't sure that she wasn't as frightened of him as she was of Charles Decker. Perhaps he should release her from her promise—so much had happened since, surely the Tafts would not turn their backs on her.

Anne could simply continue as she was—utterly dependent on the charity of others. Without family, home— He could give her that much, at least!

No happier than he had been since that ill-fated night when he'd attempted to seduce her and in doing so lost her friendship, Matthew strode into Decker's store on Fort Street. The scent of linseed oil and tobacco mixed with the less savory odors from the street, where a wagonload of squawking chickens in crates rattled its way between half-naked natives driving cattle toward the waterfront.

This was the first time Matthew had been in here. He glanced around. A good portion of the storefront held dry goods and was designed to entice women. Bolts of cloth lay heaped on a countertop, vivid satin beside crisp red calicos and indigo blue sheeting. The glass case was filled with ribbons, kid gloves, China slippers, silk and cotton hose and handkerchiefs, crepe shawls, mother-of-pearl buttons, and umbrellas. On the opposite side, another glass case held anything a gentleman might require, from suspenders, cigars, playing cards, half-bound foolscap books and gold and steel pens to snuff in bottles and shaving brushes.

Beyond the sunlight coming in the front windows were tall shelves and rows of barrels. Wandering, Matthew found baking pans and brass bedsteads, door hinges and saws, dressing cases and salt cellars. Ship's supplies were available as well, according to a sign; he had only to ask should he wish to acquire marlinspikes, a nautical almanac, or Russian or English canvas cordage, not to mention blubber hooks and spyglasses.

When a clerk scuttled toward him, he said, "I should like to see Mr. Decker, if he is available."

"Your name, sir?"

He was not surprised that his name brought Decker out of the inner sanctum. The man must be anxious this morning, wondering what Anne had said of her suspicions, whether she had somehow recognized her assailant last night, what he ought to do next.

But in shirtsleeves, red suspenders, and striped trousers, Decker looked so much his usual complacent self, no more than surprised to see Matthew again so soon, that Matthew's certainty suffered a minor jolt.

"What brings you here this morning, Doctor? Are you a customer, or would you care to come back to my office?"

"I confess to curiosity, and boredom," Matthew said. "I am rather out of sorts this morning and thought to distract myself by taking a look at your establishment."

"Out of sorts?" Decker raised his brows. "Not your health . . . ?"

"No, no." Matthew glanced at the clerk. "Perhaps we should go back to your office, if you can spare me the time."

"Naturally," Decker said with aplomb.

He listened, frowning, to Matthew's tale of the previous

night. "Thank God she suffered scrapes only," Matthew concluded, "but she professes not to have any idea who might wish her harm."

"She must be in a state of hysteria!"

Matthew gave a crack of laughter. "Come, you know Mrs. Cartwright better than that! No, she's seeing a patient today and attending some social function or another tonight—a sewing circle or a ladies' aid or something—at which my presence was not desired." He let a troubled look steal over his face. "I can't feel secure about her when I'm not with her. The maddening thing is that I feel sure she knows something. When I accuse her she says I'm absurd, that her *thoughts* must be absurd, that she must consider more thoroughly before she babbles to me. She assures me she will be more careful in the meantime." He leaped from his chair and went to the window, which looked over lower buildings toward the fort and the harbor. "What the devil can she mean?"

His spine fairly tingled as he waited through a pause.

At last, "I have no idea," Decker said, "though were I you, I would give her tonight only to think about it, then press her for answers. Perhaps she could move to a safer place—"

"She refuses." Matthew flung himself into the chair again. "Says with her window locked, she'll be safe." He rubbed a hand over his face. "Stubborn woman."

"Aren't they all?"

"Mrs. Decker, too, eh?"

The other man smiled. "Yes, but fortunately there are ways around them. And they can be so . . . delightful. Compensation, indeed."

"Easy for you to say! You're married." Matthew grinned ruefully. "Can you hear the frustration? Take pity on me; will you join me for dinner this evening? If Mrs. Decker can spare you?"

"Why not?" Decker slapped his desk with an open palm. "At the Commercial Hotel? Say, seven o'clock?"

That evening, Decker arrived as promised. The hotel was known for its food and fine French wines—which, Decker pointed out, would have cost less had it not been for the ridiculous tax imposed by the government. The conversation ranged widely. Decker sneered at local attempts to grow cotton, encouraged by the Royal Hawaiian Agricultural Society, which gave an annual premium to the best woven native cloth: thus far, vastly inferior to imported, according to him.

"They're groping desperately for some alternative to sugar," he said gesturing with his cigar. "I suppose you've heard about the Reverend Green's attempt to grow wheat at Makawao—"

"Quite successfully, from what I can gather."

"Indeed, but can it compete on the open market? I'll be astonished. Oranges are still being grown in large quantities, but for whom? They can't be kept on the voyage to New England. Now the experiments with pineapple in the uplands have far more promise, I believe—"

They discussed the previous year's revision of the constitution, which provided for annual legislative sessions, expanded the power possessed by the lower house, and allowed for election by universal manhood suffrage, instead of property owners.

"My fellow *haoles*"—the merchant said the word mockingly—"are more afraid of autocracy than democracy. Yet they offer allegiance to a king. Ironic, is it not?"

It was ironic as well that, despite the expansion of the electorate, the numbers of voters in Honolulu, at least, had been steadily dropping. "Around two thousand voted in 1851; it was less than one thousand this January."

"And the smallpox may have made further inroads in the electorate," Matthew said. He found the conversation stimulating and informative, even as his tension did not abate. What was Decker thinking? Planning? Could he be so amiably sipping wine and throwing out ideas if he were a murderer who intended to commit his next crime this very night?

Matthew remembered the informant in the alley behind the newspaper offices. Matthew had asked whether Decker was surprised to find Landre had betrayed him. *Him?* the informant had scoffed. *Not likely. Or he didn't show it. No saying with one like him.*

Was he this smooth? Well, they'd find out, for Decker himself had suggested, "I would give her tonight only to think about it, then press her for answers." That gave *him* tonight only, were he to keep Anne from giving those answers.

The day was one of the longest of Anne's life. She was grateful to be occupied, although she would have liked those occupations to have something to do with the crisis at hand. Yet she was disconcerted when she arrived to see Makalika to find that the Reverend Griggs was before her.

He looked up, his expression cool. "Ah, Mrs. Cartwright. I shall be out of your way in a moment, if I might have a word with you first?"

She agreed; he tenderly patted Makalika's hand and promised to return. "I shall attempt to reason with your husband," he said. "Perhaps his concern for you will open his heart to the truth."

If Makalika simpered, Anne didn't think she could bear it. But Kaipoleimanu's wife merely smiled and removed her hand. "I will be grateful for your prayers, *makua* Griggs."

Outside the hut, the reverend and Anne were momentarily alone. Stiffly he said, "I must ask your forgiveness for my harshness that day. Perhaps I . . . reacted with too great severity."

Disarmed she said, "I thought that you would welcome Napua's change of heart."

."We will not discuss that." His mouth thinned. His gaunt face would have looked skeletal were it not for his glittering eyes. "It is your pardon I seek, not hers."

"I see." She didn't try to hide her contempt.

"I don't believe you do." He sighed. "If you had a child of your own, you might better understand."

"She was not your child."

"We took her into our hearts—"

"And shut her out the moment she disappointed you? Christ was all-forgiving."

Griggs was silent.

"Good day, Reverend." Anne ducked back inside the grass hut.

Makalika had increased in girth even in the few weeks Anne had been attending her. She began to scold her for overeating even as she pressed the bell of her stethoscope to the swelling abdomen.

"But, Mrs. Cartwright, I've followed your advice—"

Anne held up her hand for silence. "There," she said. "I hear the heartbeat." But she frowned and moved the stethoscope, for today the quick flutter sounded peculiar, as though it echoed within the womb. Was something wrong?

She listened again, moved the stethoscope. She felt the mother's anxiety as she strained to hear the echo, to separate one sound from the other. And then she did, and began to smile.

"Makalika—" She straightened and seized the native woman's hands. "You may have a son *and* a daughter. Today I hear *two* heartbeats!"

Makalika gave her own belly a comical look of astonishment. "Two—? I am to have twins?"

"Yes, and here I blamed you for eating too much! I beg your pardon."

"Two?" Still she was dazed.

"Indeed, and both sound healthy. Do you wish to tell your husband yourself?"

At last she gave a crow of delight. "Two! We have been blessed."

"I have never delivered twins. Perhaps you'd like to consult a doctor—"

"No, no." Makalika waved away the suggestion. "I trust you. Only you."

Anne thought of the still, blue face of Nettie's baby and suffered a qualm, but she had begun to believe his death had been in God's hands and not hers.

"You'll let me tell my husband?" Makalika begged. "Say only that all is well."

"Of course."

As though by chance, Kaipoleimanu stepped out of another doorway the moment Anne left his wife's hut. Dressed formally in European clothing, he was a handsome man, the white cravat effective contrast to his dark skin. "Ah," he said. "How do you find her?"

"Very well." Anne couldn't help her smile. "She has news for you."

"News?" he repeated in quick alarm.

"Go to her," Anne said gently.

He took a step; checked himself. "Napua—you told her I would help?"

"I've written her. I don't know whether she has received my letter."

"So she left Oahu." Face expressionless, he nodded. "Very wise. And you, Mrs. Cartwright. Are you being careful?"

"Careful?" Her heart speeded. How could he know about last night's attack, unless *he* had been the man in her bedroom? But that man had spoken English— As did Kaipoleimanu, when he chose.

"It would be reasonable for Napua's enemy to think she might have told you anything she knew. It might have been wise if you had gone with her." He glanced toward the doorway beyond which his wife waited. "Perhaps you would accept my protection and come to stay here. I owe you anything in my power to give."

"I thank you for the offer." Anne was proud of her calm response. "I'll think about it this evening. But you owe me nothing. I believe God means you to have a son or daughter." *Or both.*

"Thank you." He sounded as stiff as had the Reverend Griggs. "Good day, Mrs. Cartwright."

Anne never had a chance to tell Matthew about her two encounters. As they'd arranged, she and Mary Taft attended the ladies' aid society meeting at Sweet Home, then returned to town with other missionary wives as part of a parade of carriages. They were met at their own door by Reverend Taft.

"Dr. Cabe is here, concealed outside," he said quickly. "Constable Mahaulu is with him, as we planned. I believe it is late enough that we can seem to go to bed." He bolted the door behind them. "With your curtains drawn, anyone watching won't know that I snuff the candle in your room instead of you."

His wife clutched his sleeve. "You will not stay?"

"No, we've padded the bed, so it appears as though someone sleeps there, should he get so far. I'll wait just inside the parlor, where I can see both the hall and the stairs, in case he confounds us and breaks in through another room. You'll be safe up above."

Safe perhaps, but no less terrified. The two women made no pretense of going to sleep, only sat fully dressed in straight-backed chairs and waited, speaking occasionally in whispers. If no one came, it would be a very long night.

Would he come? He must know that the doors would be barred and the windows locked. Matthew was convinced he would take the risk of breaking a pane to thrust a hand in to un-latch and lift the window.

That morning, Matthew had said, "He must be convinced that, if you speak, all is lost. No, if he thinks he might succeed, he'll take any risk."

Staring into the darkness, tensing at every small creak or scrape as a branch fingered the clapboards, Anne tried to imag-ine the scene outside. The half-moon was tonight intermittently concealed by wind-driven clouds. *He* was creeping forward even now, choosing his way in the moments of silvery light, moving in the pitch darkness. A breeze rustled the leaves, startling him. God willing, he would not see Matthew or Mahaulu lurking within the shrubbery. For if *he* would murder a woman, lying asleep, he would surely kill either of the men. Even now, he lifted a rock to shatter the glass—

She jerked at Mrs. Taft's sharp whisper. "Did you hear some-thing?"

"No!" She listened hard. "Nothing."

The clock downstairs bonged the hours, as they passed: ten o'clock, then eleven, at last midnight. Anne heard the moment Mary fell asleep, her head sagging to one side. But she couldn't sleep, and had to face the fact that her terror was not for her-self, but for Matthew.

What if the murderer guessed that this was a trap? What if Matthew was wounded, or died, trying to protect her? And she had doubted his love!

Anne's thoughts jumped as unpredictably as a flea on a dog's back. Poor Nettie! To lose her son, and then her husband, and in such a horrible way! But she could go home, back to her mother and sister. Decker would surely hang, and she could re-marry. Though she would not see that as consolation, not for a long time to come.

But what if Charles Decker was *not* the murderer? Did that

mean no one would come tonight? Anne shivered, thinking of Kaipoleimanu's flat, expressionless countenance: *And you, Mrs. Cartwright. Are you being careful?* Or the Reverend Griggs, face bereft of flesh and as waxy as though he had risen from the grave himself: *It is* your *pardon I seek, not hers.*

The stairs creaked; Anne stiffened. The Reverend Taft's voice drifted quietly up, "Patience. He'll come."

Oh, Matthew, she begged. *Don't be foolish.*

A gunshot exploded through the night, shattering glass. By instinct, Anne fell to her knees before she realized that, however loud it had been, this window was intact. Downstairs, then. She crawled to Mrs. Taft, who awakened gasping and turning her head wildly. "What is it? What—"

"Hush!"

Outside, men's voices shouted with alarm. Another gunshot came, then thudding feet. Curses, grunts. Something slammed into the side of the house.

Mary whimpered. Anne couldn't bear it any longer. "I must see," she whispered and crawled to the window. Just as she pushed the curtains aside, moonlight illuminated the scene of struggling bodies below. The gun went off again. One of the men fell to the ground.

"Oh, God!" Anne whispered, then screamed, "Matthew!"

Snatching up her skirts, she raced down the stairs, stumbling, clutching at the banister. At the bottom, the Reverend Taft put out a hand to stop her.

"You mustn't go out!"

She tried to yank herself free of his grip. "Matthew. He's been shot."

His grip tightened. "How do you know?"

"I saw— Oh, please, please."

"He charged me with your safety. We must wait."

Tears running down her face, she railed at the lot of women.

Why must they always wait? As though they were so fragile. If only men tried childbirth, they would change their minds!

A fist hammered on the door, and a voice called, "It's over! Let me in."

Matthew? Could it be Matthew?

Reverend Taft let her go. The two of them lifted the bar together. He wrenched the door open, and Anne fell into Matthew's arms.

"You're alive," she whispered. "But I saw you fall—"

He held her so tightly, she felt him tremble. "Decker's dead. He turned the gun on himself when he saw that he couldn't escape. You saw him fall. I'm not hurt."

She was wetting his shirt with her tears. "Oh, Nettie!"

He lifted his head suddenly. "How did you see anything? You weren't idiot enough to look out the window?"

Idiot, perhaps, but one who understood herself at last. "I love you," she said.

Matthew groaned and kissed her. She didn't care if the Reverend Taft disapproved. She cared about nothing but Matthew and the future she was finally brave enough to reach out and grasp. She saw the two of them on the beach at night, wading barefoot in the waves as they rushed over the warm sand. But no, they would not be here; Atlantic waves were icy cold.

He lifted his head. "You're not afraid of me?"

"Not of you. Only of my memories. Perhaps of myself."

He groaned again and deepened the kiss. "I should have known you wouldn't stay out of harm's way," Matthew muttered against her lips.

"I'll be a staid, married woman from now on. A Boston matron." Such euphoria gripped her, she couldn't even feel depressed about that part. "Can Nettie go with us, when we sail for home?"

"I'm not so sure we'll sail for anywhere." Matthew lifted his head and smiled down at her. Someone had lit a candle sconce, but Reverend Taft had been tactful enough to leave them alone. "I seem to have a thriving practice here, and I find I'm curious about the future of this little kingdom. What do you say? Shall we become Hawaiians?"

Why, she was crying again! "Yes, please," she whispered and then rose on tiptoe to kiss him. Without any fear at all.

Epilogue

Huddled inside every stitch of clothing she owned, wrapped at last in a woolen blanket, Anne more nearly resembled the plump, flightless chick of the white tern, *manu-o-ku*, than she did a human being. Even so, she shivered from both cold and awe as she gazed at the vast lake of black lava, crumpled and rent as though a storm had raged across its surface. Mauna Loa's great crater, Moku'aweoweo, stretched unimaginably far to a distant rim. Though the surface of the lake didn't move, it murmured in deep, hushed tones, a chant that might have come from the Kumulipo, the Hawaiians' story of creation:

> At the time when the earth became hot
> At the time when the heavens turned about
> At the time when the sun was darkened
> To cause the moon to shine
> The time of the rise of the Pleiades
> The slime, this was the source of the earth
> The source of darkness that made darkness.

She ought to be feeling herself before the throne of God, not thinking about Pele and wishing she had brought some red berries of the *ohelo*, sacred to the goddess, to cast into the caldera as an offering.

Far across the sea of lava, a fountain of fire shot skyward, fifty feet or a hundred, an incandescent geyser.

"Magnificent," Matthew declared and seized Anne's hand. "Shall we camp here? Watch the fireworks by night?"

She looked around at the tormented shapes of lava that formed a hideous landscape, so high above the world she had known that she had trouble drawing each breath. Here, they were even above the clouds, which spread pale gray and downy several thousand feet below, as far as the eye could see, blotting out the ocean.

But she felt such triumph at having arrived, at looking down into one of Pele's homes, that she was reluctant to leave. "Yes, but not too close to the edge," she agreed. "It's hard to be certain what ground is solid."

"A metaphor for life." He cocked an eyebrow at her, and she had to smile. Indeed it was. How drastically her life had changed in these last two years!

Here in the presence of God at His most terrible, she was also exquisitely aware of Him at His most joyful, for beside her was her husband, the man who had brought her unlooked-for happiness. And within her, at last, after a year and a half of marriage, stirred new life. Even now she felt the first tiny flutterings of fingers uncurling, arms outstretched. She hadn't told Matthew that she suspected she was with child, for she knew that he would have refused to bring her on this arduous climb up Hawaii's largest volcano, and she had wanted to come. Despite her years in the islands, the nearest she had ever been to the elemental forces of vulcanism was her sight of the great column of fire from Mauna Loa's 1852 eruption, visible even from Oahu.

Matthew's medical practice was a great success; when called upon, he sometimes traveled to the other islands, taking her with him when she didn't have a patient near childbirth. They crossed the Pali frequently to visit Napua and Henry Turner on the plantation at Kaneohe, awarded by the courts to Matthew and Kuokoa jointly. It thrived under Turner's benevolent management. The United States' tariff on sugar still hindered Hawaiian growers, but Matthew and Henry Turner found adequate markets for their processed cane.

With Charles Decker's death, the movement for revolution had lost its most able leader. Annexation to the United States had appeared imminent, for in February of 1854, the king sent Foreign Minister Robert Wyllie to negotiate with the new U.S. commissioner, David Gregg. Opposed to statehood and citizenship for natives, the Committee of Thirteen schemed once again to recruit filibusterers from California. Government troops drilled, and annexationists courted the Hawaiians.

But by this time, Prince Alexander Liholiho had gained a strong voice on the Privy Council, and he managed to stall the negotiations. In December 1854, King Kamehameha III died, and the independence of the Hawaiian kingdom was reaffirmed by the new king, who took the name Kamehameha IV.

Napua, of course, had married Henry Turner. Anne had not been altogether in favor of the match; Turner was twelve years older than Napua and content as a planter. Napua had been bred and trained to be a chiefess; she might even have been chosen to become Liholiho's queen! Her beauty and wit and education were wasted as a farmer's wife. Yet she seemed happy enough thus far; already she and Turner had a daughter, Keola, which meant "life" in Hawaiian. Henry Turner said his wife and daughter had given him the gift of life.

He and Matthew had vowed to become sugar barons; just this year they had leased back Henry Turner's acres on Maui and hired a *luna* to manage the plantation there. They had the only native foreman in the islands.

Anne thought her own child would be a daughter, also. She

had chosen a name: Abigail Puaho'ohiki Cabe. Abigail was for Matthew's mother. The Hawaiian name meant "daughter of the promise." Fitting, Anne thought.

So it was that night, when stars glittered with pure white light across the canopy of darkness and the sea of lava had come to fiery life, its molten heart glowing through the veneer that disguised it by day, that Anne leaned her cheek against her husband's arm and said, "We're to have a child."

Seated beside her on the crater's rim, he jerked. "A child! You mean—?"

Her smile unseen in the darkness, she took his hand and laid it as close to her belly as she could manage, given the layers of skirts. "Yes."

"Now you tell me!" He crushed her in an exuberant hug. "Of course, now you tell me! I wouldn't have brought you had I known."

"But I've come to no harm," she pointed out.

"I believe we'll carry you down."

She straightened. "Don't you dare!"

"I prescribe rest," he said, in his physician voice.

"And *I* prescribe vigorous activity," she argued, a confident midwife.

His mouth hovered above hers. "Then I bow to your authority, my dear."

She shivered again, but not from cold this time, for his hand had slipped inside her blanket and overcoat and found her breast. When he touched her so, her blood seemed to thicken and heat until it was very like the lava that Pele flung at the sea.

"I should have brought some *ohele* berries." The words having slipped out, Anne realized what a non sequitur this remark would seem.

But Matthew said smugly, "I did. Napua gave them to me. In the morning, we'll toss them in."

"Why, Dr. Cabe! What would the Reverend Taft say?"

Her husband strung kisses against her cheek, a precious lei. "Ah, but why toy with unknown powers? Aren't we Hawaiians now? We're astride two worlds. I refuse to offend the old gods."

She smiled against his mouth. "You're a very wise man. Now, can we go to bed?"

Of course, that bed was no more than a heap of blankets atop a floor of lava inside a tent made of ship's canvas, but for all that she must admit to unseemly eagerness. Mary Taft was right: such closeness with her husband could be joyful.

On their wedding night, Matthew had very cleverly erased the last of her fears, not by kisses and caresses, although those had wooed her to a state of mindless acceptance, if not anticipation. But he must have sensed her secret fear, for when the moment of penetration arrived, he shocked her by rolling onto his back and drawing her above him.

"You will be in charge," he whispered.

Although scandalized, she had also been exhilarated. She had come, in the nights since, to enjoy his weight upon her, although occasionally she loved to sit astride him and control the pace of their lovemaking. In fact, perhaps tonight, she would let *him* pay the price of their lava bed.

Oh, yes, life was good.

Historical Note

As is often the case in historical novels, real characters are mixed with fictional in *The Island Snatchers*. Gerrit Judd and Robert Wyllie played leading roles in Hawaiian history; Edward Landre and Charles Decker are fictional, as was the second attempt to import California filibusterers and the rumored scheme to assassinate Prince Liholiho.

Following the events of this novel and the death of Kamehameha III on December 15, 1854, Alexander Liholiho ruled as Kamehameha IV until 1863, when he was succeeded by his brother Lot, Kamehameha V, who reigned until 1872. By then whaling had fallen into decline, in part because of the discovery of the uses of petroleum. The sugar industry became the most powerful economic force in Hawaii. A reciprocity treaty, under which sugar from the islands could be imported into the United States duty-free, was signed in 1875, tying the U.S. and the Hawaiian kingdom more closely together.

However, Kamehameha V in 1864 helped write a new constitution, which vested more power in the monarchy than the American-missionary-influenced constitution of 1852. Despite the resentment of American residents, this constitution stayed in effect for twenty-three years.

Like several of the kings before him, Kamehameha V died without having had children. With him ended the dynasty begun by the remarkable Kamehameha. The three remaining monarchs were chosen by the legislature. The second of these, Kalakaua, faced revolt on the part of established planters, lawyers, and merchants, who formed an organization called the Hawaiian League and, with a show of arms, forced the king to agree to the "Bayonet Constitution" of 1887, which limited the powers of the monarchy and imposed a franchise based on property, which excluded most native Hawaiians from the vote. Also in 1887, the reciprocity treaty with the U.S. was extended, with the additional proviso that the U.S. had the right to develop and use Pearl Harbor as a naval station.

Dissatisfaction among the natives grew, and in 1889, 150 men stormed the Iolani Palace and briefly occupied it, their goal being the overthrow of the "Bayonet Constitution." Although they were forced to surrender, their leader was acquitted of treason by native jurors.

In 1890, the United States legislated a bounty on home-grown sugar, which threw the Hawaiian sugar industry into a depression. For the first time in nearly forty years, an annexationist movement gained momentum among Americans in Hawaii.

Kalakaua died in 1891 and was succeeded by his sister, Liliuokalani. She sought to gather power back into the hands of the monarchy; on January 14, 1893, she dissolved the legislature and declared her intention to proclaim a new constitution. The annexationists took up arms. By January 17, they were in control of the government buildings in Honolulu. Liliuokalani surrendered, and a provisional government was set up.

In 1898, the political climate in the United States became right, and the Hawaiian Islands were at last annexed. Sanford

B. Dole, one of the revolutionaries and a descendant of the Protestant missionaries, became the first governor of the territory of Hawaii.

However, the distance of the islands from the mainland and their racially mixed population prevented Hawaii from becoming a state until 1959, 106 years after the close of *The Island Snatchers*.